CRESTWELL

THE LEPIDOPTERA VAMPIRE SERIES

BOOK FOUR

SUSAN HODDY

CRESTWELL

First Edition published in 2021

Copyright © Susan Hoddy 2021

ISBN #978-0-6485531-2-0

Front cover image and book cover design by The Book Cover Designer, Artist – Beti Bup.

Editing by Scout Media – Brian Paone.

Formatting by KH Formatting – Kari Holloway.

Printed by Ingram Spark, in Dandenong South, Victoria, Australia 3175.

A catalogue record for this book is available from the National Library of Australia. www.nla.gov.au

Website www.susanhoddy.com

OTHER BOOKS BY SUSAN HODDY

The Lepidoptera Vampire Series

Attraction
Awakened
Affirmation
Crestwell

Other Works

Security

PART ONE
CRESTWELL

PROLOGUE

Concealed by the dense trees that outlined Pete Park, the Debauched vampires lurked behind her in the shadows of the heavy clouds that covered the night sky.

Even though the young teenager could feel from every nerve ending in her body that something was following her, she wondered why they hadn't shown their faces yet. With her pace quickening and adrenaline fuelling her every step, she doubted if she had any hope of outrunning her pursuers. Hearing a twig snap, her heart climbed into her throat, and she decided to make a run for it toward her home, which was only at the end of the street ahead.

"Master, can we proceed?" the sentinel asked.

"Take her," the Debauched leader said.

The nearly one-hundred-kilogram, muscular sentinel jumped in front of the young girl, and stopped the girl in her tracks.

"Shit."

Without speaking a word, the sentinel grabbed her and punched her to the ground, making her cry out in pain.

3

As she watched two more sentinels approach from the shadows, she tried to scramble to her feet and fumbled in her bag for the can of pepper spray. She held the can to the first sentinels face but, she didn't even get time to spray it in his eyes.

In a fraction of a second, too fast for her to follow, he had knocked the can from her hands.

"Stupid bitch, now what are you going to do?" He lunged at her and forced her to the ground.

As she hit the back of her head on the pavement, she was knocked unconscious.

"Pick her up, and let's get out of here," the Debauched leader said.

"Like, fuck will you, Debauched," the large female Griffin said.

CHAPTER ONE

The big day had arrived; with their final exams over and excitement high, college friends Analyse, Bronwyn, and Shelley boarded the airplane to Zurich, Switzerland, and a stewardess showed them to their seats.

"Wow! These seats are awesome. So much room and I even have my own TV screen to watch the latest movies," Analyse said, fiddling with the remote.

"Yeah, and the seat lies down flat so we can sleep if we want to." Bronwyn adjusted her seat into the upright position again and clicked her seatbelt buckle to fasten it tight.

"I am glad we booked first-class seats for this flight," Shelley said, remembering what she had read on the internet about their flight being over eleven hours long.

*****

As the seatbelt sign turned off, Shelley looked out the small airplane window and watched the white fluffy clouds thicken. Nervous but excited, she couldn't wait for the steward to come around with the drinks trolley so she could settle her anxieties. Hearing the clanking of the trolley coming, she looked down the aisle, only to see an attractive guy approaching her, who smiled briefly at Shelley and took his seat in front of her.

Where did he come from? I don't remember seeing him when we boarded the flight and sat down. Shelley eyed Analyse sitting across the aisle to see if she had noticed him too. But Analyse had her nose in a book, so she hadn't noticed the tall stranger at all.

"Drink, ma'am?" a steward now standing next to Shelley's seat interrupting her thoughts asked.

"Umm … yes, please. I'll have a glass of white wine if you have some."

"Yes, ma'am. Would you like sweet or dry?"

"Sweet, thanks."

He nodded and poured Shelley's wine into a glass then placed it on her tray table.

"Thank you," Shelley said and watched the steward ask the good-looking guy in front of her if he would like a drink.

When Shelley heard his deep, American accent for the first time, she was attracted to his voice and tried to eavesdrop on his requirements. She noticed the steward, as he poured the man's drink, smiled at her briefly, and she realized he knew she was listening to their conversation. Reclining in her seat, she quickly looked away and felt her cheeks redden.

Get a life, woman. She took a sip of her wine and looked out the airplane window.

"Can you believe the selection of food we have to choose from?" Analyse asked, interrupting Shelley's thoughts.

"I haven't had a look yet at the menu. What's on there?"

"A choice of steak, chicken schnitzel or fish, and these all come with either salad or vegetables, depending on what you want." Analyse thumbed through the menu. "And desert is crème brulee or cheesecake, and we even receive a small bottle of wine with our dinner. It's like eating at a restaurant."

"Sounds awesome." Shelley noticed a couple of stewardesses approaching them with a trolley. "Here they come now, by the looks of it. Mmm … something sure smells good."

"Mmm … smell that," Bronwyn said from behind Shelley. "My stomach is growling."

Shelley turned in her seat to face Bronwyn. "Yeah, I'm starving."

*****

After dinner, the three girls settled into their seats and either watched a movie or read a book, all eventually falling asleep with their seats lowered for comfort. By the time they woke again, they only had just over an hour before the airplane would be landing in Zurich.

*****

As Shelley walked down the cabin's aisle toward her seat from her much needed toilet break, the plane's turbulence gently jostled her. Holding onto each chairs' headrest as she walked toward her seat, the plane hit a turbulent spot and threw her into the lap of the handsome guy sitting in the seat in front of her. "Sorry," Shelley mumbled, quickly pushing herself off him and smiling politely.

"Good morning. Are you alright, miss?" he asked in a husky voice, smirking at Shelley.

"Morning. Yes, I'm fine. Thank you for asking," Shelley said, awakened by his beautiful deep-blue eyes looking at her. Taking her seat, her heart fluttered, and she felt her cheeks redden. *Down girl … Down*! Noticing her breakfast had been delivered while she was in the bathroom, Shelley couldn't believe the choices on the plate of pancakes, bacon, eggs, tomatoes, toast, and cooked mushrooms. Once again, everything looked delicious, and she sure felt spoilt as she tuckered into her food, all's the while watching the back of the attractive stranger' head.

"Did you two get much sleep during the night?" Shelley asked as she cut her bacon into bite size pieces.

"Yeah, I fell asleep watching a movie. I had about six hours, I recon." Bronwyn eyed Shelley and Analyse.

"I probably had around seven to eight hours' sleep, but I still feel a bit tired. What about you Shelley?" Analyse asked, smearing the maple syrup on her pancakes.

"I slept most of the way, actually. I'm glad we booked first class. At least we will feel a bit refreshed by the time we reach our hotel." Shelley watched the stewardess approach her with the metal trolley.

"Yeah, it sure was a good idea." Analyse placed her knife and fork on the plate.

As the seatbelt sign alighted in the cabin, the captain spoke over the PA system. "Good morning, ladies and gents. As you can probably tell, we have started to descend. Arrival into Zurich might be a bit bumpy. The weather is a tad windy on the tarmac this morning, so the control tower is telling us. Please fasten your seatbelts, stow your trays and any loose items and place your seats in upright position. The cabin crew will be coming around soon to collect any rubbish you have. Thank you."

"Can I take your plate, ma'am?" the stewardess asked.

That was quick. Shelley quickly placed her last forkful of food into her mouth and handed over the plate. "Thank you."

The stewardess smiled. "Do you have any other rubbish you would like to get rid of, ma'am?"

"No thanks." Shelley noticed the other stewardess taking Bronwyn's and Analyse's plates and placing them on the trolley. As she secured her tray into position and her seat upright, Shelley buckled her seatbelt again and watched Analyse and Bronwyn do the same.

*****

Once they had disembarked and collected their luggage, the trio

8

seemed to clear customs fast. As they entered the airport terminal, they soon found their driver whom they had organized with the Crestwell Hotel. He had their names on a sign, and he showed them to his car. With about a thirty-minute drive to the hotel, the three girls couldn't help but to crane their necks as they looked out the window at the passing sights.

"Where are you ladies from?" the driver asked with a French accent.

"We're all from Portland, Oregon in the USA," Shelley said as she looked at the driver through the rearview mirror.

"Is it your first time to Switzerland?"

"None of us have been to Europe before. Can you suggest any good sights to see while we are here?" Shelley asked.

He told them all about Zurich and what to do and see there. He even told them about some places to see they didn't know about.

"It is always good to talk to the locals. Sounds like you seem to know all the good spots of Zurich and what to see and do." Bronwyn watched the driver in his rearview mirror.

"If you need a tour guide via car, please don't hesitate to ask for me. I would love to show you lovely ladies around Switzerland."

"Thanks, we'll keep that in mind. So, what is your name, so we can ask for you?" Shelley said.

"It's Carson, ma'am."

"We will be sure to remember your name."

He nodded and smiled while paying attention to the traffic.

*****

When they arrived at the Crestwell Hotel, the three girls looked at each other in disbelief at how beautiful the place was. Yes, they had seen it on the internet, but the pictures had not done it justice. With its scaloppini-colored exterior walls, spicenut rooftiles, and large windows, it resembled a grandiose castle, situated directly across the road from the Rimmat River.

A doorman opened the car door for them and proffered his hand.

I feel like royalty, Shelley thought, smiling at the doorman and placing her hand in his.

The three girls watched as the driver took their bags from the car trunk and place them on a trolley. "The bellboy will help you inside with your luggage, ladies."

"Thank you, Carson," Shelley said, already impressed beyond belief with the service.

Bronwyn tipped the driver. "Thanks, Carson."

"Enjoy, ladies." Carson smiled and returned to the driver's door, pocketing his tip

Analyse, Bronwyn, and Shelley linked arms, giggled like schoolgirls and followed the bellboy pushing the trolley through the glass sliding doors and into the hotel's foyer.

The first thing Shelley noticed was the opulence of the antique white-painted room with its indented ceiling and the Indian- and Madurai-colored large granite floor tiles in the foyer, which automatically made her feel welcome. Farther in to the left was a lounge area adorned with large zebra-striped couches, accompanied by chocolate-colored leather one-seaters and a couple long white cylindrical mood lighting floor lamps and small timber tables. To the right of the entrance was a bar area with leopard-print seats and rich dark-colored walls and black and white paintings of Zurich. The lavish hotel foyer certainly was furnished with royalty in mind and for entertaining.

"Have you ever seen anything like this in your life? So beautiful," Analyse said as she followed the bellboy past the elevators to the reception desk.

Shelley and Bronwyn nodded, and from their gleaming smiles, they too couldn't believe how impressive the hotel was.

As the bellboy stood to one side with the trolley, Shelley retrieved the paperwork from her handbag and handed it to the receptionist, who stood behind a black marble counter. "Good morning, we are here to check in."

"Good morning, ma'am," the receptionist said with a German accent and took the paperwork as she searched their names in her computer. "We have you all in individual rooms on the fifteenth floor. I will need a signature from each of you, and after that, the bellboy will show you to your rooms." She placed three separate sheets of paper on the counter with pens for them to sign, along with their room keycards.

As the receptionist explained a bit about the hotel and where everything was located, a tall brown-haired guy in a charcoal-colored suit approached the receptionist from behind. "Have you given these lovely ladies their welcome drinks, Sarah?" He smiled politely at each of them.

"No, sir. I was organizing their room keys and paperwork first." Sarah placed the paperwork in a folder. "Give me minute, ladies."

Analyse, Bronwyn, and Shelley smiled politely and watched Sarah enter a room situated behind reception.

"Sorry, ladies, I haven't introduced myself. I am Alex Crestwell, owner of the hotel. How do you do?" He proffered his hand to shake their hands. "Actually, I think we were all on the same plane together this morning."

"I thought you looked familiar." Shelley's cheeks reddened as she shook his hand and remembered how she had fallen into his lap.

Analyse and Bronwyn smiled politely, shook his hand and watched the receptionist return with their welcome drinks on a tray.

"Here we go, ladies. Tequila Sunrise on ice. These should quench your thirst."

The three girls each picked up their drinks and took a sip.

"So, where are you ladies from?" Alex asked.

"We are all from Portland, Oregon. What about yourself? You seem to have an American accent instead of Swiss," Bronwyn asked ogling him up and down.

"I was born and raised in San Francisco. I have only moved here about two years ago."

"Shelley is from San Francisco, too. Actually, her parents still live there," Bronwyn said.

"Whereabouts in San Francisco did you live, Shelley?" Alex asked.

"I used to live in Sunnyside. What about yourself?"

"Westwood Highlands."

"Do you still have family there?"

"No, but I do own some businesses there and some of my friends still live there. I try to go back when time permits. Are you ladies here on vacation or business?"

"We are here on vacation for two weeks," Analyse said as she eyed him up and down. *Mmm ... nice suit.*

"I hope you lovely ladies enjoy your stay at the Crestwell Hotel. If there is anything I can do to make your stay more pleasant, please don't hesitate to ask." Alex moved to stand next to them, took their empty glasses and placed them on the reception counter.

"Thank you," Bronwyn and Analyse said together, eager for his attention.

Alex escorted the three girls to the elevator and pushed the up arrow. As the elevator doors opened and they walked in, and Alex said, "The bellboy will deliver your bags in about two to three minutes."

"Thank you," Bronwyn said.

When the doors closed Bronwyn placed her keycard into the slot and pressed the button for the fifteenth floor. "Wow ... what a hunk, and so nice too."

Analyse and Shelley both agreed with Bronwyn.

When their elevator reached the fifteenth floor, the doors opened into a deep-blue and swirly white-carpeted, with antique white walled corridor. As they exited the elevator, the bellboy greeted them with their bags. He had come up to their floor in the servants' elevator.

"Follow me, ladies. I will take each of you to your rooms and show you how to operate everything in them."

He dropped off Bronwyn first, next was Analyse, and Shelley was last. Their rooms were next to each other's.

The bellboy took Shelley's keycard from her, unlocked the door and held it open, waving her in. "After you, ma'am."

"Thank you." Shelley entered the already lit antique white-painted room with rustic-colored timber flooring.

Wow, this is exquisite, Shelley thought when she saw the large queen-sized bed with white linen sheets and pillows, a burgundy woven coverlet at the end of the bed, and three burgundy chenille throw pillows to match against a rich, burgundy-painted wall with a rustic-colored wooden headboard. With a smile from ear to ear, Shelley approached the window and spotted a small light green metal table with two bistro-type wrought iron chairs through the glass double-door entrance to a small balcony.

Turning around, she located the bathroom and was blown into another dimension, firstly noticing the elegant gray and white floor-to-ceiling granite tiles, with a gold trim and classic golden faucets handles and showerhead. She marveled at the size of the large glass-door shower, which looked like it could hold about ten people. On the right-hand side under a window was a separate white oval-shaped bath containing golden spa jets. On the left-hand side was a black and white granite, free-standing vanity, and cupboards with a mirror above and a gold heated towel rack next to it.

Wow, this is better than I could have ever imagined. They must have upgraded the bathrooms, because I don't remember them being like this on the website when I booked the accommodation, Shelley thought.

Popping his head around the doorway, the bellboy said, "Ma'am, would you like me to show you how to use everything in the room?"

"No, thanks. I am sure I can work it out for myself," Shelley said noticing the bellboy had placed her luggage on a small low cupboard near to the bathroom doorway.

"Will there be anything else I can get for you, ma'am?"

"No, thank you." Shelley took some money from her handbag and handed the tip to the bellboy.

"Thank you, ma'am." The bellboy pocketed the twenty Swiss franc note, left the room and shut the door.

Shelley unpacked her suitcase, hung a few clothes in the wardrobe provided and placed her toiletries into the bathroom vanity. She stood in front of the mirror and thought, *I wonder what the rest of the hotel is like. I can't wait to have a look around. But I might take a shower to freshen up first.*

The hot water usually felt good on her neck and shoulders and always seemed to make her feel alive—except for today. Shelley wasn't sure if it was the long flight or her high anxiety that had brought on a neckache, which had turned into a headache. After dressing, she searched her toiletries bag and found the Panadol and pressed two out the packet to have with some water, hoping it would help with the pain. After swallowing the Panadol, Shelley took one last look in the long mirror next to the doorway and decided she would see what Bronwyn and Analyse were doing.

CHAPTER TWO

To her surprise, as she opened the door to her room, Shelley found Bronwyn and Analyse standing there, about to knock.

"Hi, girls. Come in. You must have read my mind. I was coming to see what you both were up to."

"Analyse and I were discussing what we would like to do tonight." Bronwyn closed the door behind her. "Did you feel like seeing a show at the theatre?"

"Yeah, that sounds great. Actually, I know the hotel does the bookings for the theatre cheaper than booking it elsewhere." Shelley recalled the research she had done on the internet in Portland.

"Let's go to reception and see if we can book something," Bronwyn said.

*****

Bronwyn entered the elevator, pressed the ground-floor button and frowned at Shelley. "Are you feeling okay, Shell? You look pale."

"I have a horrible neckache, which has turned into a headache. I've taken a Panadol, so hopefully, in about ten minutes, it should be gone." Shelley rubbed the back of her neck.

"That's no good." Bronwyn placed her arm around Shelley's shoulders for Shelley to rest her head on Bronwyn's arm.

Shelley nodded and blinked slowly as she enjoyed her friend's kind gesture and waited for the elevator to reach the ground floor.

*****

As the three girls stood in front of reception, waiting to be served, the hotel owner entered from the back office. "Hello, ladies," Alex said, his handsome demure shining through. "What are you all up to tonight?"

"We were thinking about going to the theatre," Bronwyn said.

"We can organize that here if you like." Alex looked from Bronwyn to Analyse then to Shelley, noticing Shelley rubbing the back of her neck and her pale appearance. "Are you okay, miss? Sorry, but you look extremely pale. Can I get you a drink of water or something?"

"I seem to have a neckache type of headache. I have taken a Panadol, but it doesn't seem to be working. Actually, girls, I hope you don't mind, but I was thinking that maybe I won't come to the theatre with you. I might lay down in my room to get rid of this pain. It does seem to be getting worse."

Analyse placed her arm around Shelley. "We won't go either. We'll stay with you, Shell"

"Nah, that's okay. I don't expect you to stay with me. You both go and enjoy yourself. I'll probably take a nap."

"Can I suggest something that will help your neckache-headache?" Alex moved in front of a computer. "We have a great massage spa here, and they can help relieve your pain. I believe you have one free massage with your package. So, what do you say?"

"Umm ... I'm not sure. I'm not big on letting anyone massage me. Sorry, I am sure your staff are fully qualified, but—"

"I can guarantee you, Miss Landers, that you will feel a lot better once you have a massage. I can tell them to only massage your neck and shoulders first if you like. If you feel comfortable with that, maybe you will be all right with a full body massage. You won't believe how wonderful you will feel afterward."

"Go on, Shelley. You will probably love it." Bronwyn rubbed Shelley back.

Taking a deep breath and exhaling, Shelley rolled her eyes and harrumphed. "Alright. But only my neck and shoulders first. I will let the masseuse know if she can do the rest. It *will* be a woman, wont it?"

"Yes, definitely, Miss Landers. If you two ladies would like to see Sarah over at the desk, she will book the theatre for you both." Alex pointed to the counter behind them. "I will book your massage, Miss Landers."

"Okay. Thanks," Bronwyn said as she watched him gesture to Sarah at the counter.

"I will see you both tomorrow. Have a good time tonight," Shelley said.

"Take care." Bronwyn hugged Shelley. "See you tomorrow."

Analyse gave Shelley a hug. "Hope you'll feel better tomorrow, Shell. Call us if you need us, okay. See you in the morning."

"I'll be fine. I am sure it will be gone by tomorrow," Shelley said remembering how quick her previous neckache-headaches had been, especially when she had been cramming for her final exams prior to this vacation.

Bronwyn and Analyse approached Sarah to make their booking for the theatre.

Shelley stood at the reception counter, feeling uneasy, as she waited for the manager to let her know about the massage.

"Come this way, Miss Landers. I have booked you in already." Alex indicated for her to follow him.

"Please, call me Shelley. Miss Landers is a bit too formal for me. And thank you for organizing this so quickly. I certainly do appreciate how kind you are being."

"You're welcome, Shelley."

*****

"Here we are." Alex held open a white smoked-glass door to the hotel's beauty spa so Shelley could enter.

"*Guete morge*, Mr. Crestwell, ma'am," the beautician said with a French accent as she looked up from her paperwork. Dressed in a white uniform, with her dark hair in a bun, she approached them.

"Hello." Shelley smiled politely at the olive-complexion woman, surveying the décor and products displayed in the reception area.

"*Guete morge*, Sonya. This is the lovely lady I called you about. Shelley. She only wants her neck and shoulders done first, and, if she is feeling comfortable, you can do the rest."

"Yes, sir. It's lovely to meet you, Shelley. Come with me, ma'am, and we will get you changed into a robe."

"It's nice to meet you too."

"I will leave you ladies to get acquainted," Alex said.

"Thanks for your help," Shelley said.

"You're welcome. You are in good hands, and you should be feeling a lot better afterwards." Alex walked toward the doorway and left the beauty spa.

"This way, ma'am." Sonya showed Shelley into a small dim lit room with a massage table in the middle and soft flute music playing in the background. "On the bed is a white robe to put on. You will need to get undressed fully—no bra, no knickers, and no jewelry. Only leave on the robe, and wait for me on the bed. I will be back in five minutes to start your neck and shoulder massage."

"Thanks, Sonya," Shelley said, watching Sonya walk toward the doorway.

*****

Dressed in the white robe, Shelley placed her folded clothes on a seat near the door and sat on the bed, as instructed. With her legs dangling over the side of the bed, she scanned the dark olive-toned room and spotted a lit candle. *Mmm ... that smells like strawberries.*

"Knock, knock. Are you ready in there?" Sonya said, startling Shelley, from the other side of the door.

"Yes, I'm dressed," Shelley said anxiously.

Sonya opened the door. "This water is for you to drink after your massage. It will help to rehydrate you." She placed the plastic bottle with Shelley's clothes. "So ... Mr. Crestwell tells me you have a neckache-head ache. Which part of your neck hurts?"

Shelley pointed to the back part of her neck that ached the most.

"Right! Can you pull the robe from your shoulders a bit, and I will massage that area? Here is a hair tie to put up your hair." Sonya handed Shelley the lackey.

Shelley did as instructed.

Sonya poured some brown-colored oil into her hands and rubbed them together. Standing behind Shelley, she massaged her neck and shoulders. After about ten minutes, Sonya felt

Shelley relax as she kneaded Shelley's neck and shoulder area. "How does that feel?"

"Wonderful. Thank you." Shelley rounded her shoulders with her face pointing toward the floor.

"Good." Sonya massaged Shelley's neck and shoulders for about another ten minutes. "How are you feeling, now?"

"Extremely relaxed. Umm … I think I might take you up on the full-body massage if that's okay."

"Sure, that's no problem. What I will get you to do now, is to take off your white robe and lay on your front. Don't worry, I will place a towel over your private areas. I will massage your back, legs, and feet. After that, I will get you to turn over on your back, and I will massage your neck, shoulders, arms, legs, and feet. Again, I will put a towel over your private areas."

Shelley nodded, and even though she was a bit apprehensive about having a full body massage and laying there naked, she did as instructed.

With the soft white towel draped across Shelley's body, within minutes of Sonya starting the full body massage, Shelley felt completely relaxed. Her headache had now disappeared and was as the hotel owner had described it—relaxing. She was glad he had talked her into it. After Sonya had finished the front, Shelley turned over, and Sonya worked on the back. Within ten minutes, Shelley's eyes became heavy, and she fell asleep.

*****

Shelley woke to Sonya's voice.

"Shelley, ma'am, I am finished." Sonya with her hand on Shelley's back, rocked her to awaken. "How do you feel"?

"Huh …? Sorry, Sonya. The massage was so wonderful that I fell asleep. Thank you." Shelley sat upright and slipped on her white robe.

"You are most welcome. Maybe I might see you again whilst you are staying at the hotel."

"Definitely," Shelley said, standing. "Actually, my neckache- headache is completely gone."

"*Meravigliosa*. If you want to have a shower to get rid of the oily residue from your skin, there is one through that door." Sonya gestured toward an open doorway. "And don't forget to drink your water I put with your clothes earlier." She smiled politely.

"I will. Thank you." Shelley watched Sonya walk toward the doorway to reception.

*****

I can't believe how rejuvenated I feel from the massage. Shelley placed on her jeans after the hot shower. Hearing her stomach grumble, she checked her watch. 8 p.m. I might get some dinner at one of the hotel restaurants.

Shelley walked from the bathroom and into the spa reception and noticed Sonya standing at the desk. "Thank you again, Sonya."

"You are welcome, ma'am. That's what I am here for. Hope to see you again whilst you are here," Sonya said, watching Shelley walk toward the doorway.

"Bye," Shelley said as she opened the door.

"*Adieu.*"

With her cellphone in hand as she closed the door, Shelley realized she had a text message from Analyse. She opened it and saw a picture of Analyse and Bronwyn in their seats at the theatre with the message, *Hope you are feeling better.*

Shelley smiled and replied, *Yes, feeling much better. See you both tomorrow morning. Have a great time.* Placing her phone into her handbag, Shelley noticed the hotel owner approaching her.

"Good evening, Shelley. How are you feeling after your massage?"

"Rejuvenated. My headache-neckache has completely gone. Actually, I was on my way to get some dinner. Can you suggest which hotel restaurant is good?"

"They are all good, but for you, I would suggest the Italiano restaurant. The menu has a wide variety of meals. I wanted to ask, err … would you mind if I joined you for dinner? I've been so busy tonight I haven't had a chance to eat yet."

Shelley looked into Alex's eyes. *Why is he being so nice to me? Maybe he is nice to everyone. I am being paranoid. Usually men steer clear of me; they don't hang around.*

"Umm, yeah … okay. That would be nice

Alex smiled. "Great. Let's go." He linked his arm with hers, and they walked down the corridor toward the reception and into the Italiano restaurant.

*****

As one of the restaurant managers showed them to their table, he asked, "What would you both like to drink?" He set the menus in front of them on the table and placed their napkin on their laps.

"Umm, I'll have some water at the moment." Shelley looked from the manager to Alex.

"I'll have the same. Thanks, Charles."

Charles nodded, and used the bottle of water on the table to pour two glasses for them. "We have a lovely selection to choose from on the menu tonight, sir, ma'am. I will return in a few minutes to take your orders." He placed the bottle of water on the table and attended to another table to take their orders.

"So, how long are you on vacation for, Shelley?"

"It's meant to be only two weeks, but, if the girls and I want to stay longer, we can! We made sure our tickets were changeable. At this stage, it may be two weeks, but it might be longer. We all want to go to London, Paris, and Rome, etcetera, but we aren't sure if we will make it there."

"Have you traveled anywhere else prior to this trip?"

"No. This is my first time, and so far, I love it. I have lived in America for forever, so I thought it would be nice to see some of the rest of the world. What about you? Have you traveled much around the world?" Shelley asked, noticing his blue eyes and rugged looks again.

"Some. Mostly America and Europe. But it's a tad lonely when you travel by yourself." Alex raised his glass of water to his lips.

"So, you don't have a partner or friends you can go with?" Shelley asked as she watched him sip the water.

"Yes, I'm single, and most of my friends are too busy working. Being rich, it's not all what it's cracked up to be, Shelley. People look at you differently, and I can't always trust people either, as some do take advantage." Alex placed his glass on the table.

Shelley furrowed her eyebrows and frowned. "God, I'm so sorry. I didn't realize how hard it would be. You know, I have always thought being rich could bring you anything, but after talking with you, it seems not. Is there anything I can do for you?" Shelley asked, her naivety showing. "Maybe you could come with us when we are traveling around Europe?"

Alex glanced at Shelley in bewilderment and frowned. "You would do that for me, but why? You don't even know me. Not that I'm not flattered, because I am, but I—"

"Listen. Don't overanalyze what I said. It's only a thought, and I feel you need to enjoy life. Working and building an empire is one thing, but when you can't enjoy life, that's not an even balance. Sorry, but I've recently finished my physiatrist degree, so I know what I'm talking about."

How right she is, Alex thought.

"You have recently finished college? I bet you feel good now, knowing you don't have to study anymore."

"Sure do, but don't change the subject. I'm serious. If you want to come with us and enjoy Europe with people who are genuine, you are most welcome to. But I will warn you, I'd say my two girlfriends will hit on you, so you had better be prepared for that." Shelley smirked. "Otherwise, it will be fun"

"That is kind of you to offer. Can I think about it and get back to you?" *Where has this woman been all my long existence?*

"Sure."

"And, by the way ..." Alex gazed into her eyes. "I am not interested in your girlfriends. I like your company instead."

Shelley felt her cheeks heat up. She took a quick gulp of water to cool herself off.

"Sorry. Obviously not the thing to say. I shouldn't be so forward," Alex placed his hand over Shelley's.

"I should be the one apologizing. It's ... well ... I have had my head in books for four years and have lost touch with relationships of any sort. Men, especially, never seem to be interested in a bookworm. Years ago, that was all I thought about—finishing my studies to get a great job. Nothing else at all," Shelley said, enjoying his touch too much.

"I haven't had a relationship of any sorts for years either, as I have been too busy working. So it looks like we are in the same boat."

The restaurant manager cleared his throat as he neared the table. "Are you ready to place your orders sir, ma'am?"

Shelley slowly took her hand from Alex's and scanned the menu. "I'll have the chicken masala and salad, please."

"I'll have a penne pasta and salad. Thanks, Charles."

Charles wrote their order. "Any desserts?"

They both shook their heads.

"Okay. Thank you." Charles headed to the kitchen to submit their order to the chef.

*****

24

The night seemed to go by fast, and before Shelley knew it, her clock showed 10 p.m. "Thank you for a lovely night. I've enjoyed our meal together and your company, Alex. We will have to do this again sometime but please, do think about coming on vacation with us."

"I've enjoyed myself too. And yes, I'll think about it." He leaned in and kissed her ever so tenderly on the lips.

Shelley didn't pull away from him. She enjoyed every second of his kiss and didn't want it to end.

When Alex eventually backed away, he looked into Shelley's eyes and, with a low, rugged voice said, "Sorry. Am I being too forward?"

Shelley shook her head and kissed him on his lips. Shelley could feel the wanton in his body and panicked.

She retracted quickly.

Alex frowned. "What's wrong? Please, tell me?"

"I do like you a lot, Alex. But this is a bit too quick for me. I am only being honest, that's all. And I don't want to lead you on."

Alex frowned and was a bit taken aback, by what she had said. "Truthfully, I would love to cuddle up in a corner with you somewhere. That's all. I have only met you today and would like to take it slow and get to know you better too, if that's okay."

Shelley breathed a sigh of relief and smiled. "That sounds good to me."

"How do you feel about going to the rooftop? There is a lovely view from up there."

"I would love to." Shelley stood and placing her handbag over her shoulder.

"Great!" Alex stood and checked the time on his wrist watch. He took Shelley's hand and pulled her gently toward the restaurant's front doors.

"*Guet nacht* sir, ma'am." Charles opened the glass door for them.

"Night," Shelley said, politely as she walked through the doorway with Alex. *Hmm, maybe the meal just goes on my room bill. I'm sure I'll soon find out when I checkout.*

"*Guet nacht*, Charles," Alex said, nodding once.

＊＊＊＊＊

When the elevator doors opened, Shelley stepped out with Alex and was surprised at how appealing the rooftop was, with its wooden flooring, wooden-framed, black-cushioned lounge chairs, cream-shade sails, gas heaters, and green plants all around. "Wow. This is beautiful."

"Thanks. It's one of the many places I love at the hotel. What do you think of the view?" Alex point at the river and pulled her toward the black iron balustrading.

"The lights off the buildings in the distance look like a thousand jewels all shining at once. So beautiful," Shelley said, mesmerized, as she looked all around in wonderment and leaned on the balustrading.

"Come, sit over here." Alex indicated to the double-seater lounge chair with a low pine-colored table in front of it.

Shelley followed Alex to the lounge chair, and they sat there for a few hours, chatting.

As the night sky darkened more and the fresh air filled her lungs, Shelley yawned and realized the jetlag was kicking in. She noticed her cellphone read midnight. "Would you mind walking me to my room? I'm getting a bit tired."

"Sure, no problem." Alex stood, and proffered his hand.

＊＊＊＊＊

As they stopped in front of Shelley's doorway, Alex gently pushed Shelley against the wall and passionately kissed her soft, warm lips. Shelley's heartbeat quickened, and the butterflies in her stomach fluttered when he continued onto her neck and, eventually, her ear. Even though Shelley enjoyed every moment

26

of his touch, she knew it would not be right taking this any further, as she had only just met him hours previous. Pulling away slowly from their embrace, Shelley looked into Alex's eyes. "Thank you for tonight. See you tomorrow, sometime."

"I have enjoyed our night. And yes, I will see you tomorrow." Alex tried to calm himself as he watched her take the room keycard from her purse.

Shelley opened the door. "Night."

"Night." He headed toward the elevator before she could see his eyes dilate and his teeth protrude. *Man, she sure is beautiful. Calm yourself, Crestwell.*

*****

Shelley leaned against the closed door and took a deep breath in and out. With a grin from ear to ear, she thought, *That was unexpected. Alex sure is a nice guy and so good looking. Actually, his cologne smelled sweet, like a little powdery and floral, but still delicate. I truly felt an attraction to him.*

As she walked farther into the room, Shelley noticed a colorful bunch of flowers in a vase that had been delivered to her room while she was out.

"I wonder who these are from." She grabbed the attached card.

Thank you for a lovely evening. Love, Alex.

How nice is this guy? Wow, they sure are beautiful, and their scent is exquisite. I am one lucky girl. She inhaled their perfumed scent then sat on the bed and picked up the phone to call reception to see if she could get Alex's number to thank him.

"Miss me already?" Alex teased when he answered.

"Thank you for the beautiful flowers. They are lovely," Shelley said, beaming from ear to ear, when she heard his voice.

"You're welcome. I'm glad you liked them. Beautiful flowers for a beautiful lady. Sleep well, and I will see you tomorrow, sometime. Night."

"Bye." Shelley placed the phone on the receiver. With a warm feeling all over and a sense of happiness running through her body, she shrugged on her nighty and hopped into bed. She turned off the light and laid on her back, staring at the darkened room's ceiling and replaying the night's conversations with Alex, until she fell asleep.

That night, she dreamt of Alex.

CHAPTER THREE

The next morning, Shelley woke feeling dazed to someone knocking at her door. She jumped quickly from bed and looked through the peep hole, noticing Analyse and Bronwyn on the other side.

"Morning, girls," Shelley said, yawning, as she opened the door and spotted the breakfast trays Bronwyn and Analyse were holding. "Mmm ... that smells good."

"Good morning, sleepyhead. How are you feeling?" Bronwyn asked, entering.

"Good. Once I had the massage, I felt better right away. You both need to check it out. It's amazing, and you feel rejuvenated when they have finished." Shelley shut the door and watched the two girls place the breakfast trays on the end of bed.

"Wow, these are beautiful flowers," Analyse said, reading the card inscription. "You went out with Alex Crestwell last night? Mr. Gorgeous? You lucky bugger!"

"So, what happened? Spill." Bronwyn smirked as she placed her hands on her hips.

"There's not much to tell. We went out for dinner at one of the hotel restaurants, and afterward, we went to the rooftop and … we cuddled and kissed. By the way, he is a great kisser and such a gentleman too. When I got back last night, these were in my room. Aren't they beautiful?" Shelley was smiling from ear to ear.

"Hmm, someone is smitten," Bronwyn teased.

"Smitten. I wouldn't call it that," Shelley said with her hands on her hips. "I hope you don't mind, but I asked him if he'd like to come with us on vacation when we leave Switzerland."

"Actually, that is a good idea, having a guy with us. I would feel a lot safer. So I don't mind," Bronwyn said.

"I would love for him to come with us, but do you think that's a good idea, seen as we have only just met this guy? I'm not saying he is a—"

"I really don't think he would do anything wrong or hurt us, do you?" Shelley interrupted. "Anyway, I don't even know if he can come yet. He said he would let me know."

"So, you think he could be the one?" Bronwyn asked, knowing Shelley had not had a boyfriend or any man in her life for the last four years.

"I don't know. It's a bit early to tell," Shelley said, taken aback by what Bronwyn was inferring. "And I think I need to get to know him better first before I can say he is the one."

"Are you seeing him today or tonight?" Bronwyn asked.

"I'm not sure. I was going to wait for him to call first. What was the theatre like last night? Any good?"

"Yeah, we loved it. We ended up having dinner before the show, which worked out well, because the show finished at eleven o'clock," Bronwyn said.

"Great. So, what are we doing today? Some sightseeing, maybe?" Shelley asked.

"Sightseeing sounds good. Why don't we eat this breakfast, take showers, get dressed and meet in reception in about an hour, and we can book something down there?" Analyse said, sitting on the edge of the bed.

"Sounds like a plan. This breakfast looks nice. Thank you. Let's eat. I'm hungry." Shelley snatched a piece of fruit.

*****

Shelley exited the elevator at reception, only to see Analyse and Bronwyn talking with Alex.

As she got closer to them, Alex said, "Good morning. How did you sleep?" He pulled her in close for a kiss.

Shelley slowly pulled away from their kiss and looked into his blue eyes. "Good morning yourself, and yes, I slept well, thanks to you." Her cheeks were hot from their embrace. *Wow, he smells good this morning.*

"That's good. Bronwyn and Analyse were telling me that you are all going sightseeing today. I was saying to them that I could take you myself, as I know Zurich like the back of my hand, and I could organize a car to take us too if you all like. What do you think?"

"I'm happy if the girls are," Shelley said, looking from Bronwyn to Analyse.

"Looks like that's settled," Bronwyn said with raised eyebrows.

"If you girls want to wait out the front of the hotel, I will organize for a car to pick us up."

They nodded and watched Alex walk toward the reception desk to organize a driver.

*****

As the three girls waited for the car, Analyse said, "How nice is Alex for organizing to take us sightseeing, and in his car? Talk about lucky."

"You can tell he likes you, Shelley. The way he looks at you ... Oh, and I wouldn't mind someone kissing me like the way he pulled you in for a good-morning kiss. He is a keeper, girl," Bronwyn said.

"He sure is nice," Shelley said, remembering his touch. "So, now you trust him?"

"As I said, you can tell he likes you, and he seems sincere, so yes, I do feel like we can trust him. Plus, being that he owns multiple businesses, that says it all," Bronwyn said, who had researched Alex's profile on Google before she had come down to reception and found numerous good reviews on him.

With their reflection appearing in the mirrored windows, the three girls giggled and smiled when a black limousine pulled in front of them.

When the door opened, Alex exited the limousine and gestured for them to step into the car. "After you, ladies."

"This is what we are going sightseeing in?" Analyse asked excitedly.

"Yes. It's more comfortable than the sedans, for all of us to fit in here."

"Cool." Analyse entered the car and sat near the window, rubbing her fingertips over the smooth black leather seat.

Bronwyn and Analyse sat together, both grinning like Cheshire cats. They couldn't believe how lucky they were to even be riding in a limousine, let alone sightseeing in one.

Shelley took her seat, and Alex got in last and sat next to her. Placing his hand in hers, he instructed the driver where to take them.

*****

"For someone who hasn't lived here long, you sure know a lot about Zurich and Switzerland," Shelley said to Alex. She could tell he liked history and enjoyed telling them about the monuments and museums they had visited already.

"To be fair, I did study up on Switzerland before I moved here. Plus, in my spare time, I have tried to do as many tours as

I can." Alex felt his phone vibrate in his pocket. "Excuse me again. I won't be too long." Being an owner of a busy hotel, Alex's phone had rung a fair few times during the day whilst they were out.

Shelley watched him talk on his phone. *He sure is one busy guy. No wonder he doesn't have time for relationships or friends; he is always working. Life balance, that's what he needs.*

The lush green bushland and trees lined the road on both sides as the limousine wound up the mountain to a restaurant Alex had instructed the driver to take them to for lunch.

"Wow, absolutely magnificent view," Analyse said as she looked out the window at the beautiful greenie-blue lake which had mountains behind it with snow lapping at the peaks. "I have only seen views like this on the TV or in the magazines."

"Yeah, I never tire of them," Alex said.

"Sir, we are here." The driver looked in the rearview mirror at Alex and steered into a steep driveway.

"If you could pull up to the front and let us out, that would be great," Alex said as he looked in the rearview mirror.

"Yes, sir," the driver said, knowing how busy it usually was at the entrance to the restaurant.

*****

"Thank you for bringing us up here for lunch. Not only is the food good, but the company is great too, and the view … it is absolutely stunning." Shelley placed her knife and fork on the middle of her plate.

"Yes, the view is stunning. I can agree on that," Alex said, gazing into Shelley's blue eyes as he pushed a stray strand of her brown hair behind her right ear.

Shelley's face reddened. She hadn't had this much attention from a guy in a long time. "You sure know how to make a girl get embarrassed."

"What? You shouldn't be embarrassed about me telling you that you are beautiful. Because you are, and, if you were mine, I would tell you this all the time. The way you smile and hold yourself, it's so mesmerizing. I could watch you all day long." Alex held her hand and gently caressed it with his thumb. Looking into Shelley's eyes, Alex pulled her closer to him, placing his arm around her shoulder, and lovingly kissed the side of her forehead. He lingered to take in her enticing powdery and floral but still delicate scent.

Is this guy too good to be true, or what? I am still wondering why he even wastes his time with me. Shelley unconsciously slapped herself. *God, stop with the low self-esteem already. He does like you and has said so. So go with it and lap it up.*

"Penny for your thoughts," Alex said.

"Umm … I am self-doubting myself, that's all." Shelley nervously looked away from his mesmerizing eyes and noticed Bronwyn and Analyse outside, admiring the view.

Alex frowned. "What about?"

Hmm … should I tell him? Here goes … Shelley anxiously picked at the cuticles on her fingernails. "You may think this is silly talk, but I'm wondering why you want to spend time with me. I know you said I'm beautiful and stunning, but that's only words. As you know, I haven't had much experience with guys, and I do tend to be shy. It's one of my many flaws. I guess what I'm saying is, why would a gorgeous, confident, generous, and most of all, sexy guy like you want to be with me? You could have anybody you want, but you seem to like my company. Does not compute, if you know what I mean." Shelley looked from her glass to Alex's face, nervously smiling.

Alex frowned then smiled. *What the hell …* "You think I'm sexy?" Alex snickered.

Shelley nodded and smiled. "You sure are, and I enjoy being around you all the time."

Alex gazed into her eyes. "You know, I don't want to sound arrogant, but yes, I could probably have anyone I want, but they are not you. In the short time I have known you, I actually see that when you talk, you are confident; when you smile, it makes my heart melt. You are caring toward not only me but others, and you put everyone else before yourself. You also make me feel like I'm the most important person alive when we are together, and, in my eyes, you are the most beautiful girl I've ever met. All these qualities you have are priceless."

Shelley gulped. "Wow, you see all that in me?"

He nodded, leaned in and passionately kissed her.

Shelley's stomach fluttered, and her face flushed as she fervently kissed him back.

"Get a room, you two," Bronwyn teased as she and Analyse returned.

"Don't say that, Bron. They're in love. Can't you see?" Analyse gently slapped Bronwyn's arm.

Shelley regarded them with flared nostrils and gave them her best get-lost look.

"The view is stunning, isn't it ladies?" Alex asked.

"Sure is. I have never seen anything like this in my entire life," Bronwyn said.

"It's like something from a magazine," Analyse said.

"Would you ladies like to go back to the hotel now? I can organize a massage for you if you like. I'm sure Shelley can tell you how good they are."

"Actually, I wouldn't mind doing some retail therapy this afternoon," Bronwyn said.

"Right. I can have the driver drop you off where all the shops are. Actually, Carson knows all the best spots for bargains. I'm sure he won't mind waiting for you while you shop."

"Wow! Thanks, Alex. That would be awesome," Analyse said, flabbergasted by his generosity.

"So, are the three of you going shopping, or would you like to come with me, Shelley?"

"Girls, would you mind if I went with Alex this afternoon and caught up with you tonight for dinner?"

"No problem, Shell. I'll text you this afternoon after we get back, and we can catch up," Bronwyn said.

"Thanks, girls."

*****

As the limousine arrived at the front of the hotel, Alex said to Shelley, "I have a little bit of paperwork and a few staffing issues I need to attend to, which should only take about forty-five minutes, at the most. But after that, you have me all afternoon to yourself."

"Okay. I'm sure I can find something to do while you're working."

"Analyse and Bronwyn, if you wait near the front glass doors, Carson will come by in about fifteen minutes and pick you up. Have a good day."

"Okay," Bronwyn and Analyse said together.

Alex opened the car door and stepped onto the pavement. Proffering his hand, he helped each girl exit the car.

"Thanks for organizing the car to take us shopping," Analyse said.

"You're welcome. I'll see you ladies later." He gave Shelley a quick peck on the cheek. "I'll collect you from your room, Shelley." He smiled politely at Bronwyn and Analyse and headed inside.

"Alex sure is smitten with you, Shelley," Bronwyn said as she entered the elevator with Analyse and Shelley and pressed their floor button.

"The feeling is mutual." Shelley watched her reflection appear in the mirrored doors as they closed.

"I'm looking forward to our retail therapy this afternoon. Are you, Bron?" Analyse took her keycard from her purse.

"Sure am." Bronwyn searched through her purse for her keycard too.

As the elevator pinged and the doors opened, Shelley said, "I will see you later this afternoon. Give me a call when you get back."

"Okay. Have a good afternoon with Alex," Bronwyn said, leaving the elevator with Analyse.

*****

Shelley placed her handbag on the bed. *What should I do while I wait for Alex? Hmm ... I could swim in the hotel's indoor swimming pool. Yeah, that sounds nice and relaxing.*

*****

When the elevator doors pinged and opened, Shelley entered a huge cream- and olive-painted room with a large-squared, heated, concrete pool in the middle and a marble bar with stools at one end while a pool boy distributed towels to the guests. As she walked along the cream-colored square tiles toward the lounge seats, Shelley noticed the green mountain design wall paintings on the left-hand side, which looked hand painted inside a half-hexagon-shaped indented wall featuring pillars adorned with imprinted olive-colored trees.

Hmm, this is nice. As she reached the black rattan seats accented with cream-colored cushions, Shelley removed her emerald-green sarong and placed it on the chair. She dove into the deep end of the pool and emerged seconds later next to the edge. She pushed her long brown hair off her face and propelled from the edge of the pool to swim.

After about ten minutes of completing laps, she stopped at the shallow end steps and looked up to see Alex sitting on a chair, watching her. She waved to him, climbed the steps and wrapped a towel around her body.

Alex smiled and waved back.

"Hi," Shelley said, coming to stand in front of him. "Sorry. How long were you waiting?"

"I've only been here a few minutes, and don't be sorry." Alex stood. "I enjoyed watching you swim. You looked like you were enjoying that."

"I love to swim. It feels invigorating. I used to swim a lot when I was younger. I was on the school swimming team, but I don't seem to find time these days. How did you know I was down here?"

"When I called and you didn't answer, I figured you had to be somewhere in the hotel. Once I called a few places, I eventually found you. Was easy."

"Right. What would you like to do this afternoon? It's my treat."

"Umm, would you like to go to the movies? I haven't been for ages."

"I would love to. I need to go to my room and get ready though. Give me ten minutes and I am all yours."

"That's funny, I thought maybe you already were all mine," Alex teased, chuckling.

Shelley leaned in and kissed him on his lips. "I'd love to be all yours, and I won't be long, okay? I'll meet you in reception."

Alex smiled. "Okay." *Cheeky, I like that.*

*****

Shelley walked toward reception, spotting Alex already waiting for her sitting on the bright yellow leather lounge which hugged the silver grained wall next to reception.

Shelly smiled politely as she approached him. *God, he is gorgeous.*

"Hello." Alex stood to greet her and placed his arms around her waist to pull her close. He leaned in and kissed her lips wantonly.

As Shelley followed his lead and their lips opened, she moaned quietly into his mouth, kissing him back fervently.

Alex's breath staggered as he hesitantly pulled away from their moment of passion, and he looked into her eyes. "Come on. We better go. My driver is waiting for us out front."

Shelley nodded and breathed deeply to calm her libido.

*****

By the time they were seated next to each other in the car and the driver was pulling away from the Crestwell Hotel, Alex couldn't hold back any further. Her scent was driving him wild. After raising the divider between them and the driver, he kissed Shelley with a passion he hadn't felt for a few hundred years. *Calm yourself, Alexander.*

The attraction he has for me has awakened my whole body. God, I feel like I'm on fire and about to explode. I wonder if he feels like this. Shelley slowly leaned back to catch her breath then blurted, "I love you," and searched his eyes for a reaction.

Stunned, he blinked slowly. "I love you too, my dear, sweet girl, but I think we need to slow this down a bit, otherwise, I'll want to take this further, and I know you are not ready yet."

"I'm sorry." Shelley looked at her hands. "It's ... I've fallen for you—and in a big way."

Alex placed his hand under Shelley's chin and lifted her face to his, their eyes meeting. "Don't be sorry. I feel the same way about you too. But we need to be a bit more careful, that's all, beautiful."

"Alex, I want to tell you something." Shelley's heart pounded. "But I'm not sure if you already might have guessed."

He searched her face.

"The reason I don't let you take it any further is I'm still ... a virgin." Shelley breathed a sigh of relief that her secret had come out.

"I wasn't a hundred percent sure, but I did guess you may be a virgin. I wouldn't want you any other way, Shelley, and I don't want to lose you. I love what we have so far, so I'm prepared to wait until you are ready."

"I don't know if I will ever be ready. I have trust issues, and I don't want to jump into bed with ... anyone." Shelley recalled when she was a teenager, the harrowing night a stranger had nearly raped her on the way home and how it had changed her life. "Also, what'll happen when I go home to Portland? I don't know if I could do the long-distance relationship thing. I'm sorry, but I'm only being honest." Shelley watched the sadness in Alex's eyes and knew this was not something he'd want to hear right now.

"So, when you say you love me, do you love me enough to move here with me?"

"I could say the same to you, Alex. Would you move halfway around the world to be with me?" *God, I have only known you for a couple days and we are already at this stage.*

"Fair point, I suppose. But I don't want to lose you, Shelley. Not now that we have found each other." He searched her face for answers.

"I don't want to lose you either, Alex, but this will eventually come up when it's time for me to leave Switzerland and go home. Actually, the girls don't know this yet, so please don't say anything; I'm contemplating moving back to San Francisco soon. I miss it there, and that is where I want to open up my practice."

His brow furrowed. "Right ..." *Why is it that I'm attracted to this human so much, and why can't I read her thoughts? It seems she has awakened something in my heart. Humph, I don't know what to think of this right now.* "Can we forget about this for the time being and try to enjoy each other's company?" Alex traced his hand down the side of her face.

"You mean you still want to spend time with me, knowing I'll eventually leave?"

Alex nodded. "Of course I do. I care for you a lot, Shelley, and … I can't just turn off my feelings."

Shelley cuddled into him tight, and her vision blurred as the tears rose to the surface. "I've found the most amazing guy, and soon I'll have to leave. My world will fall apart, I know it will." Shelley wiped her tears as they rolled down her face.

Alex picked up Shelley with ease and placed her onto his lap and hugged her tightly. "I won't let you go," Alex said with a furrowed brow.

"God, what are we going to do?"

"We can figure this out later. Let's enjoy the time we have together."

She nodded and kissed him passionately.

*****

"Sir, we are here," the driver said through the intercom as the car stopped next to the curb.

"Do you still want to go to the movies?" Alex asked.

Shelley cuddled into his chest. "No."

Alex pressed the car's intercom button. "Change of plans. Please take us home, Chase."

"Yes, sir." The driver shifted into gear and pulled away from the building.

*****

"Where are we?" Shelley asked as she watched a huge limestone wall with a wrought iron gate come into view.

"This is my home."

"Your home! I'd assumed you lived at the hotel, because you always seemed to be there." Shelley shifted from his lap onto the leather seat.

The car drove through the opened gates and down a long autumn-toned paved ground with sculptured plants on either side of the driveway. Shelley took a deep breath as the elegant and grandeur triple-story house came into view. *Wow* ... "You have a beautiful home, Alex."

"Thank you," Alex said, watching her captivation. When the car stopped, Alex opened the door to exit the car. "Come on." He held Shelley's hand to help her step out of the car.

Interlacing their fingers, they walked side by side up the steps to the front door and into his house.

Shelley's eyes widened as she noticed the crystal chandelier hanging from the foyer ceiling. *Beautiful. Oh my god, look at that white-and-gray-marbled staircase with the black balustrading. Elegant.*

"*Guten abend*, Sire," the butler said.

"Good evening, James," Alex said.

"Will Sire be joining us for dinner tonight, or can I get you anything?"

"At this stage, James, I'm not sure if we will be dining in tonight. But could you bring us a bottle of white wine and two glasses? Sorry, I've forgotten my manners. This lovely lady is Shelley. Shelley, this is my butler, James, who has been with me for a long time."

"Lovely to meet you, Shelley," James said with his German accent, slightly bowing his head.

"Nice to meet you too, James. How long have you been with Alex?" Shelley proffered her hand to shake his.

"I looked after Sire when he was a child, ma'am. So I have known Sire for most of his life."

"Wow, that is a long time."

"I will bring your drinks in, Sire, ma'am." James slightly bowed and headed toward the back of the house. *Hmm, that's a bit strange. I can't read her thoughts.*

Yeah, me neither, James, Alex mind-thought then grabbed Shelley's hand to pull her to the left-hand side of the foyer. "Come on."

The lights were already on as they entered the double-doored entry, antique white-painted room sporting a roaring fire. Shelley's heart fluttered when she saw the long L-shaped, white leather lounge and a huge TV screen, surrounded by numerous DVDs stacked from floor to ceiling in their individual shelving.

"This is my TV, and or what I call my relaxation room," Alex said as he watched her expression when they entered the room.

"It's a big room, isn't it? I can see what you mean, that it's a great room to relax in." Shelley noticed the marble floor tiles adorned with an expensive black, gray, and red rug and the walls which featured some historic scenery paintings.

"When I'm not at the Crestwell, I spend a lot of my time in here. It's one of my favorite rooms in the house." Alex directed her to the lounge to sit.

James cleared his throat when he entered, carrying a tray with the drinks. He rested an ice bucket containing the bottle of white wine and the two glasses on the table in front of them. He poured two glasses of wine and handed them to Alex and Shelley.

"Thank you," Shelley said, taking the glass from James, drank it down fast and placed the empty glass on the table in front of her.

"Will that be all, Sire?"

"Yes," Alex said, taking the glass. *Shut the doors on your way out.*

James nodded slightly and closed the doors behind him as instructed.

Alex took a sip of his wine. "You drank that fast. Are you okay?"

Shelley sat ridged on the edge of the couch. "I'm a bit nervous, that's all. From what I've seen so far, this house sure is huge. I can't say I've been in anything like it before. It's … a bit intimidating, that's all."

"I suppose it would be intimidating," Alex said, considering his lavish furnishings. "I think I've been here so long I'm used to it. Nonetheless, try to relax. Maybe take off your shoes and rest your feet on the lounge if you want. The switch on the side of the lounge arm pulls out the footrest."

"Okay." Shelley watched Alex pour her another drink as she removed her shoes, reclined in her seat and pressed the footrest button.

"Now, drink this one a bit slower. It's a lovely white wine made here in Zurich, one of my favorites." Alex handed her the glass.

Shelley smiled and took a sip. "Mmm … that is nice. It has a fruity flavor."

"I knew you'd like it." Alex leaned against his chair, pressing the button for his own footrest.

"How long have you lived in this house, Alex?"

"I moved in two years ago." Alex took a sip of his drink and placed it on the small table next to his seat. "The only others who live here are my staff, who have quarters down the back of the property. I have a butler, cook, driver, and gardener/pool person. Even though the staff are here, it does get a bit lonely sometimes in this big house. That's why I think I spend most of my time at the hotel. I like to be around people."

"That's understandable." Shelley set her glass on the small table next to her seat.

Alex placed his arm around Shelley's shoulder and gently pulled her in close for a kiss. As their tongues met, she moaned into his mouth, and he heard her heartbeat quicken as he caressed her right breast through her blouse.

Shelley nervously slid her hand down his abs to his penis.

Alex's breathing became ragged, and his pupils dilated when he felt her touch his enlarged penis through his trousers and stroke it gently.

With her breathing stammering, she felt a fire ignite in her stomach as she stroked his penis through his trousers. "I want you."

"All in good time, my love," Alex said as he kissed her neck and grazed her ear with his teeth.

With her eyes closed and her breathing heavy, Shelley felt him undo her blouse buttons and enjoyed his sensual caress of her right breast. Her mouth became dry, and she moaned as he laid her on the couch and placed her erect nipple into his warm mouth, sucking it soft at first then hard, nipping at it, tormenting her. Arching her back off the couch and thrusting her nipple farther into his mouth, she felt a craving like no other when he teased her further by doing the same to her other nipple. *I'm about to come apart at the seams.*

Her scent is intoxicating, Alex thought as he kissed her stomach and lapped at her skin near the top of her jeans nearing her pelvis.

She moaned loudly as he kept kissing her pelvic area.

"Do you want me to stop?" Alex asked, panting.

Suddenly, Shelley was pulled back into reality, hearing him say those words. "I … I don't know. I'm on fire here and need to be … put out, Alex."

Alex grinned and slowly came back up to her neck. First he caressed her neck with his warm lips, then he sucked her earlobe.

I don't think I can stand this much longer. The intense pleasure Shelley felt was so deep, and her body needed a release. She pushed him onto his back, pulled his shirt from his trousers and undid the buttons. *His chest … so muscular and soft.* As she kissed his chest, his intoxicating scent nearly sent her into a frenzy. Finding his left nipple, she sucked it hard and grazed it lightly with her teeth. She did the same to the right nipple.

With his head pushing back in the chair, Alex moaned.

Lapping at and nearing his pelvic area, Shelley undid his zip.

Alex placed his hand over hers. "Are you sure?"

She didn't answer; instead, she swatted his hand and swiftly yanked down his trousers and boxer briefs to his thighs.

As he lifted his buttocks off the lounge, his penis sprung free.

She grabbed his engorged penis and placed her mouth over it to suck it slowly, relishing the taste and feel of it in her mouth. Shelley happened to look up as she slid his cock in and out of her mouth and watched Alex enjoy every moment, hearing him moan every time she sucked it harder. Frenzied by the taste and his scent, she barely heard him call her name.

"Shelley ... Shelley. Please ... stop ... I'm about to come."

With her pupils dilated and her breathing heavy, she gave the tip of his penis a quick kiss and traveled up his chest, lapping and kissing it as she went. She then lay next to Alex and kissed his lips fervently.

Alex slowly pulled away from Shelley and heaved up his boxer briefs and trousers. "That felt too good. Have you ever done that before?"

"No. You are my first. I must say, I think I enjoyed that probably as much as you did." Shelley smirked, gazing into his eyes then tenderly kissed his lips again.

Alex rolled onto his side, watching as she buttoned her blouse and her breasts bulged at the top of her bra. He wanted her in every way possible. "Would you like to go to my room?"

Shelley eyes widened, and she gulped hard. "Umm ... I'm not sure."

Calm yourself, Alexander. She is not ready. He pulled her close so she could lie in the nook of his shoulder. "That's okay. I know you're not ready, and I want you to feel comfortable here. Would you like to stay for dinner? I'd love to have you try my cooking."

"I'd love to, especially if you are cooking." Shelley snuggled into him. "But I might need to text the girls to let them know I won't make dinner with them. I'm sure they'll understand."

CHAPTER FOUR

"Are Analyse and Bronwyn okay with you staying for dinner?" Alex asked, watching Shelley walk into the lounge room toward him.

"Yeah. Cheeky buggers told me to go for it and stay the night."

Alex raised his eyebrows, smiled and snickered. Standing, he placed his hand in hers. "Come on, I'll show you my kitchen, and maybe we can do some cooking together. Are you allergic to anything?"

"No, not that I know of." Shelley shook her head as she took his hand, and they exited the lounge room toward the back of the house.

*****

Wow! Shelley's eyes widened as she entered the kitchen. Surveying the vast macaroon-cream-colored room with its light graying-toned marbled floor tiles, she noticed the high white ceilings with exposed beams that had been painted in the same coloring as the walls, which had three square black metal-framed and glass-paneled lights hanging from them.

"So, you like?" Alex asked, watching her reaction.

"What's not to like? Look at that double stainless-steel oven and cooktop. They complement the charcoal-colored cabinets and the light grey marble bench tops. I love the look of the stainless-steel double fridge and freezer. They're enormous." She released his hand and sat on one of the black metal-framed high-backed chairs surrounding the light pine-colored high island counter. "This kitchen is every woman's dream."

Alex smiled. "Do you cook much at home, in Portland?"

"Sort of. Analyse and I usually take turns. I do enjoy cooking though. In fact, when I was choosing my profession, I had to decide between being a chef and a psychiatrist."

"Right. So, what do you feel like cooking for dinner with me?"

"Umm … do you have any fresh chicken in the fridge or freezer?"

Alex retrieved a tray of boneless chicken thighs from the freezer. "Sure do." He placed the tray on the island in front of Shelley.

"What about chicken stir fry? Does that sound alright?"

"Mmm, I haven't had that for ages. Sounds great."

"What if we cut the food together, and I can cook it for you?"

"Okay. Where do I start?"

"Can you get me a nonstick frypan, cutting boards, and chopping knives?" Shelley opened what looked like a pantry door. Scanning the shelves, she located all the sauces and spices she needed then placed them next to the cooktop, along with the olive oil.

Alex placed the chicken thighs in the microwave to thaw them out too. "Did you need anything else?"

Shelley opened the fridge door. "Nah, that should be fine. I'll get the rest of the fresh ingredients out of the crisper."

"You sure are one great cook, Shelley. I don't think I have ever tasted a chicken stir fry that tastes as good as this one." Alex poured a glass of white wine for them as they sat at the island.

"Why, thank you, kind sir. Would you like some dessert?"

Alex smirked. "The only dessert I want is you, but that is off the menu tonight."

Shelley raised her eyebrows and snickered. "I can make a crème brulee?" Shelley suggested, diverting his mind from her to the dessert.

"One of my favorites."

"It only takes me about twenty minutes to cook, if you want."

"Maybe another night. At the moment, I would like you all to myself." Alex leaned in and tenderly kissed her lips.

Shelley's lips craved his tender touch, and as her mouth opened and their tongues met, she felt the affirmation of his affection. Standing but still enjoying his lips, she placed her arms around his waist and pulled him even closer.

Calm yourself, Crestwell. She is not ready. Alex slowly retracted from her sensual lips. With his breathing rapid, he kissed and lapped at her neck.

"Mmm, you not only smell good, but you taste good too. Would you like to stay the night with me in my bed? We don't have to have sex, but it would be nice to cuddle up to you in bed."

Shelley realized Alex was serious, but she wasn't sure whether to say yes or no. After all, they had only known each other for a couple days, and she didn't want this to become a vacation fling. Pulling away from him, she looked Alex in the eyes. "Umm … I'll let you know later. Can we go back to your lounge room and cuddle up in front of a movie instead?"

"Sure!" Alex said, trying to compose himself and calm his breathing. "What type of movies do you like?"

"I'll watch anything. My favorite movie is *Con Air*. I love Nicholas Cage in that movie. Actually, he is one of my all-time favorite actors. What about you?"

"I like most movies, but my favorite at the moment is *End Game*." Alex stacked the two plates and cutlery and took them to the sink.

"I love that movie. The girls and I went to see it last year. Can we watch that one?" Shelley stood and pushed her chair underneath the island countertop.

"Sure." Alex slid his chair underneath the countertop too.

They returned to the lounge room, wine glasses in hand.

Shelley laid in front of Alex on the long lounge, and he cuddled into her from behind. As the movie started, Shelley felt relaxed, and her eyelids became heavy. It had been a long day, and with the good food and wine sitting heavy in her stomach, she soon drifted off to sleep.

*****

When Shelley eventually woke, the movie had finished, and the credits were rolling on the screen. Turning to face Alex, she found him cuddled into her, fast asleep. *He looks so adorable when he is asleep.* She traced every inch of his face with her eyes. She reached for the remotes on the coffee table to turn off the TV and DVD player. With the log fire being the only thing lighting the room, Shelley cuddled back into Alex and drifted off to sleep.

*****

The next morning, Shelley woke feeling disorientated. *Where am I?* She rubbed the sleep from her eyes. *How on earth did I end up in here?* Sitting upright, she scanned the room, noticing its lavish contents, and watched Alex open his eyes.

"Good morning, sweet girl." Alex noticed her concerned expression. "Everything okay?"

Shelley's heartrate increased. "Morning. Did you carry me up here last night?"

"Yes. You must have been pretty tired, because you didn't even wake." Alex propped himself up with one hand under his head.

Man, he must be strong to carry me up the stairs and all the way to here.

"Yeah, last thing I remember is turning off the TV and DVD and cuddling into you on the lounge. Where are we?" Shelley laid on her side with her hand propped under the side of her head, facing him.

"Still at my house but in my bedroom, upstairs."

"I guessed as much."

Alex leaned toward Shelley and kissed her lips tenderly.

Shelley slowly pulled away from their kiss. *Why is it that every time he kisses me, my stomach is on fire and doing somersaults?* "Would you mind if I showered?"

"Sure. It's through that door there." Alex pointed to a doorway on the righthand side of the room.

"Thanks." Shelley pulled back the covers and got out of bed.

"Spare towels are in the cabinet under the vanity," Alex said, watching her walk toward the bathroom.

"Okay. Thank you," Shelley said before closing the bathroom door.

*****

Checking herself one last time in the mirror, Shelley ran her fingers through her hair and headed out the bathroom to see Alex. As she entered the bedroom, she noticed he was nowhere to be seen and, with a frown, wondered where he had gone. *Maybe he's downstairs.* She placed on her shoes and walked toward the bedroom doorway.

The house seemed quiet as Shelley strode toward the marble staircase. Reaching a long window first, she spotted Alex outside swimming in a pool below. Taking a deep breath, she felt her heartbeat quicken at the sight of his well-toned body. She continued downstairs, holding the rail. *I know, maybe I can make Alex some breakfast. I'm sure he'll be hungry after all those laps. Actually, I wonder if his staff has already made breakfast for him.*

Walking into the clean kitchen, the aroma of the freshly brewed coffee hit Shelley's senses, and she noticed there were no staff to be seen anywhere. *Mmm, that coffee sure smells good, and it looks like the staff hasn't made breakfast for Alex yet.*

*****

Once she had found everything she needed, Shelley started to make breakfast. With her back to the door as she whisked away at the eggs in a bowl, she unexpectedly felt two arms engulf her and a cool, bare body against hers. "Hello," Shelley said, glimpsing Alex's face.

He placed his chin on her shoulder. "What are you making there?"

Shelley placed the bowl on the counter. "I thought I'd make you some scrambled eggs and bacon for breakfast."

"Thank you," Alex said and kissed Shelley's cheek.

Turning around, Shelley said, "This kitchen is so good to cook in. I'll remember this when I'm home cooking in my tiny kitchen."

"Yeah, it's pretty darn good. Can I make you a tea or coffee?"

"Yes, please. I'll have a tea, white with one sugar."

"Right." Alex pulled away from her mesmerizing smell to make the hot drinks.

Shelley watched him walk to the coffee percolator, spotting that he was wearing only a pair of gray track pants. *That body ...*

it turns me on. She refocused on the eggs and turned on the cooktop.

Alex smiled when he allowed his mind to hear her thoughts for the first time as he poured the milk into the two cups.

*****

Alex placed his knife and fork in the center of his plate. "That was nice. Thank you for making breakfast. I'm not sure of your plans today, but I don't have to work, so you have me all to yourself. I was thinking, would you like to go to Paris with me? I have a private plane, and we could be there in no time. I can show you around, and maybe we can visit some romantic places."

Shelley sat there dumbfounded, not knowing what to say, with her mouth open. "Yes ... Yes, I would love to go with you." She stood quickly and hugged him.

"Excellent. What if we take Bronwyn and Analyse with us? I can organize for a car to take them around separately so they can see the sights and we can go off on our own. If that's okay." Alex watched her reaction at being once again separated from her friends and their vacation together.

"Wow. That's nice of you to offer. Thank you. I'll call them now and ask." Shelley, grinning from ear to ear, took her phone from her jeans pocket. *I'm starting to feel guilty for not spending much time with them on our vacation together. I wonder what they will say ...*

*****

After pressing the end button on her phone, she placed it into the back pocket of her jeans. "They are so excited. I told them to be ready in an hour. Expect to be hugged when they see you though. Analyse and Bronwyn are grateful for the chance to go. Actually, if it's okay, I need to go to my hotel room to change before we head to Paris."

SUSAN HODDY

"No problem. And don't worry, I'm sure the girls will enjoy themselves." Alex took their plates to the sink. "Before we go, I need to shower and get dressed, and after that, I can take you to the hotel."

"Okay, thanks!" Shelley said, carrying the cups to the sink.

*****

While Alex is showering, I might to go into the bathroom and brush my teeth. I'm sure he won't mind. "Knock, knock," Shelley said as she opened the door and stuck her head around the corner. "Is it okay if I come in and brush my teeth?"

"Sure, no problem. Spare toothbrushes are under the vanity!" Alex shouted as he washed his body with the dark gray shower scrunchy.

"Okay. Thanks," Shelley said, entering the bathroom. Walking toward the vanity, she couldn't help but notice the silhouette of his naked body in the shower. *Don't look, Shell. Brush your teeth and leave. Oh god, why didn't I wait until he finished his shower first? What was I thinking?*

Squeezing the toothpaste onto the toothbrush, Shelley watched her own reflection in the mirror lean over the sink and brush her teeth, trying all the while not to peek at his silhouette moving about in the shower, which was stirring a desire to get in there with him. After quickly rinsing, she reached for the towel next to the vanity to wipe her mouth and swiftly headed for the door.

"Can you hand me that towel?" Alex popped his head around the glass shower door and gestured to the linen closet as he turned off the water.

Shelley gulped hard as she placed her hand on the door-handle and looked over her shoulder. "Umm … okay." Trying not to look at him, she grabbed the first towel she saw and held it out to him. "I'll wait in the bedroom."

"Thanks," Alex said, smirking as he took the towel from her.

She strode toward the doorway and left the room before he could say anything else, all the while trying to avert eye contact. *Oh my god.* The magnetism she felt toward him was immensely becoming apparent.

When the door opened and Alex entered the bedroom with only a towel wrapped around his bottom half, Shelley's heart skipped a beat. *Goddamn, look at that body.* Her eyes followed him to his closet.

Alex dropped the towel and selected his clothes. *Would love to see her face*, he thought as he listened to her thoughts, smirking as he pulled on his jeans.

Oh my god, look away … look away. Mmm, cute ass. Shelley's breathing became ragged as she watched him out the corner of her eye. "I know what you're doing, you know."

"What? I'm not doing anything." Alex smirked as he approached her, shrugging on his shirt.

"Sure … You drop your towel and show your cute, naked little ass to anyone, do you? And that's nothing?" Shelley bounced her eyebrows up and down and smirked.

"Sorry, its habit, that's all. But I bet you didn't look away either."

Shelley grinned. "Why would I look away, when I liked what I saw?" *Man, did I say that out loud? God, if I don't leave this room right now, I won't be able to hold back any longer. His scent …* "I'll meet you downstairs." Shelley strode toward the doorway, her heartrate accelerating.

"Okay," Alex said, frowning. *Hmm, what happened?*

*****

With her elbows resting on her knees and her palms supporting her chin, Shelley sat at the bottom of the stairs, waiting for Alex to come down. *I wonder what he thinks of me. For god's sake, why did*

I suck his cock? He must think I'm some sort of teaser. What am I going to do? I should be ashamed of myself.

The soft clicking of Alex's shoes as he descended the steps stirred Shelley from her thoughts. "Sorry," Alex said as he sat next to Shelley and looked into her eyes. "I can see I've upset you."

"No, not at all. I-I want to take it slow, that's all." *If he only knew.* "I'm looking forward to Paris though!"

"Yeah, me too," Alex said, listening to her thoughts. *What is she hiding?* He stood and proffered his hand. "Let's go. My driver is waiting for us out front."

Shelley took his hand and followed him toward the front doorway.

*****

On the drive to the Crestwell Hotel, Shelley snuggled into Alex's side and placed her head on his shoulder, all the while watching out the front windshield of how the driver navigated the morning traffic.

Alex sat quietly and listened to Shelley's thoughts about him as he leaned into her and held her hand. Even though he had only recently met Shelley, he sensed something was different about her and fantasized what it would be like to have a human life partner. After all, being a vampire had its drawbacks sometimes, especially as the human and vampire relationship was not permitted amongst his kind. *Why are you pursuing this woman, Crestwell?*

*****

"I won't be long getting ready. I'll meet you in reception in about thirty minutes, if that's okay?" Shelley asked when the car arrived in front of the Crestwell Hotel.

"Take your time. I have a little bit of business I need to attend to anyhow." He raised her hand to his lips and kissed the back of it and smiled.

*****

When the elevator reached the ground floor and pinged, signaling the doors would be opening, Shelley checked her appearance one last time in the elevator's mirrored doors. Happy with how she looked, she stepped into the reception area and noticed Bronwyn and Analyse were waiting for her.

"There you are. We were wondering what was taking you so long." Bronwyn extended her arms to hug Shelley.

"Sorry. I didn't realize the time," Shelley said, returning her hug.

"How was last night?" Analyse asked.

"It was great," Shelley said, hugging Analyse. "We had dinner, and after that, we watched a movie."

"So …?" Analyse pulled away from Shelley and placed her hands on her hips. "What else?"

"What do you mean?"

"Chemistry … you know. Do tell!"

Shelley snickered. "A lady never discusses those details."

"What lady?" Bronwyn teased as she tapped Shelley's upper arm.

God, if they only knew I didn't have sex with Alex. I'm sure they wouldn't understand. Especially after I sucked his cock. Jeez, I'm such a tease, giving him head and not following through. What he must think of me …

"Leave it, Bron." Analyse raised her eyebrows and shook her head.

"So, you both excited about the trip to Paris?" Shelley asked, trying to change the subject.

"Excited? How lucky are we?" Analyse's grin spread from ear to ear. "Alex sure is one lovely guy."

"I can't even believe he asked us to not only fly in his plane, but woohoo, we get to sightsee *and* shop in Paris," Bronwyn exclaimed. "Look, here comes Mr. Perfect now."

The three of them watched Alex strut toward them.

Alex spotted the three girls chatting and waiting for him. As he neared them, he said, "Sorry I'm late, ladies. I had to get a last-minute item."

"That's okay, Alex. We were catching up with Shelley on what happened last night, that's all," Bronwyn said, panning from Alex to Shelley, and smirked, even though she didn't know any of the intimate details.

"Right. Why don't we get going? My driver is waiting for us outside to take us to the airport." Alex gestured to the front doorway. *Nosey busybodies … typical females.* Taking Shelley's hand, he smiled politely at her and rolled his eyes, knowing from reading her mind that Shelley didn't want her two friends knowing what did or didn't happen last night.

*****

The small jet came into view as the car pulled near the metal stairs leading to the plane.

Alex opened his door. "Ladies, all you need to do is board the plane and make yourselves comfortable. I need to speak with the pilot before we take off."

They nodded and followed Alex out the car door.

Bronwyn and Analyse couldn't contain their excitement as they took the metal single-file steps two at a time to board the plane. Reaching the entrance first, Bronwyn was taken aback by the simple but smooth and classic design, which had understated luxury and elegance inside the airplane cabin. "Wow, isn't this luxurious?"

"Sure is," Analyse said, looking past Bronwyn at the eight sleek cream-colored, single- and double-seater leather chairs, each situated next to a window. "Look, there is a bar at the back of the plane."

"Yeah, I see it," Bronwyn said, noticing the fully stocked bar and its opulent-styled stainless-steel and antique-white appearance.

Bronwyn looked over her shoulder. "What do you think, Shell?"

"Nice!" Shelley pushed past Analyse and Bronwyn to get to a seat first.

"Hey! No fair," Analyse said, watching Shelley scoot by fast.

"You snooze, you lose, ladies," Shelley teased, taking a seat and securing her seatbelt. She smirked and watched Analyse and Bronwyn sit in front of her, leaving a seat beside Shelley for Alex.

"Aren't these seats comfortable?" Analyse wriggled her bum in the seat.

"Prestigious, isn't it?" Bronwyn said, feeling the small teak-colored, smooth-textured marble table protruding from the plane wall.

"Talk about spoiled rotten," Shelley said, beholding the plane's lavish interior, which would supply their every comfort and efficiency.

As the girls chatted about the plane and their trip to Paris, Alex joined them and sat next to Shelley.

"All buckled up, ladies?" He smiled as he placed his hand in Shelley's and looked from Bronwyn to Analyse.

They said yes at the same time as the plane moved backwards from the Zurich terminal.

"Everything okay?" Shelley asked, noticing Alex staring straight ahead, deep in thought.

He leaned in and kissed Shelley on her soft ruby lips and whispered in her ear, "Yes, everything is good, sweet girl."

Shelley smiled, rested her head on his shoulder and cuddled into his side.

*****

Once the private jet had landed and stopped on the tarmac near the terminal at the Charles De Gaulle airport in Paris, Alex said, "Ladies, a car will be waiting for you when you get off to take you shopping and sightseeing." He watched Bronwyn's and Analyse's faces light up with excitement. "I hope you don't mind, but I've organized for Shelley and me to go off on our own in another car while we're here." Alex looked from Bronwyn to Analyse, all the while listening to their thoughts.

"Thank you, Alex. You're so kind. And no, we don't mind sightseeing and shopping on our own. Do we, Analyse?" Bronwyn looked from Alex to Analyse, smiling politely.

Analyse shook her head. "No, that's okay. Although, since we've been on vacation, we haven't spent much time with you, Shell." She looked from Alex to Shelley. "But I'm hoping we can spend some time in the next couple days though."

"Yeah, sorry about that, girls," Shelley said.

"It's okay. We understand. Don't we, Bron?"

"Yeah, it's all good."

"Now that has been sorted, are we all ready to go?" Alex unfastened his seatbelt and stood.

They nodded and did the same, following him to the plane's open doorway and down the steps.

Walking onto the tarmac, Shelley took a deep, cleansing breath and looked skyward. *The air is different here. It seems cleaner and cooler in Paris.* "Have a great day, girls. See you back here at midnight." Shelley gave them each a quick hug goodbye.

"Yeah, you too, Shell," Bronwyn said, pulling away slowly.

"You too. Enjoy," Analyse said.

As they walked to their car, Analyse and Bronwyn waved goodbye to Alex.

"See you later, ladies," Alex said as he opened the car door for Shelley, indicating for her to step in first. "Come on, let's go. We have a lot to see in one day."

Shelley smiled and entered the car, taking her seat next to the window. As she looked out, she saw the Eiffel Tower in the distance and felt excited at what the day would bring.

*****

The many beautiful monuments and sights they visited that morning had overwhelmed Shelley, and Alex being able to explain each one in detail had surprised her even more.

"Paris sure is beautiful, and the architecture ... it's magnificent." Shelley took a photo with her cellphone through the car window.

"It sure is." Alex watched the wonderment on Shelley's face. "Are you getting hungry yet?"

"Starving!" Shelley checked her cell for the time. "Wow, it's one p.m. Where has the morning gone?"

"Time flies when you're having fun. Actually, I know a great restaurant close by. It's one of my favorites. Let's have some lunch." Alex placed his hand in hers and pulled her toward the waiting car.

Shelley smiled and followed his lead.

*****

"Penny for your thoughts," Alex said as he watched Shelley behold the gray cobble-stoned street and Café Central's red awning.

"I'm trying to soak up the ambience of France, and I still can't even believe I'm sitting at a café in Paris, let alone sitting with you. It's not something I thought would happen. I feel privileged indeed." Shelley grabbed her glass of strawberry milkshake. "I mean, this is fancy, eating lunch near the Eiffel

Tower. This may be the norm to you, but to me, I never in my wildest dreams thought I would be doing this one day."

"Yeah, I get it. I remember feeling the same way when I first visited Paris. So, how was your food?"

"I've never eaten anything like this before. I thoroughly enjoyed the mince steak and pan-fried egg. Did you like your salmon?"

"Sure did. The avocado tartar sauce was nice with it too. Do you feel like some dessert?"

Shelley rubbed her stomach. "No, thanks. I'm so full I couldn't eat another thing."

"Yeah, me neither. Have you heard from your friends yet?"

"Yep. I got a text message from them, telling me how much they were enjoying themselves. They even sent me a few selfies. Can't wait to see what they brought today."

"That's good. Actually, speaking of shopping, I saw this today and thought of you. I hope you like it." Alex removed a dark blue velvet box from his jacket pocket.

"You didn't have to buy me anything." Shelley nervously took the box from Alex and felt a bit dubious about opening it, as she didn't know what a box that small could contain.

Listening to her thoughts, Alex swallowed hard as he watched her open the box.

When she opened it, she saw, to her delight, a beautiful silver butterfly pin adorned with a few sparkling diamonds. Shelley's eyes widened. "Wow, this is beautiful, Alex. I love it. Thank you." She took it out of the box and pinned it on her blouse.

"Beautiful pin for a beautiful lady." Alex leaned in and kissed Shelley's soft lips.

Shelley slowly pulled away and looked into his eyes. "Thank you. You are so good to me, Alex, and I ..." Shelley leaned back in her seat and looked into her lap. Tears formed in her eyes and spilled over her cheeks.

"Why are you crying, sweet girl?"

"You're always so good to me, and I love the way we have connected so far. I can't believe you fell into my life. What will we do when I have to go home? I don't want to leave you, and you don't want to leave Switzerland. I-I can't stop thinking about it. This is why I am unhappy." Shelley wiped the tears from her cheeks.

"I feel the same way, my sweet girl. But I'm trying not to think about it, as it always brings me down. It's like this morning when I woke up; I was so happy you were still there with me, but when you left to shower, I thought about when you have to go home, and it made me feel miserable. This is why you found me swimming. I needed to vent my frustration at it all. I feel I have, after all these years, found someone I have connected with but, in the end, can't have. It doesn't seem fair to me either." Alex placed his hand over hers.

Shelley watched the tears welling in his eyes. "Let's get out of here and find somewhere we can be by ourselves and talk."

"I know a lovely place I can take you to, and we can get some privacy. Come on," Alex said, standing.

Shelley nodded, pushed her chair back from the table and smiled at Alex. She wrapped her arms around his waist, cuddled into his chest and breathed a sigh of release.

*****

"Where are we going?" Shelley asked, watching through the windshield as she cuddled into Alex's side.

"A place called Bagnolet. We are nearly there."

The car slowed and pulled in front of a black wrought iron gate embossed with a butterfly design on each side and a large *C* in the middle.

"This is my house. It's my home away from home when I have to travel for work," Alex said, watching the front gates open inward.

"It's so lovely, Alex. You never cease to amaze me. How many houses do you have?"

The luxurious cream bricked, black-tiled house with its manicured lawn and gardens came into view.

"I have five houses, but I own many businesses too."

"Wow, you must have worked hard to accumulate so many assets."

Alex nodded. "Sure have." *If she only knew …*

As the car approached the house and drove around the back through the garage, Shelley's jaw dropped open in amazement. *Wow, so breathtakingly stunning.*

At the back of the house was a lovely, manicured green-grassed area which had a long, square, dark blue almost black-colored pool with a cream-colored paved boarder around it and dark gray-toned marble-style paving surrounding it.

"This is stunning, Alex. No wonder you bought this house. I love the cream and wrought iron outdoor furniture and all the manicured pots and lighting."

"Thank you. I love it here too. But, like my other house, it's lonely if you don't have someone to share it with." Alex's brow creased as he opened the car door. "Come on. I'll show you around."

Shelley nodded eagerly.

*****

Shelley cuddled into Alex's side on the black two-seater wrought iron, cream-colored cushioned lounge located under the outdoor main house veranda as she looked down the steps into the pool area. "This sure is nice, Alex. I like cuddling up to you and enjoying your company. I always feel relaxed."

"Me too, my sweet girl. I'll be lonely when you have to leave and go home." He took a deep breath and sighed. "So, when will you be moving to San Francisco?"

"Not sure, but it won't be too long after I leave here. Why do you ask?"

"I have a house in San Francisco, and you are welcome to stay there until you get on your feet if you like."

"Thanks, but as much as that is a lovely gesture, Alex, and I thank you for offering it to me, I would have to say no. I want to make a go of it on my own, if you know what I mean." Shelley's brow furrowed.

He nodded. "I understand. Would you like a drink or something?"

Shelley smirked. "Or *something* sounds good."

He grinned. "Come on. Let's go inside, and I can show you around this lovely house."

*****

Unlike his Zurich house, Alex had no staff at this house that Shelley could see. But she noticed the house looked like someone was tending to it daily though as she walked throughout.

"And this is the kitchen." Alex walked hand in hand with Shelley through the doorway.

"Wow!" Shelley's eyes bulged as she surveyed the huge country-style, luxurious kitchen. "This would have to be the most absolutely lavish kitchen I've ever been in."

"You like, huh?" Alex walked toward the fridge.

"What's not to like?" Shelley glided her hand over the shiny black marble countertop.

Alex opened the fridge. "Would you like some white wine?"

"Umm ... okay. Why not?" Shelley noticed the wine stock in the fridge as he opened the door.

"Dry or sweet?"

"Sweet, please."

Alex selected a bottle and pointed to a cabinet next to the range-hood. "Can you get two glasses from the cabinet over there?"

Shelley chose two long-stemmed wine glasses from the cabinet. "Are these ones okay?"

"Yep, they're fine. I'll grab some ice, then we can head to the veranda."

"Sounds great!"

*****

The afternoon slipped by fast as Shelley and Alex sat under the back veranda, talking and enjoying each other's company.

Shelley grabbed her cell from the low glass and black wrought iron table in front of her and noticed the time of 5 p.m. "Look at these selfies from Bronwyn and Analyse. Looks like they're enjoying themselves."

Alex snickered. "Look at that one of them both in front of the Arc De Tromphe. Hilarious."

"Sure is," Shelley said, feeling the effects of drinking way too much wine. *All of a sudden, my head feels hazy. Must have drunk too much.* "Alex, can I get a drink of water?"

"Sure." Alex read her thoughts that she felt nauseated as he walked around to the bar behind them.

"Alex, where is the bathroom?" Shelley asked as she watched Alex approach with a glass of water.

He quickly placed the glass of water on the table, scooped her up in his strong arms and carried her to the toilet nearest to them. He set her in front of it and lifted the seat. As he held up her hair, she vomited.

"Aww ... sorry, Alex. This sure is embarrassing," Shelley said, her voice muted and her brow furrowed.

"Don't be. We've all been there." Alex rubbed her back as he leaned down beside her on the floor.

"I think I may have had way too much to drink," Shelley said, sitting back on her feet.

After a few minutes, Alex asked, "How are you feeling now?"

"A little bit better. Would it be okay for me to rest somewhere? I feel drained."

"Sure." Alex proffered his hand to her.

As Shelley pushed herself into a standing position, Alex picked her up in his broad arms and exited the bathroom into an adjacent hallway.

Laying her head on his chest, Shelley closed her eyes as Alex carried her down a hallway and into a bedroom at the end, which had a queen-size bed situated in front of a double-doored window.

"Here we go. You lay here for a while." Alex set her on the white-, blue-, and gray-flowered Sheridan quilt cover.

Shelley turned onto her side. "Thank you."

Alex retrieved a gray woven blanket from the foot of the bed and placed it over her.

"Thanks," Shelley said, snuggling into the pillow and closing her eyes.

"You're welcome." Alex left and closed the door behind him.

Relaxed, Shelley soon drifted off to sleep.

*****

With the moon shining into the room through the sheer curtains, Shelley woke wondering what the time was. Sitting up slowly, she rubbed the side of her head. *Hmm ... gross, got an awful taste in my mouth.* She heard a knock at the door. "Come in."

"Hello. How are you feeling?" Alex entered the room with a glass of water in his hand.

"A bit dry mouthed, but otherwise good. How long have I been asleep?" Shelley rested back on the gray velour cushioned bed head.

"A while. You looked so peaceful that I thought I would let you rest." Alex handed her the glass.

"Thank you." Shelley took the glass and drank a big gulp of water. "What time is it?"

"Twelve thirty." Alex sat on the bed next to her. "Don't worry. I've taken care of the girls for tonight. They're staying at my hotel in Paris. I've organized some clothes, etc. for them, and they are happy. Actually, I have also introduced them to some of my friends, so let's see what happens from there." Alex smiled cheekily.

"Thank you for organizing that for them. What did you tell them about me?" Shelley's eyebrows raised.

"It's okay. I told them you had too much to drink and were napping," Alex said, reading her thoughts.

"Thank you. God, how embarrassing. Imagine being sick in front of you. I don't know what I was thinking by drinking all that wine. I'm not a huge drinker, so it doesn't take much." She took another sip of water.

"That's okay. Actually, are you hungry?"

"Yeah, a little bit."

"Great. While you were sleeping, I made us some dinner," Alex said proudly.

"You didn't have to cook for me. But I do appreciate the thought. Thank you. Would you mind if I shower first before we have dinner?"

"Sure. It's through that door there." Alex pointed to the doorway. "There are towels in there too."

"Okay, thanks." Shelley placed the glass on the bedside table and got out of bed.

*****

With her shoulders relaxed and her arms dangling by her side, Shelley placed her head under the large square showerhead and closed her eyes. *Mmm … the hot water feels good on my shoulders and back.* She wiped the water from her eyes, and when her vision cleared, she realized Alex was standing there, naked.

"Can I get in with you and wash you?"

Shelley nodded and smirked. "You may enter at your own risk."

Alex stepped into the shower and gently pushed Shelley against the tiled wall. As the water cascaded over their bodies, he leaned in and kissed her warm lips with passion.

Oh my … his lips … they feel so tender and inviting. She kissed him back wantonly. The attraction she felt for him was immense.

With his arms wrapped around her waist, Alex pulled her even closer and tenderly kissed Shelley's neck.

Shelley's body quivered, and her breathing became staggered when the passion she felt for him increased her body's temperature as his teeth grazed her earlobe. "Alex … please … I-I don't think I'll be able to stop you this time. I want you so badly." She panted as she savored his sensual touch.

Alex shushed her as he quickly turned off the shower and scooped Shelley into his arms to take her to the bedroom where she had previously awoken. He gently set her on the bed and laid next to her. *Hmm … she smells good. I can't get enough of her.* He leaned in and sucked and nipped at her nipples one by one.

Shelley moaned with pleasure as he rolled his tongue around her nipple and gently nipped it, and when she thought all this overwhelming stimulation had ended, he moved down her body, tracing wet kisses down her stomach, around her pelvis and along the top of her pubic hair. Greedily, he pushed apart her legs to lick and suck her clitoris. As he put his tongue into her vagina, she felt him nipping her gently and moaned once again.

"Please … don't stop. That … feels … good." Shelley's chin pointed toward the ceiling with her body arched off the bed as she felt the pure erotic pleasure of orgasming.

Alex smiled as his vampire senses smelled her come. *You sure taste good, sweet girl.*

"What?"

"I didn't say anything, my love." Alex wiped his mouth, laid next to Shelley on the bed and kissed her forehead. "Was that another first for you?"

"If you mean my orgasm, yes. It felt so amazing. I didn't want you to stop." Shelley nestled into the nook of his shoulder.

Alex smiled as he looked at the roof and cuddled her. "Would you like to try something else? No sex?" He knew she wasn't ready for that yet.

"Okay."

Alex turned on his side, pushed apart her legs and placed his middle finger into her vagina. As he moved it in and out, Shelley moaned from the unadulterated pleasure, and her heartrate increased as she climaxed once again. "You sure know how to pleasure a girl."

Alex smiled, leaned in and passionately kissed her lips.

Slowly pulling away from his lips, Shelley cuddled into the nook of Alex's shoulder and closed her eyes. *Wow, could life get any better than right now?*

Not long after, she drifted off to sleep in Alex's arms.

*****

Hearing her mind quieten and her breathing become shallow, Alex knew Shelley had fallen asleep. *She sure smells good. I would love to sneak a taste, that's for sure.* His fangs extended from his gums, and his eyes dilated. *What are you thinking, Crestwell? Sneak a taste ... You know humans and vampires are forbidden.* He mentally slapped himself and forced his fangs to retract. *I better go and attend to some business while she's asleep. That will keep my mind off her sweet, like a little powdery and floral, but still delicate scent.*

As Alex slowly pulled his arm from around her neck, he felt a raised shape on the back of her neck. *Wait. What is that?* He slowly turned Shelley onto her side and pushed her hair from the back of her neck without waking her. Sure enough, the black outline of the butterfly was appearing on the back of her neck.

No wonder we are attracted to each other. She is my life partner. Alex's eyebrows raised, and his eyes widened. *Lucky we haven't had sex yet, because that would have been hard to explain, turning into a vampire.* With his breath quickening, he realized his fangs had once again extended from his gums, and his eyes had dilated. He quickly jumped up and stood at the bedside and smiled.

I wonder what her blood tastes like. Stop, Crestwell! You know this is not right. Shit, now what will I do when she goes back home? Think, man, think. I might call my good friend, William, for some advice. Plus, there aren't too many new female Lepidoptera vampires these days, so I'll need to let him know what has happened.

Alex took his cellphone from his jeans pocket, went downstairs and nervously dialed William's number.

"Hello, Alex. It's been a long time since I've heard from you. How are you, my old friend?"

"I'm well, thanks, William. How are you and your family?" Alex asked as he sat on the dark gray-toned couch in his lounge room.

"We're all good here. Renee is pregnant, which was unexpected, but we're excited about the prospect of having a baby in the house. Essentially, over the last twelve months, there have been no problems with the Debauched here, and they have gone quiet. But I'm sure you didn't call to chitchat, Alex. What can I do for you, my friend?"

"I have a bit of a problem I need some advice on. I've been seeing this lovely lady for about one week, and for some reason, I couldn't read her thoughts, which I thought was strange. At first, I thought it was because I hadn't been with a woman for years, but I was wrong. Tonight, after we had oral sex, I found on the back of her neck the outline of the butterfly forming, confirming she is a female Lepidoptera. It's a bit sad I didn't sense it before. You think I'd remember this. Anyhow, to cut a long story short, I have not told her yet about myself and what she will eventually turn into if we have sex. But the worst of it is that in about one more weeks' time, she's going home to Portland, Oregon, and later on, she's going to live in San Francisco. But because I don't want to tell her yet about our kind, she won't know to protect herself if the Debauched vamps attack her. At the moment, I'm trying to get her to stay in Zurich with me, but I'm not having much luck with that. And business is good, so I can't leave here to follow her to where she lives to protect her either. So I'm not sure on what I can do. Do you have any advice?" Alex tapped his fingers on the couch arm.

"If you can't protect her, maybe I can spare two of my family to keep her protected until you can do it yourself." William, sat in his office chair, wrote on a piece of paper, *New Female Lepidoptera – Crestwell*.

"Thanks, William. That would be great. I do appreciate your help." Alex breathed a sigh of relief.

"As you still have one more week with her, I'll wait to hear from you on if you need my family to protect her. But don't forget she'll need protection while she's in Zurich too. You don't want to let the Debauched vamps take her, as they will either kill her or turn her into one of them."

Alex harrumphed. "I know, that's what I'm afraid of. I have it covered here, but it's when she goes home to America. Anyhow, I'll give you a call toward the end of next week if I need your family's protection."

"Okay. You take care, my friend, and I'm happy you've found your life partner."

"Thanks, William. I'll speak to you soon. Bye for now." Alex ended the call and placed his phone on the low wooden table in front of him. *At least that sorts out that problem for now. I need to keep her safe without having to tell her about becoming a vampire.*

He climbed the stairs, quietly hopped into bed and cuddled with Shelley.

CHAPTER FIVE

With the sunlight shining brightly onto her face through the sheer curtains, Shelley slowly opened her eyes and tried to adjust to the glare. Rubbing the sleep from her eyes as she rested her head on the pillow, she realized Alex was not beside her in the bed. Hmm… *I wonder where Alex is.*

As she checked the bedside digit clock, which read 8:15 a.m., Shelley felt the need for a toilet break and walked towards the bathroom. *Mmm, get a whiff of that. Someone is cooking something that smells absolutely delicious*, thought Shelley, washing her hands in front of the vanity mirror. *I might have a quick shower and maybe brush my teeth, that's if I can find a toothbrush somewhere in here. I am sure Alex won't mind.*

Shelley smiled as she leaned on the kitchen doorframe and watched Alex, who had his back to her, cooking. *He seems to know his way around the kitchen. Maybe he cooks for himself a lot?* She creeped up behind him and placed her arms around his waist and cuddled into his back. "Good morning, gorgeous."

"Good morning, yourself, sweet girl. Mmm … you smell good. Did you shower?" Alex turned around and placed his hands around her waist.

"Yes, I hope you don't mind?"

"Of course not. How did you sleep?"

"Best darn sleep I have had in ages, actually. But my neck feels a bit stiff and hurts this morning. Maybe I slept the wrong way or something, I don't know." Shelley rubbed the back of her neck.

Alex released himself from her hold. "Turn around."

Shelley obeyed, pointing her chin to the floor, and felt his rough hands massage and knead her neck and shoulders. "Mmm, that feels nice. Thank you."

"You're welcome," Alex said as he massaged her shoulders. "I have made some pancakes, bacon, fried eggs, toast, tomatoes, onions, and mushrooms for us. How does that sound?"

"Wow, you have gone all out. Thank you."

"You're welcome. How do you feel now?" Alex traced the outline of her butterfly tattoo on the back of her neck with his fingers.

Shelley moved her neck from side to side. "Better, thank you." She turned to face him.

"I bet you're hungry, especially seen as we didn't eat dinner last night."

"I'm famished."

"Great. I'll get this food plated and we can eat." Alex walked to the stove.

"Would you mind if I make a cup of coffee? Would you like one?"

"That would be great. Coffee machine and pods are over there, and the cups are in the cabinet above." Alex pointed to the sideboard on the right-hand side of the room.

*****

"Mmm, you are a good cook. Thank you for spoiling me." Shelley placed her fork on the edge of the plate and picked up her cup of coffee.

"If we lived together, you would get more of this. And I do enjoy your company and spending time with you."

"Yeah, I must admit, even though we have only known each other for a few days, I too enjoy spending time with you. Over the last couple of days, that is all I've thought about—how much I love to be with you, how good we fit together and what we have in common, how much you spoil me and take care of me. We could have a great life together. But … I don't know if I want to live in Europe. My plans all along have been to move back to San Francisco when I graduate. And after I get my practice up and going, I wanted to look after my parents as they get older. I never thought I would meet my perfect Mr. Right." Shelley harrumphed, her shoulders weighted down with apprehension. "Do you ever think you could live in San Francisco with me instead of Europe?"

"For me, there is no question where I want to be, and that is with you, sweet girl. But I have so many businesses here in Europe I don't know how they would run without me here. I would have to look into hiring managers to oversee the businesses. Plus, my whole life is here at the moment. There is a lot to consider if I moved to San Francisco with you. I can't give you a yes or no on this one. My heart is one place and my head another." Alex placed his hand on top of hers.

"Maybe we might have to do the long-distance thing, but I don't know if I could handle that. It'll sure be hard to leave you in a week." A tear formed in her eyes and ran down cheek.

As he wiped away her tear with his thumb, Alex nodded in agreement. "Come on, let's go for a walk around the grounds." He leaned in and kissed her forehead, breathing in her floral scent.

Shelley nodded, smiled politely and followed him through the house to the back gardens.

*****

As they walked hand in hand throughout the grounds towards the river, Alex pulled Shelley in close, placing his arm around her waist, and kissed the side of her forehead.

Shelley placed her arm around his waist and rested her head on his shoulder as she enjoyed their peaceful walk together.

With the time getting away from them, Alex checked his watch. "We had better head back to the house, as we must catch the plane back to Zurich soon. I have organized for Bronwyn and Analyse to meet us at the airport at noon."

Shelley agreed, not realizing what the time was or that he had spoken to her friends. "Thank you for this morning. I have enjoyed spending time with you."

"You're welcome. I too have enjoyed spending time with you. But unfortunately, when we return to Zurich, I'll have to work for the rest of the day. But I'm free for dinner tonight."

"Would you mind if we all had dinner together tonight? I haven't spent much time with the girls since we've been in Europe, and I don't feel like I've been a good friend at all."

They stopped near the back entrance to the house.

"I totally understand. I've been keeping you all to myself." Alex placed his arms around her.

"Actually, do you have any guy friends who could come out with us tonight that the girls might like and have a good time with? Sorry, I know that sounds a bit cheesy."

"Umm … I'll see what I can do about the guys, sweet girl. No promises though, as it's short notice."

Shelley cuddled into his chest. "Thank you."

*****

On the way back to Zurich, Shelley sat at the front of the plane with Bronwyn and Analyse, whilst Alex sat at the rear, managing his businesses on his phone.

Shelley watched him rifle through paperwork and chat on the phone to his staff. *He is always so busy.*

"Earth to Shelley!" Bronwyn waved her hand in front of Shelley's glazed eyes.

"Sorry ..." Shelley's brow furrowed. "So, how was yesterday?"

"After our sightseeing and shopping—which, by the way, was awesome—Alex booked us into and paid for an awesome hotel called Mercure near the Eiffel Tower. You should have seen our room, Shell, so luxurious. Talk about spoiled." Analyse removed her phone from her handbag to show Shelley the pictures.

"Wow, that is luxurious."

Analyse told Shelley about the two friends of Alex's who took them to dinner and dancing at a night club and how much they had enjoyed themselves.

"Wow, and I thought my day/night in Paris was great. Sounds like you two had the best time ever. I'm happy for you both."

"We wish you had of come with us, Shell. But I'm sure you had a great time with Mr. Adorable over there." Bronwyn looked from Shelley to Alex.

Shelley smiled and nodded in agreeance. "Sure did. See what he brought me yesterday." Shelley showed them the butterfly pin, which was pinned onto her blouse.

Analyse inspected it. "That is beautiful, Shell. Looks like it must have cost him a fortune."

"Are you ladies okay over there? Do you need any drinks?" Alex interrupted.

"No thanks, Alex," Bronwyn and Analyse said together.

"No thanks. Have you finished your calls yet?" Shelley asked.

"Yeah, for the moment." Alex slid next to Shelley, placing his hand in hers. "How is your neck now?"

"Still a bit sore, but I'll be okay."

"Lean forward, and I'll give you another massage." Alex sat forward in his seat.

Shelley obliged and enjoyed his attention.

Bronwyn and Analyse eyed each other, raised their eyebrows and grinned.

"How's that?" Alex asked when he had finished a few minutes later.

"Much better. Thank you." Shelley reclined in her seat.

"God, you are so lucky. I wish I had a man to do that to my neck and shoulders," Analyse teased.

"Why don't you use your free massage when you get to the hotel? I'm sure you'll love it," Alex said.

"Hmm, that sounds like a good idea." Analyse nodded. "I had forgotten about the massage."

"Yeah, me too. I might join you," Bronwyn said.

"While you girls are getting a massage, I might get some more shut eye. For some reason, I'm feeling worn out today," Shelley said.

"Are you feeling all right, sweet girl?" Alex's brow creased.

"Yes, I'm all right, Alex. Just a bit tired, that's all. Thanks for asking."

Alex pulled Shelley into him, and they snuggled together. Eventually, she fell asleep in Alex's arms.

"We have never seen Shelley this happy ever. Thank you for making her so happy. You know she'll be devastated when she has to leave you. Have you figured out what you'll do when it's time for her to return to Portland?" Bronwyn asked, watching his reaction.

"We haven't sorted out anything yet. We have commitments that are holding us back. I can tell you one thing though, ladies, and that is I'm truly head over heels at the moment, and I too will be devastated when she leaves. I've never met anyone like Shelley before. She is so selfless and shy yet confident. I know she enjoys my company, but, in the end, will it be enough for us? Only time will tell. We don't even know if a long-distance relationship will work, either."

Bronwyn and Analyse donned regretful faces as they listened to how he felt and realized they couldn't do anything to help either of them.

*****

Once the plane landed in Zurich and they had arrived at the hotel, Bronwyn and Analyse went for their massages, and Alex returned to work, whilst Shelley took the elevator to her room for a nap.

*****

"She is asleep, Sire," Gian said, watching Alex approach him near the doorway of Shelley's room.

"Are you sure?" Alex checked his wristwatch—6:00 p.m.

"Yes, Sire."

"Remember what I said to you earlier; your job is to guard her and ensure no Debauched get anywhere near her while she is sleeping or awake. You need to shadow her wherever she goes."

"Yes, Sire."

Alex placed his hand over the doors security card slot and opened the door with his abilities. "While I'm inside the room, you keep guard out here."

"Yes, Sire." He stood rigid and to attention, ready for anything.

With the door closed and inside the darkened room, Alex found Shelley asleep on the bed, snuggled under the comforter. He could tell she was in a deep sleep because of her shallow breathing.

You sure are beautiful. I can't wait for you to be my life partner. Hmm, that sure will be difficult, telling a human they are a Lepidoptera vampire. Alex scanned the streets below from the window for any sign of a Debauched. After checking the locks, he closed the curtains and watched her sleep. *She seems extremely tired. I might leave her to sleep some more.*

As he quietly closed the door to her room, Alex asked the sentinel, "What is your one job, Gian?"

"To guard the female Lepidoptera with my life, Sire." Gian's eyes remained straight ahead.

Alex nodded and approached the elevator. He knew Shelley would be safe in the hands of one of his most trusted and experienced sentinels.

*****

Alex knocked on Bronwyn's door. As the door opened, much to his surprise, both girls stood there. "Hello, ladies."

"Hello, Alex. What's up?" Analyse said.

"I wanted to let you both know that Shelley is still asleep."

"Is she sick or something?" Bronwyn inquired.

"I don't think she's sick. I think she's tired, that's all."

"Yeah, she looked tired when we got back this morning," Analyse said.

"How were your massages today?"

"That was the best massage I ever had. The woman sure knows her stuff. Thanks, Alex," Analyse said.

"Yeah, thanks, Alex. Sure was nice and relaxing," Bronwyn said.

"You're welcome. I'm glad you both enjoyed it. I hope you don't mind but I have organized a dinner at a lovely restaurant down the road, and two of my friends are coming as well. But, seen as Shelley and I won't be going, do you both mind entertaining these two guys yourselves?"

"Sure, if they are anything like the two from last night, we'll have a blast. Thank you, Alex," Bronwyn said brazenly.

Alex could tell from listening to both of their thoughts that they were happy about it. "Great. I'll text you the details of the restaurant soon and will let my friends know what is going on. I'll check on Shelley later and see how she's doing. And we'll see you both tomorrow, okay?"

"No problem. Give Shell our love," Analyse said. *I hope Shelley is okay!*

Alex nodded and walked from the doorway to the elevator. "Have a good night," Alex said, over his shoulder.

Bronwyn smirked. "I'm sure we will."

*****

Shelley woke dazed, feeling a body cuddled into her back and an arm wrapped around her waist. Turning around quickly, she soon realized, with the little bit of light shining into the room, Alex was laying behind her. She ran her fingers through his soft brown hair.

Alex opened his eyes and smiled at her. "Hello."

"Hi, gorgeous. Sorry, I didn't mean to wake you. You look so adorable when you are sleeping. I couldn't help myself; I had to touch you."

"That's okay. I love to be woken up by your touch. Are you hungry?"

"Mmm, extremely," Shelley said cheekily.

Alex leaned in and kissed her lips so passionately it lit a fire in Shelley's belly. As he tried to slowly pull away from her lips, she went to suck his bottom lip but bit it by mistake.

"Ouch," Alex said as his lip bled a little.

Shelley didn't notice; the smell of his blood sent her into a frenzy as she tried to suck it off his lip with vigor. With her eyes closed, she moaned in his mouth as she sucked his lip, and her breathing grew heavier. *Mmm ... his blood ... He tastes so good. I want—no, need—more.*

Alex quickly pulled away from her. "Shelley, don't do that!"

Shelley sat upright. "What's wrong?"

He scooched up and shook his head. "You shouldn't drink my blood."

"What? I wasn't drinking your blood. I licked the blood off your lip because I bit it by mistake and made it bleed." Shelley frowned. "Sorry." *I don't know what's the big deal.* Shelley looked away from him. *He seems annoyed at me now.*

Alex placed his hand under Shelley's chin, lifted her face to his and looked deeply into her eyes. "Sorry, I probably overreacted a bit. Forgive me."

"Of course, I forgive you. Are you okay, though?"

"I'm worn out with concern for what will happen with us. It's taking its toll on me, and now I'm taking it out on you, which isn't fair. Sorry." Alex's brow furrowed. *If she only knew the real reason. It's not if I could tell her that drinking my blood will send her into a frenzy and she will probably turn into a Lepidoptera.*

"I have an idea that may help. Why don't we both do some laps in the pool, and after that, we can get some dinner. How does that sound?"

"Sounds perfect, sweet girl. Thank you." Alex pushed a stray lock of hair behind her ear. "I'll need to get my shorts, and I can meet you in the pool in about ten minutes."

Shelley nodded and leaned into his sensual touch, closing her eyes as she took a deep breath.

*****

As the elevator doors opened and Shelley stepped onto the cream-colored tiles, she scanned the pool area and smiled at Alex when she spotted him leaning against a wall in his shorts. *Mmm ... love his tanned, bare chest. God, what I wouldn't do to touch that right now.*

"You sure look beautiful in that bikini." Alex eyed her from head to toe as she approached. *Yeah, and I know what I would like to do to that body. Down, boy, down.*

"Thank you." Shelley gave him a quick peck on the cheek. "How's the lip?"

"It's fine. Come on, we can put our room key and phone over here if you like." Alex took Shelley's hand and lead her to one of the sofa beds.

As Shelley bent to put her room key and phone on the sofa bed, Alex quickly scooped her in his arms and jumped into the pool.

As she resurfaced, Shelley said, "Catch me if you can!" She pushed him away and swam quickly towards the other end of the pool, giggling.

Cheeky ... I like that.

With Alex on her tail, she nearly reached the other end of the pool but wasn't quick enough.

"Got ya!" He grabbed her leg and pulled her into his arms. "Now that I've caught you, what will I do with you?" Alex panted, pretending to catch his breath. "Where did you learn to swim so fast?"

"I used to be on the swim team, and we did laps to warm up, but the coach made us swim fast." Shelley smirked as she tried to catch her breath too.

Alex gently pushed Shelley against the side of the pool and kissed her lips. As their mouths opened, his tongue searched, wanting hers, and when they intertwined, a spark ignited in his body, something he hadn't felt for years—that was, until he had met Shelley.

With her arms around his waist, Shelley vigorously kissed his wet lips. As she moaned into his mouth and felt his passionate need for her, he quickly pulled away before she could have her fill of him. "So now who's teasing who?"

Shit, I can now hear her thoughts again and feel her needs for me. I couldn't hear or feel her before, so why can I now again? It must be from when she bit my lip and took my blood. I wonder how long this will last. Hopefully not long.

"Earth to Alex. Are you listening to me?" Shelley said with a furrowed brow.

Alex was staring off into space and straight through her. "Hmm? Sorry. I'm a bit tired and hungry. Did you want to get some dinner?" Alex pulled back from her. *Fuck, what are you doing, man?* He raked his hand through his dark thick hair.

"Umm, sure. But what about Bronwyn and Analyse? Aren't we meeting them for dinner?"

"Sorry, I forgot to tell you. When you were asleep, I organized for them to go to dinner with two of my male friends. I didn't think you were going to wake, so I told them to go without us. Hope you don't mind."

"That was nice of you, and no, I don't mind. I hope they have a good time."

"What about if I meet you at the elevator in reception in, say … thirty minutes?"

"Sure."

"Great. I'll get going then." Alex quickly hoisted himself from the pool, grabbed a towel from the bar and wrapped it around his waist whilst striding to get his phone and to the elevator. *Watch her, Gian.*

Yes, Sire, Gian thought, waiting in the wings.

Shelley propped herself on the poolside ledge. *That sure was strange. Wonder what his problem is? Did I do something wrong?*

✶✶✶✶✶

Taking one last gander in the mirror, Shelley twisted this way and that, ensuring she looked good in her dress for her dinner with Alex. As Shelley was about to leave her room for the reception area to meet Alex, her cellphone rang. "Hello?"

"Hi, Shelley. Sorry, but I can't make dinner. Something urgent has come up, and I'll have to take a rain check."

"That's okay. I can order room service. Can I do anything to help?"

"No, but thanks for asking. I must go. I'll see you tomorrow." He hung up before Shelley could reply.

Mmm, that was short and sweet. He sure is acting weird. Maybe I'm imagining something is wrong. Either way, it'll be a long, lonely night. Shelley's shoulders slumped forward as she placed her phone on the nightstand.

*****

With her eyes closed as the hot water cascaded over her head and back, working its magic on Shelley's sleepless, tired body, she wondered what the day would bring. Most of the night, she had laid awake, thinking about why Alex had acted so strange and if, indeed, he did have to work. *Men—you can't live with them, can't live without them. I hope he isn't playing games with me.* She turned off the facet and stepped out the shower onto the bathmat.

Once she was dressed, Shelley went to see if Bronwyn and Analyse were awake yet. She couldn't wait to find out what their night was like.

*****

She knocked first on Bronwyn's door then on Analyse's, but neither answered. *Maybe they're still asleep. I'll come back later and catch up with them. I might head down to reception to see what Alex is doing.*

But she wasn't lucky there either. The ladies at reception informed her that Alex was not in his office yet.

Shelley removed her phone from her bag to call him.

Unfortunately, he didn't answer either.

I'm not having much luck this morning. I might get some breakfast instead. Shelley walked towards the hotel restaurant on the ground floor that had a breakfast buffet.

*****

After breakfast, Shelley went to the rooftop bar and restaurant and sat in the nice, warm morning sun and read her book whilst she waited for the girls to wake up and contact her. But not much reading got done, as her mind was on Alex, wondering if she would see him today or not.

Shelley retrieved her phone from her handbag to check the for messages in case she had missed any. But there were none. She scrolled through her phone for his name and dialed the number. *At least it's ringing this time.*

But he didn't answer, and the phone went to voicemail.

Shelley stared straight ahead, holding the phone to her ear. "Hi, Alex, it's Shelley. You know, your sweet girl. I miss you already. Please call me back." Shelley reclined in her seat and sighed as she pressed End on her phone and placed it on the coffee table in front of her.

After a few minutes, Shelley's phone rang, and her face lit up when she saw Alex's name on the screen.

"Hi, my sweet girl. Sorry I missed your calls. I've been sleeping. Where are you, and I'll come and get you."

"I'm at the rooftop restaurant. What about if I meet you in reception in, say, thirty minutes, and we can do something together?"

"Sounds like a good idea. What are the girls doing today?"

"I don't know. I haven't seen them this morning. I knocked on their doors earlier, but no one answered. I'll text them in a minute and ask them what they are up to today and let you know when I see you."

"Sounds good. See you in thirty minutes."

Shelley texted Bronwyn an Analyse and waited a few minutes to see if they would answer her. When they didn't reply, she returned to her room to freshen up.

*****

As Shelley waited at the elevator doors, she thought, *This elevator is taking a long time to get here. The hotel must be busy this morning.* When she heard the doors ping and open, she looked up to see Alex standing there, holding a bunch of flowers.

As he exited the elevator and the doors closed, he said, "These are for you, Shelley. They're to apologize for standing you up last night."

"They're beautiful Alex, thank you. But you don't have to be sorry about not taking me to dinner. I'm not mad or angry at you. You can't help it if an emergency comes up, and I do understand." Shelley took the flowers and kissed his cheek.

"You mean you're not angry I bailed on you last night? I thought you would have been, because you didn't sound too happy when I cancelled."

"No, it's all good." She wasn't about to tell Alex that she didn't sleep well last night because of him.

As Alex stood next to Shelley, he tried to listen to her thoughts, but he couldn't hear them again. *Thank God for that. If she only knew the reason why I stood her up last night was not because of a work emergency but because I couldn't be around her ... because I could hear her thoughts on how much she wanted my body, and I knew if I didn't leave, we would have sex. So I thought a night apart might be good for us.*

"Humph, look who's doing the walk of shame ... and has only come back now from being out all night." Shelley looked over Alex's shoulder as the elevator doors opened behind him. "Hey, you two, are you only getting back now? Must have been a good night!"

"Mmm, we both got a bit too drunk, and Alex's friends took us home to sleep it off," Bronwyn said groggily.

Shelley smirked. "Hey, you don't have to explain to me. I hope you both had a good time."

"The guy I was with ... God, he was so nice. These Swiss guys are amazing," Analyse said.

"You girls look tired. Are you going to rest in your rooms, or did you want us to wait for you so you can come out with us today?" Alex asked.

Bronwyn yawned. "I'll take a rain check, if that's okay."

"I'll catch up with you both tonight. I'm way too tired and need to get some rest," Analyse said.

"No problem," Shelley said and hugged them both. "See you both later on." She watched them walk off towards their rooms.

Tired ... humph! Alex's nostrils flared. *I can see the track marks on their neck and arms. I asked the guys to make sure the girls had a good time, not fucking drink their blood. No wonder they are worn out. Heads are going to roll. Fucking idiots. Contain yourself, Crestwell ...* "So, it looks like it's only you and me today. What would you like to do?"

"Actually, I wouldn't mind doing something fun today. You know, like getting on a cable car and hanging off the side or snowboarding or bike riding. I don't mind actually, as long as I get to spend the day with you."

"You sure are easy to please. What about if we catch a cable car up to the mountains, have lunch and maybe even snowboard, ski, or snowmobile down the mountain? How does that sound?"

"Sounds awesome. But it's my treat today, okay?"

"Okay with me," Alex said, pressing the elevator button.

*****

With it being such a lovely day outside, Shelley hung off the side of the cable car and felt the wind blow in her face as it took off from the front of the Crestwell Hotel.

Alex stood behind her, one hand holding the rail and the other around her waist as they moved up the mountain. He leaned over her shoulder. "You're enjoying this, aren't you? It's nice to see you happy."

"Sure am. We don't have cable cars in Portland, but they do in San Francisco, and I've missed doing this. It's … I don't know, exhilarating, and I feel free as a bird." Shelley leaned her back into Alex's chest.

Alex smiled and nodded in agreeance.

*****

When they arrived at the top of the mountain and got off the cable car, Shelley said, "Brrr… its cooler up here compared to down there."

Alex removed his jacket and placed it around Shelley's shoulders.

"Thank you, kind sir," Shelley said, looking up at him.

"You're welcome. Actually, it looks like a little restaurant is over there." Alex pointed to a rose-pink-colored building with an open outdoor eating area overlooking Zurich Lake. "Would you like to have lunch in there? It's probably a bit warmer too. It looks like they have a fire going inside the restaurant too."

"Sure." Shelley looked to where he was pointing and spotted the long wooden outdoor all-in-one tables with seats. "Look at the view of Zurich from up here!" Shelley's face lit up when she noticed how blue the Zurich Lake was with the snowcapped mountains on either side.

"Breathtaking, isn't it?"

Shelley nodded as she pulled Alex's jacket tighter around her.

"Come on, let's go inside and get you warmed up." Alex placed his arm around her shoulder.

Once inside, a hostess directed them to a comfortable couch located near a roaring log fire surrounded by a black fire grate.

"Can I get you anything?" a waitress asked.

Alex regarded Shelley. "Umm … what about some white wine and a pick plate, which has salami, ham, chicken, cheese, olive, biscuits—that sort of thing. Will that be all right?"

"Mmm, sounds good," Shelley replied, looking from Alex to the waitress.

Typing their order into her handheld computer, the waitress nodded. "So, I have your order as one bottle of white wine— two glasses of course—and our famous pick plate, with cheese and meats etc. I would say your wine and food shouldn't be long, as it's a bit quiet today."

Alex thanked her and watched her walk towards the bar area.

*****

As they finished their pick plate, Alex checked his watch. *Hmm … its five o'clock. The cable car would be finished for the day.* Spying the company who rented the snowmobiles, he decided it would be a good experience for Shelley to drive down the mountain with him on a snowmobile.

*****

"Hold on," Alex said to Shelley as he started the snowmobile. "We don't want you falling off."

Shelley placed her arms around Alex's waist and held on tight as he put the snowmobile into gear and slowly pulled away from the rental place.

With the snowmobile winding around trees and the cold wind lapping at her face, Shelley enjoyed the scenic ride down the mountain. But, by the time they had arrived at the bottom of the mountain, Shelley's teeth were chattering as she dismounted and removed her goggles.

"Cold?" Alex asked as he stepped off the snowmobile.

Shelley nodded as she pulled his coat around herself.

Alex smiled, placed his arm around her shoulder and pulled her in close. Holding his other arm in the air, he hailed a cab to take them to the hotel.

*****

"I had so much fun today, Alex. What about you?" Shelley asked as the Crestwell Hotel came into view.

"Me too. I enjoyed our lunch and the wine by the fire. Sure was relaxing," Alex said, taking his credit card from his wallet.

"Yeah, I enjoyed the snowmobile ride too. It's a lot like riding a motorcycle," Shelley said as the car stopped.

"I suppose it is." Alex handed his credit card to the driver.

Shelley opened her door and exited the taxi. "Thank you for today. I might go to my room to take a hot shower. Do you have to work tonight?"

"You're welcome. Yes, I do have to work but only for a couple hours. After that, I'm all yours."

"How about I cook you some dinner at your house?"

"That sounds like a great idea. What if I get Carson to take you to my place, and you can start on the food while you wait for me to get home?"

Shelley nodded.

"I'll tell Carson to pick you up out front of the hotel in, say, what … forty-five minutes? Does that give you enough time?"

"Umm … yeah. That should give me plenty of time. So, I will see you later, gorgeous. Don't be too late!"

"I'll try not to be. What about Bronwyn and Analyse? Did you want to invite them too?"

"I'll call them to see what their plans are."

"Okay. Make yourself comfortable at my house." He gave her a kiss on the cheek. "See you later. Bye."

*****

"Are you enjoying your holiday, ma'am?" Carson asked as he navigated the town car through the traffic.

Shelley looked in the rearview mirror at Carson's reflection. "I've had such a good time here that it'll be hard to leave, especially as I have grown so fond of Alex."

"I believe Sir has grown fond of you too, ma'am. I am sure he will miss you when you leave."

"Will anyone else be at the house tonight, Carson, besides me? I don't want to be alone in the house." Shelley knew the girls weren't coming to dinner at Alex's house either, as they had other plans.

"The butler lives at the house, ma'am, so you will be safe there. I will return to get Mr. Creswell and bring him to you later this evening."

"Thanks, Carson."

He smiled at her in the rearview mirror.

When they arrived at the house, James, the butler, was waiting for Shelley at the front door. As she exited the car, he said, "Good evening, Shelley. It's nice to see you again. Can I get you anything?"

"Hello, James. Yes, can you show me where the kitchen is again, as I am cooking dinner for Alex tonight? And can I ask you a favor?"

"Anything, ma'am. What is it?"

"Would you mind staying with me in the kitchen?"

"Yes, that is not a problem at all. I know this big house might be a bit intimidating when you're here alone," he said, already knowing how she felt from mind-talking with Carson. "Maybe I can even help you prepare some of the food?"

"Thanks, James. That would be lovely." She waved goodbye to Carson and followed James inside to the kitchen.

CHAPTER SIX

"Thanks for helping me with all this tonight, James," Shelley said, wiping the countertop.

James closed the dishwasher door. "It sure was nice to have some company, ma'am, and I enjoyed helping you. I'm certain Sire will love the lemon meringue pie you have made him too. I know it's his favorite dessert."

"Yeah, and thanks for the tip on the beef stroganoff with some balsamic rice and green beans for dinner. Now all I have to do is wait for Alex to arrive." Turning around, she noticed Alex leaning against the doorway, quietly listening to their conversation.

"Good evening, Sire. Would you like something to drink?" James asked.

"Yes. Thanks, James. I'll have a beer. It's been a long night, and I need to unwind." Alex walked into the kitchen towards Shelley. "Hello, sweet girl. Looks like you've been busy." He ran his hand down the side of her face and kissed her lips so wantonly she felt her stomach do somersaults.

James cleared his throat. "Will that be all, Sire?"

"Yes. Thanks, James." Alex noticed the small bottle of beer James had placed on the counter.

"James, I'll leave a plate of dinner for you in the fridge if you'd like," Shelley said.

James nodded. "Thanks, ma'am. That is nice of you."

"You're welcome," Shelley said, watching him approach the doorway.

Alex sniffed the air. "Something smells good."

"I've made beef stroganoff. But first, sit on the stool so I can massage your shoulders."

"You're too good to me, Shelley. I always feel relaxed when I'm around you. Thank you." Alex pulled the stool from underneath the island counter.

*****

Shelley kissed the back of his neck. "All done. How does that feel?"

Alex turned around quickly and picked her up in his muscular arms. "I love you, sweet girl." He kissed Shelley's lips. His touch was like heaven, and she enjoyed every moment of him.

When they came up for air, Shelley asked, "Are you hungry ... for food, that is?"

He nodded and smirked.

"I haven't made this before, so I hope you like it. And I made lemon meringue pie too," Shelley said, proud of her achievements.

"Yum! One of my favorites. I haven't had that in such a long time. Would you mind if I shower before we eat?"

"Sure. I have to heat it up and put it onto plates, so by the time you're finished showering, it should be ready."

"I won't be long." He gave her a quick peck on the cheek and walked towards the doorway.

*****

"Did you want to eat in the kitchen or in the dining room?" Alex asked, entering the kitchen.

"I have actually set the dining room table, if that's okay?" Shelley looked up as she plated the food. "I'll need a hand to carry it all in there though."

"Sounds like you have it all sorted." Alex retrieved a tray from the cabinet near the dishwasher. "You get the drinks, and I'll carry the food."

Shelley agreed and walked to the fridge.

Alex stood in the dining room doorway, holding the tray, and was speechless at how lovey Shelley had set the room for dinner.

"You like?"

The table, which one end was set for the two of them, had two sparkling wine glasses, silver cutlery laid on a white linen placemats with a napkin folded finely in the middle of each one, a single lit tealight candle, with low lighting in the room, a small vase of flowers from Alex's garden, and an ice bucket on the side of the table for their bottle of wine Shelley was carrying.

"This is nice, Shelley. I can't believe you did all this for me. Now I'm the one being spoiled. I think I could learn to enjoy this type of welcoming when I come each day." Alex entered the room and placed the tray on the table.

"I'm glad you like it. You work so hard, and I wanted to make something nice and relaxing for you to come home to."

"Thank you."

"Sit down and I'll put out the food." Shelley placed the bottle of wine in the ice bucket.

As she placed his food in front of Alex, he leaned into Shelley's side and hugged her.

Shelley smiled and kissed him on the top of his head.

*****

"Would you like some more wine?" Alex asked as he picked up the bottle.

"I might have some water instead. Feeling a bit lightheaded from all the wine."

"Okay. So … would you like to sleep over tonight?"

"I was hoping you'd ask me. I brought an overnight bag of clothes and toiletries. I love waking up to you in the morning."

"Me too, and it's nice to have someone to cuddle into during the night when I can't sleep."

"You don't sleep some nights?" Shelley's brow furrowed.

"Only when I've had a stressful day."

"You don't have anything to destress you? Like maybe swimming or exercise?"

"The only thing that has worked so far is you, sweet girl. Life is grand with you around, but that's not for much longer."

"You sure know how to sour the night, don't you?"

"Sorry. So, what would you like to do tonight?"

"I'm happy to do whatever you want. I enjoy spending time with you."

"Can you play snooker?"

"I've played it before, but I suck at it."

"Okay. How about we lie on the rug in front of the fire and cuddle up?"

"Mmm, I would enjoy that more. Come on, let's take these dishes into the kitchen and get some lemon meringue pie."

As Shelley took the pie from the fridge and placed it on the counter, Alex came over to have a look. "That looks good. Can I have some extra cream with my pie?"

Shelley smiled and nodded as she cut two pieces and placed them onto plates.

"Let's go into the lounge room. We can eat our dessert in there by the fire," Alex said, watching Shelley spoon the whipped cream on the side of each plate.

Shelley grabbed both plates, and they exited the kitchen.

With only the fire lighting the room, Shelley followed Alex to a plush red, gray, and white rug situated in front of the fire.

Alex took his plate from Shelley. "Would you like to sit on the rug in front of the fire and eat our dessert?"

"I would love to." Shelley sat on the rug, leaned against the charcoal L-shaped lounge with her legs stretched out front and kicked off her shoes.

Alex smiled as he took his place next to her and selected a spoonful of pie. Smirking, he placed the spoon near Shelley's mouth. His sensual yet arousing demur was alluring as Shelley opened her mouth.

As she swallowed the first bite and looked into his adoring eyes, Shelley placed her plate on the floor next to her then did the same with his, hoped into his lap and tenderly kissed his lips.

Mmm, she tastes good. Alex's breathing became unsteady as his tongue soaked up the flavors of her mouth. *Calm yourself, Crestwell.* After laying her on the plush rug, he unfastened her blouse buttons, exposing her nipples protruding through the lingerie and her supple bare skin.

Oh my god, I want him, badly. Shelley's eyes closed, soaking up every bit of his touch, until he unfastened the front clip on her bra and pushed each cup to the side.

He dragged his dessert plate to them and scooped a spoonful of cream and placed a little bit on each nipple, dribbling some down her stomach too.

With the back of her head pressed firmly into the rug and her chin pointed towards the ceiling, Shelley's body quivered, and her breathing became ragged as Alex licked, sucked, and nipped at each place he had positioned the cream. Arching her back off the rug, she moaned when he sucked and pulled her nipple with his teeth. *Oh my god, I feel like my body is on fire.*

"You sure smell good. Do you want me to slow it down a bit, because, if we take this any further, I'm not sure I'll be able to stop myself tonight?" Alex kissed her neck and grazed her earlobe with his teeth.

"Can we go to your room? It's a bit more private up there," Shelley said, stimulated by not only his touch but his voice too. *I want you so badly.* Her brain said she shouldn't have sex with Alex just yet—she always had wanted her first time to be magical with someone extra special—but her body was saying otherwise tonight. His teasing of her body was relentless, and she loved every minute of it.

Before she could change her mind, he scooped her into his arms and carried her up the stairs to his bedroom. But, as he laid her on his bed, he looked into her pensive eyes and realized she was having second thoughts. "Everything all right? You seem nervous."

"I can't do this. I'm sorry, Alex. As much as I love you and love what you do to me when you touch me, I-I don't think we should have sex. You must be so sick and tired of me saying that, and … if you want me to go, I'll understand." Shelley's brow furrowed.

"Hey. Where did that come from? It's okay, you know, and I am not sick and tired of you. Quite the opposite actually." Alex laid beside her with his head resting on his hand. Leaning in, he tenderly kissed Shelley's lips and outstretched his arm for her to cuddle into his chest. "I love you, sweet girl. Can I ask you something serious though?"

She looked up at him. "You can ask me anything."

"Do you wish you had never met me? The reason I ask is because … well, in two days, you'll be leaving for home, and I won't be going with you."

Shelley quickly sat upright. "No, I don't and won't ever regret meeting you, Alex. I've had such a wonderful time with you here, and I wouldn't trade those days and nights for anything. You are such a kind, loving person … the type of person I've always dreamed of and would eventually marry one day. The way I look at it now is that I'm lucky to have spent time with you. But, in saying all that, I'll miss you terribly. I'm not looking forward to leaving you, at all."

Alex sat upright and hugged her tightly. "Please come and live with me. I can make you happy, and then it won't only be a dream. It will be real. Please don't leave, my sweet girl."

Shelley cuddled into Alex, and her tears spilled onto her cheeks.

"Shh … don't cry. I'm sure we can work out something."

"I'll miss you, Alex. I hope we can make a long-distance relationship work."

"You know what? I haven't even thanked you for making such a wonderful dinner and dessert for me tonight. So, thank you. I love your cooking. It's sweet, like you."

"You're welcome. Actually, I enjoyed cooking for you. It's so nice to cook for someone you love, and it kind of felt special to cook a meal for you. It's like all the love I have for you goes into making it, if that makes sense."

"I can actually tell it does too."

"Do you have to work tomorrow day or night?"

"I've cleared my schedule, and you have me all to yourself for the next two days." Alex watched her reaction.

"For real? You don't have to work at all? Cool. Hmm … what can we get up to in two days? Lots of mischief," Shelley said, smirking.

"I've found a guy who can manage everything for me. The best thing about getting this guy in now is if he works out, I can visit you a lot more. But we'll have to see how he goes first. He's one of my old friends from years ago."

"That is such good news!"

Alex nodded. "How about we finish our dessert in front of the fire? I don't want to waste that nice lemon meringue pie you made for me."

Shelley nodded, fastening her bra and blouse buttons.

*****

After they ate their dessert, Alex placed some cushions on the plush rug in front of the fire, and they cuddled into each other. Gazing into the fire and feeling a little bit more relaxed, Shelley soon drifted off to sleep.

CHAPTER SEVEN

The next morning, Shelley woke early and found herself in Alex's bedroom, sleeping next to Alex, who was fast asleep and breathing slowly. *Hmm, Alex must have carried me up here last night after I went to sleep in front of the fire. I might let him sleep and shower.* She quietly rolled out of bed. As she walked toward the bathroom, Shelley got a whiff of some food cooking downstairs. *Something sure smells good.*

When Shelley entered the kitchen, she noticed a dark-headed woman wearing an apron at the cooktop, making some breakfast. "Good morning. My name is Shelley." She proffered her hand as she got closer.

"Good morning, Shelley," she replied with a French accent and wiped her hands on her apron to shake Shelley's hand. "It's so nice to meet you. Sire talks about you a lot, and I was hoping to meet you before you went back home tomorrow night. Sorry, I am being rude. My name is Luda, and I am Mr. Crestwell's cook."

"Oh, right. It's nice to me you too, Luda."

"Would you like a tea or coffee, Shelley?"

"Sure, but I can make it. You look like you're busy."

Luda flipped the bacon. "I'm making omelet, bacon, and waffles for you and Sire."

"Thank you. That's so nice. Can I help you make it? I love to cook."

"Sure, that would good, Shelley. Do you know how to use the waffle maker?"

"Yes, I sure do. But first, I'll make you and me a hot drink." Shelley walked to the coffee machine.

"Thanks, Shelley. I will have a strong, white coffee." Luda took the bacon from the frypan and covered it to keep it warm.

"Here you go." Shelley placed Luda's mug of coffee on the island counter.

"Thank you." Luda pulled out the barstool and sat next to Shelley at the bench. "So, where are you from?"

"Currently, I live in Portland, but when I get back from vacation, I'm moving to San Francisco. I want to open my own business there. Plus, my family lives there."

"What type of business?" *Family* ...

Shelley raised the mug to her lips. "Psychiatry."

"I'm sure Sire will miss you terribly!"

"Yes, and I will miss him too. How long have you worked for Alex?"

"I've been with Mr. Crestwell for about two years now."

"He has such a lovely house; don't you think?"

"Yes, this house is extremely comfortable, and he has spared no expense when it comes to appliances or furniture. Did you know I live on the property?"

"I didn't."

"I have a little house down the back of the property I rent from Mr. Crestwell."

"That would be handy, especially when you need to start early for work."

"It sure is. I not only do the cooking, but I also do the cleaning, amongst other things."

She sure does a lot around here. "I certainly will miss this beautiful house when I have to leave. It's something I can only imagine owning one day, but not only that, something about Alex and this house makes me feel … I don't know, comfortable, safe—like I'm meant to be here. I can't explain it. Its' a feeling I've had from the very first time I visited."

You're a Lepidoptera dear. We are family. That is why. "I know what you mean. Sire can make you feel that way." Luda took a sip from her mug.

"It's been lovely chatting with you, Luda, but I think I might make Alex a coffee and see if he's awake." Shelley stood and walked to the coffee machine.

"Yes, I have enjoyed our chat. But I had better get on with cooking breakfast. Sire wouldn't be too pleased if I didn't have it ready when he wakes." Luda headed to the waffle maker.

*****

As Shelley entered Alex's bedroom, she noticed he was still asleep, which wasn't like him, as he was usually an early riser. She placed his coffee cup on the bedside table, sat on the bed next to him and studied his relaxed face. She ran her fingers through his hair and down the side of his face whilst admiring what a wonderful view she had of her sleeping prince.

His dilated eyes opened wide, darting all around the darkened room. *Calm yourself, Crestwell. It's only Shelley.*

"Good morning, sleepyhead. You must be tired, as you have slept in this morning. That's not like you. Are you okay?" Shelley brushed her hand down the side of his face, looking into his eyes.

He took a deep breath and smiled up at her. "I'm tired, my sweet girl, that's all. But it's nice to wake up to your lovely face."

Shelley smiled. "Sit up. I made you coffee." Shelley took the mug off the bedside table and placed it in front of him.

"Thanks. Did you make it or Luda?" Alex sat upright, adjusting his pillow behind him.

"I made it."

"So, you met Luda this morning?" Alex sipped his coffee. *Mmm ... this is what I need.*

"Yes. She is lovely and easy to talk to. When I was chatting with her, it felt like I had known her for years. But I have a question. Why does everyone around here call you Sire or Sir instead of Alex or Mr. Crestwell?" Shelley's brow furrowed. "It's strange to me, that's all."

"In Europe, it's kind a respect thing. Strange, I know, but you get used to it after a while."

"Right. Are you hungry? Luda has made breakfast for us both."

"I'm a little bit hungry." Alex placed his mug on the bedside table.

*****

When they entered the kitchen, they saw Luda cleaning the kitchen.

"Good morning, Sire." *Are you not well, Sire?*

"Good morning, Luda," Alex said, sitting at the island counter with Shelley.

"Would you like some breakfast, Sire?"

"Yes please, Luda." *Not too much for me this morning, Luda. Not feeling too good.*

So, what is wrong with you?

I think I need a blood fix. I haven't had one for a few days, and quite frankly, I haven't had the time.

Would you like me to distract Shelley this morning with something so you can get some food?

Yes please, Luda. I shouldn't be gone too long.

Eat up and I'll distract her. "Shelley, what would you like for breakfast?"

"I might have a waffle this morning. There is some whipped cream in the fridge from last night and maybe some strawberries." Shelley approached the fridge.

"Right. Sire, what can I get you this morning?" Luda put a large waffle on a plate for Shelley and placed it in front of her.

"I'll have an omelet." Alex surveyed the cooktop at what Luda had made.

Luda dished up the omelet and placed the plate in front of him.

*****

After Alex and Shelley finished their breakfast, Luda returned to the kitchen to load the dishwasher.

"I'll be back in a minute, sweet girl. The men's is calling." Alex stood, kissed the side of Shelley's head and walked toward the doorway.

Luda sat on the barstool next to Shelley. "So, you say you like to cook. What are your favorite dishes to make?"

"I like to cook most dishes—anything actually. Has to have lots of flavor and color though."

"I'm sure Sire would love to taste more of your cooking. He has let me know what you have made for him so far and said he loved it." Luda had realized her distraction technique wasn't working when she couldn't read Shelley's thoughts. *Shit, that's right, because Shelley is transitioning into a Lepidoptera, I won't be able to distract her. I've forgotten about that. Looks like I'll have to distract her the old-fashioned human way.* "Would you like a cup of tea or coffee?"

"That would be nice. Tea for me. Thanks, Luda."

"It looks like Sire might be a while. How about we walk around the grounds with our tea?"

"Sure. That would be nice."

*****

By the time Alex had arrived home from his feed, Luda had already shown Shelley the grounds and was now showing her the reading room, which was jam packed with books on shelves along the two walls.

"Hello, ladies, what are you both up to?" Alex entered the room and stood next to Shelley.

"I was showing Shelley your reading room, Sire." *All good here, Sire.*

"Right. Sorry I took so long. I thought I might as well shower while I was upstairs. But the phone rang, and I got distracted with work."

"No problem. Luda showed me around your lovely home. It's so beautiful in the gardens, and what a view. The rest of the house is absolutely stunning too. Whoever decorated it sure knew what they were doing."

"I'll finish in the kitchen and see you later tonight for dinner," Luda said.

"Thanks for showing me around, Luda."

"You're welcome, dear," Luda called out as she left.

"I might shower now." Alex smirked. "You feel like washing my back?"

Shelley grinned. "Humph, don't temp me, teaser."

Alex laughed. "I won't be long. Make yourself at home."

As Shelley circled the room, she noticed Alex's library contained all sorts of books—history, politics, romance, supernatural, gardening, and many others. One thing she hadn't seen around the house yet was photos of Alex or his family. *Maybe he has them packed away, but that sure is strange.*

After walking around the house, Shelley ended up outside and sitting on the stairs that lead into the gardens overlooking the pool area. *What a beautiful day it is out here. The warm sun on my face makes me feel alive.*

"It's a beautiful view, isn't it?" Alex asked, interrupting her thoughts as he sat next to her.

"Sure is. You are so lucky. I love being outside. The sun always makes me feel alive."

"I know what you mean. I love the outdoors too. Hey, I was thinking … Do you like four-wheeling?"

"I love it, but haven't ridden one in ages. Why?"

"Down the back of the property, I have a couple four-wheelers, and we could go for a ride if you want. What do you think?"

"That sounds like fun. Yes please."

"Awesome! Let's go."

*****

Once Alex fueled up the four-wheelers, they rode into the surrounding trees and tracks, chasing each other in and out of the bushes and racing each other over the hills. When they eventually stopped next to each other and let the cloud of dirt catch up to them, they chuckled when they realized how much dirt covered them, from head to toe. All they could see was their goggle-imprinted eyes outline and white teeth.

Shelley couldn't remember having this much fun or laughing that much in such a long time. *I don't think I have seen Alex this relaxed in days.* Shelley pulled away on her bike from Alex and showered him with dust.

Impressed by her skills, Alex watched from the sidelines how Shelley raised herself off the seat as she rode over the dirt jumps with ease and tore around the property, sliding and skidding, throwing dirt sideways, and went round and round in circles, eventually pulling up next to him. "You are not a bad rider. I am surprised. Most women can't ride four-wheelers."

"Thanks. There is probably a lot you don't know about me yet. You look like you are enjoying yourself too."

"I could say the same for you." Alex snickered. "Look how dirty you are."

"I haven't laughed this hard in a while."

"Catch me if you can!" Alex sped off and flicked dirt at her.

Cheeky shit. Shelley chased after him and cut him off at the pass.

Alex pulled over next to her. "No fair. You cheated!"

Shelley smirked. "And what, you didn't?"

They both laughed loudly.

"This day has been so much fun," Shelley said.

"Sure has."

*****

Once they arrived at the house, Alex said, "You can shower first, and I'll go in after you if you like."

"Would you like to shower with me instead?" Shelley smirked at him with raised eyebrows.

"I would love to, but only if you're sure."

"I'm sure. Anyhow, I need someone to scrub my back," Shelley teased and ran up the stairs.

Alex chased Shelley. Chuckling, he tried to catch her. When they reached the top of the stairs, Alex grabbed Shelley and pulled her into his arms. They both laughed so much that Shelley's stomach hurt. Alex leaned in for a kiss on her dirty lips, and when they came up for air, Alex said, "It will be you who scrubs my back, wench." He chuckled and ran into the bathroom.

Shelley followed him, trying to catch him. *God, how I love this playful side of Alex.* When she caught him in the bathroom, she said, "Wench? Hey, I'll give you wench!" She pulled him in closer for a kiss.

Panting, they stripped off their clothes and hoped into the shower where Alex washed the dirt from her body.

*****

Shelley poured the Moroccan body wash onto the sponge and lathered Alex's back as he stood with his hands pressed onto the tiles and head under the water.

The more she touched Alex, his breathing quickened, and he fantasized how good it would be to make love to his life partner.

"Your back's done. Turn around." Shelley watched the foam disappear from his body as he faced her.

Alex tried to calm himself when he felt the blood run through his enlarged penis.

Shelley looked into his eyes and smirked. Raising one eyebrow, she rinsed the sponge and placed some more bodywash onto it. Starting at his broad shoulders, she slowly made her way to his abdomen, rubbing gently, until she reached his erection. "Hmm, what do we have here? Someone has woken." Smirking, she gingerly cleaned his penis and scrotum with the sponge. *He smells good.* She knelt in front of him and washed the dirt from his legs and feet while watching his erection grow larger.

Alex could hear her heart beating fast, but before he could stop her, she had placed his cock in her mouth to enjoy his fullness. *Oh my god … feels so good.* Alex moaned and thrust his penis in and out of her mouth whilst holding onto her shoulders. When Shelley swirled her tongue around the tip of his penis and rapidly pulled it in and out of her mouth, it tipped Alex over the edge. With his senses heightened and his body quivering from her touch, Alex's eyes dilated, and he felt his fangs extend. Quickly, he withdrew his penis from her mouth, turned off the water, scooped Shelley into his arms and carried her to his bedroom. After he laid her on the edge of his bed, she stayed there, naked, watching his every move. Slowly, he knelt in front of her, pulled her legs apart and nipped and sucked at her clitoris.

Shelley took a deep breath and quivered as she moaned from the pure pleasure.

Turned on by her scent and taste, Alex became oblivious to how this was about to play out. He laid on the bed next to Shelley and kissed her soft lips whilst he caressed her right breast.

Shelley's body felt like she was on fire, and her body shuddered when Alex sucked and kissed her neck and earlobe. *God, I can't take much more.*

"I want you," Alex murmured as he sucked and nipped gently at her left nipple.

Don't stop ...

Alex placed his finger into her vagina, pulling it in and out gently, slowly until she adjusted, and he felt her come.

"Alex ... please ... Don't stop. That feels ... too good,"

"I'll need to stop soon, sweet girl, otherwise, I'll have my way with you," Alex said, panting.

"I won't stop you. I'm ready to give myself to you. Please ... take me!"

"No, not yet, my love. As much as you want me now, you will regret it later."

"Please stop talking. I want you now, but please be gentle with me."

When Alex heard these words, his penis burned with delight as the blood rushed through, but he knew he had to withhold, as she would become a Lepidoptera. So he did the next best thing he could think of.

What is he waiting for? I've given him the green light. She watched him scoot down the bed and suck her clitoris again. With her emotions in overload, she moaned as Alex provided her further pleasure by biting her clitoris and drinking her blood. To any human, this was pure pleasure, but it also placed them into a sleeplike state afterward.

Even though Alex knew this was the only thing he could do, he now was attracted to her even more, because he had her blood in his system. When she would wake later, Alex would tell her she had fallen asleep and that they didn't have sex. The bite marks would heal too so she wouldn't feel sore below.

*****

Shelley woke to find herself naked under the covers, not remembering anything past asking Alex to have his way with her. *God, no. I hope we didn't do that. No, I should have said no. Shame on me. What have I done?* Her gaze darted around the room as she sat upright in bed.

Alex listened to Shelley's thoughts as he rinsed his mouth free of the toothpaste. Now that her blood was in his system, he could hear her every thought. *Fuck, Crestwell, you need to get back in there with her.* Alex entered the room and approached the bed. "Hello there, sleepyhead. You sure know how to make a man feel unwanted. You fell asleep on me. You must have been tired."

Shelley's heart beat fast. "Hello. So … we didn't have sex?"

"No. You fell asleep."

Thank the dear lord for that. She took a deep breath in and out. "I'm sorry for falling asleep on you. You must think I'm one hell of a tease. But I must say, I'm glad we didn't do it. I need to control myself when I'm around you. Your touch, it turns me on so much, so much that I always give in to you easily and without any regard for myself or my beliefs. Sorry, that must sound arrogant."

He sat next on the bed. "I don't think so, babe. I knew you didn't want to, but a man can only hope." Alex's brow furrowed.

"I wish I could stay longer, you know, so I could get to know you more, and, in turn, maybe I would feel comfortable about sleeping together." She placed her hand in his.

Alex leaned into Shelley and gave her a long, passionate kiss.

His lips are to die for, so soft and velvet-like to touch.

Alex pulled away slowly and caressed the side of her face. "Don't be mad at me, but I need to ask you something. When you go home to Portland tomorrow, what are you going back for? Is it that you have an interview for job, or ...? I need to know, that's all."

"No, I don't have a job interview or a reason to go back so soon, except my ticket has been booked for tomorrow. Why do you ask?"

"Why are you going back tomorrow? Why don't you stay with me for, say, another month, and we can get to know each other a bit more? As you can tell, I don't want you to leave, but I can't see why you're going back if you don't have anything planned, especially since you say you love me and don't want to leave me." He looked into her eyes with wonder.

"Actually, I was thinking the same thing yesterday. I don't have an answer either, besides that my bank accounts is nearly out of money, so I'd have to find work if I did stay. But, if I do stay, I want to earn my keep. I won't mooch off you."

Alex raised his eyebrows. "So, does that mean you're willing to stay if I can get you a job somewhere?"

"I suppose it does. Jeez, how easy was that to plan? Why didn't we think about this before? It would have saved us a lot of heartache. But I do need to go home soon, as I want to start my practice in San Francisco."

"You have made me the happiest man alive right now. I can't believe you're going to stay." Alex hugged Shelley tight.

"And, who knows, I might even like it here enough after one month that I open my practice here instead."

Alex leaned in and kissed Shelley's lips wantonly.

His lips are so soft, and now they are mine. As they came up for air, Shelley said, "I think I'll call the girls and meet with them in person to give them the news. I know they'll be happy for me, but I think they'll be sad I'm not going home with them too. What time is it?"

Alex checked his bedside digital clock. "It's only two thirty."

"So, would you be okay with us spending the next day and a half with the girls?" She looked into his adoring eyes. "I want to spend some time with them before they go back to Portland."

"That's fine. Hey, how about we all go to Rome today in my jet and return tomorrow afternoon? Their flight to home isn't until midnight, so that will give them plenty of time to pack for the trip to Portland, and we can go with them to the airport to say goodbye."

"Really? You want to take us all to Rome? That is so nice of you. I'm sure the girls would love it. What time would we leave?"

"Say around four thirty. I'm sure I can get the plane organized by then. I'll ask Carson to bring them to the airport if you like."

"Let me call them and see what they're doing first." Shelley hugged Alex. "Thank you." Shelley dialed Analyse's number.

"Hi, Shell. How are you?"

"I'm good. I have a surprise for you and Bronwyn. Would you like to go to Rome today with Alex and me?"

Analyse screamed with glee. "For real?"

"Yep." Shelley smiled from ear to ear.

"Man, thank you. Yes, we would love to go. Hold on!"

Shelley heard Analyse pull the phone away from her ear and say, "Guess what? We're going to Rome today with Alex and Shelley."

"Carson will pick you up out front in, say, thirty minutes. Does that give you both enough time to get ready? Pack an overnight bag, as we won't be back until tomorrow afternoon."

"We'll be ready. Thanks, Shelley, and tell Alex we said thank you too!"

As Shelley pressed End on her phone, she said to Alex, "I suppose you could hear how happy they are about going."

"It'll be nice spending some time with them again. Your friends are great to hang out with, and I'm glad I could organize something that makes them happy."

"Hey, now that I am staying, maybe I might get to meet some of your friends. I remember you said you had some here and some in Paris too."

He kissed the side of her head. "I'm sure they would love to meet you too, sweet girl."

CHAPTER EIGHT

Nice ride, Shelley thought as she watched Alex pull up in front of her in his sleek, black Mercedes Benz sedan.

"You ready to go?" Alex asked as he alighted from the car and opened the trunk.

"Sweet ride!" Shelley handed him her overnight bag.

"Yeah, it's one of my favorites. Handles well too." Alex placed her bag with his in the trunk and closed it. He opened the passenger's door for her, and she slid into the seat.

Nice, Shelley thought, feeling the softness of black leather and admiring the sleek, black console and illuminated dash.

"You ready for a ride of your life, sweet girl?" Alex climbed into his seat and fastened his seatbelt.

Shelley buckled her seatbelt. "Give it all you got. I love to drive fast."

Once they were on the open road, Alex mashed the gas pedal, which flattened Shelley's back into the seat.

"Wow, this certainly moves," Shelley looked from the road to Alex.

Alex smiled and kept an eye on the road as he wound through the traffic toward the airport.

"Can we listen to some music?"

Alex glanced at Shelley. "There's an iPod in the console."

Shelley opened the console and spotted the iPod and connected it to the USB port inside the console. She flicked through the playlist of songs and eventually found one she liked and pressed Play, watching Alex's expression when 'Can't Get You Out of My Head' came through the speakers.

He smiled and eyed her. "How appropriate is this song?"

Shelley smirked. "Yeah, I know." *God, he looks sexy as hell. I want to kiss his gorgeous body all over.*

Alex read her thoughts and grinned.

*****

With the plane waiting for them on the tarmac, Alex pulled next to the metal stairs and turned off the engine. "You go ahead and get yourself seated. I'll get the bags and meet you on board. The girls are already on the plane."

Shelley opened her door. "Thanks." As she reached the top of the metal stairs and popped her head around the corner into the cabin, she saw Bronwyn and Analyse jump from their seats to give her a group hug. "I've missed you both so much. Have you been enjoying your time here so far?"

"Sure have," Bronwyn said as she and Analyse slowly pulled away from Shelley's embrace.

"Alex's friends have been keeping us company and taking us places. We've had a ball. I'll be sad to leave tomorrow," Analyse said.

"That's good. I have some news for you, but I'm not sure you'll like it."

"I think we can probably guess what you're going to say, Shell," Analyse said. "You're staying, aren't you?"

Shelley watched their reaction as she nodded. "Alex has asked me if I'd like to stay with him for another month, and I said yes. But I did tell him that after that, I'd need to go home. What do you think?"

"We sure will miss you." Bronwyn's brow furrowed. "But it has been nice seeing you so happy these last couple weeks with Mr. Gorgeous."

"Yeah, go for it. Whatever makes you happy, I say," Analyse said.

"Thanks, girls. I appreciate your support."

The captain spoke over the speaker to tell them to take their seats and get ready for takeoff.

As Shelley sat across from Analyse and Bronwyn and Alex sat next to her, she thought, *I can enjoy myself and get to know Alex a lot more and not have to think about leaving.*

*****

As the plane came to a stop on the tarmac at the Fiumicino airport in Rome a few hours later, Shelley looked out the small plane window and noticed a black limousine. Leaning into Alex, she asked, "Is that for us?"

"Sure is."

Analyse and Bronwyn both looked from Shelley to the window and smiled, noticing the limousine.

"I'm going to take you all on a tour of Roma. It's such a beautiful city; you'll love it."

Analyse and Bronwyn giggled excitedly.

Shelley leaned into Alex. "Thank you."

*****

The afternoon was jam packed with tours at the Colosseum, Vatican, and the Sistine Chapel, visiting the Trevi Fountain, the Spanish Steps, and many more historical sites. And, as the evening drew near, Alex took them to one of his favorite family orientated restaurants called La Tavernaccia, which served traditional Italian food. The restaurant was well known for not only its delicious food and wine but also for playing music, which they all danced to when the band played "The Birdie Song." The night was so much fun, and Alex couldn't remember laughing this much in such a long time.

*****

That night after dinner, Alex had booked them into the Hilton Hotel for the night. Bronwyn and Analyse shared one room, whilst Alex and Shelley occupied another next door. The rooms were extremely elegant and were much like the Crestwell Hotel rooms.

"Thank you so much for today and tonight. We won't ever forget your generosity. If we can ever do anything for you, don't hesitate to ask." Bronwyn hugged Alex as they stood outside her hotel room doorway.

"Yes, thank you, Alex," Analyse said. "Our holiday has been perfect in many ways."

"You're welcome, ladies. I'm glad, and I've enjoyed spending time with two lovely ladies like yourselves. Shelley sure is lucky to have good friends like you both to protect and look after her. I'm sure she'll miss you while she's here. By the way, tomorrow, we'll be going shopping, and it's on me. You can buy anything you want at the clothes shop."

"Wow, thanks, Alex. That is so generous of you, but I wouldn't feel right taking your money. I do have some money left, so I should be okay. But thank you for offering," Bronwyn said.

"Sorry, Alex, I feel the same way. As much as that is a lovely gesture, I wouldn't feel right spending your money."

"No problem. I do understand. But, if you change your mind tomorrow, the offer still stands. I love to see you happy, that's all. Goodnight, see you in the morning." He walked toward his room doorway.

Shelley gave them both a hug. "Goodnight. See you in the morning. And think about taking Alex up on his offer. He enjoys being generous to people he likes."

Analyse and Bronwyn both said their goodnights to Shelley and watched her walk to her room doorway.

*****

Alex and Shelley entered the room, and Alex closed and locked the door behind them. Shelley pushed him gently against the wall and kissed his neck. "Mmm … you always smell good." Her breathing increased.

Her sensual touch awakened his penis, and, before he knew it, Alex pulled Shelley's top over her head and unfastened her bra then hastily discarded them both to the floor. With his hand cupping and caressing her breasts, he kissed her lips passionately.

"What you do to me …" Shelley said when he sucked and kissed her neck. *Man, I feel like I'm on fire.* Once again, she felt the need for him to have his way with her, but she knew she couldn't—not today.

Without warning, Alex picked her up in his arms and laid her on the bed. "We can play if you want. Is that okay?"

Shelley smiled at him and nodded.

Alex removed all his clothes except his boxer-briefs and laid next to her. Once he had her naked too, Alex said, "You know you have a beautiful body. It's as smooth as velvet." He ran his hand up and down, pleasuring her body.

Goosebumps formed on her, and her nipples stood to attention as Alex kissed her neck and grazed her earlobe. Traveling down to her nipples, he licked, sucked, and nipped at them, making her moan in sheer delight. The torment he was inflicting was relentless. Sliding off the bed, Alex pulled Shelley closer to the edge and kneeled in front of her. He pushed her legs apart, placed his tongue into her vagina and sucked her clitoris.

She moaned and arched her back off the bed, pushing her vagina into his mouth, as she orgasmed. Breathless, she lay there, feeling overwhelmed with passion.

Alex smiled to himself and laid next to Shelley. "Would you like to play some more?"

"Give me a minute. I'm exhausted." But, as soon as she said it, Shelley got a second wind, pulled down his boxer-briefs and gave him what she knew he needed.

Exhausted from all their play, Alex outstretched his arm for Shelley to cuddle into him and kissed the side of her forehead. "I love you, sweet girl. I'm so glad you're staying for one more month."

"I love you too, my sweet, sweet man," she said as she yawned.

They got under the covers and eventually went to sleep, cuddling each other.

*****

The next morning, Shelley woke to the smell of breakfast being brought into their room by a bellboy. The breakfast cart contained an array of delicious items to eat and drink. Unbeknown to Shelley, Alex had ordered the same for Analyse and Bronwyn.

As Shelley sat upright in bed and placed her feet on the floor, Alex approached with the breakfast cart. "Stay there. I want to give you breakfast in bed."

"Aww, thank you. This is so nice of you to organize breakfast for me. What a sweet man you are. But I need to go to the ladies room first."

Alex watched her get out of bed, noticing she was still naked from last night's escapades. *Mmm ... beautiful.*

"Thank you," Shelley said, hearing his thoughts. She pulled the sheet from the bed and wrapped it around herself and walked toward the bathroom, grabbing her bag on the way so she could get out her nightgown.

Shit, Crestwell, you need to hide your thoughts. Luckily, she didn't notice you didn't move your lips, only your mind. Note to self: got to be more careful. I don't want to scare her off.

*****

With pillows propped up behind her in bed, Shelley surveyed the scrambled eggs and bacon Alex had placed in her lap. "This looks yummy. Mmm, a cup of tea too; this is what I need."

"I enjoy doing this for you, my sweet girl," Alex said, looking over his shoulder as he got a plate of food for himself, then sat on the bed next to her.

"These scrambled eggs are yummy, probably the best I've ever had." Shelley swallowed her first mouthful.

Alex smiled at her. "Can I spoil you some more today by taking you shopping? I would love to buy you something nice. A beautiful body like yours deserves to wear beautiful clothes."

"Really? That sounds awesome! But only if I can buy you something too."

"Fair deal." Alex cut into his bacon. "By the way, I texted the girls this morning about meeting us in reception at ten o'clock. So that gives us an hour to shower and get ready. I hope they let me buy them something today. I enjoy seeing their faces light up with delight when they get something special."

"You're too nice for your own good. But that is something I do love about you." Shelley leaned in and kissed his lips. "Alex, I want to ask you something, but I'm not sure how to say this."

"What is it?" But he already knew what she was going to say by reading her thoughts.

"When I am away from you, I yearn for you. When I'm with you, I can't get enough of you. Even when you touch me, my skin ignites. When we kiss, your lips feel so sensual to me. I always feel like the attraction I have for you is more than that and has awakened something in me. I suppose my question is, do you feel like that about me?" Shelley's brow furrowed as she waited for his response.

Alex regarded Shelley as if he was thinking of an answer. "If you're asking if it's normal to feel this way about someone you're attracted to and love, the answer is yes. I've spoken with some of my friends about this, and they've told me this is normal to feel like a lovesick puppy, as they put it, when you have feelings for someone. Apparently, it starts as a feeling of attraction then escalates into a need to be with them. But, in answer to your question about whether I feel the same way; yes, I have the same feelings. You know, for days now, I've been trying to think of a way to stop you from going home, and it wasn't until I spoke to my friend William that the answer hit me. He asked me why you were leaving and if you had something you were going back to in Portland. I'm glad you're staying so we can see if our relationship will work. So, you've not had a real boyfriend previously?"

"No, not someone like you. I don't think I've ever felt this way about a guy. I have led a pretty sheltered life and have studied a lot, and there hasn't been a lot of time for guys. That's why I was wondering if this is normal. I can't believe how lucky I am to have come all the way to Switzerland to find a guy like you." She ran her hand down the side of his face.

"It should be me saying that. You're so good for me, Shelley, and for us to be together as a couple, I can't wait to shout it to the world." He looked into her eyes, leaned in and kissed her tenderly.

After pulling away slowly, she placed her plate on the bedside table and cuddled into his chest.

After about ten minutes, Alex said, "As much as I would love to do this all day, babe, I'm sorry, but we need to get a move on if we want to be in reception by ten o'clock."

She sighed, released herself from his loving arms and hopped out of bed to shower.

*****

When they arrived in reception, they saw Carson waiting with Bronwyn and Analyse, as he would drive them today.

"Hi, Carson. Nice to see you again," Shelley said.

Carson took her overnight bag. "Good morning, Shelley. Are you ready for what Alex has planned for you?"

Shelley noticed the wide smirk on Carson's face. "What does Alex have planned for us today?"

"I'm taking you ladies to Venice by plane for some shopping," Alex said.

Bronwyn and Analyse screamed in delight and thanked him.

"Thank you for the nice surprise," Shelley said to Alex.

"You're welcome, ladies. So, are we ready to go?"

They all nodded in anticipation of their day.

*****

Noticing the humidity as she departed the plane in Venice, Shelley watched Carson open the car door and help them into the limousine.

As instructed, Carson was to take them to where the good bargain-hunting was. First, they went to some street shopping, which looked like flea markets. This was fantastic, as the girls got to choose some trinkets, hats, scarves, sunglasses, and ornaments. Next, they went clothes shopping, and these shops were average-to-expensive pricing.

As Alex waited patiently for the three women to try on the clothes in each shop, he would give his opinion on whether it looked good on them. He even bought them shoes from an expensive shoe shop to match the clothing. Alex checked his watch as they stood at the shoe shop counter. "It's nearly one o'clock, ladies. Would you like to get some lunch?"

Bronwyn took the bag from the cashier. "Sounds like a plan."

Shelley nodded.

"All this shopping and walking sure has made me hungry," Analyse said, taking her bag from the cashier.

"I know a great restaurant nearby, and after lunch, I thought we might all take a gondola ride in the Venice canals and do some sightseeing. What do you think?"

"Sounds awesome," Bronwyn said.

Excited with what the afternoon would hold for them, both Shelley and Analyse smiled and nodded.

*****

Seated next to Shelley on the plane, Alex watched her flick through the photos on her phone she had taken today. "You're quiet. Is everything okay?"

Shelley snuggled into Alex's side. "Yeah, I'm okay. I was reviewing the photos I took today and was thinking about what an amazing day I've had—the shopping and sightseeing—and that I've thoroughly enjoyed myself. Thank you."

"You're welcome. But I sense something else is going on."

"I was thinking about how Bronwyn and Analyse are going home later. I sure will miss them."

"I'm sure they'll miss you too, my love. When we get to the hotel, how about I leave you three alone for the rest of the night? I can come back at about nine thirty to pick you all up and take the girls to the airport. That way you get to spend some quality time with them before they leave. How does that sound?"

"Thanks, that would be great. I'd like to spend some time with them, you know, talking about girly things and, of course, you."

"Okay, that's settled." Alex rested his head on Shelley's as the plane taxied down the runway for their few hours' flight to Zurich.

*****

As the car arrived at the Crestwell Hotel, Alex said, "I'll see you ladies later."

"Thanks for our trip to Rome and Venice, Alex," Bronwyn said.

"Yeah, thanks, Alex. I've had the time of my life on this vacation," Analyse said.

"You're both welcome. I'll see you all in reception at around nine thirty tonight. Have a lovely time at dinner." Alex stepped out the car and helped the three women alight from the limousine.

"See ya later on, Alex." Shelley leaned in for a hug.

"See you later, sweet girl." He walked inside toward reception to check on his new manager.

Turning to Bronwyn and Analyse, Shelley said, "How about we go to our rooms to pack and after we can have dinner at one of the hotel restaurants?"

"Sounds good. We can meet here in, say, an hour?" Bronwyn said.

"Yeah, that's doable," Analyse said.

*****

With her bags packed, Shelley took one last look around her hotel room to ensure she hadn't left anything behind. I can't believe how many clothes I bought over the last two weeks. The zipper looks like it might break on my suitcase. Wonder what it'll be like when I've been here for another month. She placed her bags near the doorway for when she would return later to collect them. I wonder if the girls are ready yet. Might go and see. Shelley checked her purse for her room keycard.

Shelley knocked on Analyse's door and heard her say, "One moment."

When Analyse opened the door in her blue and white satin robe, Shelley realized Analyse had company. "Sorry, Shell, I'm not ready yet. I'll see you downstairs. By the way, Bronwyn has someone with her too, so don't knock on her door."

Shelley's cheeks reddened. "Oh, right. Sorry. I-I didn't realize." *God, how embarrassing.* "See you downstairs about six thirty. Will that be okay?"

Analyse nodded and mouthed, *Sorry,* smiled politely and closed the door.

*****

"Thank you," Shelley said as the bartender placed a glass of wine in front of her. She gazed into the glass. God, how could I have not known Bronwyn and Analyse had men they were seeing and probably having sex with while we were here? They never even told me about these guys. I suppose I've been wrapped up in my own world, and this is why I didn't know. I should have told them not to worry about tonight and to have a good time with their male friends instead. But still, it would have been good to spend some time with them tonight before they go home.

As Shelley sat wondering what she would do whilst she waited for her two friends, she felt a familiar hand wrap around her waist.

"Hello, what are you doing here all by yourself?" Alex asked.

Shelley turned around. "The girls are sort of occupied with your male friends. I went to Analyse's room, and when she opened the door, she was in her robe and had male company, so I figured this must have been one of your friends. She told me Bronwyn had a guy with her too and not to disturb her either. I felt so embarrassed. I didn't even know they were seeing these guys, and I wonder why they didn't tell me."

"Maybe they didn't tell you because it's only a holiday fling, not something serious, like us. So, you're sitting here waiting for them? Why don't you text them and tell them to enjoy themselves and we can meet them in reception at nine thirty. I'm sure they'd appreciate it."

"Yeah, you read my mind." Shelley took her phone from her pocket, not knowing he *had* read her mind. *It would have been nice to spend our last night together though.*

"Can I take you to dinner, my sweet girl? There is a nice restaurant next door that I think you may like."

"That would be nice. Give me a minute, and I'll message the girls."

*****

Alex opened the restaurant door to wave Shelley inside and followed behind her. As he closed the glass door behind him, his senses were heightened when he spotted the three Debauched vampires leaning on the steel railing along the River Limmat. *I wonder what those fuckers want.*

"Table for two, sir?" the manager asked.

Alex didn't answer; he was too busy looking in the Debauched vampires' direction.

"Sir? Mr. Crestwell?"

"Huh? Yes, sorry. That would be great. Make it somewhere quiet and in the back. Thanks."

"Right this way, sir, madam." The manager walked through the restaurant. "Will this table be satisfactory, sir?"

Alex pulled out a chair. "Yes, this is fine."

The manager pulled out a chair for Shelley.

"Thank you," Shelley said, not used to this type of service.

"Would sir, madam like to order some drinks?"

"Umm, we might have some water to start, if that's okay." Shelley looked from the manager to Alex, who was watching the front windows.

The manager poured the water, placed the menus in front of them, announced the specials then left them to choose their meals.

Gian ... Gian, Alex mind-thought. He waited a few seconds for a reply.

Yes, Sire?

Three Debauched are out front. Get two of the guards and deal with them. Alex gave Shelley a polite smile across the table.

Yes, Sire.

Shelley reached across the table for his hand. "Penny for your thoughts."

"Umm ... I was actually thinking I haven't organized for a car to take the girls to the airport tonight and that I must do that when we get back from dinner," Alex lied, taking her hand. *Get it together, Crestwell.*

Shelley looked into his eyes and nodded.

Alex removed a red velvet box from his jacket pocket and placed it in front of her. "Open it."

Shelley eyed the small box. "You shouldn't have."

He smiled. "I saw this today and thought you'd like it."

As Shelley opened the box, she gulped hard and panned from Alex to the contents of the box. "This is lovely. Can I wear it now?" Shelley eyed the gold band ring with embedded white diamonds.

Alex removed the ring from the box and placed it on her right finger. "It's a friendship ring. In Europe, they say this is how to show you're taken."

She looked into Alex eyes, and her heart melted. "So beautiful, and it looks great on my finger too." She watched how it sparkled in the lighting.

"Beautiful ring for a beautiful lady," Alex said, watching the happiness in her eyes.

Shelley leaned over the table and kissed him wantonly. As she came up for a breath and leaned back in her seat, she said, "You are always buying me such lovely gifts. Thank you. I feel spoiled."

"You're welcome," Alex said, watching her delight and listening to her thoughts.

Taken ... I like that. Shelley looked from the ring to Alex and smiled.

Sire, they have been dealt with, Gian mind-thought to Alex.

Thank you. Keep guard out front until we return from dinner.

Yes, Sire.

I wonder if they have sensed Shelley or whether it's a coincidence they were in the area tonight. Either way, I need to keep her safe while she is here for the next month.

*****

With the evening going by fast, Shelley wasn't looking forward to saying goodbye to Analyse and Bronwyn. Their vacation in Switzerland had flown by, and now she was to meet them in the Crestwell Hotel lobby for their ride to the airport.

"Thank you for the lovely meal and my beautiful ring," Shelley said, walking arm in arm out the restaurant with Alex. She had enjoyed the night and especially the slow dancing with Alex.

"You are most welcome." He kissed the side of her forehead, lingering to take in her scent.

*****

When Alex and Shelley entered the reception, they noticed Bronwyn and Analyse were waiting for them with two other men.

"Of course, it's okay. You don't have to ask to make anything around here. This is your home while you're here. *Mi casa es tu casa.*"

"Okay. I think there should be some lemon meringue pie left too. I might have some of that. Would you like some?"

"No thanks, babe. But I'll come with you to the kitchen."

*****

"Here you go, one cup of tea, madam," Alex said playfully and placed it in front of her. "Do you feel a bit better now?"

"Mmm, much better. Thanks," Shelley said, picking up her cup.

"You ready for bed?"

"Yeah. Will be nice to cuddle in bed for a while." Shelley took her plate and cup to the dishwasher.

"While you are staying here, it's not *my* bedroom; it's *our* bedroom. I want you to feel at home here, Shelley."

She raised her eyebrow at him. "I'll try."

When they reached the bedroom, Alex pointed to a stack of bags. "I had your luggage delivered from the hotel, and it's over there."

"Thanks. I was wondering what I was going to sleep in."

"If you need anything washed, put it in a pile, and the staff will wash them for you."

"I'm certainly not used to anyone doing my washing. Do you have a hamper, as I do have a lot of dirty clothes? Also— and this is embarrassing, but you need to know—I'll need to go to the supermarket next week to get some black panties and some tampons, as I'll have my period soon." Shelley's cheeks felt heated. "Sorry, but it's part of being a woman, and I wasn't initially planning on staying any more than two weeks, so I didn't bring any of those items with me."

"No problem at all, babe. I'll take you shopping for whatever you need tomorrow."

"And to warn you, I get a bit moody before I get my period."

"Mmm, now that is something I can help with, if that happens."

Shelley frowned and wasn't sure what he meant, and she didn't ask either.

As she unzipped and opened her suitcase, she saw the present she had brought for Alex today wrapped up and on top of everything else and removed it. "I bought you something today I thought you might like."

Alex's face lit up when he saw the wrapped item. "You didn't have to buy me anything, babe. But I am now excited. What is it?"

Shelley handed him the present. "Open it up and find out."

Alex sat on the bed with excitement and unwrapped the gift. Two presents were inside, wrapped individually. He opened the flat one first, and inside was a white T-shirt with a picture of the Venice gondola ride on it. He put it up to himself and looked in the mirror. "This is awesome, babe. I love it." Excited, he opened the long present and saw the gold designer cufflinks. "Wow, these are nice, babe. Thank you so much."

"Look at the back of them."

Alex turned them over and saw the engraving: *I will love you forever, Luv Shelley.* Alex walked over to Shelley, pulled her in close and kissed her passionately. As he came up for air, he said, "I will love you forever too, my sweet girl. I will never let you go either. No one has ever bought me such a great gift like that before. Thank you."

Shelley beamed. "You're welcome. I wanted to buy you something so when you wore them, you would think of me."

"They certainly are extravagant. What an awesome end to a perfect day."

Shelley nodded and cuddled into his chest. *He always feels good to cuddle into, and I always feel safe and loved while I'm in his arms.*

"Would you like to go with me tomorrow to Paris? I have business in Bagnolet, but it's at a friend's place, so I would love for you to meet his family. Maybe we can stay a couple days if you are enjoying yourself. What do you think?"

"I would love to go, and I would love to meet some of your friends." Shelley walked over to her suitcase.

"Great. We'll probably leave about eleven o'clock in the morning. That should give the staff plenty of time to clean your clothes and for us to pack a bag. And when you wake in the morning, you will find that I won't be here. Don't worry; I have to go into work early. I should be back about nine thirty, if not earlier."

"How's the new manager working out?"

"He's turning out to be good, actually. Are you ready for bed?"

"Umm, I might get into my nightie. Won't be a minute." Shelley retrieved her clothes and toiletries and headed for the bathroom. "I'm glad your new manager has worked out good for you."

"Yeah, me too." Alex watched her close the door. "Don't be long in there, as I need to brush my teeth too."

"Ok!" Shelley called through the door.

CHAPTER NINE

"Morning," Shelley said to Luda and Alex as she entered the kitchen. "Something sure smells good."

"Good morning, Shelley," Luda said, looking up.

"How are you doing, Luda?" Shelley approached Alex sitting at the island counter.

"I'm well. Thanks for asking. What would you like for breakfast, dear?"

"Some cereal would be nice." Shelley leaned into Alex's lips. "Mr. Crestwell ..."

Alex pulled away slowly. "Good morning, sweet girl. Did you sleep well?"

"Yes, thanks for asking. I'm all ready to go to Bagnolet. I only need to put my clean clothes in my suitcase."

"Your laundry should be dry soon, my dear. I'll bring it up to you," Luda said.

"Thank you so much for doing it. I'm not used to other people doing my laundry."

"That's what I get paid for, dear, and I'm happy to do it for you. I'm so glad you're staying for another month."

"Me too."

"I bet you're tired. You didn't get much rest last night, and this morning you had to get up early," Shelley said to Alex.

"I don't need much sleep, babe. I'm okay, no need for you to worry."

Luda placed Shelley's cereal on the island counter. "Here you go. Would you like a cup of tea?"

"Thank you for making breakfast, Luda. No, I won't have a cup of tea."

"If I'm not needed, I'll go finish your clothes." Luda looked from Alex to Shelley.

"That is all for the moment, Luda," Alex said.

She nodded, smiled and left the kitchen.

Shelley leaned over her bowl to mix the milk with the cereal. "Have you had breakfast, Alex?"

"I had some earlier. Well, I might go pack my bag." Alex slid of the chair and carried his cup to the sink.

"As soon as I finish my cereal, I can give you a hand if you want."

"Thanks. I'd say Luda will drop off your clothes soon. I cleared a draw and one side of my wardrobe for you to put clothes if you want. Eat up, and I'll see you upstairs."

*****

I could get used to this type of service. How nice, Luda has not only hung my clothes in the wardrobe but also placed my lingerie into the draw Alex cleared for me, Shelley thought as she packed her bag. When she had finished packing, she went to help Alex with the rest of his folding and packing.

"We make a good team, huh?" Shelley said as Alex exited the bathroom.

"We sure do." Alex wrapped his arms around her waist, pulling her in close for a kiss. "By the way, you sure look lovely in that dress, sweet girl."

"Thanks. I'm wearing the butterfly pin you bought me too. It's beautiful!"

"You are the one who is beautiful. I could gaze at you all day."

Shelley cuddled into his chest and closed her eyes. *God, what you do to me.* "You certainly know how to make a girl feel good."

"I could say the same. I feel like something has awakened in me since I met you." Alex placed his cheek on the top of her head.

Shelley smiled and was looking forward to the next month of spending quality time with the man of her dreams.

*****

"So, what are the names of your colleagues?" Shelley watched out the small round plane window as they landed at Charles De Gaulles airport in Paris.

"William owns the business, and his partners name is Renee. But others live at the house who you'll meet too. They are mostly our age and work for William. It's a bit of a long story, and I'll tell you about it one day, of how each of them came to live with William and Renee," Alex paused to remember how he had first met William more than two hundred years ago.

"The way you make it sound is like William and Renee take in people who need help."

"Sort of, but it's not like that." Alex felt the plane come to a halt. "I'll explain it later to you."

Shelley unfastened her seatbelt. "I'm looking forward to meeting them all. I hope they like me."

"I'm sure they'll love you." Alex stood. "Come on, the car is waiting for us on the tarmac."

Shelley slung her handbag over her shoulder and grabbed Alex's hand. As she followed him out the plane, she noticed Carson waiting for them, holding open the car door.

*****

"Sure is a lovely city," Shelley said, watching out the car window.

Alex took her hand in his. "I'd like to show you more of Bagnolet while we're here."

"I'm looking forward to it." Shelley noticed the car slowing in front of a limestone fence.

William said the code for the keypad is 7984, Carson, Alex mind-thought.

Thank you, Sire. Carson rolled down his window and entered the code into the keypad.

Shelley watched the black iron gates open inward. She surveyed the manicured lawn and gardens as the car traversed the driveway, and her jaw dropped when she noticed the size of the mansion as it came into view.

"Beautiful, isn't it?" Alex asked, watching her face.

"Sure is. I can't wait to see what the inside looks like. I can't believe we are actually staying here!"

As the car stopped outside the front entrance, a doorman opened the car door and helped Shelley exit the car.

"Thank you."

He nodded, waited for Alex to follow and indicated to proceed to the foyer. "I will let Sire know you are here."

Alex nodded and watched him walk toward the rear of the house. But Alex already knew William was aware they had arrived via mind-thought.

Shelley noticed a tall, muscular man flanked by two men in black leather approach them.

William proffered his hand as he got closer. "Alex, my old friend. It's so good to see you again." He hugged Alex and ruggedly patted his back.

"Good to see you too, William." Alex returned the pat.

He turned to Shelley. "Hello, my name is William. It's nice to meet you, Shelley. Alex has told us so much about you."

141

"Hello. Nice to meet you too." Shelley leaned in to hug him. "Come on through. Everyone is out back, waiting."

Shelley grabbed Alex's hand, and, as they walked through the house, Alex could tell from her heartbeat that she was nervous.

"It's okay. I'm here for you," Alex leaned in and whispered.

Shelley squeezed his hand in thanks. *These people sure must be wealthy. Look at this outdoor patio area under the main roof. So grand ...*

"Look who I found lurking at the front door," William said to everyone seated in the patio area.

William's family turned and greeted Alex with either a hug or a slap on the back.

Shelley smiled politely and stood by his side. *He must have known all these people for a long time.*

Alex introduced Shelley to them one by one, explaining who was their partner.

"Hi, my name is Annabelle." She leaned in and hugged Shelley. "So, where are you from, Shelley?"

"I'm originally from San Francisco, but I'm living in Portland at the moment."

"Are you here on holidays?"

"Yeah, long story actually. I came to Zurich on vacation with my two best friends. We had just finished college a few days before and came to Europe as a graduation present to ourselves. Fortunately for me, I met Alex at the Crestwell Hotel, where we were staying, and the rest is history. Actually, my two best friends went home to Portland yesterday."

"How long do you intend on staying, or are you staying for good?"

"I plan to stay for another month, but I'm not sure at this stage. Alex and I have grown close, and I don't know if I could leave him after one month. Must sound silly, I know, but even though I have only known him for two weeks, I don't want to live apart from him."

Alex squeezed Shelley's hand.

"No, that doesn't sound silly at all. Once you fall for someone who you love, it sure wouldn't be easy leaving them."

Annabelle seems like a nice person, Shelley thought, feeling a lot calmer. Little did she know, Annabelle had the ability to calm people by touch.

"Stop hogging the guest of honor," a man said as he stepped in front of Shelley with his partner. "Hi, Shelley, my name is Grayson, and this is my partner, Samantha."

"Hello, it's nice to meet you both." Shelley hugged them. "Sorry if I don't remember your names later—too many names to remember."

"Yeah, I know what you mean. I remember meeting everyone for the first time. It's a bit daunting," Samantha said.

"Actually, Alex, whilst we are all together, we wanted to ask if you and Shelley would like to go out on mopeds tonight with us. We can show Shelley the sights of Paris at night," Grayson said.

"Thanks, Grayson. That would be great. So, who'll be coming?" Alex said. *Shelley needs guarding.*

"Annabelle, Samantha, myself, and you two."

That's fine, Alex mind-thought to Grayson as he nodded. "You up for a moped ride later, sweet girl? It will be fun, I promise."

"Sure! What time would we be going?"

"Say, around eight thirty?" Annabelle said.

"Awesome. Thank you, that's lovely of you all to take me out sightseeing."

"The sights are a lot better at night on a moped—better than a car, any day. You get to see more," Annabelle said.

"Alex brought me to Paris the other day, but we didn't get to see everything. I'm excited to go."

"Shelley, I'd like you to meet my partner," William stood in front of Shelley and Alex.

143

Renee gave Shelley a warm hug. "Hi, I'm Renee. It's nice to meet you." She gave Alex a warm hug too. "Did you two eat on the plane, or can I get the cook to make you something?"

"We haven't eaten yet. That would be great if Lamiae could make us something. I'm a tad hungry, and I'd say this sweet lady is too."

Shelley nodded and noticed Renee's belly. "When are you due to have your baby?"

Renee rubbed her stomach. "Any week now."

"Do you have a nursery, or will you have it in your bedroom?"

"At first, we will probably have it in our bedroom. But we do have a nursery for it. Come on, Shelley, follow me, and I'll show you the nursery, and afterward we can get you both something to eat." Renee took Shelley's hand and walked to the front of the house, up the marble staircase and into the nursery. *Don't worry, Alex, she is safe with me.*

*****

"Man, is she pretty, or what, Alex? You lucky bastard," Brock said as he shook Alex's hand.

Alex bobbed his eyebrows up and down. "I can't believe after all these years I've found my life partner. She came halfway around the world on vacation and happen to be staying at my hotel."

"She seems nice, but why can't I hear her thoughts?" Annabelle asked.

"I don't know. I had trouble at first too. It is strange." Alex shrugged. "Actually, I was going to ask William if I could see the queen downstairs and ask her."

"I'm sure our queen will have some answers."

"So, has William filled you in?" Alex eyed each of his Lepidoptera friends. "That Shelley doesn't know about our kind yet, and so far, she only has the outline of a butterfly on her neck?"

They all said yes together.

"Are you hoping that having her here might change her into a Lepidoptera?" Annabelle asked.

"Hate to state the obvious, but we must have sex for that to happen, and she is not ready yet. I was hoping that meeting some of my family, and the longer she stays with me, that it will happen. But I don't want to push her."

"You are a true gentleman, Alex," Samantha said.

Alex nodded at her.

"How long are you staying?" Brock asked.

"Not sure. It depends on Shelley."

"We'll treat her as one of our own family," Violette said, walking up the limestone steps, holding hands with Michael.

"Thank you, Violette." Alex gave them a hug and slapped each on their backs.

*****

"Your nursery is lovely, Renee. I think your baby will love it," Shelley said, exiting into the hallway.

"Thank you, Shelley. You are too kind. Let's get you something to eat." Renee took Shelley's hand and walked her down the staircase and into the kitchen. "Lamiae, this is Shelley, Alex's girlfriend."

Lamiae looked up from buttering the bread. "Hello, dear. How was your flight?"

"It was good, thanks. Do you prepare all the food for the Gramaze household?"

"Yes, dear. Sometimes Violette likes to help me though. But mostly, it's me who does all the cooking."

"Shelley hasn't met Violette and her partner, Michael, yet."

"You must be pretty busy, as there are a lot of hungry mouths here to feed. I don't mind helping out while I'm here, so please don't hesitate to ask."

Lamiae nodded. "What would you and Alex like to eat?"

"Maybe a bread roll with some meat and salad. That would be nice."

"Sure. I'll bring it out to you both soon, dear."

"How about I show you around my home?" Renee said.

Shelley agreed, starting to feel more comfortable.

*****

Renee held open the door for Shelley to enter. "This will be yours and Alex's room whilst you're here, Shelley."

The first things Shelley noticed in the huge, wallpapered room were a four-post bed, elegant Parisian furniture, and a double door entry window. *You could throw a ball in this room; it's that big.*

Renee showed her to the en-suite bathroom.

"Thank you for letting us stay here, Renee. The bedroom and bathroom are so grand. I'm not used to so much elegance."

"You're welcome, my dear. Whilst you're here, you'll have to ask Alex to take you horse riding. We have stables down the back of the property."

"I will. Your home is so beautiful, like something from a magazine." Shelley noticed her bag was at the foot of the bed.

Renee sat on the bed, placing her hand on her stomach. "Make yourself at home whilst you are here, dear. We want you to feel comfortable."

"Are you okay?" Shelley sat next to Renee, noticing her pale complexion.

"Yes, dear, it's only Braxton Hicks. They are painful sometimes. They are the pains you get prior to going into full-on labor, and they can come and go for weeks prior to birth."

"Can I get you anything to make you more comfortable?"

"No thanks, dear. I'll be fine in a few minutes."

William entered the room. "How are you, my love?" He bent down in front of her.

"I'm okay. I need to rest a bit." Renee took focused breaths.

William scooped Renee into his arms. "Come on. You need to get some rest. You've been overexerting yourself today."

Shelley followed William as he carried her out the bedroom.

"You should go have a good time with Alex," Renee said to Shelley, cuddling into William's shoulder.

Shelley furrowed her brow, feeling useless. "Can I check on you later?"

"That would be lovely. We are only two doors down on the right."

William carried her into their bedroom and shut the door, leaving Shelley standing there.

As Shelley descended the marble staircase, she saw Alex waiting for her at the bottom.

"Hi, sweet girl. Are you okay?"

"Yes, I'm all right, but Renee is not well. Braxton Hicks, she called it. William took her to their room for a rest. I said I would check on her later. I felt so useless, unable to do anything for her."

"She'll be okay, babe. William will take care of her. Come on, our food is outside waiting for us." Alex took her hand as she reached the bottom of the stairs.

*****

The afternoon seemed to go by fast, and before Shelley knew it, Lamiae was letting everyone know that afternoon tea was being served in the dining room.

Excited to see what food would be available, Shelley followed Alex through the doorway. After selecting a pastry and a small cup of orange juice from the side buffet, Shelley squeezed next to Alex at the large wooden table with all the other Gramaze family, some of whom she hadn't met yet. "William and Renee are missing. Do you think it would be all right if I see how Renee is doing after I finish my pastry?"

"I'm sure she's fine, babe, but I think she would appreciate you checking on her."

*****

Shelley knocked on William and Renee's door and heard William say, "Enter," so she went inside.

Shelley stopped at the foot of the bed. "I hope I'm not disturbing you. I wanted to check on Renee."

"You're not disturbing us," William said, sitting upright.

"Sit down, dear." Renee patted the bed next to her.

"How are you feeling?"

"Much better. I needed to rest, that's all." Renee sat upright and leaned against the headboard.

"Have either of you eaten yet? I can get you both something if you like."

"Actually, I am feeling a bit hungry. That would be nice, dear."

"I'll come with you, and we can both get something for Renee and me," William said, standing. "We won't be long, my love."

She smiled and followed William toward the doorway.

As they descended the staircase, William said, "I appreciate your kindness toward Renee, but I have to wonder—and don't take this the wrong way—why are you so ... drawn to her?"

"I-I like to help, that's all." She furrowed her brow, wondering why William would even ask that.

Fuck, why can't I read this woman's mind? Is she genuine? William listened to her heartbeat quicken as they entered the kitchen,

Shelley following behind. "I appreciate your kindness towards my partner. No wonder Alex thinks the world of you. You know he wants to marry you one day." William watched her reaction as they came to stand at the island counter.

"No, I didn't know that, and … well, I think it's a bit too early for a wedding, don't you?"

William nodded. *Sensible, I like that.*

"Don't get me wrong, I do have strong feelings for Alex, and our relationship so far feels right. It's strange; even though I've only known Alex for two weeks, I already feel like I can't be apart from him."

"I know that feeling all too well. It's called love. You know Alex hopes you won't leave after one month, don't you?" William selected a plate from the cupboard.

"In all honesty, I don't know if I could leave after one month."

William placed a pastry and sandwiches on two plates sitting on the sideboard. "What is stopping you from making a commitment to Alex?"

"I don't know. I-I don't have an answer to that. I suppose I'm scared in a way. I don't want the bubble to burst, if you know what I mean."

"Alex is one hundred percent committed to you. I can assure you he'll make you one happy lady." William walked to the fridge. "The friendship ring he bought you is only the beginning. This is his signature of devoting his life and love to you."

"Wow, I didn't know that. But I don't have anything to give him in return besides myself, and will that be enough?"

"It will be plenty, my dear." William poured water into two glasses then placed the food and drinks onto trays to carry to their room.

*****

"That looks delicious," Renee said, watching William and Shelley place the trays in front of her on the bed. "I'm famished."

"You are looking better. How do you feel?" Shelley asked.

"Much better." *Hmm, I can't read her mind.* She eyed William. *What's going on?*

I am not sure, my love. William shrugged.

"That's good. I'll leave you both to eat. I'm glad you're feeling better."

"Thank you, dear. I'll see you tomorrow morning."

Shelley turned for the doorway. "Thank you for the chat, William."

William sat next to Renee and smiled at Shelley.

*****

Shelley checked her watch. *I might shower before we go out tonight.* When she entered the room, Shelley found Alex asleep on the bed. Quietly, she lay next to him and snuggled into his muscular body.

Once Alex registered she was there, he opened his eyes. "Hello, sweet girl. How is Renee?"

"She's doing okay. But you don't look too good. Are you all right?"

"I'm feeling a bit tired, but don't worry, I'm fine." Alex sat upright.

Shelley heard someone knock on their door. "Come in!"

"Sorry to interrupt. I've brought Alex a protein shake. It might make him feel better. He said he was feeling lethargic." Annabelle approached the bed with a covered cup.

"Thanks. You didn't have to do that for me." Alex outstretched his hand to take the cup.

"No problem at all. That's what family is for."

No sooner than Alex drank it down, the color returned to his cheeks. "Nice shake. I feel better already." He licked his lips. *That's what I needed. Thanks for the blood, Annabelle.*

You're welcome. You'll have to look after yourself a bit more. You can't burn the candle at each end and get away with it, you know. "I better go. I'll catch you both later at dinner." Annabelle walked towards the doorway.

Alex placed the cup on the bedside table.

"That sure was nice of her."

"Yeah, she is always like this with everyone, such a caring person. How are you doing, sweet girl?" Alex kissed the side of Shelley's head.

"I'm a bit tired, actually. I think I might lay down before dinner." Shelley got under the covers with Alex and cuddled into his chest. "I'm looking forward to the sightseeing tonight, though. You sure have some nice friends here. They didn't even know me at all, and already, they've asked me to go sightseeing." Shelley looked at Alex. "I had a good chat with William this afternoon, about you."

"I don't think he wouldn't have told you anything you didn't already know."

"He told me one thing I didn't know: one day you'd like to marry me. He also told me the friendship ring is a sign of love and devotion."

"How do you feel about that?"

"Like I told William, but he told me I was being silly, you are a rich and a powerful man and have a lot to give, but I don't have anything to give you in return. I only have myself. But will this be enough in a few months when you'll probably be sick and tired of me? I do love you a lot, Alex, but I can't commit to you yet. Plus, I'm afraid if I do give my all to you, that my heart will be open to be hurt. I know I'm rambling, but do you understand what I mean?"

"This is how you feel? You think you have nothing to give me but yourself and you won't open your heart to be hurt? Wow, that sure is sad, especially since you know how I feel about you. As you said before, the friendship ring is a sign of love and devotion, which, in my eyes, is a symbol of how much I do love you and want to spend my entire life with you."

Shelley thought he sounded sincere as she looked deeply into his eyes. "I wake up every day and watch you sleep, and I wonder why you would want to have me as your partner. I suppose it's the physiatrist in me who questions everything that happens in my life and around me." Shelley cuddled into his chest.

"I want you to be my partner for many reasons besides that you're absolutely beautiful. You're caring, you always think of others first, you're great cook, you're extremely smart and intelligent ... I love the way you smile and the way you laugh, and I can tell you have a good heart. Please don't ever question if I love you, as that will never, ever change, and, if you would have me, maybe one day I'd love to be your husband. You're someone I could wake up to each day and feel fulfilled by in every way. Life is not all about money and power, you know."

"Wow, you've thought about this long and hard, haven't you? I think I'm only now starting to realize how much I mean to you."

"You mean everything to me, sweet girl, and never, ever forget that, okay?" He leaned over to kiss her lips passionately.

As Alex reassured Shelley of his love and devotion, she felt like she could let her guard down and let him into her heart. As she lay cuddled into his chest with his muscled arms around her, she eventually fell asleep.

CHAPTER TEN

"Shelley ... sweet girl, wake up," Alex said as he sat on the bedside and stroked the side of her face.

"Hmm ... What time is it?"

"Six fifteen and nearly time for dinner. I thought I'd wake you so you could get ready."

"Can you cuddle with me?"

"Are you still tired, sweet girl?"

"A little bit. I suppose if I get up and wash my face, I might feel a bit better. But I'd like to cuddle with you for another minute if that's okay?"

Alex laid next to Shelley and extended his arm so she could cuddle into his chest.

"Mmm, that's better. You always know how to make me feel safe in your arms."

"You sure know how to make a man feel good about himself."

"That's because you're a good person, and I always feel safe when I'm around you. Did you sleep, or did you get up?"

"I couldn't sleep, and I knew you were tired, so I've been talking business with William."

"Thank you. Are you still feeling all right?"

"Yes, but I do need to get you up now so you can get ready, sweet girl." Alex picked her up off the bed and carried her into the bathroom.

She snuggled into his chest, thinking how good he smelled. "I love how strong you are, Alex."

Alex placed her on the edge of the bath.

She stood and kissed his lips wantonly. *God, what you do to me.*

I wonder what you would think of me when I tell you about my family and our secrets. "Maybe we can continue this tonight when we get back from sightseeing?" Alex raised an eyebrow, smirking at her.

"You're a tease, you know that? But that's one of the many things I love about you."

Alex slapped her back side and said, "Get ready," as he left the bathroom smirking and shaking his head.

*****

When they arrived downstairs for dinner, Shelley noticed more people were seated at the table and the room was quite noisy.

"Shelley, this is Michael and Violette, and Christian and Danielle. Violette and Danielle are sisters and are both from L.A." Alex gestured to each of them and sat next to Brock.

"Nice to meet you all." Shelley shook each of their hands across the table and sat next to Annabelle. *Wow, so many people.*

"Did you get much sleep, Shelley?" Annabelle asked.

"Yeah, I got a couple of hours, which was good. Now I'm ready for tonight."

"You'll probably need to wear jeans and a jumper. It tends to get a bit cold on the mopeds."

Alex placed his hand on Shelley's under the table, and when she turned, she found him staring at her and smirking. "Yes, I like what I see, so I like to stare."

Shelley leaned into him. "That's okay, my sweet man, you can stare all you like. It's comforting to know how much you love me."

Smelling it first, Shelley looked around and noticed Lamiae enter the dining room with a tray of food, along with a couple of male waiters following her. They each placed a plate of food in front of everyone. Surveying the plate as Lamiae placed it in front of her, she saw they were having chicken Kiev with asparagus, boiled potatoes, baby carrots, and a lovely side dish of a mustard-colored sauce. She readied her knife and fork. "This looks delicious."

"Sure is," Alex said, already enjoying his meal.

Shelley scanned the table, leaned into Alex and quietly asked, "Why does everyone at this table look like they workout at a gym?"

"Because William and Renee have a gym and an instructor here at the house."

"What type of business does William have?"

"A security firm, and everyone at this table works there."

"Wow, I'm impressed," Shelley said, cutting her Kiev.

"Shelley, what did you study at college, and have you graduated yet?" Violette asked.

"I studied psychiatry for four years and graduated about three week ago."

"I have one year left of a teaching degree at university. I mainly want to teach English or science," Violette said, placing her knife and fork in the middle of the empty plate.

"Do you have any school in mind where you want to teach?"

"Yes, hopefully I can teach secondary schooling here in Bagnolet. I won't know until I graduate." Violette grabbed her glass of water. *If she only knew, that being a Lepidoptera Princess, I may not be able to pursue my career even if I do have my degree. Life sure sucks sometimes, but we do have bigger things to worry about than my career path.*

"So, if you move permanently to Zurich with Alex, would there be any opportunities to open a clinic there?" Danielle asked from across the table.

"I'm not sure. I haven't looked into it yet. But when we get back to Zurich, I'm hoping to see what I can do." Shelley panned from Danielle to Alex, noticing his happy expression. She leaned into Alex and whispered, "I'll discuss it with you later."

Alex nodded and smiled.

As the dinner progressed, everyone around the table had spoken to Shelley, and the more she talked with Alex's friends, the more she felt comfortable around them all.

*****

"You both ready to go in about twenty minutes?" Brock asked as he stood behind Alex and Shelley with his hand on each of their shoulders.

"I need to get a jacket, and I'll be ready to go," Shelley said.

"We'll meet you in the foyer in twenty," Alex said to Brock.

Alex and Shelley excused themselves from the table and went to their room to get ready.

"Shelley, I want to ask about what you meant downstairs, when you said you would search for a practice?"

"I've been thinking, why don't I move permanently to Zurich with you and start my practice there? I don't see the point in moving to a place where I can't be with you. I love you way too much to lose what we have, and after you told me today that you love me with all your heart, I know for sure that my heart won't get broken."

Alex picked up Shelley and whirled her around the room. "I love you so much."

"I love you too, my dear sweet man."

"But we had better go; they'll be waiting for us," Alex said, standing her up.

*****

As she reached the foyer, Annabelle said, "The mopeds are out front. Shelley, you and Alex will be on one moped, and Grayson and Samantha on another, and Brock and I will be on single mopeds. Alex is a good rider, so he should be able to keep up with us when we hit traffic. We all have mobiles with us, so we shouldn't get separated. We will probably stop for a coffee later at a great café we usually go to. They make the best lattes. Right, let's get going."

Once they were outside, Shelley felt the cold night air setting in and shivered. "Could I borrow a warm parker or something from you, Annabelle? I'm feeling the cold already, and that's without even going for a ride."

"Sure, come with me, and we can pick one out." Annabelle took Shelley's hand.

When they were out of ear shot, Grayson said to Alex, "If anything goes wrong tonight, like if the Debauched vamps smell Shelley out, don't worry, we have back up following us. We have taken every precaution possible so they won't take her."

"Are you sure sightseeing is a good idea?" Alex's brow furrowed as he secured his helmet.

"Should be okay. We'll stick close to you both."

Alex's nostrils flared. "I tell you, if those fuckers lay one hand on her, I'll kill each and every one of them, slowly and painfully."

Annabelle mind-talked to Grayson, Alex, Brock, and Samantha to tell them she and Shelley were not far from the front door.

*****

"I can't believe how beautiful this place is at night. On a moped, you get to see so much more," Shelley said, looking around in wonderment.

157

"Sure is beautiful," Alex said, who had been detailing all the monuments as the rode along.

Grayson pulled his moped next to Alex and Shelley in the traffic. "Park your bike; that café is only across the road."

Alex saw the café across the road from the Seine River.

*****

"Can we go for a walk along the Seine River later?" Shelley asked Alex. "Looks romantic, don't you think?"

"Sorry, Shelley," Brock interjected. "It's not safe at night. You might get mugged. It's all right during the day. Maybe Alex can take you whilst you are here during the day?"

"Oh, right. Thanks for letting us know." Shelley took her coffee cup from Annabelle, who had returned to the table with a tray of lattes for everyone.

Heads up, Lepidopteras, a Debauched sentinel has walked in, Grayson mind-thought to everyone. *I'll take care of him.*

"I might get a cake. Does anyone else want something whilst I'm up there?" Grayson asked, noticing the Debauched now standing at the counter and taking a deep breath, knowing he could smell the female Lepidopteras in the room, especially Shelley.

Everyone said no except for Brock.

"I'll come with you, bro," Brock said, standing.

Brock and Grayson approached the Debauched soldier on either side of him to see what he would do. But he did nothing.

"Fuck off. She is ours, and, if you think you can take us all on, you have another thing coming, jerk," Grayson said.

The Debauched soldier glanced at the Lepidopteras and knew he was outnumbered. Turning around, he shouldered Brock on his way out.

*****

With the café closing and the café owner bidding them a goodnight, they crossed the road to their mopeds, only to find all their tyres slashed.

"Bloody bastards," Brock said.

Grayson took his mobile phone from his jacket pocket and called the Gramaze house. "William, some asshole has slashed our moped tyres. Could you please send a car to collect us and a truck for the bikes?"

"Debauched?" William asked, annoyed.

"I would say so. We sent one packing earlier," Grayson said, trying to talk quietly so Shelley didn't hear.

"We'll be there in ten minutes to pick you all up. Keep an eye out." William hung up abruptly.

Grayson pressed End and placed his phone into his jacket pocket. "William said they'll be here in ten minutes." *Keep an eye out, Lepidoptera's.*

"Who would do this, Alex?" Shelley asked, surveying their moped's tyres.

Alex wrapped his arm around Shelley. "Some idiots who don't have a clue."

"I am a bit scared," Shelley said, cuddling into Alex's side.

"It's okay, babe, you'll be all right. Everyone here knows some form of combat fighting, so we'll be safe," Alex said, noticing six Debauched standing across the road looking in their direction.

Let's deal with these fuckers, Grayson mind-thought to Samantha, Brock, and Annabelle. *Alex, you stay with Shelley. We will deal with them.*

Alex nodded once.

"Who are they?" Shelley asked as she watched Grayson, Samantha, Brock, and Annabelle approach the six huge Debauched soldiers dressed in black leather battle gear.

Alex's nostrils flared. "Not sure." *Fuck, we might be in trouble here.*

*****

"We're here for the girl. Hand her over, and there won't be any trouble," the Debauched soldier in charge said.

"Fuck off, Debauched. If you think you can take us on, try it. We have back up over there waiting for our signal and more on the way. So, unless you back off, you will die." Annabelle clenched her fists on either side of her body. She heard Shelley scream and watched Alex try to fend off an attack from behind them from two other Debauched sentinels.

As Grayson tried to run at vampiric speed to Alex and Shelley, a Debauched clotheslined him to the ground. Brock, Samantha, and Annabelle were left to fight the six other Debauched soldiers standing before them.

Shelley watched her newfound friends and Alex fight but also noticed Michael, Violette, Danielle, and Christian appear from what seemed like out of nowhere, and they fought the Debauched too. Terrified, Shelley tried to run but didn't get far before a tall Debauched caught up to her and held her captive while watching his comrades fight. Shelley tried to wriggle free from his hold, but it was futile.

"Hold still, bitch, or I will drink from you."

Drink from me? Ha! What is he talking about? Shelley watched everyone fight and soon realized everyone from the Gramaze house and the large men who were attacking had fangs. *Vampires? No ...!* Shelley wiped her eyes for clarity, only to see Alex approaching her.

"Let her go." Alex's nostrils flared as he stood in front of the Debauched.

"Fuck off, Lepidoptera." The Debauched soldier pulled Shelley closer to him.

"Let her go, or I will break your neck, asshole." Alex pushed the Debauched soldier away from Shelley. "Run, Shelley!"

Scared out of her mind, Shelley obeyed. When she reached the café entrance across the road, she pulled the door handle to see if they would budge open, but they were locked, and the lights in the café had been turned off. "Fuck." She turned and scanned the area for a safe place while watching the battle from the corner of her eyes. When Alex broke free from the Debauched's hold on him, Shelley watched in horror from across the street as Alex beheaded the soldier with his bare hands, and his body disintegrated in front of her eyes.

Alex spotted Shelley and ran toward her, but she tried to back away from him.

"Get away from me. What are you?" Her voice was shaky.

Fuck, what am I going to say?

Annabelle rushed to Alex and Shelley. "We need to get out of here. Our car has arrived. Alex, you need to help Grayson finish off these bastards, and I'll take Shelley to the car."

Alex nodded and ran toward Grayson, only to watch Grayson behead a Debauched with his bare hands.

Annabelle placed a hand on Shelley's arm. "Shelley, are you all right?"

"No ..." was all Shelley got out before she went limp and fell into Annabelle arms.

Alex watched from across the road as Annabelle carried Shelley to the waiting car and placed her inside.

*****

"Is everyone all right; no one is hurt?" Grayson scanned their faces as the car tyres squealed away from the café.

They all said yes together.

"How in the fuck did they know we were even there?" Alex asked.

"They could smell her." Annabelle eyed Shelley now laying in Alex's arms.

"The sooner I get her home, the better." *I can't believe I put her life in danger like this. What was I thinking even agreeing to sightseeing?*

She is safe, and that is all that matters, Violette replied.

Alex frowned and nodded once in her direction, remembering that Violette was a multi-colored vampire who was next in line to the throne, so she could hear any thoughts he had, even if he was blocking everyone else.

*****

As the car arrived at the Gramaze residence, William was waiting at the front door, and from the look of determination on his face, he wanted an explanation.

"We will debrief in the operations room," Grayson instructed. He opened the door and alighted from the car.

They all nodded in agreeance.

"Alex, take Shelley to your room. Annabelle, you can go with them to keep her calm," William said, watching them alight from the car.

"Yes, Sire," Annabelle said.

Alex nodded once and carried Shelley inside.

*****

Shelley opened her eyes and sat up slowly, noticing Annabelle sitting next to her on the bed. "Where am I?"

"You're at the Gramaze residence," Alex said, coming to stand next to the bed. "How are you feeling?"

"I'm ... Get away from me!"

Annabelle placed her hand on Shelley's arm. "It's okay. You're all right."

"But I saw ..."

"You're safe now. No one will hurt you in this house," Annabelle reassured.

Shelley eyed Alex and Annabelle. "Am I correct in assuming every one of you is a vampire?" She pushed herself against the headboard with her legs bent into her chest. "And, if that is true, why do you have me here?"

"You're a vampire too, Shelley. Only, you don't know it," Annabelle said.

"Don't give me that bullshit! I would know if I was a vampire. I don't have fangs like you all do!" Shelley's nostrils flared. *Fuck, how can I get out of here?* Her eyes darted around the room.

Annabelle pushed herself off the bed and proffered her hand. "Come with me, and I'll show you something."

"Like fuck!" Shelley swiftly jumped off the bed and ran past Alex and Annabelle for the double door window to escape.

As Shelley neared the window, Annabelle had moved with vampiric speed and was waiting for her, arms crossed and shaking her head. "Where do you think you're going?"

What the fuck? How did she get in front of me so fast? "Anywhere but here. Get out of my way!" Shelley tried to weave past Annabelle.

"Stop!" Annabelle sidestepped into Shelley's path. "You're not safe out there." Annabelle grabbed her and pushed a reluctant Shelley into the bathroom.

"Let me go, you fucking bitch." Shelley tried to wriggle free of Annabelle's hold. Then Annabelle's calming touch soon quietened Shelley. "What is so important in here that you want to show me?"

"You'll see."

Shelley watched Annabelle get a small handheld mirror from the cupboard under the vanity.

"Lift up your hair."

Shelley frowned but obeyed while watching Annabelle's reflection in the large vanity mirror.

Annabelle placed the handheld mirror near the back of Shelley's neck and watched the reaction on Shelley's face when she noticed the butterfly outline.

"Where did that come from? What have you done to me? I've never seen that tattoo before. I …" Shelley traced her fingers over the tattoo.

"It's not a tattoo. It's a marking from our kind. It only appears when you have found your life partner," Annabelle said, looking at Shelley's reflection in the mirror.

Shelley frowned and turned to Annabelle. "What … What are you saying? Your kind? That doesn't make sense. You mean …" She eyed Alex standing in the doorway. "Alex is my life partner?"

"Yes." Annabelle placed the handheld mirror on the top of the vanity.

"None of this makes sense. I … I …" Shelley watched Alex walk away. "I want to leave!"

"I'm afraid that is not possible. Sit." Annabelle directed Shelley to the bathtub edge. Annabelle tried to explain in a bit more detail about the transition into becoming a Lepidoptera and their world. "I know this is a lot to take in, but I need you to listen to what I'm about to tell you."

Shelley gulped, her heartrate skyrocketing. *Fuck, what else is she going to tell me? I want to get out of here.*

Annabelle sat on the edge of the bath with Shelley and touched her arm. "Does that help?"

Shelley wondered what Annabelle was talking about until she felt calmer and nodded. "Yes, but how …?"

"I have the ability to calm you by touch. It's a neat ability to have." *If she is a Lepidoptera, why can't I hear her thoughts?*

"Wow, that would be wonderful. I do feel calmer." Shelley's heart stopped hammering, and her thoughts became a bit clearer.

"Good. What I'm about to tell you is something you need to know about your transition. So please listen carefully."

Shelley nodded and took a deep breath.

164

"If you have sex with Alex, you will turn into a full Lepidoptera vampire. And believe me, the transition is not an easy thing to endure. What you also are not aware of is Alex has prevented that from happening so far only because he wanted it to be your decision of when you become a Lepidoptera. His feelings for you have not changed either. He loves you more than anything and is willing to do whatever it takes to earn your trust."

Although it seemed impossible, her frown lines deepened as Shelley stared straight ahead and listened to Annabelle.

Alex listened from the other room, hoping Annabelle could convince Shelley of not only their world, but his love for her as well.

"So you're saying that if I have sex with Alex, I will turn into a vampire? Unbelievable ..."

"Yes, and the outline on your neck will color itself in. Everyone has a different color, and this color determines what strength and ability you have. Like mine is to calm people." Annabelle lifted her hair from her neck and showed Shelley her deep-blue butterfly.

Pretty. Shelley went to touch Annabelle's butterfly but pulled her hand away. "This is"—Shelley gulped hard—"Unbelievable. I never thought vampires ever existed, except in the books or movies."

"I know this is hard to comprehend, but we are good vamps, Shelley. The ones you met tonight are the bad vamps. If they had gotten hold of you, they would have turned you into one of them, and they are nasty creatures. They sell their women to the highest bidder for sex. It's so disgusting and degrading."

Shelley swallowed hard. "Can I get a drink, preferably alcoholic? I don't care what it is as long as it numbs the fear I have right now." Shelley's heart beat rapidly as she picked at her cuticles. *I can't believe this sort of life even exists.*

"Let's get you settled in the bed, and I'll sort out a drink for you, okay?" Annabelle stood, proffering her hand.

Shelley nodded and followed Annabelle into the bedroom where she spotted Alex waiting for them on a chair in the corner.

Annabelle walked toward the doorway. "I'll be back in a minute." *Talk with her, Crestwell. Try reassuring her.*

With her brain trying to absorb everything she had been told so far, Shelley rested her back against the fluffed pillows and pulled the quilt to her chest, only glancing at Alex and quickly looking away.

What do I say to her?

"You can sit closer, Alex," Shelley said. She was still afraid, but something inside told her he wouldn't hurt her.

With vampiric speed, he sat at the end of the bed. "How are you feeling about all this?"

"I'm still trying to process it all. It's a lot to take in." Shelley looked into his worried eyes.

"I know you probably don't feel like you can trust me anymore, Shelley. But please, I need to know if you … if you could ever love me again?"

"At this stage, I'm not sure of anything. I-I need time to understand all of this." Shelley's brow furrowed with sorrow. "I know one thing for sure; I don't want to become a creature of the night. It frightens the hell out of me."

Alex smirked. "Creature of the night? You've watched way too many horror movies. It's not even like that. We can go out during the day or night. And no, we don't drink from humans— for their blood, that is."

"Right. So, what would we do about not having sex, because I don't want to turn into a Lepid … I can't pronounce it, vampire. I'm sure you won't want to wait for sex. Am I right?"

"I'm a man of morals, and I would never pressure you into having sex with me … not unless you wanted to. And even if you did, I would ensure you knew all the consequences first. Listen. I would love to have had sex with you, but, as you know,

166

I've been a true gentleman." Alex moved closer to her on the bed.

"I appreciate what you're saying, but I need to know how long you are prepared to wait."

"I don't know. How long is a piece of string? All I know is I love you, and I'll do whatever it takes. I need you to give me a chance so we can see where this goes."

"Knock, knock." Annabelle entered the room. "Here you go." She handed Shelley a glass of wine. "Would you like me to leave you alone with Alex?"

"Umm ... I don't know. I suppose so." Shelley looked at a disheartened Alex then back to Annabelle. "Thank you for the drink."

"You're welcome." Annabelle headed for the door. "Call if you need me, okay?"

"Okay." Shelley quickly gulped down the entire glass of wine to calm her nerves and watched the door close.

I love you, sweet girl. That has not changed. Alex shifted closer to Shelley and ran his hand down the side of her face, adoringly looking into her eyes.

Shelley closed her eyes, and her breath stammered as she leaned in and enjoyed his touch. *Mmm ... safe.* "Alex, can we cuddle on the bed for a while?"

"I'm surprised you want to. Are you sure?"

Shelley nodded, leaned in and gave Alex a long, warm, affectionate hug. "Yes, I am sure."

Alex pulled away from their embrace and lay on the bed with Shelley. He outstretched his arm for her to lay into the crook of his shoulder, pulled her in close and kissed the side of her head.

Closing her eyes, Shelley breathed a sigh of relief. Even though she wasn't sure what would happen with her and Alex—or even her transformation, if it happened—she did know one thing for sure; she always felt safe in his arms.

CHAPTER ELEVEN

The next morning, Shelley woke to a darkened room. After feeling for her cell on the side table, she activated the screen to check the time. With the screen dimly lighting the room, she noticed Alex on his side, turned away from her, still asleep.

I might go for a run. Shelley hoped out of bed, and with her cell still lighting the room, she found her suitcase and put on her track suit and sweatshirt. *I need to clear my head.*

The cool morning air felt good on her body as Shelley ran around the edge of the property and sorted through what had happened the previous night and what she had witnessed—creatures she didn't even know existed, until now. But one thing was certain; she did still love Alex, no matter if he was vampire or not. He had never hurt or bitten her—which she knew of—and he had only shown her love. As Shelley approached the house, she saw Violette standing in the doorway.

"Can we talk?" Violette indicated for her to sit on the limestone steps.

"Sure." Shelley said, a bit taken aback, and sat on the step next to Violette.

"How are you feeling this morning?" Violette placed her hand on Shelley's arm to calm her.

"I'm not sure. I've been replaying everything that has happened in Zurich and now Paris, and, even though I'm still a bit scared and overwhelmed by knowing vampires exist in the world, I also think something feels comforting about being part of a large family."

"Yeah, it's a lot to take in, I know. And the Gramaze families are a wonderful family to be a part of. I was in the same situation as you a few years ago."

"Okay. So, Michael is your life partner?" Shelley's eyebrows raised as she remembered everything Annabelle had told her the previous night and was now putting everything together.

"Yes, but I didn't transform from having sex with him. I turned because I became livid from a situation the Debauched had put me in. It can happen that way too—not very often but it can happen. I also want to speak with you about one other thing. You can never tell anyone—and I mean *anyone* at all— about our kind. Even your human parents and your best friends, they won't understand. Do you comprehend what I'm telling you?"

Shelley swallowed hard and nodded. "You have my word."

"Good! I better let you go. Remember, Alex does love you and will protect you from the Debauched, no matter what you decide If you need anything or want to talk more, I'm always here for you."

"Thanks." Shelley hugged Violette and headed up the marble staircase. *She sure is nice.*

"Thank goodness you're still here," Alex said, watching Shelley climb the staircase. "I thought you might have tried to take off."

"Can we talk outside?" Shelley stopped and watched Alex approach her.

"Sure. Where did you go this morning?"

"I went for a run to clear my head," Shelley said as they walked together towards the back doorway.

"Did that ... help? What did you decide?" He stopped walking and looked into her eyes.

Shelley passionately kissed Alex.

Alex slowly pulled away. "You still love me and want me, even though I'm a vampire?"

"Yes." Shelley tenderly ran her hand down the side of his face. "And I know you love me, because, if you didn't, you wouldn't have stayed with me last night. This morning, I had a bit of time to think about everything, and I don't want to lose you, so I'm asking you to bear with me for a little while longer while I come to terms with all this."

Alex nodded.

"Also, I know your friends mean well, but I'd prefer to work this out on our own. If I learned one thing at college, it's couples need to sort things out without interference from others."

"I'll tell them to back off. Did you want to go back to Zurich, or are you happy to stay here for a few days?"

"I don't mind either way."

Alex picked up Shelley in his muscular arms, pulled her close to his chest and tenderly kissed her lips. "I love you, sweet girl."

"I love you too. I think even more than before if that's possible." Shelley gazed into his blue eyes, drinking in his scent.

"By the way, everyone here can read minds. But, for some reason, none of us can read yours. I'd say that will change if or when you turn." Alex placed her on the seat inside the gazebo. *I need to find out why too. It's certainly strange.*

"There's probably a lot you'll need to teach and show me. Alex, if the Lepidoptera vampires have been around for thousands of years, how old are you?"

Here goes. "I'm about three hundred years old, but I still think of myself as about twenty-eight—the age when I turned."

"You've been on this earth for three hundred years ..." Shelley raised one eyebrow, trying to fathom it all. "You sure must have seen a lot in those years. And you must have given up thinking you would find your life partner."

"I sure did. I think that's why I poured myself into my business. I couldn't believe the day you walked into the Crestwell Hotel and how lucky I was."

"How did you know I was a Lepidoptera vampire?"

"I didn't at first. But when I couldn't read your thoughts and eventually saw your butterfly outline, I knew for sure."

"So, have you had many girlfriends over the three hundred years?"

"I've had a few girls in my bed, but I wouldn't call them girlfriends. The Lepidoptera laws are quite clear—a vampire cannot date or marry a human."

"You must've been pretty lonely. No wonder you're a workaholic."

"At least now I can pour myself into you instead of my work."

"Alex, I don't want you to give up anything because of me. Life has to be a balance that keeps you happy."

"Right!"

"Even though I now know vampires exist, I still think I might wake up and learn it's not true. It's still hard for me to believe, you know, and I'm trying to come to terms with it." Shelley frowned and took his hand. "Something that does explain itself though, is on my birth certificate, the mother's and father's names were left blank. So I've never known who they might be, but now I know why. Life sure has a funny way of making you take stock, doesn't it?"

"Sure does. Life can be funny sometimes with what it throws at you. I take it a day at a time. By the way, I need to tell you a few rules. One is you can't go out anywhere without Lepidoptera vampire protection, before or after you turn. It's not safe. This is why I've always gone with you while you've been on vacation, to protect you and your friends. If the Debauched vampires do take you—God, I don't want to even think about that; it's so ugly and disgusting what they do to our kind. If you want to go out from now on, you'll need a Lepidoptera vampire with you at all times. Also, you cannot, and I mean this seriously, you cannot tell anyone—and I mean *anyone*—about our kind. They would not understand at all."

"You're making me feel scared again. Please, I'm frightened enough as it is. But yes, I do understand what you've told me." Shelley let go of his hand. "And Violette told me the same thing this morning, about not telling anyone."

"I'm sorry, I didn't mean to frighten or scare you. I just don't want anything to happen to you, that's all."

"Why didn't any Debauched vampires try to take me in Zurich?"

"I'm not sure. Even William thought it was strange too. I told William last night that maybe it'd be better if I take you back to Zurich, as it's safer there. But he disagreed. He said there is safety in numbers."

"That makes sense. But I don't want to stay here forever. I want to go back to our home."

"I'll speak with William today, and maybe he can release some of his family to come and live with us for a while so they can help protect you. I don't want to stay here forever either. I want to start our life together, in our home."

"I've noticed from talking with some of the other women in the Gramaze house that even though they are life partners, they are not married. Whys is that?"

"It's the males choice on whether they marry or not, and the female has to talk them into it if that's what they want."

"Humph, right!"

"We've discussed this. You know I want to marry you."

Shelley breathed a sigh of relief. "That's good to know, because I have values, and when a couple has been together for a while, they need to seal their relationship with a marriage, as this is a final commitment of their love for each other." Shelley's brow furrowed.

Alex took her hand in his. "Yes, I agree."

"I'm getting a bit hungry. What time is it?"

"We have probably missed lunch, but we can go to the kitchen and make something if you like. Come on," Alex said, standing.

*****

"Hello, you two. How has your day been so far?" Annabelle asked, sitting at the kitchen island counter with Grayson.

"Not bad. Alex has explained a lot to me already about the Lepidoptera's, and I'm starting to understand it all. I'm glad I have Alex to fall back on though. Also, I'd like to thank you both for saving my life last night." Shelley hugged Grayson. "I won't ever forget what you did for me, and hopefully one day, I can repay your kindness."

Grayson returned the hug. "Hey, you don't have to thank us. You're family, and we would do anything for family."

"Thank you. That means a lot." She hugged Annabelle. "Thank you for being so kind to me, Annabelle."

"Anytime," Annabelle said, hugging her back

"How come you two missed lunch?" Shelley asked.

"We were out on patrol and didn't get back in time."

"Patrol? What is that?"

"We all take turns to patrol certain areas so we can rid this earth of the Debauched vampires. It's a bit like security."

"You mean you *kill them* when you find them?"

Annabelle nodded. "Sorry, Shelley. This sort of talk probably frightens you. But, if we don't exterminate them, they would kill not only vampires but humans too. They've already tried experimenting on humans by draining their blood and injecting their experimental drugs into them. God, it's awful what these bastards will do; you have no idea."

Stop talking. You're frightening her. Can't you see that? Alex mind-talked to Annabelle as his nostrils flared.

Shelley noticed Alex shoot Annabelle a dirty look. "I know you two are mind-talking. Please don't do that in front of me. I'd prefer to hear, even if it does frighten me. I have to get used to this world, so I need to toughen up."

Annabelle apologized then raised her eyebrows at Alex. *I told you she could handle it.*

Alex rolled his eyes at Annabelle and took a deep breath. "What would you like for lunch, Shelley?"

"Maybe a peanut butter and jelly or honey sandwich? Two rounds and a glass of milk."

"You're easy to please. Actually, that sounds good. I think I might have the same." Alex said.

"How much longer are you staying for, bro?" Grayson asked Alex.

"I was thinking we might go home tomorrow. But I need to speak with William first about security in Zurich for Shelley."

William entered the kitchen. "So, you're thinking about going home tomorrow?"

"Yes, sir. But I wanted to ask if you could spare some of your family to stay with us so Shelley has security until this all dies down."

"I'm sorry to be so much trouble, William," Shelley said, frowning. "You probably already have more important things to deal with here, and don't need this sort of problem in your life."

William regarded Shelley, troubled. "Dear girl, you are family, and we protect family. You must understand that no matter what happens, you are not trouble nor a problem, and we will always be here to protect you from the Debauched. Also, if anything ever happened to Alex, we would look after you and protect you. 'You Are Family Always.'"

Shelley gave William a warm hug. "Thank you."

William turned to Alex. "I'll organize for two or three of my family to protect Shelley. I'll let you know who it is when I talk with everyone tonight at the operations meeting."

"Thanks, my old friend." Alex shook William's hand. "I appreciate anything you can do for us."

"How is Renee today?" Shelley asked, sitting at the island counter.

"Our doctor recons she's only days from delivering; otherwise, she's doing okay."

"Would it be all right if I sit with her for a while?"

"I'm sure she'd like that. She's fond of you."

"Here's your sandwich." Alex placed a plate in front of Shelley. "Maybe you can take some up for Renee too?"

"Does Renee like peanut butter and jelly sandwiches and milk, William?" Shelley asked.

"Hang on, I'll ask her," William said then mind-talked to Renee. "She said that would be great."

"Can you make a couple more, Alex, and I'll pour the milk?" Shelley asked, standing. "I still can't wrap my head around the mind-talk thing."

Alex placed bread on the counter, ready to butter. "You'll get used to it eventually."

Once they were made, Shelley went to Renee's room.

*****

"How are you coping, dear, now that you know about our kind?" Renee asked, leaning against the headboard.

"I'm a bit apprehensive of the unknown, and I'm unsure if I want to become a Lepidoptera vampire yet. Alex has told me all about the transformation, but can you tell me what it's like as a female?"

Renee tried to read Shelley's thoughts but couldn't and wondered whether to inform Shelley of the transformation process. "Well, at first, your skin will feel like it's crawling with something inside it. Also, you'll hear everyone's thoughts—and I mean *everyone's*—and you'll think you're going mad. You'll smell human blood and hear it running through their veins. The best thing to do is to get to a quiet room and quickly get some A-positive blood into you. This stops the craving to drink human or vampire blood. It will also stop all the other symptoms. But you must keep your A-positive blood supply up, because if you don't, the symptoms will return." Renee reached for Shelley's hand. "It seems to take two to seven days, depending on the person, for the cravings to stop and you feel some sort of normality. Alex should be able to help you through this time, but you must remember to keep your blood supply up daily."

"That doesn't sound like too much fun at all." Shelley sighed. "But I suppose it's inevitable. What if I can't control myself?"

"Don't worry, Alex won't let you get out of control. But be warned; do not drink Alex's blood until you are fully transformed. When I say fully transformed, I mean the color on your butterfly has fully colored itself in. If you drink Alex's blood prematurely, you won't be able to stop, and you'll drain him, and he'll die."

"Oh my god, Renee, how will I get through this? I'm more frightened than ever."

"You'll be all right, dear girl, I know you will. We all felt like you do now, and we have all come through it okay. You need to trust Alex, and he'll see you through it. When are you going home?"

"Tomorrow, I think."

"Maybe we should send Annabelle home with you to calm you when your transformation happens. She's extremely good at this, and it'll make a difference to your transformation. The calmer and accepting of the ability you are, the quicker it'll happen and—" Renee clutched at her stomach and doubled over in pain. "Shelley, I think the baby is coming. You need to get help. I'm in a lot of pain, more than usual," Renee said through clenched teeth; she couldn't mind-talk to anyone because she was in too much pain for it to work, so Shelley tried.

Alex, Alex, can you hear me? Alex, Alex, I need help. Renee is in trouble.

Before she knew it, Alex, William, Annabelle, and Grayson burst in the room.

"My dear, are you all right? What can we do to help?" William kneeled on the floor beside the bed.

"Nothing. The baby is coming."

Remembering her training at college, Shelley asked, "Renee, are you having a water birth or a normal birth?"

"Water birth."

"We need to get Renee to a warm bath."

"Are you sure this'll work?" William asked.

"Yes. Annabelle, can you try to calm Renee's pain?"

Annabelle sat on the bed next to Renee and nodded.

"William, can you please get someone to half fill the bathtub with warm water?" Shelley asked.

"Grayson, you can do this."

"Yes, Sire." Grayson headed into their en-suite bathroom.

When William could see Renee was a bit more settled, he picked her up in his muscular arms and carried her into the bathroom. He sat her on the chair next to the bath and looked at Shelley. "What can I do to help?"

"You boys can leave now. We women will help Renee undress and get into the bath," Shelley said authoritatively, kneeling beside Renee.

William regarded Renee, and she nodded. He kissed Renee's forehead, and all the men left the bathroom and closed the door behind them.

"Let's get you undressed," Shelley said.

Renee nodded and stood slowly.

Annabelle helped Renee undress and ease into the warm water.

"That feels better already. Thank you."

"When you have the next contraction, you need to let us know when it starts and stops so we can time their length and how far apart they are. This will give us an indication on how far along in the delivery you are. Annabelle, can you please mind-talk to William and ask him to call Renee's doctor and ask her to come straight away; that's if he hasn't done it already."

"Already done. He said she is five minutes away."

"Renee, did you practice any breathing techniques for when you are in labor?"

"Yes."

"Great. When the contractions start, you need to try to forget the pain in your body and concentrate on your breathing. Can you do that for me?"

Renee nodded as the pain started again.

Annabelle timed the contractions on her wristwatch. "This time, it's a fifty-five-second contraction."

"You're doing fine, Renee. Do you think you could do that breathing technique again?" Shelley wiping Renee's brow with a cold compress.

Renee nodded. "Could you please rub my back? It's extremely sore." She leaned forward.

Annabelle massaged Renee's neck, back, and shoulders.

"Here it comes again," Renee said, scrunching her face.

"Breath for me, Renee. In and out, in and out. That's a good girl," Shelley said.

Annabelle set her timer again. "This time it was one minute and six seconds contraction. The time between contractions was two minutes."

Renee's contractions seem to be getting closer and closer. The baby will come any time. Where is this doctor? Shelley thought.

"I feel like I want to push. Can I push?" Renee asked Shelley.

"Lift you vagina out the water and let me have a look at how dilated you are." Once she lifted, Shelley could see she was fully dilated. "Right. Put your vagina back into the water and push hard."

With each contraction, Renee pushed harder, and eventually, the baby was delivered in the water.

Shelley grabbed it out the water, cleared its airways and tapped its back.

Within seconds, they heard the baby cry for the first time.

"It's a boy," Shelley said, grinning from ear to ear.

With a furrowed brow, Renee smiled, knowing her child had survived the birth. "William will be happy."

Shelley quickly found a pair of scissors in the vanity cupboard, cut the umbilical cord and clamped it off with a hairclip.

Annabelle wrapped the baby in a white towel she found hanging in the bathroom and handed the baby to Renee.

Renee beheld the tiny face of her little boy and smiled, kissing his forehead for the first time.

"Renee, you need to push one last time to get the placenta out of your body, otherwise you'll get an infection," Shelley said.

Renee handed her baby to Annabelle and gave one almighty push, and the placenta came out whole.

As Annabelle returned the baby to Renee, the doctor entered the bathroom.

"Your late. You should have been here sooner," Shelley said, her brow creased. "You can take over now, as I don't know what to do from here on."

"Yes, ma'am," the female doctor said.

As Shelley went to stand, Renee grabbed her hand. "Thank you, dear sweet girl. And thank you too, Annabelle. I couldn't have done it without you both. Can you please ask William to come in now?"

Annabelle and Shelley both smiled and said, "You're welcome," together.

"You can go in now, William," Shelley said as she and Annabelle entered the bedroom where William, Alex, and Grayson were waiting.

He ran quickly towards the bathroom.

Annabelle and Shelley took one look at each other and giggled.

"We need to shower and get these bloodied, wet clothes off. Can you believe how exhilarating that was? I've never helped someone with a birth before," Annabelle said.

"Yeah, I couldn't believe what I had remembered from my training at college. We did a great job in there. At least Renee and the baby are okay."

"Well, don't keep us in suspense. What did she have? Boy or girl?" Alex asked.

"It is a boy, and he has lots of dark hair," Shelley said.

"Awesome. Someone to carry on the name."

"Yeah. I'm going to get out of these clothes and shower," Shelley said.

"Me too," Annabelle said, walking towards the doorway.

Alex followed Shelley to the bathroom and sat on a stool. "How did you know I would hear you today when you tried to mind-talk to me?"

Shelley entered the shower and turned on the water. "I didn't know if you could hear me or not. I tried hard to concentrate on an image of you in my mind, and it worked. I think I was lucky."

"Now it seems I can hear your thoughts all the time. I'll have to show you how to turn it off."

"You're joking. You can hear my thoughts *all the time?* Unbelievable. I wonder why all of a sudden it has started to work. But hang on, I haven't heard your thoughts. Why is that?"

"Because I'm not letting you in. We use a technique so we can't hear each other's thoughts. I'll teach it to you. Let me see if you can hear this." *I love you, sweet girl.*

"Say that again." Shelley popped her head out from under the shower.

I love you, sweet girl.

"I heard that, and I love you too, my sweet man." Shelley smiled. "It's certainly strange not seeing your lips move and, instead, hearing you speak. That will definitely take a bit of getting used to." Shelley turned off the faucet and stepped out the shower. As she reached for the towel, she watched Alex eye her body, and she smirked. "Like what you see?"

Love what I see and wouldn't mind a piece of that.

Shelley shook her head. "You are incorrigible, my sweet man." After she towel-dried, she got dressed. "I might go to the kitchen and make something to eat. Would you like anything?"

"I'll come with you so we can make something together."

Renee, are you hungry? Would you and William like something to eat or drink? Shelley thought to Renee.

Yes please. Anything will be okay, Renee replied.

I'll bring you something soon.

"You are so thoughtful," Alex said and kissed her.

*****

Shelley prepared an omelet and milk for Renee and an omelet and wine for William. Alex delivered their food whilst Shelley made their own food.

CHAPTER TWELVE

Later that night, when everyone was seated for dinner in the dining room, William entered the room, carrying Renee and their baby.

Everyone stood and clapped, each congratulating the proud parents.

"Please, please. Thank you all. Take a seat." William placed Renee and baby on a seat at the head of the table and gestured for everyone to sit. Once they were all quiet, William stood tall with his chest puffed. "Today our son was born, and we have named him Samuel Allan Isaac Gramaze. Please welcome our son into the world by raising your glasses for a toast."

Everyone raised their glasses and said, "To Samuel."

"Also, we would like to thank two beautiful girls who helped my lovely partner, Renee, give birth today, and that is Annabelle and Shelley. Please raise your glasses for a toast to Annabelle and Shelley."

They all did so, and Shelley felt honored.

Alex placed his hand over hers and squeezed it. He kissed the side of her forehead and smiled.

Annabelle smiled from ear to ear. *Welcome to the world and our family, Samuel.*

Samuel was passed to each Lepidoptera to hold, cuddle, and gaze at him. After all the women had finished clucking over him, William took Renee and Samuel to their bedroom to rest.

"Isn't he adorable?" Shelley asked Alex.

"Sure, and they are proud parents too. Do you still want to go home tomorrow, or would you like to stay longer?"

Shelley pondered it. "I'd like to go home if that's okay."

"No problem." Alex leaned in and kissed her.

*****

After dinner, Alex and Shelley went to their room. Shelley was exhausted from the day's events, and all she wanted was for Alex to cuddle up to her and go to sleep. As they were about to turn off the lights, they heard a knock at their door.

"Enter," Alex said and watched the door open as he sat upright.

William entered. "I wanted to give you some news. I have organized for Annabelle, Grayson, and Brock to accompany you to your home tomorrow. They'll stay with you for as long as you need. You'll also need to keep me informed of when you fully transform, Shelley."

"Yes, for sure, William," Shelley said, sitting upright.

"Thank you, William. We appreciate all you are doing for us. We'll call you each week to update you on how everything is going too. As soon as everything is copacetic, we'll send them back to Bagnolet. We know Grayson and Samantha haven't been together long, so if Samantha wants to come too, that is fine with us."

"That is most gracious of you, Alex. I'm sure Samantha will appreciate it. I'll see you both in the morning before you go." William turned to leave.

"Night, William," Shelley said as she lay down.

"Goodnight," William said, closing the door.

"I'm glad Annabelle is coming with us, because Renee said to me today that Annabelle could calm me while I transform if needed. That was nice of you to consider Grayson and Samantha. You're such a romantic, my sweet man."

Alex smiled and turned off the bedside light. As he cuddled into Shelley, he could hear her mind replaying the day's events and not being able to switch off. "I can hear you. Would you like some help to sleep?"

"What do you mean?"

"One of my abilities is to be able to make you drowsy and sleep."

"Thank you, but no. I'd prefer to go to sleep on my own terms. Sorry to keep you awake. Is there any way you can switch off from my thoughts?"

"Yes, I can switch off from your thoughts. But I don't want to in case you need something answered that I can help with."

"I'll be fine. Switch off. You need your rest too."

He pulled her closer and kissed her forehead. "Goodnight, my sweet girl. I love you."

What a wonderful man he is. Within minutes, her mind quietened, and she fell asleep.

*****

Shelley woke feeling panicked, remembering the nightmare she had awakened from. She was sweaty but breathed a sigh of relief as tears flooded her eyes when she recalled the dream: Prior to her transforming, the Debauched vampires had taken, tortured, and eventually killed Alex. They also took her and turned her into a drug-addicted, bloodsucking prostitute.

As she lay there for a few minutes, looking at the ceiling and wiping away the tears, she thought about how much she loved Alex and how much he meant to her. Startled into reality by his voice, she watched Alex enter the bedroom.

"You're awake, sleepyhead. I thought I'd have to wake you up, as you have slept late." Alex sat on the bed next to Shelley, noticing her red eyes. "Have you been crying? What's wrong?"

"I had a bad dream, that's all, and when I woke, it felt so real. Don't worry. I'll be okay. It's only silly thoughts, that's all."

"Can I get you anything?" Alex laid on the bed next to her, outstretching his arm for her to cuddle into the crook of his neck.

Shelley firmly cuddled into his body. "No. I need to get up, shower and get ready to go home. I feel safer there with you."

"Would you like some breakfast? Lamiae has prepared some for you, and I can bring it up here if you'd like." He kissed the side of her head.

"That would be nice. Thank you. Can I have a cup of tea too?"

"Sure. You go shower, and by the time you come out, breakfast will be ready for you."

Shelley leaned up, kissed his lips, thanked him and headed to the bathroom.

*****

"Thank you so much for having us," Shelley said to William and Renee then hugged them. "Tell Samuel we'll miss him."

Renee returned the hug. "You're welcome. We hope you come back soon."

After they said their goodbyes, William organized a car to take them to the airport.

On the way to the airport, Samantha said, "I've never been to Zurich. I'm looking forward to some sightseeing on my days off."

"I can organize for someone to take you and show you the sights if you like," Alex said.

186

"That would be nice. Thanks, Alex," Samantha said as she held Grayson's hand.

*****

"Please take your seats and secure your seatbelts, as we are about to take off," the captain said over the PA system.

I can't wait to get back home. I've missed being there and feeling safe. I don't feel safe at all in Paris, Shelley thought as the plane taxied from the terminal.

Alex placed his hand in hers, and Shelley laid her head on Alex's shoulder—before she knew it, they had landed on the Zurich runway.

"Hello, Carson, how've you been?" Shelley asked, noticing him waiting for them at the bottom of the stairs on the tarmac.

"Good. Thanks for asking, Shelley." Carson opened the limousine door and watched the six Lepidoptera's enter the car. He placed everyone's luggage into the trunk. *It's been all quiet here on the home front, Sire.*

Thank you, Carson. I'm glad to be home again, Alex replied as he sat next to Shelley and held her hand.

*****

When the limousine arrived at the front doors of the Crestwell residence, Alex noticed James waiting for them.

"Hello, Sire. Can I get you anything?" James asked, holding open the door.

"Please let Luda know we're home and to come see me about meals etc. I'd like you and Carson to show our guests to their rooms."

James nodded once. "Yes, Sire."

Once they were inside, Alex turned to his guests. "I'll give you a quick tour of the house and grounds, and after, you can have a good look around at your own pace. I'll also show you where the weapons, cars, bikes, etc. are."

The four Gramaze Lepidoptera's nodded, knowing full well what their job was whilst they were staying at the Crestwell residence.

There sure is a lot to do before we can relax, Shelley mind-said to Alex. *While you're showing everyone around, I'll help Luda, James, and Carson.*

Alex mind-thanked Shelley.

*****

"Hello, Luda," Shelley said, entering the kitchen, and hugging her.

"Hello, dear sweet girl." Luda returned the hug. "I heard you had a terrible time of it in Paris. I'm so sorry. But I suppose the best thing that came out of it is you now know about our kind."

"So, you're a Lepidoptera too? Why should I be surprised at that?" Shelley raised an eyebrow. "Actually, I came to help you plan meals for our guests from Paris."

Luda smiled and nodded. "I already have made the menu, but I wanted to run it past Mr. Crestwell first before I bought the food." Luda indicated to the menu on the island counter.

"Alex is happy for me to make a decision. Would you mind letting me see what you've planned?" Shelley grabbed the menu to ensure the meals contained a good selection of food groups. "The menu looks fine, Luda. Go ahead and buy the food you require. No need to bother Alex with this, as he has his hands full. Did you want Carson to go with you, as this is a lot of food?" Shelley handed the menu back to Luda.

"Actually, dear, that is a great idea."

"Once we bring in the guests' luggage from the car and put it into their rooms, you can go with Carson. If you need a hand with anything, don't hesitate to ask me, as I love to help. I want to keep busy, and I don't like sitting around, being waited on hand and foot; it's not me.

"Thanks, Shelley. I'll probably take you up on that later on, as long as Mr. Crestwell says that's fine."

"Listen. Don't worry if Alex thinks that's okay or not. I'll tell him I offered."

"You are too kind. I can see why Mr. Crestwell loves you."

"I might go help James and Carson bring in the luggage and put them in the guest rooms." Shelley walked towards the doorway. "See you later."

*****

"Do you need a hand? I'd like to help," Shelley asked James as he descended the staircase.

"That would be great, but only if that's okay with Sire."

Shelley put her hands on her hips. "Don't worry about Alex and what he'll say. He knows I'm helping you."

"Okay, come to the car. There are still a lot of bags to bring in."

*****

"Why don't we take all these bags out the car, and that way, Carson can take Luda food shopping," Shelley said, standing at the trunk with James and Carson.

"Yes, ma'am. That sounds like a good idea," James said.

*****

"Thank you for helping me today, Shelley. That was nice of you." James handed Shelley a glass of white wine.

"It's not as if I had anything else to do. Anyway, I enjoyed helping you." Shelley sat on the stool at the island in the kitchen. "So, where is the blood stored around here, as I would say our guests would like a drink soon?"

James opened a secret door to reveal, sure enough, a fridge full of blood.

"How will I know if they want blood or a normal drink?"

"You only need to ask them, ma'am. Vampires are a lot like humans when it comes to food and drink."

Alex, can you ask everyone what they would like to drink. I can bring it out for you all, Shelley mind-said.

Thanks, sweet girl.

*****

"Here we go," Shelley said as she and James walked out to the back patio with the drinks for everyone.

"Thanks, babe," Alex said when Shelley joined them at the table with her own drink.

"Have you shown them where everything is now, Alex?" Shelley asked.

"Everywhere, except for the armory and training room. After we have these drinks, I'll show them."

"Would it be okay if I came with you, as I don't know where that room is either?"

"Are you sure? It's a bit of an eye opener."

"Yes, I am sure."

*****

"This is my training, combat, and weapons rooms," Alex said as they descended the stairs into the first room. "Take your time and have a look around."

Samantha, Grayson, Brock, and Annabelle studied the room, as they knew they would need to become familiar with these weapons.

As Alex watched and followed the four Gramaze soldiers through the rooms, he turned to Shelley. "What do you think?"

Shelley gulped hard, and her eyes widened when she noticed the type of weapons hanging from the walls as she walked through. Swords, knives, stars, blowtorches, cabinets with grenades and bombs—there was anything and everything she could think of to kill a Debauched vampire.

"A bit overwhelming in here, isn't it?" Alex asked Shelley.

"That's a bit of an understatement. But I think I understand why you have all this. Maybe one day when I'm up to it, you can train me in combat so I can at least protect myself."

"Sure, one day ..." Alex said, hoping she would never have to protect herself, ever. "Everyone, that's everything. I'll draw up a roster tonight and put it on the wall in here. Do you have any questions?"

Annabelle smirked. "What time's dinner?"

"Usually about seven o'clock, but if any of you are hungry or thirsty, you are welcome to raid the kitchen at any time. Right, now that I've shown you where everything is, you should be good to go. Make yourselves at home here. Our cook's name is Luda, but she only makes breakfast, lunch, and dinner, so if you want anything in-between, you make it yourself. We'll see you all later on."

They all nodded once.

Alex took Shelley's hand and pulled her towards the basement stairs.

"Where are we going?"

"To our bedroom."

*****

As they entered their bedroom, Shelley noticed a lovely bouquet of flowers on her bedside table. She rushed over to read the note attached. *"To my sweet girl, I will love you forever. Love Alex."* Shelley turned to see him smiling at her, and she ran into his arms, passionately kissing him. "Thank you for the beautiful flowers and the lovely card. They are perfect, like you, my sweet man."

"You're welcome, but it is me who should be thanking you for everything you've done today. Helping with the luggage to everyone's rooms and helping with the menu. That was nice of you to do that, and you didn't complain once. There are not too many women like you around, that's for sure. I am such a lucky man."

"Like I said a few days ago, I want to work, and I won't sponge off you. Being your girlfriend doesn't mean I can't do some chores"—Shelley smirked—"but I won't clean toilets."

Alex laughed. "Now that we're home, what would you like to do tonight?"

"After being cooped up in the Gramaze house, I need to get out. Do you think we could go out for dinner? Maybe one of the Crestwell Hotel restaurants would be nice. I'd like to get dressed up ... and maybe some dancing with you."

"Yeah, it sure would be good to get out. I'm not used to being cooped up either. I'd love to take you on a dinner date and some dancing."

"When do you have to go back to work?"

"Whenever I feel like it. The new manager is working out fine so far, so I'm all yours for the time being."

"I like the sound of that. The more time we spend together, the more I can get to know you. Hey, do you like games? You know, Scrabble, Monopoly, chess, snooker, cards?"

"I like some of those. Can you play pool?"

"I'm not good at it, but I like to play for fun. What about you? Are you any good at pool? What other games do you like?"

"I'm a pretty average pool player, but I do like to play Upwords, chess, and cards. We actually have all those games here, including the pool table. There is probably some of the house you haven't seen yet."

"I love to play games, sitting by a fire and drinking a few wines. But I warn you, I do cheat." Shelley smirked.

"Who doesn't cheat? That's half the fun of it."

"How about I make some reservations for tonight at the restaurant for seven thirty? That means we'd need to leave by six forty-five. I'll also have to let security know, who'll be looking after us tonight, and Carson can take us in the limo."

"Sounds good."

"I'll be back in a minute. I need to sort out the security for tonight and draw up a roster for the next two weeks, at least." Alex walked towards the doorway.

"Okay," Shelley said, approaching the wardrobe to select something to wear for tonight. *God, I still can't believe supernatural creatures exist in this world. I have lived such a sheltered life. And to think that maybe one day, I'll become a vampire. I don't know if I'll ever wrap my head around this or will ever be ready. What about my parents, my friends, or my job prospects …?* The tears welled in her eyes until she heard Alex's calming voice.

Don't over think it, my sweet girl …

CHAPTER THIRTEEN

"Knock, knock," James said.

"Come in," Shelley said, looking toward the doorway.

"I hear you need an iron and ironing board," James said, carrying them in.

"Yes, but how did you know?"

"I can hear your thoughts, dear." James set up the ironing board next to the window and plugged in the iron. "You know, you do need to work on keeping your thoughts to yourself."

"I wish I knew how," Shelley said, walking toward James.

"I can show you if you want."

"That would be awesome."

With patience, James taught Shelley how to control her thoughts so others couldn't hear her.

"When I'm done with the iron and ironing board, where do they get stored?" Shelley asked, checking to ensure the iron had reached the appropriate temperature.

"They belong in the cupboard next to the laundry room. But you don't have to bother yourself with that; I'll do it later on."

"Thanks, James, but I'd prefer to do it myself."

"If you change your mind, let me know."

Shelley smiled and watched the door close. *Right. Let me look again at what I have to wear for tonight.*

By the time Shelley had gone through her clothes and had picked her emerald-green full-length, strapless with a love heart neckline dress and ironed it and chose what shoes and accessories she would wear and how she would style her hair, the afternoon had slipped by.

Jeez, where has the time gone? I had better get in the shower.

*****

Shelley stood in front of the long mirror in the bathroom, admiring how well the dress hugged her body in all the right places. She was glad she had brought her corset on vacation so she could wear it under the dress to keep in all her bits and bobs too.

Hmm, not bad, and it covers the butterfly outline on the back of my neck. She admired how she had managed to put her hair half up and half down, with some soft curls. Slipping on her shoes, she took one last look in the mirror, smiled and was ready to go.

As she neared the bottom of the marble staircase, Shelley saw Grayson and Alex, who had his back to her.

Grayson took a deep breath, and his eyebrows rose when he saw Shelley approach them. "Bro, turn around," he said as his eyes widened.

Alex's heartbeat quickened, and his senses heightened when he watched, with pleasure, his life partner coming to stand before him. "Wow, you look stunning. That dress is lovely on you." He gave her a sensual kiss on her lips.

Shelley slowly pulled away and looked into his eyes. "Thank you, kind sir."

Grayson cleared his throat. "Sire."

"Right," Alex said, turning to Grayson.

"You need to get ready," Shelley said, self-conscious of their intimacy in front of Grayson.

"It will only take me ten minutes." Alex excused himself and climbed the stairs.

Grayson beheld her emerald-colored dress. "You looked nice tonight, Shelley."

"Thanks. Who's going to be keeping us safe tonight?"

"Brock and I will be looking after you. Don't worry, you'll be all right with us guarding you."

"Thank you, but I am a bit worried that the same thing will happen tonight, as what happened in Paris. It makes it not worth going out."

"That won't happen, will it, Grayson?" Alex asked from behind them.

"No, Sire. We are more prepared this time around. Those fuckers won't even get near you, ever again. Sorry about the language, ma'am."

Shelley smiled politely at Grayson.

"Meet us out front in five minutes, Grayson, with Brock. You'll be following us in the car at a close range, won't you?" Alex asked authoritatively.

Grayson nodded once. "Yes, Sire."

*****

Alex held Shelley's hand as they sat next to each other in the car on the way to the restaurant. "You have learned to turn off your thoughts to me."

"Yes, James taught me how to do it this afternoon."

"Good, I'm glad you mastered it so quickly. You look stunning in that dress. When you were coming down the stairs today, I kept thinking what a lucky man I am to have such a beautiful girl like you on my arm tonight. You look worried though, and you keep fidgeting. Are you all right?"

"I'm worried about a repeat performance of Paris tonight. Probably best if I have a few drinks to calm me down, oh, and some great company. I've been looking forward to dinner and dancing all afternoon. By the way, you look handsome in your black suit, and I too was thinking what a lucky girl I am."

Alex kissed the side of her forehead and inhaled her scent as they cuddled closer to each other whilst they travelled to the Crestwell Hotel.

*****

"Good evening, Mr. Crestwell, Miss Landers. I have your table ready for you. Come with me," the restaurant manager said.

Shelley's face lit up as she walked through, noticing the refined dining restaurant interior and its dancefloor to one side with a small orchestra playing.

"Here we go." The manager stopped at a table next to a full-length window overlooking the Limmat River. He pulled out their chairs and waited for them to sit. "May I take your drinks order?" He laid their napkins in their laps.

"We'll have a bottle of pink champagne, and could you put it into an ice bucket?" Alex said.

The manager nodded and left them with the menus to ponder what they wanted for their meals.

*****

Nervous, Shelley didn't wait for the waiter to pour Alex's glass of champagne so they could make a toast; she drank hers fast. Not only was she thirsty, but she was also hoping it would calm her anxieties.

When the waiter left them, Alex poured Shelley another glass of champagne. "Sip this one and tell me if you like it or not."

Shelley nodded and smiled. She took a sip. "Mmm … that is nice." She quickly drank the whole glass.

Alex watched her place the empty glass on the table. "How do you feel now?"

"Better, but I'm looking forward to my meal. Those two drinks went straight to my head."

For the entrée, Alex and Shelley had ordered asparagus wrapped in bacon with a spicy dipping sauce on the side. Shelley had never tried anything like this before.

Alex watched her take the first bite. "What do you think?

"Now, that is yummy! Can I have some more?" Shelley opened her mouth for him to put in another piece, as he had done previously. Her heart fluttered with the sensual, almost erotic way he fed her.

As the night progressed, they enjoyed each other's company and conversation. Shelley sipped on her drink and thought about how much she was enjoying herself and realized she had completely forgotten about the vampires.

Standing, Alex proffered his hand. "Would you like to dance?"

Shelley smiled and nodded. Taking his hand, she followed him to the dance floor. She felt safe in his muscular arms as Alex pulled her in closer to him, and they danced, cuddling each other.

God, how I love this man more than life itself, she thought as she drank in his scent.

When the music stopped for a break thirty minutes later, Alex asked, "Would you like to dance some more or go home?"

What, no dessert? Shelley mind-asked as she smiled up at him.

Alex smirked. "What dessert would you like, sweet girl?"

"I'll have you if that's available tonight."

"I'm sure we can accommodate that, my love." *Carson, bring the car around to take us home. Grayson, Brock, I expect you will be ready.*

They all mind-said together, *Yes, Sire.*

"Let's go." Alex grabbed Shelley's hand and walked toward the front entrance, collecting another bottle of pink champagne on the way out, which he had organized via mind-talk talk to the restaurant manager.

On the way back to the Crestwell home, Alex and Shelley couldn't seem to keep their hands off each other. When they arrived home, Alex carried Shelley out the car and up the stairs to their dimly lit bedroom and closed the door behind them.

"Woman, what you do to me," Alex murmured, as he cupped her breast through her dress.

"Undress me," Shelley pleaded as he grazed her earlobe with his teeth.

"Turn around."

After she obeyed, he unzipped her out of the dress, only to watch it fall to the ground and realize she was wearing a corset.

"Does my sweet man like this?" She gestured her hand down the corset.

"You look lovely, my sweet girl." He kissed the tops of her breasts and lapped at her cleavage as Shelley leaned against the wall with her head back. "Mmm, you smell damn good too."

Shelley smiled, knowing she had earlier that afternoon lathered her body with a nice-smelling lotion for her man. With her senses in overload, his touch was like pure heaven to her.

Alex unzipped her corset, pulled off her panties and carried her to the bed. As his loving eyes beheld her supple body, he hurriedly undressed and discarded them to the floor. Lying beside her, he ran his fingers up and down her body. "You are so beautiful."

She loved the way he made her feel, and she felt a fire ignite inside her when he teased her body with his tongue, gently nipping her as he went. Her body climaxed with many multiple orgasms when he lapped at her clitoris. *Oh my god, I want him so badly.*

"Would you allow me to make real love to you tonight, my sweet girl?"

She nodded because she couldn't answer. Shelley knew she was ready, and she wanted it as much as he did, even though it would bring on her transformation. When she eventually found her voice, she said, "Please be gentle with me."

He nodded and kissed her lips.

As their mouths opened and their tongues found each other— for what seemed like the first time—it ignited the fire in her again.

Alex inserted two fingers into her vagina. *Lovely ... so wet.* Watching her reaction, he gently pushed apart her legs, hovering over her, then placed his pulsating penis into her vagina.

It felt foreign at first, and Shelley's brow furrowed as she felt a stinging sensation inside her. But as he slowly rocked his penis in and out, the stinging sensation disappeared, and all she could now feel was unadulterated pleasure as she moved in time with his body.

Once Alex felt she was enjoying herself, he pounded his cock in and out of her.

"It ... feels ... so ... good. Please ... don't stop ..."

Alex smiled, enjoying the pleasure he was inflicting on her as their bodies gyrated in sync.

With the back of her head pressing into the bed, Shelley moaned, feeling a release as she orgasmed again.

Not long after, Alex came. He dropped beside her, panting and with sweat beading on his top lip. "Was that worth waiting for?"

"Is sex like that ... all the time or only the first time? As that was"—she caught her breath—"awesome. I've never felt so alive and pleasured like that in my whole life." She cuddled into the crook of his arm.

"Yes, it's like that all the time. But when you're a vampire, your senses heighten, so it seems ten times better." Alex placed his arm around her and pulled her into his chest. "How are you feeling now?"

"Umm, I feel good, actually. Do you think we could do that again?" Shelley looked up at Alex and smirked.

"You don't have to ask me twice. But would you like to try it a different way? Most women say this is better than missionary position."

"I'm game."

Alex sat upright. "Turn onto your stomach and get on all fours."

She obeyed.

He placed his cock into her vagina from behind.

Shelley moaned with the enjoyment of its fullness as Alex pumped it in and out of her, faster and faster. With her whole body tingling from the erotic pleasure, she moaned loudly, and before she knew it, Alex had come again, and she orgasmed.

Sated but exhausted, they lay on the pillows and cuddled into each other.

When Alex regained his breath, he said, "You sure know how to please a man. That was amazing."

Shelley cuddled into Alex tighter. "Sure was." Then she felt her anxiety build. *I wonder how long before I'll start to change.*

"It'll be all right. I am here with you to help you through it, my sweet girl," Alex said, responding to her thoughts. "But to answer your question, you should start feeling it soon. I might get the doctor to put in an IV drip for you, that's if you don't want to drink the blood we have in the fridge." Alex wrapped both arms around her and pulled her in tight. He kissed the side of her head.

"Can I try to see if I can stomach it first, and, if I can't drink it, you can get the doctor? What do you think?"

"Sure. Let's get dressed and go to the kitchen."

*****

When Shelley entered the kitchen, she noticed Annabelle was

already waiting for her and had poured some blood into a cup with a lid so Shelley couldn't see what she was drinking.

"Sit down." Annabelle indicating for Shelley to sit at the island counter. "Drink it slowly. Don't gulp it down, as it will make you sick."

As Shelley sat next to Annabelle, Annabelle placed her hand on Shelley's shoulder. Shelley took the first sip and nearly gaged on it. "Aww, that is disgusting." Shelley placed the cup on the counter and pushed it toward Annabelle, shaking her head.

"Take another drink." Annabelle held the cup in front of Shelley as she proceeded to calm her anxiety.

Shelley gulped hard, trying to keep down the saliva. She placed the cup to her lips, closed her eyes and took another sip. But this time, the blood tasted good.

Alex watched her gulp down the entire contents. "It's good, huh?"

Shelley licked the blood from her lips. "Mmm … unbelievably good. How much do I need to drink?"

"Maybe another cup?" Annabelle removed her hand from Shelley's shoulder.

Shelley hastily nodded as she watched Annabelle walk to the fridge and pour more blood into the cup. Within seconds of drinking the second cup of blood, Shelley started to scratch her forearm, because she was experiencing the sensation of something crawling under her skin. With her senses heightened; she could see better, smell odors she hadn't smelt previously, hear voices that seem to be getting louder, by the minute.

"Make it stop," shouted Shelley, placing her hands over her ears, shaking her head.

"Here, drink some more," said Annabelle, handing her another cup of blood. With every drop, the blood seemed to dull the heightened senses she was experiencing, a bit more. Shelley kept gulping down, cup after cup, but neither the blood or Annabelle's calming touch was doing her any good.

"I feel extremely hot. I need to take a cold shower." Shelley fanned herself with her hand. "And this sensation of feeling like something is crawling under my skin, I want to rip it out."

Alex and Annabelle regarded each other and gulped as they watched Shelley's eyes dilate.

"Alex, can you either put me in the swimming pool or in the shower? I need to get rid of this sensation. It's driving me mad." Shelley scratched at her skin with fervor and rocked to sooth herself. "Why is it so bright in here? Can we turn off the lights please?"

Alex collected Shelley in his arms and ran with vampiric speed to their bathroom where he stripped her down and placed her under a cold shower.

Shelley put her head under the showerhead and rested her hands on the tiles. "God, that is freezing, but it feels good. Can you please turn off the lights? It hurts my eyes."

Alex walked to the switch.

"Alex, this is getting worse." Tears formed in her eyes. "I still feel like I want to rip open my skin and get rid of the insect crawling inside me."

Annabelle entered the bathroom. "Get Shelley out of the shower and take her to the pool. It's a lot colder and might help."

With vampiric speed, Alex turned off the faucet, collected Shelley in his arms, ran down to the pool and placed her into the cold water.

"Oh my god, this is freezing!" Shelley said, her teeth chattering as she felt the release.

Annabelle knelt in front of Shelley and handed her another cup of blood. "Drink. It will help."

Shelley's body shook as she gulped down the entire contents. "I don't think this blood is working. My head feels like it's about to explode." Shelley's dilated eyes widened, and her nostrils flared when she noticed Annabelle's pulsating vein in her neck and pulled her into the water. Shelley held Annabelle with brute force, not allowing her to pull away.

Annabelle hadn't felt this type of power from a new Lepidoptera in a while. *Fuck! Alex, help!*

Alex jumped into the water and knocked Shelley off her feet, which allowed Annabelle to wriggle free from Shelley's clutches.

Shelley lunged forward. "She is mine!"

Annabelle's eyes widened, and she stood in the pool with clenched fists.

Alex slapped Shelley, immediately feeling bad that he had wounded his life partner. *Shit ...*

Rising out the water with her swollen, bloodied mouth, Shelley retaliated against Alex. Quicker than the eye could see, she grabbed Alex's arm, pulled him toward her and bit his wrist. As she vigorously sucked his bloody, she growled, and her eyes darted back and forth, like he was her prey.

"Get the fuck off him, you bitch!" Annabelle clocked Shelley with a piece of wooden furniture from behind, knocking her out. Annabelle pulled Alex and Shelley out the water and laid them next to the pool. "Alex, are you all right?" Annabelle gently shook Alex, noticing the bite marks on his forearm.

"Yes, I will be in few seconds. Thank you." Alex slowly sat upright. "God, that was close. She is strong, and so fast. I'll take her to our room and put her to bed."

"I think it's going to be a long night, so you might want to restrain her. I'll give the doctor a ring right now and get him to put in the IV drip, as I think this will work faster than those cups of blood." Annabelle watched Alex collect an unconscious Shelley. "I'm sorry you had to see and go through this, but don't let her drink from you for at least a week. It'll probably take that long for her transformation. You can't take her out anywhere either, as she will be unpredictable for that week. When a female slowly transforms, it is hard not to bite a human, as you can hear their blood pumping through their veins, and it sort of turns you on."

"I appreciate any words of wisdom and help you can give us," Alex said, carrying Shelley inside.

Are you both all right? Grayson mind-asked, listening to their mind-chatter.

Annabelle replied for the both of them.

*****

Quickly sitting up in bed, Shelley woke, wondering where she was. She checked the bedside clock—2:30 a.m.—and realized she was in her own bed. With her heightened senses, she smelt blood and felt the IV drip in her arm. Frowning, she ran her fingers over the cannula in her arm. *I wonder how that got there. Aww, jeez, my head hurts.* Shelley rubbed her temples and realized Alex was in the room, from his scent. "Alex, can you please get me some headache medicine? My head feels like it's splitting open."

"Here." Annabelle handed her a tablet with a glass of water. When Annabelle placed her hand on Shelley's head to feel her temperature, her touch-induced a calming sensation which stopped Shelley's head from throbbing.

"Thank you, Annabelle. Can you please put me back to sleep again?"

Within seconds of Annabelle's touch, Shelley was out like a light for another four hours.

During the night, Alex and Annabelle swapped places with Samantha and Grayson to ensure everyone was plenty rested in case Shelley caused trouble the next day.

*****

Shelley startled awake and realized from the scent in the room that she had company. Sitting upright, she spotted Samantha and Grayson sitting at the back of the room. "What the fuck are you two assholes looking at? Get the fuck out of my room."

Grayson and Samantha didn't bat an eyelid; instead, they silently watched Shelley to see what she would do.

Shelley got out of bed and pulled her IV drip and its stand with her toward the bathroom while glaring at Grayson and Samantha as she passed them. After slamming the door, she quickly headed for the toilet. *Fuck off. I don't want you here,* Shelley mind-said to Samantha and Grayson.

But they didn't answer her.

Shelley stripped down, disconnected her IV from the bag, turned on the faucet, stepped into the shower and closed the glass door behind her. Sitting on the shower floor, she pushed herself backward against the wall tiles. With her forehead pressing into her knees and the hot water running over her body, Shelley rocked herself as tears streamed down her cheeks.

God, what have I done? Poor, Alex. I'm meant to be his life partner. How could I have done that to him? I wouldn't blame him if he kicked me out and told me to never come back.

Sweet girl … Shelley, if you can hear me, say so.

Alex, I can hear you. I'm sorry for what I did to you … truly. I'd understand if you want me to leave. Shelley sobbed.

Don't cry. I can't be near you at the moment because you might try to drink from me again. It's for the best if I stay away. I know you're hurting, but try to keep your chin up, sweet girl. I love you, and that won't ever change. Don't forget that.

I love you too, Alex, and I don't want to lose you.

I know you do. Would you like some breakfast or a drink?

Yes, please, that would be nice. But I don't know if I can keep breakfast down. My stomach is in knots, and I feel miserable. I feel like I … I want to die.

As Shelley sat on the shower floor, crying, she felt a friendly hand extend to her. Annabelle had come to help calm Shelley. Within seconds, Shelley felt better.

Annabelle turned off the shower. "Come on, let's get you dressed and back to bed."

Shelley nodded and eventually followed Annabelle to the bedroom where she drifted off to sleep for a few more hours.

*****

Shelley woke at four o'clock in the afternoon after sleeping all day.

Grayson and Samantha were still watching over her in the back of the room.

Shelley remembered what she had said to them earlier in the morning. Sitting upright, Shelley swallowed hard. "Samantha, Grayson, please forgive me for what I said to you both. I feel awful, and I know you didn't deserve to be treated like that."

Samantha stood. "It's all good, Shelley. It's forgotten, okay? Are you hungry or thirsty? Can we get you something?"

"Thank you for being so understanding. Umm ... could you please ask Luda to make me an omelet and maybe a cup of tea to settle my stomach cramps?" *Girl, you need to sort your shit out.* Shelley hopped out of bed and decided to shower, get dressed and brush her teeth and hair. *At least doing this will make me feel sort of normal again.*

*****

"Knock, knock," Luda said, entering with a tray. "Here you go, my dear." She placed the food tray on the bed. "How are you, dear? I hate to see you going through this."

"I'm a bit better." Shelley sat on top of the now made bed. Her eyes widened when she noticed Luda's neck vein pulsating with blood.

"That's good, dear. If you need any food or drink, mind-talk to me, and I'll bring it up to you!"

"Thanks, Luda, but ..." She took a deep breath to calm herself. "Don't get too close. Actually, you're better off staying away from me. I am not a good person. I have done some horrible things in the last two days that I'm ashamed of."

Luda leaned in to give Shelley a reassuring hug, but Shelley felt like she wanted to drink her blood.

"Get out, Luda, before I hurt you!" Shelley's eyes dilated once again at the smell of fresh blood.

"Shit." Luda strode for the door and ran out the room.

Grayson stood, watching her every move. "Calm yourself, Shelley."

Sorry, Shelley mind-said to Luda as tears welled in her eyes.

*****

After Shelley ate the omelet and drank some of her tea, she felt a little better; even her headache was gone. But something still didn't feel right, and she knew it. With her fists clenched, she paced like a wild cat trapped in a cage, wanting to punch something or someone.

"Knock, knock," Brock said, entering the room.

"Now what?" Shelley asked.

"Calm down, girly. Sit on the bed. I'm going to unplug your IV drip. Keep still."

Shelley obeyed and watched him place a bandage around the cannula.

"Come with me." Brock said, walking toward the doorway.

"What for?"

"Can you do as you're told for once?" Brock raked his hand through his light brown, crewcut hair.

Shelley took a deep breath then quickly exhaled and followed Brock downstairs and into the training and combat room.

Grayson and Samantha flanked behind them.

Reaching the padded mat area, Brock said, "Now, fight me, or try to hurt me. I won't break. You need to get some of your anger out of your system before it eats you alive."

Shelley clenched her fists. "I'm not doing that, you fucking idiot."

"Chicken are we, you fucking bitch?"

Grayson and Samantha smirked at each other as they sat on the steps.

"Fucking bitch, huh? If that's the way you want to play it, come on, you bastard. I'll flatten your ass on this floor right here and now." Shelley raised her fists to fight.

Brock pushed her, which angered Shelley even more, so she shoved him, and he landed on the floor with a thump.

Shelley laughed and pointed. "Who's the bitch now, huh?"

Brock got up quickly, slapped her face, laughed and stood in a fighting stance.

"Asshole," Shelley said, looking into his brown eyes, and threw the first punch. She knew she couldn't beat him, but she had to try, and it made her feel good too. After about ten minutes of fighting, Shelley said, "Stop. I give up."

But Brock kept pushing her until she started to fight him again. By the time he had finished with Shelley, she was black and blue all over and drenched in sweat.

Brock slung a resisting Shelley over his shoulder like a sack of potatoes.

Shelley vigorously punched his back, trying to get away from him, as tears stung her eyes with frustration.

When he reached her bedroom doorway, he put her down.

"Fucking bastard. You fucking asshole! You'll pay for that one day!" With tear-stained cheeks, she stormed to her bathroom and slammed the door.

*****

After her shower, Shelley reinserted her IV drip into her arm to start the blood transfusion again and hopped into bed. Lifting her top, she noticed her bruising was nearly gone.

Ha, must be a vampire thing, she thought as she lay down.

*****

When she woke at 9:30 a.m., Shelley was hungry. As she sat upright in bed, she saw Brock and Annabelle watching over her from the back of the room. Rolling her eyes, she lay down again and stared at the ceiling while exhaling.

God, I am sick and tired of being babysat. She mind-talked to Luda, requesting breakfast. *I can't believe she is even talking to me after the way I screamed at her yesterday. Alex, can you hear me?*

"He's gone to work, Shelley," Annabelle said, "because he can't bear to see you like this. He needed something to occupy his mind because he was going mad. He can hear you, but he is choosing not to listen, because he is so upset about what he did to you."

Shelley's brow furrowed. "He never did anything I didn't want him to do, and I'm the one who tried to drain him. I should be the one apologizing for what I've done."

"Knock, knock," Luda said, entering with Shelley's breakfast tray. She set the tray on the bed. "How are you feeling today, dear girl?"

"Not bad. I don't feel like I want to drink anyone yet. I am hungry though."

"That's good. I'll leave you to eat your breakfast, dear girl." Luda nodded once and walked toward the doorway.

Shelley rolled her eyes and thought, *Yeah, still a leper.*

After Shelley finished her breakfast, she felt energized. "Hey, you. Do you want to go another few rounds with me in the combat room? I feel like I could whip your ass this morning,"

"No worries. Let's go, bitch," Brock said, standing.

*****

In the training and combat room, Brock was the one who did the ass-whipping, and once again, Shelley was black and blue from the fighting.

"Not bad today. You're getting better, bitch," Brock teased.

Shelley laughed. "Thanks, asshole."

When they returned to her bedroom, Shelley spotted Alex waiting for her on the bed. She ran over and kissed him ever so passionately.

"I've missed you too, my sweet girl," Alex said, looking into her eyes.

"I love you, my sweet man."

"Do you still crave the blood?" Alex's brow furrowed with worry.

"No, but I still don't feel myself yet. Whatever that is now!" Shelley said, glancing into her lap.

"It seems like you're over the worst of it, I think, babe." Alex stood. "Let me look at the back of your neck." He lifted her hair off her neck only to find her butterfly had nearly finished coloring itself in. "It's purple and white so far, Shelley. Wow, you're going to be powerful."

"Can you stay, or do you have to leave because I'm dangerous to you?"

"I think I'll be safe to stay with you now. But we can't have sex or drink each other's blood; do you understand me?"

Shelley nodded. "Can we cuddle up together? I've missed you and your strong arms."

"Sure, come on." Alex indicated for her to lay on the bed with him.

"I need to shower first. I'm a bit on the smelly side from the combat training with Brock. Then plug in the IV drip. After that, I'm all yours."

*****

The next day, Shelley woke early only to find Alex not in bed with her. Sitting upright, Shelley noticed Brock sitting in the back of the room. *Boy, I would like to whip your ass.*

"Give it your best shot, bitch. Let's go."

She had forgotten for a second that he could read her thoughts if she didn't block him out.

*****

Once Shelley had gotten rid of all her pent-up energy, she said, "Same time again tomorrow, asshole?"

Brock smirked. "Bring it on, bitch."

Shelley laughed and walked toward the stairs with Brock only to spot Alex waiting for her on the steps.

"Man, you sure kick ass. You're not too bad."

"Thanks, babe. I'm going to shower. Catch up with you in the kitchen in thirty minutes."

Alex pulled her close and kissed her lips.

"As much as I would like to take this further, we can't. So I'll see you in thirty." Shelley pulled away from his alluring scent.

Alex smiled and watched her walk up the stairs.

*****

"Good morning, Shelley. How are you feeling today?" Luda asked as Shelley entered the kitchen.

"I feel good today, Luda. Can you please pour me a drink of blood? I'm not sure I can pour anything at the moment. I have the shakes." Shelley showed Luda her shaky hands.

"Yes, sweet child." Luda removed the jug of blood from inside the fridge's secret compartment.

Shelley drank the first glass fast and polished off another one straight away. "Thanks, Luda, I needed that."

"You're welcome, dear. Are you hungry?"

"Famished."

"Sit, and I'll get you some breakfast." Luda prepared a plate of bacon and eggs for Shelley.

"Where is everyone today?" Shelley asked, cutting the poached eggs.

Alex entered the kitchen. "I've given them the day off. As you are now better, they won't need to watch you for me. How do you feel?"

"Yeah, good. Though I still feel strange. It's hard to explain. I don't feel whole, if that makes sense."

"That is because you haven't fully transformed yet," Luda answered, glancing back at Shelley as she loaded the dishwasher. "Once that happens, you'll feel whole again."

"Okay. That makes sense."

"You, at least, have another three to four days before you fully transform." Alex sat next to Shelley at the island counter. "We must keep you busy for those days so sitting around waiting for it to happen doesn't make you crazy."

As sex is off the menu for three to four days, what will we do? Shelley mind-said to Alex, blocking Luda from hearing.

Naughty girl. "Would you like to play a game or watch a DVD?"

"I wouldn't mind playing Upwords with you, as long as we can use a dictionary."

"Sure. You finish breakfast, and I'll set up the game in front of the fire. It will be how you like it."

"You remembered," Shelley said, smiling.

CHAPTER FOURTEEN

Mesmerized, Shelley stood at the window and watched the snowfall covering the ground in wonderment. *Magical* ...

"Beautiful, isn't it—the snow?" Alex wrapped his arms around her waist from behind, snuggling into her neck and shoulder.

"This is the first time I've ever seen snow. It's calming and magical to watch it fall from the sky onto the ground. I could watch it fall all day and not get sick of it."

"It's our winter season, so we have another two months of snow to come. Do you need me to plug in your IV drip?"

"Yes, please."

"I have the game all set up next to the fire, along with a dictionary." Alex plugged in the IV drip. "You still want to play?"

"Do you mind if we play later?" Shelley sat on the rug in front of the fire. "I don't feel like it right now."

"What's the matter, my sweet girl?" He sat next to her, peering into her eyes.

Shelley sighed. "I don't know. I wish this transformation would hurry up and be over. How much of the butterfly is colored already?" Shelley turned her back to Alex and lifted her hair off her neck.

"Hang on. I'll get a couple mirrors so you can look yourself." Alex stood and walked toward the doorway.

"Ok!" Shelley excitedly tapped her foot while waiting for Alex to return.

Within seconds, Alex was sitting next to Shelley again with the two mirrors. "Here, you hold this so you can see your butterfly while I hold up your hair."

"It's ... It's so beautiful, and it's purple with some white, like you described." Shelley moved the mirror around so she could see it from all angles and noticed the butterfly had nearly fully colored itself in; it wouldn't be too much longer before she was fully transformed. *To think only a few weeks ago, I was a normal girl, who had finished her college exams, to now, I am a Lepidoptera vampire, and that I have a long life ahead of me with such a wonderful partner.* Shelley put down the mirror and faced Alex. "What abilities will I have, Alex?"

"As I said before, you'll be pretty powerful. Female Lepidoptera vampires usually have one color on their butterfly, but you have two. You'll play an important part for our kind in the future, I know this. But to answer your question, you'll be able to touch any vampire and copy his/her ability; it's called mimicry. You also have the power to control the elements, like the wind, rain, sunshine. Extremely powerful."

"So, say for instance, when I'm fighting someone, if I touch them, I will absorb their strength?"

Alex nodded.

"Cool. That means I can put Brock on his ass. You know, he has egged me on so much in the last couple days that I would love to whip his butt." Shelley smirked.

Alex's brow furrowed. "He did that for your own good, you know that, right?"

"Yeah, I know. But he called me a bitch, and I ain't no dog. Don't worry, I am not mad at Brock, and I know he was only doing this to help me with my pent-up energy. But it would be nice to see him suffer a bit."

Alex shook his head, smiled and laughed. "Give it your best shot. None of us can beat him. He is the best fighter around. Don't say I didn't warn you."

"Hey!" Shelley playfully slapped his arm. "You're supposed to be on my side!"

The afternoon passed quickly, and by four o'clock, Shelley felt she needed to rest. As she lay on their bed, Shelley said to Alex, "You don't have to stay with me if you have work you need to get done. I'll be all right. I need to rest anyway."

Alex kissed the side of her forehead. "Okay. I won't be far away, sweet girl. Call out if you need anything, and I'll come for you."

Shelley nodded and smiled. Closing her eyes, she drifted off to sleep, thinking of what a wonderful day she had with Alex.

*****

Shelley woke late into the night, and Alex was sitting in a chair next to the bed, watching over her. "Hello there, sweet girl."

"Hi. How long have you been watching me sleep?"

"Not long. I didn't want to disturb you, and I do love to watch you sleep; you are peaceful to watch."

Shelley smiled and patted the bed for him to lay next to her.

As he lay on the bed next to Shelley, Alex extended his arm so she could cuddle into the nook of his shoulder.

I have missed this, Shelley thought, inhaling his scent.

"Are you hungry?"

"Yeah, but not the hungry you're talking about."

"That would be good … but not today. How about I take you to the kitchen for some food?"

Before Shelley could answer, Alex had unplugged her IV drip and picked her up in his arms and headed for the stairs.

"Wait. I need to go to the ladies room first."

"Sorry. There's a bathroom downstairs you can use instead," Alex said, arriving at the kitchen doorway.

"What's the rush?"

"Nothing. The toilets are through there." Alex pointed to the doorway.

When Shelley returned to the kitchen, she found Alex sitting at the island counter.

"Are you hungry?"

"Not at all."

"How are you feeling?"

"I feel fine. What's going on, Alex?" Shelley asked suspiciously.

"Nothing. I wanted to show you another part of the house you haven't seen yet." Alex stood, grabbing her hand, and pulled her into another room not far from the kitchen. As they entered the room, Alex said, "This is my office."

Shelley surveyed the room. "I thought it might be, especially with the furniture and the way it's placed. Do you spend much time in here?"

"A little bit. I mainly use the computer at my desk over there." Alex pointed to it.

Shelley wandered over and stood in front of his desk, which had a laptop on it. The lid was open, and when she sat down, the screen illuminated to reveal an image of Bronwyn and Analyse.

"Surprise!" they yelled together.

Shelley's face went from sad to happy. "Hello! I miss you two so much. How are you? What have you been up to? God, it's good to see you both!"

"One question at a time," Analyse said, smiling back at Shelley. "Alex tells us you were in a car accident a few days ago and that you're still recovering."

Shelley eyed Alex quizzically, and he mind-said, *You look pale, so they would have asked questions about what's going on. I had to make something up.*

I never thought of that. Thanks, babe.

"Yeah, idiot came out of nowhere and smashed into me. Luckily, I didn't break anything, only bruising, and I'm a bit sore all over. But the doctor said I should be okay by Friday. Alex has been looking after me though."

"Besides looking pale, babe, you look pretty good. So, are you still enjoying it over there?" Bronwyn asked.

"Yeah, I love it here, but I need to tell you both something … Umm … I've decided to stay here and live with Alex. He loves me, and I love him, so I figure, why leave something so good? I think I'd probably die inside if I couldn't see Alex anymore."

I will leave you to talk with your friends, Alex mind-said.

Thanks. Shelley smiled at him and watched him leave the room.

"We sort of thought that would happen. So, this means you're no longer a virgin, am I right?" Bronwyn smirked.

"Why didn't you two let me know how good sex is? This man is such a great lover."

"Let's get off that subject. Since we've been home, we both have had interviews and are waiting for callbacks," Analyse said.

"Wow, good luck, girls. So, any men on the home front for you both?"

"No, only a bunch of losers. I sure do miss the guys we met in Zurich. Yeah, we knew they were only after us for one thing, but at least they treated us good. I always felt like I was his princess," Analyse said.

"Mr. Right is out there, waiting for both of you. You have to be in the right place at the right time. You wouldn't believe how good Alex is to me. I've met such a great guy, and he looks after me and treats me like his partner. It's like living in a dream, except I never wake up; that's how good it is."

"Wow, you are one lucky girl. But we miss you bunches. So much so we're saving to come back one day. And, who knows, maybe our Mr. Right is over there, waiting for us this time," Bronwyn said.

"Analyse, could I ask you a huge favor? Would you mind boxing up my clothes and stuff and sending them to me? I've give you a list of what to send to me and what to send to my parents' place. I'll pay you for the postage."

"Sure, babe. No problem. You'll need to give me your address though."

"Thanks, Analyse. I appreciate you doing this for me. I hope you find a new roommate to share the rent. I'm sorry to leave you in the lurch like that."

"It's okay. I'll get it organized, and all will be good. I don't want you to worry about any of that. What do you want us to do with your car?"

"Sell it for whatever you can, and keep the money for the back-rent. Hopefully that will help until you find a roommate."

"Wow, that is nice of you. Thank you."

"It's the least I can do."

"Do you think you might start a practice in Zurich?" Bronwyn asked.

"That's the plan. Alex said he'd help me, but I kind of want to try stand on my own two feet. I don't want to sponge off him."

"You sure have a great man there. I hope you appreciate him and everything he does for you."

"I sure do know what a great man he is, and I do appreciate him. You know, he actually took me to Paris again last week. We even went moped riding to sightsee at night together. How romantic. I met some of his friends in Paris too, and they were nice. Everything sure is feeling right about being here with Alex. So much so that I think I could marry him one day."

"Wow, that is serious, babe, and so soon."

"When will you tell your parents that you're moving to Zurich?" Analyse asked.

"Once I get better, I'll either call or Skype them."

Shelley talked to Bronwyn and Analyse for another hour, and before they logged off, they promised to Skype each other every couple of weeks to catch up.

That is one thing I sure miss, not having any friends here, only Alex's friends. It's not the same as having my own friends. But now that I'm a vampire, I suppose everything is different. As she stared at the screen, Alex's screensaver started, and she watched pictures of her that she didn't even know he had taken revolve. There were also pictures of her and Alex. Closing the laptop lid, Shelley smiled and headed for the kitchen, as she was getting hungry.

"Hi, Annabelle," Shelley said, walking to the sideboard.

"Hello, Shelley. How you feeling?" Annabelle asked from the island counter.

"Yeah, not bad. Do you want one?" Shelley took some bread from the breadbox.

"Sure. What are you going to put on it?"

"Peanut butter and honey," Shelley said, spreading the ingredients.

"Ooh, sounds yummy. I've not tried those two together before."

"Here you go." Shelley placed the plate with the sandwich in front of Annabelle.

Annabelle took a bite of the sandwich. "Mmm, this is good. I might make another one. You want another one?"

"Yes, thanks. Annabelle, have you ever had a life partner?"

"Yes. A long time ago. He died at the hands of the Debauched vampires."

"I'm sorry. That must have been horrible for you. Do female Lepidoptera ever get a second chance at love?"

"I have not heard of any in my lifetime."

"That is harsh. So, what do you do when you want, you know, sex or to feel like a woman?"

"I don't. I haven't been with anyone since my partner died. I have never felt the urge to fuck anyone else. And no other vamp male has shown any interest in me yet. I think I may be destined to stay single."

"We'll have to see about that. A lot of male vamps who work at the Crestwell Hotel are hot. And Alex has some hot male friends, which I think you may like. Leave it to me."

"Hey, that is kind of you, Shelley," Annabelle said, scrunching her face. "I don't know if I'm ready yet either."

"Of course, you are ready. Female to female, don't you miss not having sex? It's so hot and awesome and … I think you get the message."

"Yeah, I do miss that feeling. Oh my god, how I miss that feeling, but as I said, no male vamp seems to look twice at me."

"I don't see why not. You are beautiful. Great body, great looks, nice personality—what's not to like? Maybe you have been looking in all the wrong places. Paris is full of hotheads, whereas Zurich is full of lovely vamps. Even my two best friends said the men here were awesome."

"Thanks. You are one cool chick, Shelley. Thanks for the compliments too. I hope I get to stay a bit longer here. I don't want to go back yet, and I'm enjoying getting to know you and Alex."

"I'll talk with Alex and see what we can do."

"Thanks, babe." Annabelle leaned in and hugged Shelley.

"Talking of Alex, have you seen him around?"

"Last time I saw him, he was in the combat room." Annabelle took their plates to the dishwasher.

"Right! Umm ... I might catch up with you tomorrow if that's okay. I want to go see my man."

"No problem, and thanks for the chat."

*****

Shelley sat on the steps, watching her man fight, and became aroused by his muscular body as he trained with Brock.

"Get up, bitch," Brock said, looking at her sideways as he sparred with Alex.

She hadn't realized Brock had noticed her sitting on the steps. Her brow creased. "Fuck off, bastard. I'm not in the mood for your shit tonight."

Brock moved with vampiric speed and quickly pulled Shelley into a standing position then slapped her face a few times. "So, you think you can whip my arse, eh? I'd like to see you try, bitch."

"Why are you so mean to me all the time? You know, don't worry about that." Shelley kicked him square in the balls.

"Low blow, even for you, bitch," Brock said, doubling over and grabbing his crotch.

"Bring it on, fucker." *He always brings out the worst in me.*

Alex smirked and stood to one side whilst Brock and Shelley sparred.

Brock knocked her flat on her arse, and Shelley did the same to him a few times.

"Mmm, you're getting stronger by the day. Have you been training in here without me?" Brock asked.

"Nope, but as I said to you yesterday"—Shelley held her fists in front of her—"one day, I will whip your ass, and that may not be today, but it could be tomorrow, as I seem to be getting stronger by the minute. After that, you won't be calling me a dog, fucker."

"Bring it on, babe. No one has beaten me yet."

"I'm not your babe or your dog. My name is Shelley, and don't you forget it." Shelley kicked him in the chest, sending him against a wall and falling to the floor.

"Shelley, that is enough! You either fight fair or not at all. Brock is only training you in combat. It's not personal!"

"You guys always stick together. Fuck this, I'm out of here."

Brock grabbed Shelley and held her tightly until she stopped wriggling. "You need to calm down. Alex is your life partner, and he deserves your respect. I'm the one you're mad at, so take it out on me. But just so you know, I've been goading you since you turned. It's the only way for you to get rid of your pent-up anger, and it has worked so far. But in the end, I'm on your side, and hopefully one day, we can be friends, not like this now."

Shelley eyed Alex and shook herself free from Brock's arms and stood there for a few minutes, considering what Brock had said to her. "Listen. I'm not usually a violent person; in fact, I don't usually like violence of any kind. But, as you've been provoking me each day, my blood seems to boil, especially when you call me a bitch. I don't like being called a dog. I do seem to have a lot of pent-up anger, and I'm hoping this will subside, but, if it doesn't, I'm hoping, as a friend, you can show me a way I can control it." Shelley raked her hand through her hair. "I'm sorry for the way I've acted toward you. There is one thing I'd like you to do though, and that is to teach me combat training. I need to learn how to protect myself and kill them fucking Debauched vamps."

Brock nodded once. "Tomorrow I'll teach you, but tonight you need some time alone with Alex." He turned and left the room.

"I'm sorry for the way I acted toward you," Shelley said to Alex standing at the bottom of the staircase. "As Brock said, you do deserve my respect, not my bad-mouthed attitude. Can you forgive me?"

He hesitated. "Yes, I forgive you. But don't ever talk to me like that again, especially in front of others." Alex's nostrils flared as he left the room, leaving Shelley standing there, feeling awkward.

I suppose I deserved that. She climbed the stairs toward the kitchen for some blood.

*****

Shelley rested her back against the lounge as she sat on the plush rug in front of the fire and watched its flame dance all around whilst sipping her mug of blood. *I hope I can get this anger under control.* After placing the mug on the side table, Shelley retrieved a pillow from the lounge and lay in front of the fire, staring at the flames. Eventually, she drifted off to sleep.

*****

The next day, Shelley woke to Alex stroking the side of her face and watching her eyes open. "Good morning."

"Hi," Shelley said, leaning into his hand and smiling.

They gazed into each other eyes for a moment, not saying anything—verbal or mind.

"How are you feeling this morning?"

"Umm ... okay, I think."

"Would you like some breakfast?"

Shelley sat upright. "Not right now. I might go shower."

"Would you like some company?"

"Umm ... if you don't mind, I think I'd like to shower by myself." Shelley pulled away from his touch and quickly stood. *Oh my god, his scent is driving me crazy. I want to drink his blood.* Her eyes dilated as she tried to control her thirst. Shelley strode away from Alex, leaving him sitting on the floor.

Alex frowned, not knowing what was going on in Shelley's mind, as he watched his life partner leave the room.

God, what is wrong with me? Why am I acting this way toward the man I love so much? Shelley quickly grabbed some clean clothes and headed into the bathroom.

With her back to the tiles and her chin on her chest, Shelley enjoyed the hot water cascading over her body. As the steam filled the shower, Shelley's eyes filled with tears, and her heart grew heavy. She collapsed on the shower floor.

*****

Her eyes opened wide, wondering where she was, only to realize she was in her bed. Shelley noticed the IV drip had been reapplied to her arm.

"How are you feeling?" Alex asked, sitting on a chair next to the bed.

Wiping the sleep from her eyes, she slowly sat upright. "Umm … I feel fine. What happened?"

"You fainted in the shower." Alex leaned toward her. We think it's because it's the first night you had been without the IV drip."

Shelley inspected her hands. "I should be more careful."

Alex sat on the bed next to Shelley and lifted her chin to meet his eyes. "Its okay. Can I cuddle with you?" His soulful eyes searched hers.

"I would love that." She smiled and pulled back the comforter. *I always feel safe and loved in his arms.* "Are you still mad at me for what I did and said?" She cuddled into his chest.

"No, I'm not mad at you, babe. And I'm sorry for the way I acted toward you. You didn't deserve the way I treated you either. I think I too have some readjusting to do." Alex placed his arm around her.

"Our first fight."

"Yes. Plus, I should have known that in this day and age, women do not like men talking down to them, even if they are wrong. I think I have a lot to learn when it comes to having a life partner."

"I think we both have a lot to learn. More patience is required from me too. And the transformation into a vampire has not helped us one bit. It sucks actually."

Alex laughed. "No pun intended."

Shelley chuckled.

"So, let's have a look at your butterfly."

"Do we have to? I personally am over this. I'd like to be normal for one day. Can we do that, or is it too late for that now?"

"Sorry, babe. I need to see if it's fully transformed." Alex released his hold on her.

Shelley sighed and turned around so he could check the back of her neck.

"It's fully colored in, which means you're fully transformed."

"So, what does that mean?"

"We should be able to remove your IV drip for good, as long as you can maintain your blood supply. You can now leave the house. You don't have to be cooped up here all the time. Also, we can have sex again."

"Make-up sex would be good, but I like romantic sex more." Shelley smirked. "Can we do a repeat of our dinner at the restaurant the other night and maybe come back here for some fun?"

"Mmm, that sounds promising. I'll surprise you tonight. Can you get dolled up again in something nice, like the dress you wore the other night?"

"That is the only nice dress I own."

"We'll have to fix that. Annabelle can take you today to look for a new dress if you'd like. "And before you say anything, I'll buy the dress for you."

"Thanks, Alex. You are too kind. Speaking of Annabelle, I was talking with her yesterday, and did you know her life partner died by the hands of the Debauched vampires?" Shelley's brow creased as she sat upright.

"Yes, those bastards. Must have been devastating for her."

"You know, she is so lonely, not that she would admit it. Do you think you could, maybe, introduce her to some of your friends while she's here? She hasn't been with anyone for eighty-five years, and … that's a long time to not be loved by someone. I'd like to help her, that's all."

"Do you think she's ready for a commitment?"

"I do. I know this from talking with her yesterday. She thinks no vampire would look at her twice. How sad. Even though she's a great vampire warrior and has a great personality, she seems to have a low self-esteem of herself when it comes to men. Annabelle told me she thinks she's destined to be alone for the rest of her life, because she thinks you only ever get one chance at a life partner. I told her to not think that way and that she is gorgeous and that any vampire would want her. But I suppose you have to find that someone first."

"I do know of a guy, but I don't know if he'd be interested. Would you mind if I ask him and Annabelle to join us at dinner tonight to see if they hit it off?"

"As much as I want you all to myself tonight, no, I don't mind. Who is he?"

"Actually, he's my new manager. His name is Bryant. I know he lost his life partner years ago, but I don't know if he's ready for a new one. But even if he isn't ready, maybe they still could hook up. I do have other friends who would be interested in Annabelle, but they're not ready for commitment and will only break her heart. We sure are a pair of matchmakers, aren't we?"

"Yeah. I'll tell Annabelle to come with me to pick a new dress and that she is coming to dinner with us tonight—not as security but as a friend."

"And I'll make the restaurant booking and call Bryant to tell him he's joining us for dinner tonight. We'll meet Bryant at the Crestwell Hotel reception at, say, around seven o'clock. How does that sound?"

"Sounds great."

"So, are you hungry?"

Shelley smirked. "Yes, but not for food."

Alex's eyes widened, and he dislodged Shelley's IV grip plug. He removed her clothes and his own.

I need him so badly inside me ... Shelley thought, aroused by his scent.

"You are beautiful, my sweet, sweet girl." Alex caressed and showered her body with his mouth.

Shelley whimpered with delight and curved her body toward his mouth as Alex inflicted pleasurable torment upon her body and her vagina.

CHAPTER FIFTEEN

"Good morning, Sire, Shelley. Would you like some breakfast?" Luda asked, watching them enter the kitchen.

Shelley headed to the fridge. "Yes please. Could I have some fried eggs, fried tomatoes, onion, and mushroom, with a slice of toast?"

"Mmm, that sounds good. Make that two, Luda," Alex said.

Luda nodded once and smiled.

"Here you go, babe." Shelley sat next to Alex at the island counter, placing a cup of blood in front of him.

Alex raised the cup. "You remembered. Good girl."

Luda placed the bread in the toaster. "Everyone is still in the dining room, eating their breakfast, if you want to join them. I can bring your breakfast in for you if you'd like."

"Thanks, Luda. Let's go join them." Alex stood, and Shelley followed him into the dining room. "Good morning, everyone."

They all said, "Good morning," together.

"How are you feeling today, Shelley?" Brock asked.

"Umm, actually, I feel good, and I have fully transformed." Shelley placed her hand on his shoulder and smiled then sat next to him. "I want to apologize for the way I've treated you. Can I do anything to repay you for your kindness toward me?"

Alex stood behind her with his hands on her shoulders.

"Thank you, but I don't need repayment. I'm happy to see you're now fully transformed and feeling like one of us. It's a good feeling being part of the Lepidoptera vampire family. And I recon now you are fully transformed you can whip my arse. I don't want to be beaten by a female; you know. I have a reputation to protect." Brock smirked and hugged her. "Welcome to our family."

When Brock pulled away, Shelley had tears welling in her eyes.

Brock wiped away the tears streaming down her face. "What are the tears for?"

"I am so happy right now. I don't think I've ever been this happy and felt so loved in my entire life." Shelley sniffed back the tears.

Brock hugged Shelley again and said to Alex, "You better look after her. She is special to me."

Alex nodded. "You have my word, bro." He sat next to Shelley and watched Luda approach with their breakfast.

"Would you two ladies like to come clothes shopping with me today?" Shelley asked Samantha and Annabelle.

"Sorry, I can't. Brock, Grayson, and I are going home to Bagnolet today," Samantha said.

"What time are you leaving for the airport?" Shelley asked.

"Around one p.m." Samantha checked her wristwatch.

"That soon? I won't be here to see you off." Shelley's brow furrowed as she looked from Samantha to Grayson to Brock. "I'd like to thank you for looking after me and putting up with my shit. I'll sure miss the three of you. You must come and stay again someday."

Samantha leaned across the table and placed her hand on top of Shelley's. "I will miss you too."

"I look forward to seeing you again one day, and hopefully, soon. I have a feeling you'll be one tough vampire to beat," Brock said, leaning into Shelley's shoulder.

Shelley smiled at Brock.

"Thank you, Shelley. I sure will miss you too. It's been a pleasure to look after you, and we're glad you're now one of us," Grayson said from across the table.

Shelley smiled and nodded once.

"Alex, when is Annabelle leaving?" Shelley whispered.

"She's here for one more week, and after that, she must return to Paris. William needs her back because the Debauched vampires are causing trouble in Paris," Alex said, cutting his food.

"Okay. Annabelle, are you up for some shopping today? I want to buy you something nice, as we are taking you out for dinner tonight."

"Sure, but you don't need to buy me anything. I do have my own money."

"Can you be ready, by say, around eleven thirty to go?"

"Sure, babe," Annabelle said, standing.

Alex placed his hand on top of Shelley's, noticing her sad demure. "Are you okay?"

Shelley nodded and leaned into Alex. "I've grown fond of them in the short time they've been here looking out for me. I sure will miss them."

Alex scanned the table. "Yeah, I know what you mean. They certainly are good friends indeed. I will miss them too."

"What do you think about having everyone from Paris here for Christmas? Your house certainly is big enough for everyone. I'd love to celebrate Christmas with them."

"Hmm, that sounds like a great idea. I'll run it past William first and let you know what he says. But, for New Year's, I'm taking you home to see your parents. I'd like to spend a couple weeks there, if you want to, that is." Alex watched Shelley's reaction as he smiled.

"Wow, we're going back to my hometown, for New Year's? I can't wait. Thank you!" She lovingly kissed his lips.

"I was going to surprise you, but I thought that if you planned something else, we couldn't go."

Shelley hugged Alex. "You are too kind."

*****

After breakfast, Shelley said her goodbyes to Samantha, Grayson, and Brock and went to her bedroom to get ready for shopping with Annabelle. Taking one last look in the mirror, Shelley smiled and went to find Alex. *Hmm, this vampiric speed thing sure is awesome*, Shelley thought as she ran throughout the house. She eventually found Alex in his office on the phone.

"Hang on a minute, Bryant." Alex placed the call on hold when he saw Shelley open the door and approach him.

"See you later on," Shelley said, hugging him.

"Carson will be waiting for you out front to take you and Annabelle to all the shops. You'll be safe with them both. Have a good day shopping, my sweet girl. Remember to buy a nice dress for tonight for you both." Alex kissed her goodbye and handed Shelley his credit card.

"Thanks, babe. See you later. We should be back by about five o'clock." Shelley placed the credit card in her purse. She smiled, kissed him goodbye and left the room.

*****

Excited, Shelley sat next to Annabelle in the back of the car. "Hopefully, I can find a nice dress to wear tonight."

"Yeah, me too. I haven't been clothes shopping for a while!"

"Carson, did Alex tell you where we wanted to go?" Shelley asked, looking at his reflection in the rearview mirror as the car pulled out the front gates.

"Yes, ma'am. He told me to take you clothes shopping and to ensure you both buy a lovely evening dress and anything else you may need too." Carson eyed them through the rearview mirror.

"So, can we count on you for your opinion on whether our evening dresses look nice or not, Carson?" Shelley asked.

"Of course, ma'am. I know you'd like to see Mr. Crestwell's eyes light up."

Shelley smiled at Carson, sat back and enjoyed the ride.

*****

With arms linked, Annabelle and Shelley navigated the shopping mall, proud of their day's achievements. Not only had they bought their full-length evening dresses with spaghetti straps, a love heart-shaped bustline that fitted and hugged their bodies in all the right places, but they had purchased lingerie and shoes to match their dresses.

"Sure has been a fun day," Annabelle said to Shelley as they approached the car.

"I've enjoyed myself. Thanks for coming with me." Shelley handed her many shopping bags to Carson to place in the trunk. "I love the color of your evening dress. Pearly green suits you"

"Thanks. I thought your choice of emerald-blue looked awesome on you. It accentuated the color in your eyes. And the silver shoes look good with the dress too." Annabelle handed her shopping bags to Carson.

"I can't wait to see Alex's face when I give him the pair of gold cufflinks, I bought him."

"I'm sure Sire will love them," Carson said, holding open the door. "And thank you both for buying me that nice gray tie today. I love it."

"You're welcome," Annabelle said, stepping into the car.

"It looked good on you, too," Shelley said sitting next to Annabelle.

Carson smiled and closed the door.

Shelley furrowed her brow. "I wanted to ask you something, Annabelle."

"You can ask me anything, babe. What is it?"

"You know how I bit Alex when I was transforming and I nearly drained him? Do you think that will happen again now I'm fully transformed? I suppose my question is, how do you know when to stop?" Shelley swallowed hard.

"When I was with my life partner, the way I knew to stop drinking was listening to him breathing. If his breathing became shallow or not at all, you'd know you've gone too far. Plus, when you are drinking from your life partner, it will feel euphoric to him, and he will be moaning that he loves the way it makes him feel. It's pure pleasure, you know—better than sex even. I wouldn't worry too much, because Alex will guide you anyhow."

"I can't believe how good sex is now that I'm a vampire." Shelley raised her eyebrows and grinned. "Sorry, Annabelle. You probably don't want to know about that."

"It's okay. I'm glad you can talk about it with me. I don't get to talk about anything like this when I'm at the Gramaze house. It's all work, work, work or combat training. For once, I'd like to be made to feel like I'm still a lady." Annabelle's brow creased. "So, where are we going for dinner tonight?"

"To the hotel Alex owns. It's called the Crestwell Hotel, and they have five restaurants there. But I'm not sure which one the four of us will be going to."

"Four? Who's the other one?"

"Alex invited his friend Bryant. He currently runs the business for Alex, and Alex wanted to take him out to dinner to say thank you for a job well done."

SUSAN HODDY

"What type of restaurants does the Crestwell Hotel have? Are they dressy or jean and blouse type?"

"They are all dressy. This is why Alex bought us the evening dresses, so we could wear them tonight. Alex told me we need to be in the foyer at home by six thirty, as we have reservations for seven thirty. Carson will be taking us three in the limo. I do know that each restaurant at the Crestwell has a dancefloor, so you and I can boogie. I love to dance fast or slow."

"Me too. I'm looking forward to getting dressed up and having a lovely meal out. I haven't done it in so long!"

"If you need help with your hair, I'm good at putting it up. Give me a yell if you want some help."

The car pulled up next to the front doors of the Crestwell mansion.

"Thanks, Shelley. I appreciate the offer. And thanks for today."

"You're welcome."

They exited the car and headed for the front door.

Shelley placed her handbag straps over her forearm. "Carson will bring your shopping bags to you soon."

*****

When Shelley opened her bedroom door, she noticed Alex asleep on the bed. She crept into the room, closed the door behind her, quietly put her handbag on the chair and lay next to him. *Poor thing, he must have been tired. He has had a lot to deal with in the past week—I bet more than he ever though he bargained for. I still can't believe how lucky I am to have even found him and how much he loves me. It's like a match made in heaven.* Shelley ran her fingers through his soft hair and down the side of his face and watched his eyes open. *God, could he look any more gorgeous.*

"Hello. You feeling tired?" Shelley asked.

"Mmm … I thought I'd catch up on some rest before our big night. Have you had some blood today, my sweet girl?"

235

"Yes. We took some with us in a cooler in the car. I've had more than enough today already. And Annabelle made sure I drank heaps. She sure is such a great person, you know. I had so much fun with her today. I haven't giggled like that with a friend for what seems like ages."

"I'm glad."

"So, have you drunk enough blood today? You look pale. Don't answer that; I already know the answer. I'll be right back." Shelley hopped off the bed and headed for the bar fridge on the right-hand side of their room. "Here you go. Drink this down."

As soon as he gulped down the blood, Shelley thought, *You look better already.*

"Thank you, babe. It's what I needed. I have been a bit lax today with my blood drinks." Alex reclined against the headboard.

"Now that you don't have me to worry about, I'll make sure you get enough blood drinks during the day, every day." Shelley sat next to him.

Alex lovingly kissed the side of her head.

"I bought you a present today." Shelley got off the bed and searched through her handbag for the gray velvet box. Sitting back on the bed, she handed him the box.

"You didn't have to buy me anything," Alex said, excited.

"I know, but I wanted to."

Alex's eyes lit up when he saw what the present was. "Wow, Shelley. These are wonderful! Thank you so much. I will wear them tonight. You are so thoughtful."

"You're welcome, my sweet, sweet man."

"Did you find a nice dress for tonight?"

"Yes, I found something I think you might like."

"I can't wait to see it on you."

"I need to shower and get ready." She gave him a kiss on the lips.

With vampiric speed and before she could blink, Alex gently pushed Shelley onto the bed. Looking into her eyes, he leaned in, and vigorously kissed her lips. Overwhelmed by her scent and the touch of her soft lips, Alex's mouth consumed Shelley's, searching for her tongue, soaking up the flavour. "So beautiful …"

She looked into his carnal eyes and watched as he unbuttoned her blouse and pulled down her bra straps.

His breath stammered when her nipples stood erect and were ready for him to suck. Taking the left one first, he teased it with his teeth and then his tongue, tormenting her.

Shelley moaned with pleasure as she thrust each of her breasts one by one into his mouth and panted when she felt his warm tongue lap at her stomach.

"I want you," Alex murmured as he pulled down her skirt and panties and discarded them to the floor.

"No … more … teasing," Shelley said, her breathing rapid.

Alex stood next to the bed and beheld her supple body as he removed his own clothes and hastily discarded them to the floor. "Turn over." His blood-pulsing penis stood erect as he moved Shelley close to the edge of the bed, pulled her bum into the air and thrusted his cock into her vagina, fucking her at a fast pace. "Mmm… so wet, my love."

Shelley moaned with delight. "Don't stop … Feels so good." *God, I loved being fucked this way.*

No sooner than she said this, they orgasmed simultaneously. Wiping the beading sweat from his lip, breathless from their shenanigans, Alex lay on the pillow and outstretched his arm for Shelley to cuddle into him.

But Shelley wasn't quite ready for that yet, even though she felt sated from their lovemaking session. "Can I drink from you, my sweet man?"

He nodded, as he had read her mind and knew she was in control.

CRESTWELL

Shelley gently pushed his face to one side and bit into his neck. As she sucked the blood, she grunted with the pleasure of how alive it made her feel. "Tell me when you want me to stop, please."

Breathless yet overcome by how much he was enjoying her drinking from him, Alex said, "Yes." He moaned when she sucked harder.

Shelley pulled away from him, panting and feeling satisfied she had drunk enough. Lying next to Alex on the pillow, she looked at the ceiling. "That was too good."

Alex snickered, laying flat on his pillow. "Lick the wound holes and they will heal straight away."

Shelley did as instructed and watched the bite marks disappear.

Alex turned his face to look at her. "Can I drink from you?"

Shelley nodded.

With his eyes dilated as he watched the pulse in her neck vein beat hard, Alex pushed her head to one side and quickly bit into her skin.

The initial puncture of his teeth into her skin hurt. But once he started to drink her blood, she felt pure erotic pleasure. With her eyes closed, she moaned. "Oh my god, that feels good."

Alex smiled as he drank. Once he'd had enough, he licked the two holes, watched them heal and laid next to Shelley on the pillow. "Your blood, it tastes like ... like drinking something you enjoy the taste of but can't get enough, if that makes sense." He outstretched his arm so she could cuddle into his chest. "How was that for you?"

"Your blood tasted like heaven, and it made me feel warm all over and the feeling of, like, euphoria. I didn't want the pleasure to stop. That could be extremely addictive, you know."

"You are not wrong. I think we'll need to be careful when we do this. I felt like I couldn't get enough, but luckily, I am old enough to control myself."

Shelley checked the bedside digital clock. "My sweet man, we have to get a move on! It's five thirty-four, and I take a long time to get ready."

He kissed her hair. "You have the first shower, and I'll take mine after you."

*****

As Shelley was making the last-minute changes to her hair and makeup in the mirror, Alex came up behind her. "Woo-wee, woman. Don't you look beautiful in that dress."

Shelley smiled, turned and gave him a sensual kiss. "Whoops!" She wiped the lipstick from his lips. "Don't you look handsome in that suit, too?"

"Will you help me put these on?" Alex opened his hand to reveal the new cufflinks.

Shelley inserted them one at a time through the hole of each shirt sleeve. "They look nice." She collected her purse from the bed and retrieved her phone from it. "Let's get a photo before we head downstairs."

Alex straightened his suit and came to stand next to her.

"Smile!" Shelley pressed the button on her phone camera. "Let's have a look if these are any good. I want to print off a copy for my purse wallet."

"Can you print one for me too? Actually, one for my wallet and one for my office desk."

"Sure, babe," Shelley said, reviewing the pictures on her mobile phone.

Alex placed his wallet in his suit jacket. "We better get going."

"One sec. I need to put on my perfume," Shelley said, walking toward the bathroom.

"Mmm, you smell good with that perfume on."

"Control yourself, my sweet man. I told Annabelle to meet us in the foyer at six thirty, and we don't have time for any hanky panky now," Shelley said, smirking.

Alex nodded and grinned. "God, woman, you and your body are driving me crazy. I can't seem to get enough of you today. I must say I've never felt like this before, but I will say it's got something to do with you being my life partner and that we drank each other's blood."

"I feel the same way, and I think you're right. Come on, let's go." Shelley placed her arm through his and walked toward the bedroom door.

*****

When they reached the foyer, they saw Annabelle waiting for them at the bottom of the steps. "Wow, Annabelle, you look stunning in that dress," Alex said.

"She sure does. You look absolutely beautiful." Shelley retrieved her phone and took a photo. "I'll send you a copy."

"Let's get going. Carson is out front waiting for us." Alex opened the front doors and took them both arm in arm on either side of him to the car.

*****

When Annabelle, Alex, and Shelley arrived at the Crestwell Hotel, Bryant was waiting for them, as planned, in the reception.

"Evening, Bryant," Alex said, proffering his hand.

"Evening, Sire," Bryant said, shaking Alex's hand.

"Annabelle, Shelley, this is Bryant Dune. He is managing my business for me and is coming to dinner with us."

"Pleased to meet you, Annabelle, Shelley," Bryant said, his Swiss German accent apparent. "Shall we?" He took Annabelle on his arm and lead her toward the restaurant.

Alex and Shelley followed with their arms around each other.

"You look lovely in that dress tonight, Annabelle. Is it new?" Bryant asked as they walked along.

"I bought it today, and thank you for the nice complement. I haven't had too many nice comments like that for a few years. My husband always used to tell me how lovely I looked before he died. Its little things like that which I miss. What about you? Do you have a life partner?"

"No, I don't. My life partner died a few years ago too. She used to enjoy going to dinner and getting dressed up too."

"Right, sorry for your loss. Where are you from, Bryant?"

"I'm from Zurich, originally. But I've been living in Rome for the last two years. Alex and I are old friends from years ago, and when he offered me a position here, I thought I would give it a go and see if I like living here again. So far, so good." Bryant raked his hand through his light brown, shoulder-length hair. "What about you?"

"I live in Bagnolet, in France. I've been here for about a week, working for Alex as security. But I'm going home at the end of next week. I sure will miss Zurich; it's such a beautiful place." Annabelle pushed her long blond hair behind her ear.

They sure are hitting it off. They haven't stop talking since we left reception, Shelley mind-said to Alex.

There is chemistry already. I can feel it.

Once they arrived at the restaurant and the waiter seated them, everyone ordered their drinks and meals.

"So, Annabelle, which family do you live with in France?" Bryant asked, looking into her blue eyes.

"The Gramaze family. I've been with them for about eighty-five years. They took me in when my husband was killed, and I've lived and served them since."

"William Gramaze, you mean?"

"Yes," Annabelle said, noticing his deep-blue eyes for the first time.

"William is an old friend of mine. Great family too."

"Oh right. His life partner had a baby boy about two weeks ago."

"I'll have to give William and Renee a ring to congratulate them. How wonderful. Whilst we are waiting for our dinner, would you like to dance?"

"I'd love to!" Annabelle said, standing.

The music was slow, and, as he took her into his arms, they danced beautifully together; in fact, it was apparent something had awakened in them both with the attraction they both had for each other.

"Do you feel like a third wheel here tonight?" Shelley asked Alex, watching Bryant and Annabelle dance.

Alex leaned into Shelley. "Yeah. They seem to be hitting it off."

"Bryant and Annabelle are so wrapped up in each other they aren't even noticing us or making conversation with us. Do you think after dinner we could excuse ourselves so they can have some private time together?"

"I was thinking the same thing, babe. Good idea. But I want a dance with you before we leave."

"I'd love to." She kissed his lips. As she slowly pulled away, she noticed the waiter approaching with a trolley of food. *Bryant, Annabelle, dinner is here*, Shelley mind-said as she glanced at the dancefloor.

Shelley and Alex ate their meals in silence but, every so often, sideways smiled at each other as they watched the banter between Annabelle and Bryant continue throughout dinner.

"What's your meal like?" Bryant asked Annabelle.

"It tastes nice. Try some." Annabelle placed some on her fork and put it into his mouth.

"Mmm, that is good. What's that called?"

"Chicken carbonara. What about you? How's yours?"

"A bit spicy. Here, try some." Bryant fed Annabelle with his fork.

"Mmm, I like hot and spicy food."

"I'll have to take you to this restaurant down the road. They serve the best hot and spicy food I've ever tasted."

"Would you like to dance, my sweet girl?" Alex asked Shelley.

"I thought you'd never ask."

Alex held Shelley close, and they danced slowly to the music.

Shelley rested her head on his chest. "You smell really good, Mr. Crestwell. Can I take you home yet?"

Alex looked down at her. "You are incorrigible, Miss Landers, and when I get you home, you'll be begging me to stop. Are you sure you want to leave so soon?"

"Yes, I'm sure. And you will be the one begging, gorgeous," Shelley said, giggling. "Let's go." She pulled Alex by the hand and headed to the table to get her purse.

"Annabelle, Bryant, we're heading off home," Alex said. "We're a bit tired. Bryant, will you be okay to make sure Annabelle gets home safely?"

"Yes, of course. Actually, I was saying to Annabelle that they have a great night club here at the hotel. So we might as well head off there, that's if you want to, Annabelle?" said Bryant, looking from Alex to Annabelle.

"Sure, I'd love to. But I need to powder my nose first. Shelley, could you please come with me to the ladies?"

"Sure," Shelley said and followed Annabelle into the restroom.

Annabelle removed her lipstick from her clutch purse. "Shelley, Bryant sure is lovely. He seems to like my company so far, and I his. Do you think I should go to the nightclub with him, or should I go home with you and Alex?"

Shelley looked at Annabelle's reflection in the mirror. "You two certainly have some chemistry going on there, and you can see there's an attraction between you both. Yes, I think you should go to the nightclub with him. But remember one thing; as a lady, we don't have sex on the first date. So even if you're attracted to him, don't do it. You'll find he will respect you more the next time you meet. I know it'll be hard, and, of course, it's totally up to you whether you have sex or not, but remember you are a lady not a hooker."

"Thanks for the advice. I had forgotten about that side of a relationship with a man. I'll remember what you said."

"He is hot though. He looks like he works out too, which means he'll have a great body. Have a good time, and you never know, he might ask you out on a real date if you hit it off."

*****

"Don't keep her out too late, Bryant. She is a lady and likes to be treated like one too," Alex said to Bryant as Shelley and Annabelle returned to the table.

"Yes, Sire."

"Have a good time you two. And nice to meet you, Bryant," Shelley said as she hooked arms with Alex, and they walked away.

As the two couples headed in separate directions, Shelley mind-said to Annabelle so she could only hear her, *If you get in trouble, text me, and I will come for you.*

Annabelle and Shelley turned back to each other and nodded once.

"Hopefully, this isn't a one-off night for them," Shelley said as they approached the car.

"I spoke with Bryant while you ladies were powdering your noses, and he told me that he likes Annabelle, so yeah, hopefully they are a good match," Alex said, opening the car door.

244

Shelley slid into the car. "Speaking of good matches, thank you for taking me to dinner tonight and dancing with me. You are quite the dancer."

"I can't wait to get you home and have my way with you." Alex smirked as he cuddled into her side, holding her hand.

*****

Eagerly stripping off their clothes and lying on the bed, Alex kissed and lapped at every inch of her body. When he reached her pubic area, Alex bit into Shelley's clitoris and drank her blood.

Shelley convulsed off the bed, and she moaned in sheer delight as her whole body gave way to waves of extreme pleasure, and her body orgasmed. *We haven't even had sex yet, and I'm already exhausted.* "Babe … you need to stop. I … can't take anymore … pleasure. It's tearing me … apart inside."

Alex heard her plea, licked the two puncture holes and lay beside her, outstretching his arm for her to cuddle into his chest.

My favorite position …

"Are you all right now I've stopped?"

"I felt like I was floating, with extreme erotic pleasure building and building. If you didn't stop, I thought I might explode. It felt that good. I loved it. But now, I'm exhausted."

"You blood, it tasted so damn good. I didn't want to stop."

"Can we lay here for a few minutes until I get my breath back?"

He nodded. "I know when I was drinking from you, it felt like the feeling I get when I am fucking you. I was so turned on by your blood that I came. Talk about euphoric. I can't believe after all these years that my sex life is this good. We sure are great together."

She lifted her head and kissed his lips.

CHAPTER SIXTEEN

The next morning, Shelley woke early and thought, *I wonder how it went with Annabelle and Bryant last night.* She hopped out of bed and walked to Annabelle's room. Reaching the slightly opened doorway, she popped her head into the room to find Annabelle and Bryant fully clothed on top of the bed covers asleep. Beaming, she closed the door and returned to her own bedroom. *Good girl, you did it. You held out on your first date.* Shelley hopped into bed with Alex.

"Is Annabelle okay?" Alex asked.

"Annabelle and Bryant are asleep in her room still fully clothed on top of the bed covers. Maybe they fell asleep talking?"

"I'm glad Bryant was a gentleman. I wonder what time they got in. I was so exhausted that I didn't hear anything. I don't think I've ever been so exhausted that I slept through the night—vampire thing, you know." Alex kissed the side of Shelley's head.

Shelley smirked. "Glad to be of service, my sweet man."

Alex smiled and pulled her in close.

246

"Alex, when I'm cuddling you, I always love the way you smell. It's not like your cologne smell either. Why is that?"

"I have the same feeling when I'm near you too. I think the reason is that we are life partners, and we will always love the way each other smells and feels. I think it's normal. You know, since you have fully transformed, I can sense the way you feel from even miles away."

"Yeah, it's like we are connected on all levels now, because I can sense you too."

"What time is it?" Alex sat upright to check his phone. "Hmm, five thirty. I better wake Bryant; he needs to start work soon."

"Can't you find someone else to replace him for this morning?"

"Sorry, babe. It's either me or him." Alex pulled back the covers and got out of bed.

*****

As Alex approached Annabelle's room, Bryant was attempting to sneak out.

"Good morning, my friend. Sleep well?"

"Yes, Sire. Thank you for sharing your house with me," Bryant said quietly, closing Annabelle's door.

"I'll get Carson to give you a ride to the Crestwell Hotel. Will you be seeing Annabelle tonight?"

"If it's all right with you, Sire, I'd like to take Annabelle on a date tonight."

Alex looked at him for a moment and read his thoughts. "Yes, that would be fine, but only if you're serious about her. Annabelle is too much of a lady to be fucked around."

"She is such a delight, Sire. We had a great time, and I haven't felt that alive since … since my life partner died. And I know she is a lady, as her intent was quite clear last night."

"What time will you be collecting her tonight?"

"Is seven o'clock all right with Sire?"

"That will be fine. But I'm warning you. If you hurt her in any way, you'll have me to deal with. Also, have you contemplated what will happen when she has to go back to Paris?" Alex put his hands on his hips. "If she falls for you, it'll break her heart when she leaves. If you're serious about Annabelle, you'll have to speak with William about releasing her. Believe me when I say there is a lot to consider, as I have been through the same with Shelley."

"Thank you for your advice, Sire. I am quite aware of what will happen if we fall for each other. I suppose I shouldn't get my hopes up, but I am … I am hoping she'll be interested in a guy like me."

"I'll help you in any way I can. Now, you better go, otherwise you'll be late for work, and I've heard the boss is a real tyrant," Alex said, smirking.

Bryant shook Alex's hand and ran at vampiric speed down the stairs and to the car where Carson was waiting for him.

*****

Shelley watched Alex enter the bedroom and get into bed. "You're a great friend and such a romantic. I'm sure Annabelle would be pleased you have her back."

Alex cuddled into Shelley, and once again, they made love.

*****

"Good morning, all," Annabelle said, entering the kitchen and spotting Alex and Shelley sitting at the island counter, eating their breakfast.

"Good morning, Annabelle. How was your night?" Shelley asked.

Annabelle went to the coffeemaker. "Fantastic. I haven't had so much fun like that for a long time. Bryant took good care of me, and he was a gentleman all night."

"So, are you seeing him again?" Shelley placed her knife and fork in the middle of the empty plate.

"Actually, I received a text from him about a minute ago, and it said he would pick me up here tonight at seven, so yes, it looks like I'll be seeing him again. That is, if I'm not needed here, of course, and it is all right with you, Sire?"

Alex grabbed his cup of coffee. "That's fine. You have my permission to go and enjoy yourself. Now that Shelley is feeling better, we won't need you for security. But, if we do, I'll let you know."

"Thank you, Sire. I appreciate you letting me go tonight." She sat next to Shelley with her coffee. "Shelley, he makes my heart come alive."

"He likes you too," Alex said.

"Does he? How do you know?"

"I spoke with Bryant this morning before he left for work. He said he enjoyed your company and asked if it would be okay to spend some more time seeing you. I told him yes, as long as he didn't break your heart."

"Thank you, Sire. That was nice of you. Do you know where he's taking me tonight? I don't have a lot of nice evening dresses."

"Text and ask him if it's dressy or casual, and you will know what to wear," Shelley said.

"Good idea." Annabelle took her phone from her back pocket.

When the answer came back straight away, her face lit up. "It's casual ... thank God. Can you help me pick something to wear tonight, Shelley?"

"Sure. How about we get together, say around four o'clock? I can help do your hair too if you like." Shelley raised her cup of tea to her lips.

"Sounds great. Thanks!" Annabelle made her breakfast and headed into the dining room.

"Do you have to work today, Alex?" Shelley asked.

"No. You have me all to yourself."

"Have you ever snowboarded in your back yard or built a snowman?"

"I can't say I've done either of those in the back yard. I suppose it would be fun."

"Seen as it's been snowing a lot, this would be a good opportunity before the snow melts to do it."

"I'm game if you are."

After they finished their breakfast, Alex and Shelley headed upstairs to put on some jeans, a warm jacket, and boots.

*****

"All we need is a bit of a slope and we can snowboard," Shelley said as Alex handed her the two snowboards he had found in his back shed.

"There's a little bit of a slope over there we could use." Alex pointed to the back of the property.

"Cool! Let's go," Shelley said, carrying the two boards to the spot.

*****

They had so much fun snowboarding around trees. They both kept falling off and ploughing into the snow but laughing as they went. In the end, they were drenched from the wet snow and looked like they had been playing in the rain.

"Did you want to build a snowman?" Alex asked.

Shelley pushed her wet hair from her face. "Love to."

"Come on!" Alex pulled her toward the front yard.

Wearing their snow gloves, Alex and Shelley built the snowman's body and head.

"Hang on a sec. He's missing a few vital characteristics. I'll be back in a minute," Alex said and headed toward the front doors. When he returned, he had an orange carrot for the nose and an old black hat and scarf. "Now he looks perfect," Alex said, adjusting the hat.

Shelley smiled and loved this silly, carefree side of Alex.

"Let's get some photos." Alex took his phone from his jacket pocket.

Shelley stood next to Alex and the snowman and smiled as Alex took the photos.

"What a great day, Shell. We must do this again. I've enjoyed myself so much." He pulled her close. "What about you?"

Shelley cuddled into him. "I've had a ball."

Alex leaned down and passionately kissed her lips. "Let's go inside and shower."

"Can we lay by the fire after our shower? I love to watch the flames dancing around the fire."

He smiled at her. "Sure, babe."

As they headed toward the front doors, a van arrived. "Delivery for Annabelle," the driver said as he approached them.

"Yes, we'll accept the delivery," Alex said, holding Shelley's hand and pulling her toward the van.

"Sign here, sir." The driver handed Alex an electronic notepad. He opened the van to reveal a huge bouquet of colored flowers.

"I'll take them and give them to her," Shelley said, accepting them from the driver.

Alex handed the notepad to the driver, and they walked inside.

"Annabelle! Annabelle!" Shelley yelled from the foyer. "Come have a look at what's been delivered for you!" Shelley watched Annabelle appear at the top of the stairs and run down to collect them.

"They're for me? From who?"

"There's a card attached."

Annabelle retrieved the card while Shelley held the flowers, watching the excitement in her face.

To Annabelle, I had a great time last night. Looking forward to seeing you again. Love Bryant xx

"They're from Bryant. How sweet is this guy?" Annabelle said, picturing his face.

"There are vases in the kitchen to put the flowers in," Alex said.

"Thanks, Alex. I can't believe he sent me flowers. I'll have to ring him." Annabelle took the flowers from Shelley and walked toward the kitchen.

"That sure was nice of Bryant to send Annabelle some flowers. He must like her," Shelley said.

"I'd say so. Let's get out of these wet clothes and shower."

"You don't have to tell me twice. I'll race you up the stairs." Shelley giggled as she ran up the stairs.

She reached the top of the stairs first, but Alex caught up to her and swept her into his arms. He kissed her lips and carried her into their bedroom and had his way with her.

*****

"Mmm, this is nice, sitting here with you, enjoying each other's company and eating lunch. What could be better?" Shelley said, sitting in front of the fire on the plush rug.

Alex looked into Shelley's eyes. "Will you marry me?" He pulled a ring box from his pocket and opened it to reveal a gold band ring with a huge sparkling white diamond in the middle with resplendent diamonds along either side of it.

Shocked, Shelley was lost for words. Besides the friendship ring, this was the most beautiful engagement ring she had ever seen. She looked from the box to his face and back again.

"Is it too soon for you?" Alex's brow furrowed when she didn't say anything.

"No, it's not too soon. I'm … speechless, and it's … it's not something I had expected." Shelley watched the ring sparkle in the light.

Alex took the ring from the box and placed it on her finger. "It looks lovely on your finger."

Shelley moved her hand all around, admiring how stunning the ring was on her finger. Looking into Alex's eyes, she said, "Yes, I will marry you. I love you so much. Nothing in this world could make me happier than to marry you." She leaned in and adoringly kissed his lips.

Alex pulled slowly away from their embrace. "If you didn't already know, Shelley, I adore you and want to spend the rest of my life with you. You have made me the happiest man in the world."

Shelley smiled and placed two pillows from the lounge onto the floor. As they lay on the pillows, looking into each other's eyes, Shelley brushed her hand through his soft hair and down the side of his face, soaking up his gorgeous features. And when his lips touched hers again, it ignited a fire in her stomach. Before they knew it, they were making love and drinking from one another in front of the fire.

*****

Annabelle cleared her throat as she entered the lounge room and saw Alex and Shelley cuddling in front of the fire and stopped near the couch. "Sorry. Are you still okay to help me pick some clothes for tonight?"

Shelley sat upright. "Sure. Give me a couple minutes, and I'll meet you in your bedroom."

Annabelle nodded and walked toward the doorway.

"Sorry, babe. Got to go. I did promise Annabelle I'd help her," Shelley said to Alex. "Is it okay if I tell Annabelle that we're engaged and show her the ring?"

"Sure, but only Annabelle. I want to speak with your parents and ask your father for your hand in marriage tonight before we tell anyone else. I want the world to know you'll be my wife."

Shelley smiled. "Me too. I had better go. Annabelle is waiting. I'll see you later, my fiancée."

Alex raised an eyebrow. "Mmm, I like the sound of that."

*****

"Knock, knock!" Shelley opened Annabelle's door and entered, seeing scattered clothes covering her bed, and that she was in such a tither. Shelley walked to Annabelle and hugged her, knowing that as soon as she touched her, Shelley would gain her ability and could calm down Annabelle.

After a few seconds, Annabelle pulled away slowly. "Thanks, Shelley. I needed that."

"No problem. Now, the dress tonight is casual, so as you're still going out to dinner, it should be a dress. You want to look sexy but not sluttish. So, we can put some of these blouses and jeans back in the closet and see what else you have." Shelley collected the discarded clothes and returned them to the closet.

"Wow, you're good at this, girl," Annabelle said, hanging up her clothes.

"Now, we have two dresses to choose from—plain emerald-green and colorful. Hmm…" Shelley panned from one dress to the other. "I'd choose the emerald-green dress. It's sexy, looks comfortable and will show off all your assets. Try that on and let me see what it looks like."

Annabelle removed her clothes and tried on the dress.

"Nice ... but something is missing. Wait there, I'll be back in a minute." Shelley walked toward the doorway. When she returned, she had a necklace, earrings, and a beautiful wrap to wear with the dress. "Put these on and wear the shoes you wore last night."

Annabelle did but decided not to wear the wrap.

"Now, your hair. I might put it up with some bobby pins and a beautiful green clip and leave some hair down and also with some curls at the front to soften your facial features and some curls in the back to make your hair look naturally beautiful. I'll need to get the clips and pins from my bathroom, so I'll be right back." Shelley headed toward the doorway. "We can do your hair after you shower."

When Shelley returned to Annabelle's bedroom, she said, "With your makeup, don't put on too much. You only need mascara, lip gloss, and some concealer. Keep your lip gloss in your bag to retouch after dinner. Do you have some nice-smelling perfume and body scents?"

"Yes, I have both."

"After you shower, apply the body oils, and before he picks you up, put on the perfume. It will drive him wild. Men like the smell of nice scents and perfumes."

"You sure know your stuff. I feel so out of the loop since I haven't been on a date in more years than I can count."

"It comes from years of watching my family and friends. You end up picking up a few tips or two. Okay, now that everything's sorted, you have an hour and a half to get ready. Plenty of time before Bryant gets here at seven." Shelley sat on the bed. "Are you nervous?"

"No, not nervous. I'm excited more than anything."

"That's good. I have some exciting news, but it's a secret, so you can't tell anyone until tomorrow."

"I can keep a secret. Tell me! What is it?"

Shelley pulled her engagement ring from her shirt pocket, placed it on her finger and showed Annabelle. "Alex proposed, and I accepted."

"You are one lucky girl, Shelley! Not only have you found your life partner, but he also wants to marry you. Not too many vampires want to commit to marriage. That ring is beautiful, isn't it? I love how it sparkles. I'm so envious. Congratulations, Shelley!" She hugged Shelley.

"Thanks. Once we tell my parents tonight via Skype, we can tell everyone else. Alex is asking my dad for my hand. How sweet is that? I sure do love that man. I better let you get ready for your big date." Shelley stood. "Give me a holler if you need some help."

"Congratulations again. I'm so happy for you both. And thanks for all your help. You're such a great friend."

*****

"There you are! I've been looking for you everywhere," Shelley said, standing in Alex's office doorway.

Alex looked up from his computer. "I had to do some last-minute business. I'll probably be another ten minutes, then you can have me all to yourself."

"No problem. I'll leave you to it." Shelley closed the door behind her. *Hmm, Alex looked a bit pale. I think he may need some blood.* Shelley ran with vampiric speed to the kitchen.

By the time she had returned to Alex's office, Alex had finished his business and sat at his desk, reclining in the chair with his eyes closed. Shelley stood there for a moment, watching him.

Alex opened his eyes, sat upright and smiled when he saw her worried face. "Hi, babe."

"Here, have some of this. It'll make you feel better." Shelley handed him a cup of blood. "You look worn out, my love."

SUSAN HODDY

"I'm feeling a bit tired, that's all, my sweet girl. Nothing to worry yourself about." Alex ran his hand through his hair. As he drank the blood, his color returned, and he felt better.

"Alex, you need to slow down and remember to feed; otherwise, you'll make yourself sick. Tonight after dinner, how about we cuddle and watch a DVD on the sofa?" Shelley's brow furrowed as she ran her hand down the side of his face with affection. "Do you think the number of times we have drunk from each other and had sex might have something to do with why you're so tired?"

"You're probably right, my love. And what you have planned sounds good to me. I need a night off from everything, and I do need to look after myself. Thank you for looking after me. I love you. I still plan on Skyping your parents to ask for your hand tonight though. Is Annabelle all sorted out now?"

"Yes. And I am sure Bryant will be extremely happy with how lovely she looks."

*****

Calm yourself, Dune, Bryant thought as he stood at the front doorway, waiting for someone to greet him.

Shelley opened the door and gestured for him to enter. "Hello, Bryant. Come in."

"Good evening, Shelley. Is Annabelle ready?" Bryant stepped into the Crestwell mansion foyer.

"I'm ready," Annabelle said, walking down the marble staircase toward them.

Bryant's jaw dropped when he saw how beautiful she looked.

"Hello, Bryant," Annabelle said as she came to stand in front of him.

"Hello ... Wow, don't you look beautiful in that dress?" Bryant's eyebrows raised as he beheld his date.

Annabelle blushed as she looked into his eyes.

257

"We had better be off. The restaurant is booked for seven forty-five. I have a car waiting for us outside," Bryant said, taking in her fruity scent.

Annabelle smiled. "Ready when you are."

"Have a great time tonight, you two," Shelley said.

They both thanked her and headed to the car.

Shelley closed the front door. *What an adorable couple.*

*****

"It will be a grand affair, Luda," Alex said, sitting at the kitchen island counter.

"What will be a grand affair?" Shelley asked, entering the kitchen, and sat next to Alex.

"I was discussing Christmas with Luda."

"Does this mean the Gramaze families are coming for Christmas?"

"Yes. William and his family are so thrilled that we asked them all to come."

"Awesome! It sure will be a Christmas to remember."

"Would you like me to employ more cooks and waitstaff to help with the days they're here, Luda?"

"Yes, Sire, that would be good. I can review the menu with you and Shelley tomorrow if you like. It will be absolutely wonderful to have a lot of people here for Christmas. I'm looking forward to the cooking and preparation. So much to do though …" Luda made a mental note of what she needed to do and plan for.

"We can talk more tomorrow about their visit and Christmas," Alex said to Luda.

"It's only three weeks until Christmas, so we have a lot of planning to do. Do you have Christmas decorations, Alex?" Shelley asked.

"I do. I'll ask James to get them out for you, and we can put them up if you like."

"Great! Can we buy a real Christmas tree and decorate it together?"

Alex smiled at her. "Absolutely. Wow, you seem excited about this."

"Yes, and now that we're getting married, the tree means more to me than you know. You see, when I was a girl, my mom and dad and I used to decorate the tree together. And now you and I will be our own little family. We can do the same."

"That is sweet, and what a lovely tradition to keep going." Alex traced a hand down the side of her face in adoration.

"Hang on. Did you say you're getting *married*? When?" Luda's eyes widened, and her eyebrows raised.

Alex and Shelley smiled at Luda.

"We haven't told anyone yet. I only proposed to Shelley today, and she accepted. I'm asking her father for her hand tonight, and after that, we'll tell everyone. But, in answer to your question, yes, we're getting married. But we haven't set a date yet."

Luda walked around to the other side of the counter and hugged them. "Sire, that's the best news I've heard all year. I'm so happy for you both. Congratulations. The old house is indeed becoming a family home." Tears of joy shone in her eyes.

"Yes, I suppose it will be," Alex said.

"Will you both be eating in the dining room tonight?" Luda asked Alex.

"No. We'll eat in the lounge room tonight. We're worn out and need a night where we have no pressures or stress. We were thinking of watching some DVDs while we eat dinner and basically relax."

"It sure will be good to see you relax, Sire. I can't remember the last time I have seen you this happy."

"We might Skype your parents now. What do you think?" Alex asked, standing.

Shelley nodded and let him lead her out the kitchen and into his office.

Both seated in front of Alex's office laptop, Shelley dialed her mom and dad's Skype number and patiently waited for them to answer. When their faces came into view, Shelley said, "Hello, Mom and Dad. How are you doing?"

"Hello, sweetheart. Hello, Alex. It's nice to see you both and hear your voices. How is Zurich treating you, sweetie?" Shelley's dad said.

"I love it here, Dad. Life sure is good. Dad, Alex wants to ask you something."

"Sir, I would like to ask you for your daughter's hand in marriage."

Shelley's mom screamed in shock.

"This is quite a shock, Alex," Shelley's dad said, his brow furrowed. "I don't know. You both haven't known each other that long. What's the rush? Wouldn't you prefer to get to know each other first?"

"No, sir, we don't want to wait. Yes, we have only known each other for a short time, but we feel like we know each other well. I love your daughter, sir, and nothing would make me happier than to have your blessing. Shelley is the best thing that has ever happened to me in my entire life. You have my word and honor that I'll love and protect Shelley and treat her with respect for the rest of her life."

"Shelley, do you love this man, and is he your happily ever after?" Shelley's mom asked.

"Yes, Mom. I love Alex a real lot, and he is my happily ever after. Can you see the ring he bought me? It's so beautiful, like he is, Mom." Shelley held her hand to the computer screen so they could see the engagement ring.

"Wow, that is lovely, dear," Shelley's mom said.

"Do we have your blessing, sir?" Alex asked.

Shelley's dad stared at the screen for what seemed like ages. "I suppose if you're happy, Shelley, that is all a father can ask for. So, my answer is yes. You can have my daughter's hand in marriage. You'll have to let us know the date of the wedding."

"Thank you, sir. As soon as we get over Christmas and New Year's, we' sit down and plan a date and place." Alex looked from the screen to Shelley.

"Thank you, Daddy."

"So, what are your plans for New Year's?" Alex asked.

"Staying home and probably going to bed early. We old folks don't do much these days for New Year's," Shelley's mom said.

"Will it be okay for Shelley and me to visit for a week? I'd love to meet you both." Alex watched their reaction.

Shelley's mom screamed. "My baby girl and fiancée are coming home for New Year's! How exciting. I can't wait!"

"Sure will be good to meet you, Alex my boy," Shelley's dad said.

With the excitement of their wedding and the New Year's visit, they talked with Shelley's parents for half an hour, eventually saying their goodbyes when Luda announced dinner was ready.

*****

"For a minute there, I didn't think your dad would give us his blessing," Alex said as they sat in front of the fire, eating dinner.

Shelley nodded as she cut her food. "I know. I thought the same thing. But I think once you told him how much you loved me and wanted to be with me, he got the message. Did you see my mom? She was like a blubbering mess when you told her we were coming for New Year's."

"You have great parents, Shelley, and I can tell they love you a lot and care about your happiness." Alex grabbed his mug of blood.

"Yeah, ever since I can remember, they have always been good to me. They couldn't have children, so that was why they adopted me. Actually, there is a story behind my adoption I haven't told you about. My mom used to work at a church, helping out the priest. One night when she was working late cleaning the chapel, a lady gave me to her. She told my mom I was a special baby and that she needed to adopt me and look after me. Because my parents couldn't have children, it was like a sign from God for them. My mom always tells the story of how the woman was regally beautiful and had a powerful aura around her. And now that I know I'm a Lepidoptera vampire, I know this was my birth mother who gave me to my adoptive mom. How weird is that?"

"Unbelievable! That would mean your mom has seen the queen. I wonder if she knows about our kind. I wonder what else the queen told her. Would you mind if I look into your mom's thoughts when we get there? I'll be able to see if she knows anything about our kind."

"Sure. It's better to be on the safe side. Actually, it's probably better if we don't stay with my parents. I think my mom will see the butterfly tattoo, and I don't want her finding out. The little they know, the better."

"Shelley, humans can't see the butterfly tattoo, only supernatural creatures."

"Right!"

CHAPTER SEVENTEEN

As Alex and Shelley chatted further about the Skype call and her parents, Shelley heard a text message ding on her phone. She grabbed her phone and read, *Help ... We are at Buffalo Wings restaurant in the city.*

"Shit. Alex, I received this message from Annabelle. Somethings wrong. They need our help."

Alex took the phone from Shelley and read the message. "Fuck." With his nostrils flared, he retrieved his phone from the side table and dialed three numbers for a conference call. "Frederick, Harris, and Allan, I need you to meet me at the Buffalo Wings restaurant in the city. We have a Debauched attack on Bryant and Annabelle. I'll be there in ten minutes."

They all said, "Yes, Sire," in unison.

As Alex ended the call, Shelley asked, "What can I do to help?"

"You can help me to get some weapons ready. I need you to text Annabelle to let her know us five will be there in ten minutes. I've already mind-spoken with Carson, and he's getting the car ready."

"Right," Shelley said, texting Annabelle.

*****

With the weapons readied and packed in the trunk of the car, Carson sped toward the city whilst Shelley and Alex sat in the back seat.

Alex felt his phone vibrate and checked Bryant's message. *Get here as quick as you can. I can't hold them off for too much longer.*

"Shit! Carson, drive faster!" Alex eyed Carson's reflection in the rearview mirror.

Carson nodded once and pressed the gas pedal.

Alex texted Bryant, *We are five minutes from you, and five of us are coming.* "If those fuckers hurt one hair on Annabelle head, they'll die a slow death. A female vampire is extremely valuable. They'll kill Bryant if they have to, to get to Annabelle." Alex's nostrils flared, and his breathing became rapid.

Shelley furrowed her brow. "Fucking hell. What would you like me to do once we arrive?"

"Stay with me, okay?"

Shelley nodded and placed her hand in Alex's.

*****

Carson careened the car into an alleyway next to Buffalo Wings. With the headlights on, they could see Bryant, Annabelle, Frederick, Harris, and Allan fighting the Debauched vamps.

"Fuck. They're outnumbered," Alex said as he jumped from the car and headed to the trunk to select what weapons they would need to behead the Debauched vamps. "Stay close to me, babe," Alex said to Shelley as they ran toward the Debauched soldiers.

Scared, Shelley nodded and followed Alex and Carson into the alleyway.

Yeah, that's right, you better run, you fuckers, Alex mind-said to the four Debauched who saw Alex, Shelley, and Carson running with swords in hand toward them.

Shelley watched four disappear down the long alley but also noticed eight other Debauched stayed. As she stood behind Alex, she watched Carson run straight for one of them and decapitate him with his long sword. *Humph, and I thought he was only the Crestwell chauffeur. He is skilled in combat. Who would of thought?*

Alex joined Carson, and they played tag team with a Debauched soldier. Shelley watched in fear of what might happen as she saw Alex behead another Debauched soldier and his body disintegrate. As the combat continued and they killed more Debauched, Shelley noticed Annabelle in a fetal position on the pavement. "Alex! Annabelle is down! I'm going to her!"

He nodded and kept fighting the Debauched vamps.

Shelley approached Annabelle with caution, only to see she was bleeding badly from her head and was unconscious. Panicking, she tore off a piece of her top and wrapped it tightly around Annabelle's wound as a tourniquet, not remembering the wound would eventually heal itself. "Annabelle …?" Shelley shook her.

Annabelle didn't answer.

With her newfound vampiric strength, Shelley picked up Annabelle in her arms and headed for the car and out of harm's way. As Shelley lay Annabelle on the back seat and closed the door, Annabelle came around.

"It's all right, Annabelle. You're safe. The guys shouldn't be too much longer." Shelley surveyed Annabelle's bloodied dress and bruised face. "You've lost a lot of blood, and we need to get you some care and some blood."

"Get Bryant. He has healing abilities," Annabelle said through gritted teeth, clutching her stomach. "Aww, fuck! This hurts."

Shelley gulped hard, and, as she opened the car door, a Debauched pulled her out by the hair. Shelley shrieked. "Get off me! Let go!"

"Let her go, fucker." Bryant pointed his sword into the Debauched vampire's back.

The Debauched soldier pushed Shelley to the ground and turned to fight Bryant, but he wasn't prepared for the sword that righteously came his way and decapitated him, leaving his body to disintegrate on the pavement.

"Are you all right?" Bryant helped Shelley from the ground.

"I'm fine," Shelley said, a bit dazed from the events.

"Where's Annabelle? Have you seen her?"

"In Alex's car. She's lost a lot of blood and is weak. She needs you to heal her."

"Fuck." Bryant hoped into Alex's car and took Annabelle into his arms, used his ability to heal her then gave her his wrist.

She drank from him to replenish the blood loss.

"Are you okay, my love? You're not hurt?" Alex asked as he came to stand beside a shaken Shelley.

"Nothing a stiff drink won't fix. But you aren't; you're wounded. Let me have a look." Shelley lifted his bloodied shirt.

Alex looked down at his shirt. "I didn't even realize I was wounded."

"It's not a deep wound, but it looks painful." Shelley's brow furrowed. "Do you need some of my blood to help you?"

"No, babe. I'll heal, and it'll be fine. How's Annabelle?"

"Bryant healed her wound and gave her some of his blood."

"When we get her home, she'll need to rest for a day or so, as it takes time to heal properly. I'm glad those fuckers didn't either kidnap or kill her." Alex placed his arm around her shoulders. "Hey, you did great out there tonight."

Shelley leaned into his side and smiled.

"Frederick, Harris, and Allan are finishing the cleanup so no humans see any evidence of us being here."

"Are you both okay?" Carson asked as he approached the car.

"Yes. Thanks, Carson," Alex said.

"What about you, Carson? Are you all right?" Shelley asked.

He placed his knife in his belt. "Yes, I am fine."

"You sure can whip ass. I'm impressed," Shelley said.

"Thanks. Not bad for an old guy."

Frederick, Harris, and Allan walked to the car.

"Sire, we have finished the cleanup. Can we do anything else for you?" Harris asked.

"No, but thank you for coming so quickly. I appreciate it. Do you have a car here, or do you need a lift somewhere?"

"We'll need a lift, Sire," Harris said.

*****

Once Carson had dropped Frederick, Harris, and Allan at their homes, Alex turned to Bryant and said, "I want a debrief on what happened tonight."

"We were sitting at the restaurant, eating dinner, when a Debauched soldier walked in. He noticed us and eyed Annabelle off, but I didn't think much of it, because I thought he was alone. After we finished our dinner and were ready to go, we waited outside for my driver in the alleyway, and that's when they cornered us. Apparently, the first one who came into the restaurant was the leader, and he bought back his minions with him. They weren't about to reason with us, and Annabelle wouldn't leave my side, so we had to fight them. We were lucky you all arrived when you did, otherwise they would have killed me and taken Annabelle." Bryant raked his hand through his hair.

"Lucky? That wasn't luck, and you should've been more careful, especially regarding Annabelle. You know she's valuable to our kind, yet your stupidity nearly cost not only your own life but Annabelle's too! Next time you take her out, take backup with you!"

With his head down and his eyes averted, Bryant said, "I am sorry, Sire. This won't happen again. You have my word."

Alex's nostril's flare. "It better not; otherwise, heads will roll."

Alex, stop that. He doesn't need to be chastised anymore. He feels bad enough. Can't you see it in his eyes? Shelley mind-said to Alex.

Alex regarded Shelley with a raised eyebrow. *He nearly got Annabelle killed.*

Yes, I know, but he does need a bit of forgiveness too. You don't have to do it in front of the others. You can talk with him when you are by yourselves.

Alex placed his hand on top of Shelley's. *I must show authority, as I'm his leader.* But yes, you're right. I can chastise him later. Alex sighed.

Shelley smiled up at Alex and cuddle into him. *How's your wound?*

It needs some TLC from my sweet girl when we get home. But it's okay at the moment. "How's Annabelle, Bryant? Does she need the doctor to put in an IV drip, or can she drink blood?" Alex spied Annabelle, who was unconscious again from the blood loss.

"I think we should get the IV drip, Sire."

"Right. I'll organize that now." Alex took his phone from his jacket pocket.

*****

Bryant carried an unconscious Annabelle to her room and, as he opened the door, spotted the doctor waiting by the bed. "Will she be all right, Doc?" Bryant placed Annabelle on the bed.

Standing, the doctor cut off Annabelle's clothes and evaluated her wounds. "She needs to get some blood into her. The IV should help. Her wounds have already healed, so I'd say she'll only require rest and recuperation for the next couple days." He inserted the cannula into Annabelle's arm and connected the bag of blood and cleaned her bloodied body.

"Let's change her into some clean clothes and get her comfortable under the covers."

"Thanks, Doc," Bryant said, helping to dress an unconscious Annabelle.

The doctor finished attending to Annabelle and gave Bryant his business card. "I'll be going now. Ring me if you need anything else."

"Thank you," Bryant said as he watched the doctor collect his medical bag and approach the doorway. He sat next to Annabelle's bed and held her hand, hoping his healing abilities would help mend her faster.

"Knock, knock," Shelley said in a soft voice as she entered the room. "Here, Bryant, you need to get this into you. Drink up."

Bryant took the mug of blood from her and drank it fast.

"How's she doing?" Shelley asked, standing next to the bed, looking at Annabelle.

"The doctor seems to think she'll recover." Bryant raked his hand through his hair, beholding Annabelle's bruised face. "This is entirely my fault." He sighed. "I should have known better than to take her out without backup. Fuck, if anything had happened, I would never have forgiven myself."

Shelley placed her hand on his shoulder. "Don't beat yourself up. What is done is done. I can tell you love her a lot, don't you?"

He nodded.

"The most important thing now is to help her to get better."

"Yes, you're right. You know, I never thought I'd get a shot at love again. I've fallen for Annabelle." Bryant's brow furrowed. "I hope she still wants to see me."

"Of course, she will want to see you again. She cares for you a great deal."

Alex entered the bedroom. "How's she doing?"

"The doctor said she'll be all right, but she'll need a couple days to heal. She's still unconscious, but I would say it's probably the body's way of dealing with it all. She needs to rest, that's all," Shelley said.

"Yeah, usually vampires heal fast. I think having the IV drip will help with the blood lust too."

"What have I done, Sire? How could I have been such a fool? I should have had backup when we went out." Bryant shook his head. "But, as usual, I didn't think."

"Yes, you should have had backup, but don't beat yourself up, bro. She'll be all right. And next time, you'll know what to do." Alex placed his hand on Bryant's shoulder.

"Sire, do you mind if I stay the night to watch over her?"

"You can stay for as long as you want. I've organized for someone to cover your shifts for the next three days, but after that, you'll have to return to work."

"Thank you so much, Sire. I appreciate it. I won't let you down." Bryant turned to shake Alex's hand.

"Shelley and I will leave you to watch over Annabelle. We're only two doors down the hallway. Please keep us informed of her progress or if you need anything. You're welcome to food or drink in our house, so make yourself comfortable."

*****

With the room in darkness, Annabelle eyes opened wide, and she wondered where she was. Surveying her surroundings, she realized she was at the Crestwell manor and spotted Bryant sitting by her bed, watching over her.

"Hi, beautiful," Bryant said, leaning forward.

"Hello." Annabelle took his hand in hers.

"How are you feeling?" His brow furrowed.

"I feel like shit, like I've been run over by a truck or something. Those fuckers!" Annabelle burst out.

Bryant sat on the bed and ran his hand over her temple. "Shh … come on. You're safe now. They can't hurt you anymore."

"Life sucks sometimes. I couldn't even go out with the man I adore and enjoy myself without them bastards fucking everything up." Annabelle sat upright and noticed the IV drip in her arm.

"You'll probably need to have that in until you're feeling better."

Annabelle nodded and leaned against the headboard.

"Annabelle, I want to apologize for putting your life in danger tonight. I should've brought backup with us to protect you. Can you please forgive me?" Bryant lowered his head.

"Don't be so stupid, Bryant. I don't blame you for what happened. Those Debauched fuckers like to spoil every opportunity they can get." Annabelle placed her hand under his chin. "Hey, look at me. That was not your fault, so stop blaming yourself."

"God, if anything had of happened to you, Annabelle, I don't think I could live with myself. I love you, Annabelle, and I don't want to lose you, ever," Bryant said, shaking his head.

He loves me. Woo-wee! "I love you too. You know, since I drank your blood—which, by the way, thank you for healing me and letting me drink your blood—I now can tell how you're feeling. I feel your love for me; I feel your guilt too. Also, I feel your pain; you're wounded." She frowned. "Have you had that looked at? Let me see."

"It'll heal eventually." Bryant lifted his shirt to show a deep gash across his stomach.

"In the bathroom is a first-aid kit. Go get it." Annabelle watched him retrieve the kit.

"Don't fuss too much. It'll be fine." Bryant placed the first-aid kit on the bed.

Annabelle searched through the kit and found some solution which she dabbed onto a cotton ball. "Lift your shirt."

He obeyed, and Annabelle applied the solution to the area, cleaning the blood off his abdomen.

"There. Now it'll heal quicker."

"Thank you for caring for me." Bryant closed the first-aid kit's lid, returned it to the bathroom and discarded the used cotton ball in the bin.

"So, back to what we were discussing. As I said, I can feel that you love me, but can you feel my love for you?"

Bryant sat next to her on the bed. "Are you saying you love me and want me in your life?"

"You didn't answer my question. But yes, I do love you. I recon I could feel the connection we have from the minute I met you. What about you?"

"I too have felt the connection. I haven't felt this way for years, Annabelle, and never thought I would again." He kissed her lips ever so tenderly.

Annabelle slowly pulled away and smiled, searching his face. "Hop in with me."

Bryant lay next to Annabelle and outstretched his arm for her to cuddle into his chest.

"Mmm, this feels nice and warm and safe, being cuddled up in your arms." Annabelle breathed a deep sigh of relief.

"How are you feeling now?"

"Not bad. The blood's helping. But most of all, you're helping me to heal. I can feel your power."

"Did you want me to stay the night? We can cuddle up and go to sleep."

"I think I'd like that. To cuddle up and go to sleep in your arms would be nice."

"Alex has organized for me to have the next three days off so I can watch over you. We can get to know each other a bit more before you have to go home to Paris."

"That's nice of him. I'm so lucky to have met you, Bryant."
Annabelle said, cuddling into his chest.

"I feel the same way, beautiful."

273

CHAPTER EIGHTEEN

"So much for a quiet night, babe. You must be exhausted. How about I get you something good to drink and a little snack?" Shelley asked, slipped on her clothes after her shower.

"I could use some blood, thanks." Alex answered, shrugging on his t-shirt.

"I'll be back in a jiff." Shelley ran to the kitchen at vampiric speed and retrieved two mugs of blood. "Here we go," she said, reentering their bedroom. *Alex doesn't look good at all. In fact, he looks sick.*

He drank them both straight away.

"I'll get you some more." She zipped away and returned within seconds with a jug of blood. "Here you go." She watched him down the whole jug. "Are you okay?"

Alex wiped his mouth. "Better, thanks. This always happens when I battle the Debauched. I seem to need more blood than usual."

"Your color is returning." Shelley sat on the bed next to him.

"Thank you for looking after me," said Alex, climbing into bed with her.

"Come on, let's lie down and cuddle up," said Shelley, lying on her pillow.

"Sounds good. I need to rest," said Alex, lying on his pillow.

It had been a long night, and even though Shelley had been terrified of what she had seen tonight, something inside of her was telling her that everything was going to be alright.

With their bodies exhausted, both drifted off to sleep in each other's arms.

*****

Alex felt a bit apprehensive as he sat in his office chair and dialed William's number. Yawning, he wondered what William would say about Annabelle and Bryant and what had happened the previous night.

"Hello, my friend. You're up early this morning. Is everything all right?" William asked.

"Everything is fine now, but we had an incident last night that I wanted to discuss with you." Alex told William about the attack.

"Those fuckers. They can't help themselves. Is Annabelle all right?" Alex heard William slam his fist on the desk.

"She was badly wounded in the fight, and I had the doctor come out and hook her up to an IV drip last night. He said she'll be okay in a few days. She needs rest." Alex tapped his fingers on the wooden desk.

"I'll send Grayson and Samantha to get Annabelle and bring her home. She can recuperate here."

"I need to let you know something." Alex swallowed hard.

"What?"

"In the last couple days, Bryant—you know, the one who has taken over some of my business for me—has been taking Annabelle out, and they've become quite close. In fact, I think they're life partners. I'm not sure, but there's a strong bond there."

"How in the fuck did you let this happen, Crestwell?"

"Wasn't planned. Is it possible for Lepidoptera's to have more than one life partner?"

"I'm not sure. I'll have to consult with the queen and get back to you. So, Annabelle and Bryant have become close, eh? Who would have guessed?"

"They haven't slept together yet, if that's what you're asking. Bryant has treated her like a lady and has been a true gentleman. But once Annabelle is better, I don't know if that will last. I would say that because of what happened last night, they have become even closer. I know you need Annabelle back with your family once she is recovered, but is it possible for her to stay here with us until you all come over at Christmas time?"

"Hmm, I'm not sure I like that idea. She's needed here, but, if her mind is elsewhere, that might cause a problem. I'll give her a ring later in the morning to see how serious she is about Bryant first. After that, I'll decide. For interest sake, how would you feel about Annabelle living with you or Bryant moving here with us?"

"I'd have to give it some consideration and let you know."

"I'll give you a ring later this afternoon to discuss this further, my friend. And, in the meantime, I'll ask the queen about life partners."

"Okay, thanks, William. And again, I'm sorry for all the trouble this has caused."

"No problem, my friend. We'll work this out later. Bye for now," William finished and ended the call abruptly.

I'm surprised at how well that went. I was expecting his wrath. As Alex placed his phone on his desk, Bryant entered through the opened office door.

"Good morning, Sire. I wanted to talk with you about Annabelle if that's alright?"

"Sit." Alex pointed to the chair in front of his desk.

"Annabelle seems to be a lot better this morning, Sire, but I think she still needs a few more days to heal. I wanted to ask if …" Bryant cleared his throat. "If you and William would give your permission for me to be Annabelle's life partner. We have become really close, and I don't want to be apart from her. I love her."

"I've noticed you two becoming close, but I don't know what to tell you. I've spoken with William early this morning, and he said he wants Annabelle back home, now. He is going to call Annabelle later this morning to discuss everything. I told William how you both feel about each other too. Also, William is going to consult with the queen about Lepidoptera's having more than one life partner. I think once he speaks with the queen and Annabelle, he'll decide. How would you feel about moving to Paris if William won't release Annabelle?"

"I'm loyal to you first, Sire. But in saying that, I do love this woman. I don't have an answer. I suppose it's up to you and William to decide our fates."

"I appreciate your loyalty. We must see what William says first." Alex stood. "Have you had any blood this morning, my friend?"

Bryant stood also. "No, Sire."

"Come. I'll show you where we keep it, and we can get some breakfast too. Luda is a great cook." Alex escorted Bryant toward the doorway.

*****

"Is it okay if I come in?" Shelley said, standing in Annabelle's doorway.

"Come in." Annabelle had been lying awake in the dark, staring at the ceiling.

"How are you feeling?"

Annabelle sat upright. "Not too bad. A little sore. I'll heal soon enough."

Shelley sat on the bed and hugged her. "That's good. So ... besides the Debauched destroying your date last night, how was it going before that?" Shelley smirked. "I notice he stayed the night too."

"I was having such a great time last night. Bryant is easy to talk with, and last night, when he stayed over, he told me he loves me." Annabelle grinned from ear to ear. "I can't believe I've found love again."

"I'm happy for you, Annabelle. And it's so nice to see you happy with such a great guy too."

"I hope William sees it that way. I hope he doesn't try to split us up. Especially as I've drunk from Bryant's blood, I'm now bonded to him."

"Why don't you get in first and call William, let him know how you are feeling?"

"That's not a bad idea!".

"I'll leave you to make your phone call to William, and after that, I'll bring you some breakfast if you'd like."

"Thanks, Shelley. Could I have some toast and a coffee? But could you give it about thirty minutes? That'll give me time to talk with William, and I can shower as well."

Shelley wished her good luck and headed for the door.

Annabelle dialed the number on her mobile and waited for William to answer.

"Hello, Annabelle. How are you feeling?"

"So, you know what happened last night?"

"Yes. Alex rang me early this morning."

"I'm feeling a lot better today. In fact, I think by this afternoon they could probably remove the IV drip."

"When are you coming home? We need you here. Especially now that Alex and Shelley are okay."

Annabelle took a deep breath. "I want to ask your permission about something. I'll start at the beginning. A few days ago, Alex and Shelley introduced me to one of their friends,

Bryant. As soon as we met, we hit it off straight away. Since that night, he has taken me out for dinner, bought me flowers and has been a true gentleman and has respected me in every way." She waited from him to say something, but the phone was silent. "William, I've totally fallen for Bryant, and I love him, and he loves me. Is it possible that Lepidoptera's can meet two life partners? I ask because I feel the same about Bryant as I did my first life partner; there is a connection and a bond between us. Last night when we were attacked, Bryant had to give me his blood for me to live, so now we are truly bonded. I suppose what I'm asking you is for your permission for us to be life partners."

"The answer to your question, can we have a second life partner once the first one dies, is yes. I spoke with the queen about this, and she informed me that once our life partner dies, you can have numerous life partners. So, I would say that yes, you have found your next life partner. But now we do have a predicament. Are you and Bryant coming to live here, or are you wanting to live in Zurich with Bryant?"

"I haven't even thought about that, Sire. I'd need to speak with Bryant. I don't want to let you down either. I know the family depends on me, so you come first."

"You're correct. We do depend on you. What I'd like you to do is speak with Bryant about living with us and get back to me on when you will be returning."

"Yes, Sire. I'll call you back later this morning," Annabelle said sadly.

William ended the call without a goodbye.

Bryant, can you come to my bedroom? she mind-asked.

Be there in a minute.

Annabelle harrumphed as she put her mobile on the bedside table.

"Is everything all right, beautiful?" Bryant asked, entering bedroom, and sat next to Annabelle on the bed.

"I'm not sure. I rang William and told him about us, and he said I have to return to Paris. Umm ... I wanted to ask you—" Annabelle's brow furrowed— "would you consider moving with me to Paris to live with the Gramaze coven?"

The room fell silent as Bryant contemplated his answer. "As much as I would love to, I can't. I've made a commitment to Alex, and I do enjoy my job here. Do you recon William will release you so you could live here? How would you feel about living here with me in Zurich? I can look after you, Annabelle."

"I'd love to live with you here, Bryant, but I don't know if William will give his permission to release me. He's been good to me over the last eighty-five years. He looked after me when my life partner died, and without hesitation. I owe him my life, that's for sure."

"Why don't we Skype William and ask for his permission? If he says no, I don't know what to do."

"Okay. In the drawer over there is my laptop." Annabelle pointed. "Could you get it for me so we can use that?"

Bryant retrieved the laptop and watched as Annabelle opened the lid and launched the Skype app.

"Here goes," Annabelle said, dialing William. She swallowed hard as she waited for him to answer.

"Annabelle ..." William said as his face appeared on the screen.

"Good morning, Sire. I have someone here I want you to meet." Annabelle turned the laptop toward Bryant sitting next to her.

"Bryant, my old friend. It has been a while. I didn't know you were the one Annabelle has been seeing."

"Yes, Sire. It has been a long time, that's for sure. The reason for our call is to ask for your permission for Annabelle to live with me here in Zurich. Will you release her to me?"

"Why won't you consider living with us, Bryant?"

"I'm committed to Alex, my friend."

"I see. What can you offer her, and how will you look after Annabelle in Zurich?"

"I'm working for Alex, so I have the income to support her. I may not have a house for Annabelle to live in, but I'm looking into this. I currently live in the Crestwell Hotel's executive suite, as this comes with the job, so she could live there with me. I can protect her at the Crestwell Hotel too. I'm sure you already know the Crestwell Hotel is home to more than one Lepidoptera vampire and holiday maker, and Alex's team guards it well. William, I love this woman, and I don't want to live without her, at all."

"Annabelle, how do you feel about what Bryant said?"

"I don't mind living at the Crestwell Hotel with Bryant, and I am probably sure I could get a security position there. I'd have to speak with Alex first though. Being that you know Bryant, you'd know he's a man of his word and he'll look after me. When I was wounded last night, Bryant healed me and gave me his blood. I know he loves me, and I love him too. To be honest, William, I don't think I could live without him." Annabelle cuddled into Bryant's side.

"Hmm, I can see that. I'll consider everything you've both said and give you my decision later today. But no matter what I decide, that will be my final decision. Goodbye." The screen flickered, and he was gone.

"You didn't tell me you knew William," Annabelle said as she watched the screen go blank.

"I wasn't sure until I saw him that he was the same person from years ago."

"Hopefully that might sway his mind."

"Let's not think about it now. Let's enjoy the time we have together. How are you feeling?"

"I'm starting to feel like myself again. I would say, by this afternoon, we can remove the IV drip. Actually, I'm getting hungry. Shelley promised to bring me breakfast, so I wonder what happened to it."

Just as she spoke, Shelley entered the room with a tray of Annabelle's breakfast. "Sorry I took so long. Got caught up."

"That's okay, babe. Thank you, this looks great," Annabelle said as Shelley placed the tray in front of her. "I'm starving."

"I wasn't sure if you wanted any spreads, so I put a few there to choose from. I'll leave you to enjoy your breakfast and will catch up with you later."

*****

Might go see what Alex is doing, Shelley thought as she walked toward his office. "Knock, knock," Shelley said, overhearing voices coming from Alex's office, as she entered.

"Come over here." Alex gestured for her to sit on his lap in front of his opened laptop.

"Hello, Shelley, my dear. How are you?" William asked from the screen.

"Hello, William. I'm good. All transformed now and on top of the world. How are Samuel and Renee doing?"

"They're both good. Samuel is still adjusting to feeding. Babies sure don't know when it's night or day, do they? And they make it hard to sleep when you're dog tired. Otherwise, Renee is a great mother, and she is coping extremely well. Now that I have you both there, how would you feel—and I need to ask this as a favor, if Annabelle lived with you until Bryant could get his own house?"

"Me, personally, I'd love to have them here. But it's not my house, and I don't think I have a right to answer on Alex's behalf."

Alex looked at Shelley. "This is your house too, so yes, you do have a say. William, I have a cottage down the back of the property where they could live if they wanted. But it needs some work. I don't mind if they live with us forever. You know, William, you'll make it hard for them if Annabelle has to return home and Bryant stays here. I remember how I felt when Shelley and I were having a difficult time deciding what to do; life was miserable until we could be together. Are you considering letting Annabelle stay here?"

"Yes, I'm considering it, but I need to know that she'll be looked after. I promised her life partner, when he was dying, I'd take care of her no matter what. I know Bryant is an honorable man and he'll treat her good. It'll also be a damn shame to lose a great combat warrior like her." William's brow creased. "Could you give her work, Alex, if she needed it?"

"Sure. We're always looking for more security staff at the hotel."

"I think that settles it. Would you mind hanging up and going to Annabelle's room so we can all talk on Skype together?"

"Sure, give us a minute."

The screen went blank.

*****

"Can we come in?" Alex said, standing at Annabelle's doorway with Shelley.

"Enter," Bryant said, eyeing the doorway.

As Alex and Shelley walked in, Annabelle's laptop rang. "It's William," she said as she answered his Skype call. "Hello, Sire."

"Bryant, I want you to put the laptop where the four of you can see me."

Bryant obeyed as Alex and Shelley sat on Annabelle's bed.

"The reason for my call is to give you permission, Annabelle, to stay with Bryant in Zurich. I've spoken with Shelley and Alex, and they've agreed that you both can stay at their home. Alex said he has a cottage home down the back of the property that needs some work, but you both can stay there for as long as you like. Also, Annabelle, to repay Alex kindness, you'll work at the Crestwell Hotel, doing security. As for you, Bryant, I'm here to warn you; if you harm her or put her life in danger one more time, I will reverse my decision, and Annabelle will come back to live under my roof. Have I made myself clear, Bryant?"

"Yes, Sire, crystal clear. Alex has also said he'll have my head if I mess this up with Annabelle. But you both have my word; I love this lady a lot, and I'll be there for her and love her until the day I die." Bryant looked from the screen to Alex and Annabelle.

"Thank you so much, William, for giving me permission to live with my life partner. You won't regret it. Also, I want to thank you for looking after me all these years. I don't know what I would have done without your kindness, and it's a debt I can only hope to repay one day. You've made me the happiest girl alive!" She cuddled into Bryant.

"Yes, thank you, William. And thank you, Alex and Shelley, for allowing us to stay with you in the cottage. We'll have a look this afternoon, and I'll start fixing it up straight away." Bryant proffered his hand to Alex.

"Now this is all sorted, I'll see you all in three weeks for Christmas. The Gramaze family is excited to visit you all and catch up." William reclined in his chair, raking a hand through his brown hair.

PART TWO
GRAMAZE

CHAPTER ONE

Wicce.

Talitha's deep-blue eyes opened wide, and her gaze darted around the room. She sat upright on her bed and took a deep breath. As spine-tingling shivers ran throughout her body, she swung her legs over the side of the bed, placed her feet firmly on the floor and stood to attention with her fists clenched, ready for anything.

Wicce.

Her eyes widened, and her nostrils shuddered as she heard the voice no louder than a whisper again. "Who's there? Show yourself!" Talitha commanded, positioned now in a fighting stance, as she eyed her closed bedroom door.

No one answered.

Shaking her head, Talitha took a deep, sharp breath and scanned her table where she had previously left the old and tattered sepia-colored photo of her family in their suits and gowns. She picked up the photo and wondered if she had imagined the voice in her head—especially since she had been thinking about her slaughtered family of late and the rumours of a female First One taking over as the France Debauched leader.

Wicce.

Dropping the photo, Talitha's gaze once again darted around the room. "Show yourself, Wicce!" Talitha's nostrils flared with rage as she waited for the female's voice to appear.

I am coming for you, Talitha.

"Show yourself, coward!"

All in good time, sister. All in good time.

"Alizon?"

CHAPTER TWO

"I'm excited to spend Christmas and Boxing Day in Zurich," Violette said, zipping her suitcase shut and placing it next to the doorway.

"Yeah, me too. I'm a bit concerned about the queen coming with us though. I'm surprised she's even leaving the house," Michael said, his brow furrowed, placing his last-minute items into the suitcase.

"Yeah. I don't think it's a good idea either," Violette said, putting on her shoes. "But to leave her here in Bagnolet with hardly any security to protect her is not a good idea at all." *And that voice I keep hearing ... I want to know who it is. I need to speak with the queen about it later.*

"I agree. At least with all of us around her, she'll be protected. Plus, William told me Alex has increased security at his mansion too." Michael sat on the bed. "And it'll be good to meet Annabelle's life partner, Bryant. I believe from speaking with William that Emily and Adrian will be there for Christmas too."

"Yeah, they're arriving here soon. William has asked Adrian to portal us all to Alex's mansion instead of catching a plane to

Zurich. Apparently, it'll be safer for the queen and me. I haven't seen Emily and Adrian in such a long time, and it'll be great to catch up." Violette zipped her case. "I'm all packed and ready to go. Shall we take the suitcases down to the foyer?"

"Sure," Michael said, zipping his suitcase.

*****

"Hello, Violette and Michael," Emily said, standing at the bottom of the staircase in the foyer with Renee and Samuel.

"Hello, Emily. Good to see you again." Michael placed his and Violette's suitcases on the marble floor at the bottom of the staircase.

Emily hugged him, and, as she pulled away from their embrace, she turned to Violette. "It's so good to see you, Violette."

"It's good to see you too. I've missed you, Emily," Violette said, breathing in her motherly scent as she hugged her.

"Are we all ready to go?" William asked, entering the foyer with Talitha and Adrian.

They all said yes and bowed their heads once to Talitha.

"Where is everyone else?" Violette asked William.

"Adrian has already portaled them through. It's only the eight of us to go through, and our luggage," William said, watching Adrian open the bluey-green portal again.

"Right," Violette said, watching the portal appear. *Nice of you to tell me what is going on prior.*

William, Talitha, Renee, and Samuel walked through the portal first, followed by Emily, Adrian, Michael, and Violette. When they appeared at the Crestwell mansion, Alex and Shelley were there to greet them.

"Welcome," Alex said as he shook each one of their hands.

"Thank you, Alex," William said, shaking his hand and patting his shoulder.

Once the shimmering portal doorway had closed and all the pleasantries were done, Alex and Shelley showed their guests to their rooms.

*****

"Thank you for all your help in getting the house and each guests' room ready. I'm sure the Gramaze and Lachance families will appreciate all the finer details you've put into their rooms, Shelley," Alex said as they sat at the kitchen island counter with their hot drinks.

"You're welcome. I've enjoyed helping," Shelley said, remembering how she had organized for each bedroom and bathroom to be completely striped, washed, and remade, ready for their guests. Shelley had even ensured all the fridges were stocked with enough extra blood for their entire stay, and even longer if need be. "I can't believe tomorrow is Christmas Day already."

Alex lifted his cup of coffee. "I know. I can't even explain where the last three weeks have gone."

"I think life is like that in general, isn't it?" Talitha interrupted, entering the kitchen.

Alex turned when he heard her voice. "Good evening, My Queen. Can we get you anything?"

"No. I'm fine. You have a lovely home here, Alex," Talitha said, sitting next to Shelley.

"Thank you. I've been here for about two years."

"So ... Shelley." Talitha scanned her facial features. "Where are you from, my dear?"

"I'm originally from San Francisco, but I moved to Portland four years ago for college. And now, as you know, I live here with Alex."

"Your parents ... are they still alive?"

"Yes. Actually, they still live in San Fran."

"Do you know much about your birth mother and father?"

Shelley's brow furrowed. "Why do you ask?"

"No reason." Talitha placed her hand over Shelley's. She couldn't feel the Lepidoptera connection with Shelley like she had with her other female offspring and wondered why.

"Are you looking forward to tomorrow, My Queen?" Alex asked.

"I can't wait. I haven't been out of the Gramaze house for years or spent a Christmas with others. This certainly is a treat for me." Talitha stood. "Thank you once again for inviting us all here."

Alex stood also. "You are welcome, My Queen."

"I have some business to attend to so I'll bid you both good night." Talitha walked toward the doorway.

Shelley and Alex returned the salutation and watched her regal glow leave the room.

*****

As Talitha climbed the marble staircase, she mind-talked to Violette. *Princess, come to my room. Something is not right here.*

Within seconds, Violette was by her side. They entered Talitha's bedroom together.

"What's wrong?" Violette's brow creased as she closed the door.

"We have a problem." Talitha's nostrils flared. "I don't think Shelley is who she says she is."

"What makes you think that?"

"I don't have any evidence yet, but I don't think she's my daughter," Talitha said, pacing the room. "I don't feel a connection to her like I've had with all the other female Lepidoptera's. I can't put my finger on it."

"Do you think it has something to do with … the voices?" Violette watched Talitha's reaction to her knowing.

Talitha halted and eyed Violette. "What...? You mean you've been hearing them too?"

Violette nodded. "For weeks now. Do you know who it is?"

"No. But in saying that, it only seemed to start happening around the time Shelley visited us in Bagnolet. I'm not sure if it's a coincidence or not. I want you to keep an eye on her."

"So, you think she's a Debauched sympathizer or something else?" Violette's nostrils flared.

"I don't know. But one thing I do know is she's not my child." Talitha approached the double door window.

"Right. That doesn't make sense though. She's definitely a female Lepidoptera, but, if she's not your child, whose is she? You're the only First One, and— Wait! You don't think the Debauched have created her, do you?"

"Not sure. Time will tell." Talitha looked into the distance of the Crestwell grounds' back yard.

Violette came to stand beside her. "Who is Alizon?"

"She was my sister."

"Was?"

"The humans slaughtered her many thousands of years ago. All of my families were, but I fear she's the voice we have been hearing. I don't understand how though."

"That would make sense! Word on the streets in Bagnolet is that a First One has taken over the France Debauched as their leader—only, we haven't seen or heard of who it is yet."

"Hmm, I know. Have you heard the voice here yet, Violette?"

"No." Violette shook her head. "But we've only been here a few hours."

"That's true. We are well fortified, Violette, and I don't think whoever it is can infiltrate the Crestwell mansion, so I think, until we portal back to Bagnolet, we need to be on our guard."

"Yes, I think you're right. But getting back to Shelley; I'll keep an eye on her. If she's not who she says she is, I'll take care of her."

"Thank you, Violette. You can go now, but be vigilant, my daughter." She leaned in and hugged Violette.

"Yes, My Queen," Violette said, returning the hug.

Chapter Three

"Hello, Violette," Annabelle said, walking toward the marble staircase, spotting her closing Talitha's door.

"Annabelle," Violette said, trying to avert eye contact as she approached the staircase.

"Are you all right?" Annabelle asked, sensing something had transpired between the princess and the queen.

She sighed. "Yes, fine. Whereabouts can I find the combat and training room here?"

"Come on, I'll show you." Annabelle gestured toward the marble staircase. "All the Gramaze coven weapons are down there too."

"Right. I knew they had been sent through the portal, but I wasn't sure where our weapons were being stored whilst we are here." Violette said, walking with Annabelle down the stairs to the basement. "Where is everyone tonight?"

But before Annabelle could answer, Violette entered a large padded room, resembling the Gramaze house training and combat room, and spotted most of the Gramaze coven either training with their weapons or with each other. "Impressive."

"Yeah, I know. Right?"

"Hello, beautiful," Bryant said, coming to stand in front of them. He leaned in for a quick hug from Annabelle.

"Hello, yourself. Violette, this is Bryant, my life partner."

"Nice to meet you, Bryant." Violette proffered her hand.

"It's nice to meet you too. Annabelle has told me so much about you already that I feel I know you," Bryant said, shaking her hand.

"I hope it's all good. I'm sorry; I'm at a disadvantage. I don't know much about you at all."

"Currently, I am managing Alex's businesses for him. I've lived in Zurich most of my life. Spent a few years in Rome too."

"Who was your sire, or are you born from Talitha?"

"I was sired by Alex Crestwell, Princess." *Could she get any more personal?* He looked from Violette to Annabelle and sighed. He never did like anyone questioning his transformation to vampire or why it had happened.

What is he hiding? Violette thought as she probed his mind. "How long?"

"About three hundred years, give or take a year. You lose track after a while." *A lot longer than you, little girl.*

Violette smirked when she read his thoughts. *If you only knew what I could do, you wouldn't regard me as a little girl, fucker.* "That's *Princess* to you," Violette said and walked away from him with her nostrils flared.

Bryant frowned. "Did I say something wrong?"

"No, I don't think so, but I'll warn you …" Annabelle's brow creased. "She can read your thoughts."

"That would explain it," Bryant said, watching Violette interact with Michael, Grayson, and William. "My bad. I'll apologize later."

*****

"How are James, Micajah, Bennett, Kelan, and Taiven going at home?" Violette asked William.

"Actually, I was saying to Grayson and Michael that I need to go see Brock to find out what is happening in Bagnolet. Would you like to come with us?"

"Lead the way."

Violette followed William, Grayson, and Michael toward the doorway and out to another room, which resembled the Gramaze operations room.

*****

As the double white glass doors slid open, Brock turned to watch the four of them enter. "Sire, I was about to get you. I think you need to see this." He brought up some footage on the big screen in front of them.

Violette, William, Grayson, and Michael watched footage of four blood-raged Debauched suck their hosts dry and discard their limp bodies down the drainage system in Bagnolet city.

"Fuckers," Grayson said, his nostrils flaring.

"Wait. You haven't seen everything yet." Brock pointed to the screen.

William squinted at the screen. "Braxson? Fuck! What is that ruthless prick doing there? And who is that woman with him?"

"What is Braxson doing in Bagnolet?" Grayson asked with his hands on his hips.

Both William and Grayson had come across Braxson years previous and knew how bad it could get if this Debauched was in Paris, causing trouble.

"Fuck knows. Brock, get Taiven to check this out. I want to know why Braxson is in Bagnolet and who that woman is. Now!"

"I can answer one of those questions," Talitha said from the back of the room. No one except Violette had realized she had joined them. "She is my sister Alizon."

297

William turned to see Talitha approach him. "I don't understand, My Queen. How? She died years ago."

"I'm not sure. Brock, replay the footage."

"Yes, My Queen." Brock rewound the recording.

Frowning, Talitha watched the screen and reacquainted herself with Alizon's persona. Sighing, Talitha shook her head in disbelief. *How in the hell is she alive?* "It's definitely her. I'm not sure how, but ..." Talitha's face hardened as she turned to Violette. "It would explain the voices."

William, Grayson, Michael, and Brock eyed each other and frowned in confusion.

Violette nodded. "Yes, but how is this possible? And what is she doing with this arsehole Braxson?"

"Sire, do you think Braxson and Alizon could be the new leaders of the Debauched in France?" Michael asked.

William harrumphed as he touched his jawline and stared at the screen. "That would make sense ..."

"Brock, have Taiven, James, Micajah, Bennett, and Kelan investigate this and report back to us," Talitha said with her hands on her hips.

"They're already on it, My Queen. We should hear something back soon from them."

When the white glass doors slid open, everyone turned to watch Adrian enter. "What can I do for you, Violette?"

Violette had mind-asked Adrian to come to what she now called the operations room. "We have a bit of a situation here, Adrian. I was wondering, how would, say, a First One, who has been dead for thousands of years, suddenly reappear or even be alive?"

"There is only one way, and that is if a warlock or witch has resurrected them through casting an incantation."

"Is it possible to find out who would have cast an incantation to bring someone back to life?"

"I don't think so. Why are you asking about this?"

"Someone has resurrected a First One, and we need to know who. Show him the footage, Brock."

"Yes, Princess," Brock said, rewinding the footage.

As Adrian watched the footage, his face paled. Gulping, he pointed to the screen. "There is your culprit. Gardon. He is a warlock and has the capabilities of bringing someone back to life."

"Gardon ... yes, I remember him. He was the warlock who we came across at the chateaux in Lorie Valley last year, who was helping the Debauched slaughter humans. It's a pity we didn't kill him," Violette said, remembering how she had helped Adrian take down a shimmering invisible wall Gardon had created.

"Yes, that's the one. And yes, it is a pity we didn't kill that traitor. After our initial encounter with Gardon, I did report him to our council. They informed me Gardon had gone rogue, and they are looking to bring him in to answer for his crimes," Adrian said.

William felt his phone vibrate. Taking it from his jacket pocket, he noticed Kelan's name on the screen. Placing his phone on speaker, he took the call. "Yes?"

"Sire, we have checked most of the usual places and the streets from the footage tonight, and there is no sign of the Debauched anywhere. It's like they have vanished."

"They have a warlock by the name of Gardon with them, so it's quite possible they have vanished." William's nostrils flared as he dared to think what these Debauched were scheming. "Tell everyone to keep their wits about them whilst you're on patrol tonight, Kelan. Another First One has arrived in Bagnolet, and I would say between her and the warlock, they are there to cause havoc, alongside the Debauched."

"Yes, Sire. I'll let everyone know."

"Brock, I want you to let everyone here know what is happening in Bagnolet and tell them they must be ready for anything that may arise whilst we are here. Adrian, be ready at a minutes notice to portal us to Bagnolet."

Both Brock and Adrian nodded.

"Grayson, Michael, whilst we are here in Zurich, I want extra guards patrolling the perimeter and the queen and princess guarded around the clock. Am I making myself clear?"

"Yes, Sire," Grayson and Michael said at the same time.

"Thank you, William," Talitha said.

Violette rolled her eyes. *Humph, more guards. For fuck's sake, I can take care of myself.*

Yes, you can, my child, but you won't beat Alizon by yourself. She is supremely powerful. And now that she has teamed up with Gardon and the Debauched, you are and will be one of her targets, Talitha mind-said to Violette.

Violette gulped hard and nodded in Talitha's direction.

"Let us know if anything else comes to light tonight, Brock," William said.

"Yes, Sire," Brock said, repositioning his Bagnolet cameras.

"Right, let's all go to the combat and training room and catch up on some training." William gestured for the queen and princess to go first as he approached the sliding doors.

CHAPTER FOUR

As Shelley lay in bed, reviewing the menu and the plan for tomorrow's Christmas lunch in her head, she heard a voice calling her.

Shelley.

Sitting upright, she scanned the semi-darkened room but couldn't see anyone. She lay back on her pillow. *Must be hearing things.*

Shelley.

Frowning, Shelley sat upright quickly. "Who's there?"

But no one answered.

Alex, where are you?

I'm in the training room. Are you all right? I can sense you're frightened.

I keep hearing someone calling me.

I'm coming. Alex burst through their bedroom door at vampiric speed and sat on the bed next to her.

Shelley breathed a sigh of relief. "Someone is calling my name, but I don't know who it is."

Alex frowned as he looked into her nervous eyes.

Shelley.

"There it is again. Did you hear it?"

Alex shook his head. "No."

"I did," Violette said, entering the room. "Don't you know who it is?"

"I wouldn't have a clue," Shelley said, eyeing Violette standing next to the bed.

"It's Alizon," Talitha said, hearing the voice of her sister, as she entered the bedroom and stood at the foot of the bed.

"Who's Alizon?"

Shelley.

Shelley placed her hands over her ears. "What?"

Come to me.

Talitha's brow creased. "Alizon is my sister. But what does she want with you?"

Shelley shook her head. "I don't know."

Come to me, my child.

Talitha's eyes widened and her nostrils flared. "You are not welcome here, Alizon."

Sister, she is mine, not yours.

"What is happening?" Alex panned from Shelley to Violette then Talitha.

"Alizon, you have no influence here. Leave!" Talitha scanned the room.

We will see ... We will see.

"Can someone tell me what is happening?" Alex stood, placing his hands on his hips.

"It seems Talitha's sister Alizon wants to speak with Shelley," Violette said. "So, why is it only the three of us can hear Alizon's voice?"

"I don't know," Talitha said. "Hang on. Alizon said, 'She's mine, not yours,' and referred to you as, her child. I wonder ... I wonder if she's your birth mother. That would make sense."

"What?" Shelley frowned. "None of this is making sense!"

"Shelley, since I've met you, I haven't felt a connection to you like I usually do when I meet my daughters. I've been wondering why, and now this makes sense. If Alizon is your birth mother instead of me … shit, she can easily find you …"

"Yes, she is my daughter." Alizon appeared from what seemed like nowhere. "You will come with me, my child."

"Get behind me," Alex said to Shelley.

Frightened by the sudden appearance of Alizon in her room, Shelley quickly moved from the bed and complied. She gulped hard. "I won't be going anywhere with you."

"Leave, Alizon. You are not welcome here," Talitha said as she stood next to Violette.

Alizon outstretched her right hand. "Come to me."

Shelley's feet involuntarily slid around Alex and across the floor. "Alex!" Shelley cried out as the wind increased in the room.

"Stop!" Talitha extended her right hand to use her powers on Alizon.

For a moment, it seemed to be working, until Alizon outstretched both hands and summoned Shelley again.

"Violette!" Talitha yelled as she grabbed Violette's hand, and, as they held their ground against Alizon, the room became a whirlwind. "You will *not* take her!" Talitha shouted over the noise of the wind. Moving her hand in one quick forward motion, Talitha threw Alizon across the room and pinned her against a wall. As Talitha walked hand in hand with Violette toward her sister and stood in front of her, she shouted, "You are not welcome here, and Shelley is not going with you! Leave, or you will die."

The smirk on Alizon's face became apparent as she vanished. *I will return, and you will not stop me next time.*

Everything in the room dropped to the floor, including Alex and Shelley, as the whirlwind stopped.

"Are you all right, my dear?" Talitha asked Violette still holding her hand.

"Yes, My Queen."

"My Queen, are you all right?" William asked as he burst through the doorway with Grayson and Michael wielding swords.

"We are fine. Alizon was here. Violette and I got rid of her, for now. I'm sure she'll return to collect what is rightfully hers—Shelley."

"Huh, rightfully hers?" William frowned. "You mean Shelley is Alizon's daughter?"

Talitha nodded. "I'm afraid so."

Shelley picked herself up off the floor. "What does all this mean for me?"

"Don't worry, my love. I'll keep you safe." Alex wrapped his arm around her and pulled her close.

"Unfortunately, Alex, my sister is too powerful, so I don't see how you can keep Shelley safe. We must devise a plan."

"I'll get Adrian to put up some wards around the house and its perimeter so Alizon can't detect Shelley," William said.

"That won't stop her," Talitha stated. "She has a warlock working with her, remember?"

"The only way to stop her is to kill her." Violette eyed Talitha. "Are you prepared for that?"

"When I looked into Alizon's eyes and soul, I saw a fraction of my sister in there. She may have previously been my family, who I would have done anything for, but not anymore. To your question, yes, I am prepared."

CHAPTER FIVE

Christmas Eve was a long night, and with all that had been transpiring in Bagnolet, William was regretting his decision to have Christmas and Boxing Day at the Crestwell mansion, especially now that Kelan had confirmed that Braxson was the new Debauched leader in France and he was working with Alizon and Gardon. William knew he needed to take his family home to Bagnolet to deal with the Debauched situation, but he also recognized that his family deserved some happiness, so he decided to stay in Zurich and celebrate Christmas with his family and friends.

"Everything okay?" Renee asked as she watched William's blue eyes staring off into the distance. She knew that look all too well.

"Huh? Yes, my love." William kissed the side of her head, lingering to take in her sweet magnolia scent, which he loved. William took Samuel from Renee and held him upright on his lap. "And how are you this evening, my boy?"

"He is looking more like you every day, William."

William smiled at Renee then kissed her lips. As he pulled away, he said, "We sure are lucky to have this little one."

"Yes, we are. He is a handful though, like his father." Renee smirked. "I am looking forward to Christmas tomorrow. Are you?"

"Yes, my love," William lied, not thinking about Christmas. He was more worried about what might happen tomorrow, especially with Alizon on the loose.

"I might see if I can get this little night owl down for a sleep. It'll be a big day tomorrow, and he'll need his rest." Renee held out her hands to take Samuel from Williams.

"Goodnight, my boy." William kissed Samuel on the side of his head and handed him to Renee. "I'll be downstairs if you need me, my love."

"Okay. I'll come down after I've gotten Samuel off to sleep." Renee approached the white wooden-slatted cot.

*****

"Come," Talitha said, hearing a knock at her door.

"Was there something you needed me for?" Adrian asked, entering with Violette.

"Actually, yes. Is it possible for you to find Alizon?"

"I'd need something of hers."

"As it happens, I found some strands of her hair when she was here tonight." Talitha removed them from her nightstand drawer and handed it to Adrian. "Will that suffice?"

"Yes." Adrian nodded as he took the strands from Talitha. "Once I find her, what would you like me to do?"

"Report to me, and I'll take it from there."

"Right." Adrian frowned and spied Violette to gauge her reaction, but she silently averted eye contact.

"Off you go. Get to it." Talitha shooed him toward the doorway.

Adrian opened the door. "I'll let you know when I have something."

Talitha nodded and watched the door close. "If he can find her, we can kill the bitch. Are you ready?"

"She won't beat us together, My Queen." Violette clenched her fists. "Have you spoken with William about our plan?"

"Yes," Talitha lied.

*****

"Hello, my dear," Adrian said, entering his and Emily's bedroom.

"What did the queen want from you?" Emily asked, her straightforward no-nonsense English accent apparent.

Adrian walked to his bag. "She has asked me to find her sister."

Emily's brow furrowed. "She doesn't expect you to confront Alizon, does she?"

Adrian noticed his wife's worried face and ran his hand down the side of her strawberry-blond hair, knowing she would be nervous of the ramifications. "No, she doesn't."

She breathed a sigh of relief. "That's good."

"Don't worry, my love. Nothing will happen to me.".

Emily hugged Adrian tight.

*****

Shelley shrugged off her sweaty combat clothes and stepped into the hot shower. With her hands resting against the tiles, she placed her head under the showerhead and closed her eyes, trying to block out the constant uncertainties in her mind. *Sometimes, I wish I had never come to Switzerland with the girls. Life sure was a lot less complicated.* Shaking her head, Shelley sighed and remembered when she had first moved to Portland four years ago and met Bronwyn, her brother, Bronwyn's roommate Corey, and eventually meeting and moving in with Analyse. The biggest concerns she had back then was passing the final exam and graduating college. But that had all changed since arriving in Zurich and meeting her life partner, Alex Crestwell. Shelley pictured Alex's face and smiled, knowing how much he cared for her.

"Penny for your thoughts," Alex said, standing in his light gray tracksuit pants and white t-shirt.

Shelley startled when she heard his voice. She hadn't even heard let alone noticed the shower door opening.

"Sorry, I didn't mean to startle you."

Shelley shrugged. "It's okay."

"You've been in there a while. Are you okay?"

"Yeah. I'm trying to drown out what has been happening. You know, with Alizon." Shelley turned to wash herself.

Alex nodded. "It's a lot to take in, I know."

Shelley poured the body wash onto the shower puff. "Hmm … give me a minute to finish in here, and I'll be out."

Alex nodded and closed the glass shower door.

*****

Now dressed with her hair up in a towel, Shelley entered the bedroom and spotted Alex at the half-closed doorway, speaking with Fredrick. "Evening, Fredrick," Shelley said as she approached the doorway.

Fredrick, a man of few words, bowed his head in her direction. "Shelley."

His main job tonight was to guard and protect Shelley anywhere in the Crestwell mansion or grounds. Even though William had organized a guard for each of the female Lepidoptera's, Alex had planned for Talitha, Violette, and Shelley to each have an extra guard whilst they were all at the Crestwell mansion.

"That will be all for now," Alex said to Fredrick.

"What's going on?" Shelley asked, now standing beside Alex.

"Nothing for you to worry about, my love. How are you feeling?" Alex looked into her eyes, trying to read her thoughts.

"I'm all right. I've been thinking about how much my life has changed and now with this threat from Alizon hanging over us as Christmas nears. I'm a bit worried she'll spoil tomorrow, that's all."

"I won't let that happen." Alex directed her toward the bed.

"I think it's inevitable. I don't think anyone can stop her," Shelley said, sitting on the bed. "I'd like to ask Alizon one thing though if I get the chance."

Alex read her mind. "It would be good to know who your father is. But I'm also wondering who raised Alizon from the dead. Was it Gardon, and why would he?"

"Do you think he may be my birth father?"

"It is plausible. Especially if he was the one who raised her from the dead. It certainly is food for thought. Talking about food, would you like something to eat or drink, my love?"

Shit, I haven't had enough blood today. "With all that has gone on, I've forgotten to drink enough blood." Shelley's brow creased as she walked to the small fridge in their room to retrieve a bag of blood. She tore it open and quickly gulped the contents.

Shelley …

Shelley's eyes opened wide, and she dropped the empty bag of blood as she scanned the room for who had said her name.

"What wrong?" Alex asked, standing.

"Alizon … she's calling me again."

Shelley …

"Answer her, and I'll get Violette and Talitha." Alex headed toward the doorway.

"No, don't leave me. Alex, please. I'm scared." Shelley's voice shook as she ran toward Alex.

Violette burst into the room. "I can hear her. Are you all right?"

Shelley nodded. "What does she want?"

"You, I'm afraid." Talitha passed Fredrick on guard at the doorway and entered the room. "You're in for a fight if you think you can take her, Alizon."

She is mine, and you won't stop me this time, Wicce. Alizon appeared, grabbed Shelley, and they vanished.

"Fuck! Shelley!" Alex shouted as he scanned the ceiling and the room. *William, Alizon has Shelley. I need your help.*

William suddenly stood next to Alex. "How did this happen?"

"Alizon appeared briefly and took Shelley. How will we be able to find her?"

"This should never have happened. Why didn't you stop her?" William glared at Talitha and Violette.

Talitha furrowed her brow. "It happened all too quick, William."

"Fuck!" William raked his hand through his brown hair. "Let's get—"

Adrian entered the room, answering Violette's call for help. "I've seen where Alizon has taken Shelley. I can portal us there."

Gramaze, get your weapons packed and be ready to go in five minutes. Shelley has been taken, William mind-said to his coven.

CHAPTER SIX

Her eyes opened slowly. Dazed, Shelley's mind registered that she was no longer at the Crestwell mansion, and she quickly sat upright. With her eyes darting all around, Shelley clutched her head. She slid off the bed and headed for the door. She tried the handle—locked.

"Shit, where am I?" To her left through a large door opening was a modern-colored bathroom, and to her right were three sealed glass-paneled windows overlooking a frozen bay with some ice-capped mountainous peaks rising in the distance. Shelley heard the solid-paneled door unlock, panicked and backed herself into a corner.

"You're awake," Alizon said, entering with a drink. "Here you go, my dear." She placed it on the gray-toned bedside table and sat on the bed. Patting the black, gray, and white dooner, she gestured for Shelley to come to her.

"Why am I here?" Shelley asked, still nervously standing in the corner of the room, away from Alizon.

"Come. Sit, dear, and I'll explain," Alizon said in a calm voice.

Shelley gulped hard and obeyed.

"That's better. Are you okay?"

Shelley nodded. "Why have you brought me here?"

"I won't hurt you, my dear, if that is what you're worried about. In fact, quite the opposite. I hope to get to know you better."

"Why have you only showed yourself now?" Shelley scrutinized her facial features, only now recognizing the resemblance.

"I've been waiting for you to turn into a Lepidoptera. I'm not the enemy, Shelley. I wanted to meet you and tell you that I'm your birth mother, not Talitha."

"Who is my birth father? Is he still alive?"

"Would you like to meet him?"

"Umm … what is his name?"

"Gardon is your father, so that would make you half vampire and half witch. You are valuable to our kind."

"Your kind?" Shelley harrumphed, and her nostrils flared. "I don't want anything to do with someone who drains humans and thinks nothing of it, let alone someone who would link up with a Debauched. How could you? You ought to be ashamed of yourself!"

"Ashamed? On the contrary, my dear, I'm proud to be associated with Gardon and Braxson." Alizon snickered. "They are not only my friends but also my family. And I couldn't have asked for more loyal subjects."

"Subjects? Loyal? Don't kid yourself. They are not your subjects. You're a pawn to them—an end to a means." Shelley rose with her hands on her hips.

"You're wrong, my child," Alizon said, trying to keep calm.

"I'm not your child and never will be." Tears formed in her eyes. "Take me back home."

"Your home is here, with me."

"Actually, I live with Alex. He is my life partner." Shelley approached the open door.

"Life partner!" Alizon said, snickering.

Before Shelley could reach the doorway to make a run for it, Alizon stood in front of her and grasped Shelley's arm. "Let go, you bitch!"

"Bitch? Humph, nice. If you want to play it like that, no problem." Alizon took a syringe from her pants pocket and injected Shelley with a drug, rendering her unconscious. "You'll learn to keep that mouth of yours in line, my child." Alizon collected a limp-bodied Shelley in her arms and laid her gently onto the bed.

*****

"How's it going in there with Shelley?" Gardon watched Alizon close the door and lock it again.

"It's as I suspected—not good. She is brainwashed. Talitha will pay for what she has done!"

"I warned you this may happen when we gave her up for adoption twenty-four years ago. Give it some time, Alizon. You never know, she may come around to our way of thinking."

"I doubt that." Alizon turned to walk away.

"Braxson is waiting for us in the sitting room." Gardon followed his partner down the staircase.

"Braxson? What does he want?" Alizon asked as she entered the sitting room with Gardon.

"There you are. We have some business to attend to," Braxson stated as he watched Alizon and Gardon enter. "Sit."

"Where are you regarding the shipment coming in via the Port of Le Havre?" Alizon sat on the white cotton French provincial couch next to the window with Gardon.

"The shipment has already cleared customs at the port." Braxson sat across from them. "We're extracting the drug from the ceramic tiles at our warehouse."

"Right. So, when will it be ready for distribution?"

"I'd say, tomorrow, if all goes to plan. How did you go with your daughter?"

"Waste of time. She's not cooperating."

"You know what to do." Braxson panned from Alizon to Gardon with cold, rigid eyes.

"Yes, Sire," Gardon said, averting his eyes.

Alizon's eyes narrowed, and her nostrils flared as she sighed, trying to calm her thoughts and her mouth. *You had better think twice about harming my child, Braxson.* "Once you've extracted the drug, when will you distribute it to the humans?"

"As soon as humanly possible—pardon the pun." Braxson smirked. "These fucking Lepidoptera's won't know what happened to them once the humans take Tsoukalos's drug and become Debauched." Braxson stared off into the distance and wrung his hands at the possibility of eradicating Lepidoptera's from the world.

"Right, and meanwhile, what is your plan going forward?" Alizon approached the bar fridge located in a secret wall cavity at the back of a bookcase.

"Besides exterminating all the Lepidoptera's? Well, we will see." Braxson stood, his eyes narrowing as he looked in her direction.

CHAPTER SEVEN

"How did you know where to find Shelley?" William asked Adrian as he stood beside the shimmering blue portal in Alex Crestwell's back yard, watching each Lepidoptera walk through.

"Earlier this evening, Talitha gave me some of Alizon's hair and asked me to find her. So, I'm surmising Shelley will be at the same place."

"And you never thought to inform me, why?"

"I thought you knew. And, as this request came from Talitha, why would I question her word?"

"Right. That makes sense." William's his brow creased. He was fed up with the way Talitha was dealing with the Alizon situation. Once this battle was sorted tonight, he would have to discuss why she was not only interfering in his decisions but also organizing missions without involving him. After all, she did relinquish her duties and place him in charge years before. "That is everyone. Let's go, Adrian." William approached the portal's shimmering blue light.

After Adrian and William stepped through to the other side, Adrian closed the portal and watched William stride toward

Talitha and Violette waiting next to the property's black wrought iron gates.

"You'll both stay behind us. We don't want either of you getting hurt—or worse, beheaded," William said to Violette and Talitha.

"But I—"

"There are no buts, Violette. You will do as you are told, Princess."

Violette rolled her eyes and sighed heavily.

"William, I will be the one to kill her," Talitha said authoritatively.

"You'll get your chance. But, for now, stay behind me. We can't afford to lose you, My Queen, nor you, Violette."

Talitha knew he was right. She nodded once and averted her eyes from him.

Standing rigid, William instructed everyone how they would proceed with the battle tonight.

*****

"Check what is happening outside," Braxson said to his sentinels, hearing the explosion.

Within seconds, one of the sentinels returned. "Sire, we have a situation at the front of the property. It looks like the Gramaze coven and a few others are here."

"Don't stand there, you fucking idiot. Get the others and go kill these Lepidoptera bastards!" Braxson retrieved some weapons for himself from his cabinet. *How in the fuck did those bastards know we were here?*

*****

William, Annabelle and I have killed four soldiers near the back door, Grayson mind-said as he watched a Debauched soldier turn to ash.

Good. Get inside and see if you can find Shelley, William mind-said, blowtorch in hand, walking down the long driveway toward the house with Adrian, Brock, Talitha, Violette, Stephen, and Sharina.

Grayson and Annabelle did as instructed.

The back shed is all clear, Sire. Michael and Alex climbed the limestone steps to the back of the house.

Right, I want you and Alex to check inside the house with Annabelle and Grayson. Keep a watch out for Alizon and Gardon too.

"Let's go," Alex said, hearing William's command. *If they've hurt one hair on her head, the three of them will pay.*

Stephen, Sharina, I want you to check the rest of the property. Report to me if you find anything.

They ran toward the right-hand side of the property with their swords drawn.

Sire, you need to come quick. They have Shelley and are going through a portal, Stephen mind-said as he and Sharina ran with vampiric speed to the back of the property.

"Fuck, no!" Alex ran out the back door.

By the time everyone heard what was happening and were running to the back of the property, the portal Gardon had created was gone, and so were Braxson, Alizon, Gardon, and Shelley.

"They are going to pay," Alex said, sword in one hand and a clench fist in the other. "Where do you think they've gone?"

"Not sure, but one thing I do know is Shelley didn't go willingly." Stephen sheathed his sword. "She was unconscious and slumped over Braxson's shoulder when they went through the portal."

"Grayson, I want you to search this house room by room with a fine-tooth comb and let me know what you find. Adrian, get ready to portal us to the Crestwell mansion."

Adrian nodded once.

"Yes, Sire," Grayson said. "Annabelle, Brock, Stephen, Sharina, come with me, and we will check the house."

*****

As the last Lepidoptera walked out the portal, returning them to the Crestwell mansion, Adrian closed the shimmering doorway.

I want a full debrief in the sitting room in three minutes, William mind-said to his coven as he watched them walk inside.

Yes, Sire, they all mind-said together.

"I need you to give some of Shelley's hair, which there should be some on her brush, to Adrian so he can track her," William said to Alex, walking alongside each other.

"Yes, Sire. Adrian, follow me," Alex said, entering the house.

Adrian nodded and followed Alex inside.

William, come quickly, Talitha mind-said, her voice shaky.

William ran through the house at vampiric speed and stopped in his tracks by the sight of Christian, Danielle, and Samantha cradled in Grayson's arms. They had all been beaten and lay unconscious near the bottom of the foyer stairs. "Shit!" William raked his hand through his hair as he bent to check his family. "Get Violette to help heal Christian, Danielle, and Samantha," William said to Talitha.

Talitha nodded.

Renee, William mind-said to his life partner.

She didn't answer, but he could feel her presence in the house.

William ran up the stairs to their bedroom. He opened the door to find her lying face down next to Samuel's cot, but when William looked inside the white-slatted cot, he saw Samuel was gone. He picked up her limp body off the floor, placed her on the bed and gently rocked her. "Renee ... Renee ..."

Renee slowly opened her eyes and remembered the battle she'd had with Alizon.

"Where is Samuel?" William's brow creased.

"Alizon has him." A tear escaped her swollen eye as she glanced at Samuel's cot.

"Fuck! That bitch will pay!" William swiped at the lamp on the bedside table, pushing it onto the floor with haste. "Renee, can you feel Samuel's connection to you?"

Renee closed her eyes and imagined Samuel's face. "No, I can't ... Wait, there he is. Yes, I feel his presence. He is near." Renee quickly sat upright, not worrying about how bad her wounds were let alone the blood loss she had endured. "So, if she thinks she can substitute my Samuel for Shelley, because she missed out on her daughter's childhood, she has another think coming." *That bitch has messed with the wrong Lepidoptera.* Renee got off the bed, raced to the cot and retrieved Samuel's blue and white baby blanket. "Give this to Adrian. It might help find Samuel quicker."

*****

Sister, your life for the boys.

Talitha's eyes opened wide when she heard Alizon's voice. *Gladly.*

Violette burst into Talitha's room. "Don't even think about it. You will not trade your life for anyone's."

"I agree," William said, running through the open doorway. "Renee and I won't agree to this." This time, they had heard Alizon voice as well.

"You don't have a say. I'll do whatever it takes to keep your boy safe," Talitha said, watching a bruised and battered Renee stand next to William and Violette. "My dear ..." Talitha placed her hand over her mouth. "Are you all right?"

"It looks worse than it is. I'll eventually heal. I'm more worried about my Samuel than myself at the moment."

"The sooner we find him, the better." Talitha placed her healing hand on Renee's arm. "I'll gladly swap my life for his."

"No, you won't!" William retorted.

"Listen. My whole life I've watched on as the Debauched have ruined our lives, and I don't want to be party to this anymore. They've taken so many of our beloved family and either turned them or killed them. I won't be able to live with myself if anything happens to that dear, sweet boy. So, the answer is to trade my life for his. And there will be no arguments from any of you." Talitha looked from Renee, to William, and to Violette with tears forming in her eyes.

William's brow creased. "My Queen …"

"My word is final. Find these fuckers, and let's get on with this!" Talitha turned and walked toward the doorway.

*****

"William I've found Shelley and Samuel," Adrian said as he watched the queen pass him down the marble stairs with William and Violette in tow.

"Great. Be ready in a couple minutes with another portal, Adrian." *Gramaze, they have taken Samuel. I want you all assembled with your weapons and ready to go in the back yard again in three minutes,* William mind-said, reaching the foyer.

With her hands hovering over Danielle's body, Violette's nostrils flared when she heard William's command.

"Christian, Danielle, Samantha, will you be all right?" William asked as he stood in front of them, watching Violette wave her healing hands over them.

"We are fine, Sire. You go," Christian said, his injuries already healing.

William placed his hand on Christian's shoulder. "Thank you." He eyed Samantha, and she said the same.

"Go. Your son is more important," Danielle said.

CHAPTER EIGHT

"Sire, we didn't get to debrief at the Crestwell mansion, and there is something you don't know yet," Grayson said, walking alongside William through the shimmering portal doorway onto the wharf.

William looked at Grayson. "Yes?"

"When we searched Braxson's house, I found an email and some notes on a shipment coming into the French Port of Le Havre tonight. And now that the portal has brought us to the same French port, I think we need to check this out." Grayson handed William the printed-out email.

William scanned the message. "My first priority is to find Samuel. We'll deal with this later." He handed the printout to Grayson.

"Yes, Sire." Grayson placed the folded paper into his jacket inside pocket. "Also, I've requested James, Micajah, Bennett, Kelan, and Taiven to join us. They should be here any minute."

"Good thinking."

"William, I think Samuel is in that warehouse over there." Renee gestured to her right. "I can feel his presence."

"Yes, I feel Shelley's presence there too." Alex unsheathed his sword.

"Sire, where do you need us?" Taiven asked as he, James, Micajah, Bennett, and Kelan appeared from what seemed like nowhere.

"Thank you for joining us. Listen up!" William made eye contact with everyone standing before him. "This is a rescue mission, and the aim is to take Samuel and Shelley home alive with us. There will be no swapping of lives either. Am I making myself clear?" William waited for Talitha's response, but she kept silent. *Am I making myself clear?*

Yes, crystal, Talitha mind-said to William only.

William sneered at Talitha and instructed everyone on their jobs and his plan of attack.

Who left him in charge? Violette thought to herself.

Talitha glanced at Violette. *I did, and you had better get on board.*

Violette harrumphed, not realizing Talitha was listening.

Young and so inexperienced … You have a lot to learn, my child.

Renee, William, Violette, Talitha, Brock, Adrian, and Alex leaped up the side of the building and landed quietly on the warehouse rooftop. Walking to a skylight, they watched the goings on below of Braxson and his soldiers extracting the drugs from the crates of ceramic tiles.

I can't see Samuel or Shelley. Maybe they're in a different part of the warehouse, William mind-said to everyone. *Grayson, I want you, Annabelle, Bryant, Danielle, Christian, Samantha to go around the left-hand side of the building, and Stephen, I want you, Sharina, James, Micajah, Bennett, Kelan, and Taiven to go around the righthand side of the building. Tell me what you find.*

They nodded and obeyed. Within seconds, Stephen mind-said, *William, both Samuel and Shelley are being held by Alizon and Gardon in what looks like an office around this side. We can see through the window Shelley has been tied up in a chair near the doorway, and Alizon is holding Samuel in her arms. What would you like us to do?*

Hold your position for the moment. He waved his team to the side of the warehouse. *Let's go.* William landed firmly on the ground. *Grayson, Annabelle, Bryant, Danielle, Christian, Samantha, James, Micajah, Bennett, I want you all to stop the extraction inside the warehouse and kill these mothers. Talitha and Violette, once we are inside, you will stop Alizon so Renee can take Samuel. Alex, you will rescue Shelley. Adrian, I want you to see if you can stop Gardon. The rest of you will keep guard and stop any other Debauched from entering the office. Once Samuel and Shelley are safe and these fuckers are dead, Brock, I want you to set the explosive charges and blow this place and its contents sky high. Is everyone clear on our mission?*

*****

"What is happening?" Alizon asked when she heard the first explosion.

"You are all dead now," Shelley said, trying to wriggle free from her steel chains that bound her to the chair.

Gardon opened the office door and watch Braxson run toward them. "Shit, the Lepidoptera's are here."

"Let's get out of here, Gardon," Alizon instructed as she placed Samuel into a wool-lined calico bag. "Here, give this to Shelley." Alizon handed Gardon a drug-filled syringe.

Shelley squirmed in her seat and watched Gardon approach her. *Fuck, not again.*

Braxson burst through the door. "Let's get the fuck out of here."

William punched a hole through the tin-lined wall and ripped it wide open so he and his coven could enter the office. "You won't be going anywhere with my son."

"Gardon, quickly," Alizon said, running toward him.

Talitha and Violette stood next to William and extended their hands.

The room got windy, and its contents scattered everywhere. Braxson, with an unconscious Shelley over his shoulder, Alizon carrying Samuel, and Gardon were pushed and pinned against the wall.

"Gardon, open the portal!" Alizon shouted, holding Samuel again her chest.

"I can't! My hands are pinned!"

Alizon raised Samuel into the air. "You want this?"

Renee's nostrils flared, and her jaw went rigid as she moved with vampiric speed toward Alizon, fearing this mad bitch would hurt—or worse, kill—Samuel. "Put him down." With her fists clenched, Renee's stood in front of Alizon with hatred in her blue eyes, waiting to see what she would do.

"Catch!" Alizon threw Samuel toward Renee, and the wind caught hold of him.

With the bag flying through the air, William moved quickly to retrieve Samuel before he hit the floor.

"You fucking bitch!" Renee tried to stab Alizon with her knife.

As the wind slowed, Alizon tossed Renee with one swipe of her hand toward the roof beams.

Renee smashed into the beam, and she fell to the floor with a thud and a groan.

Talitha rushed toward a distracted Alizon with her sword drawn and beheaded her. As she watched her body turn to ash, Talitha felt not only a sense of pleasure but sadness for the loss of her sister once again.

"Alizon!" Gardon screamed as he watched her ashes blow away.

Talitha was brought back to reality when she heard Gardon's screams. Looking up, she extended her hand and twisted it, strangling Gardon as he was pinned against the office wall. "You will pay, warlock, for what you have done to my family. And you too, Braxson." She extended her other hand and did the same to Braxson, who had now dropped Shelley.

Violette stood beside Talitha and watched her queen make them squirm.

Alex ran to Shelley and scooped her into his arms, kissing her forehead as he pulled her close to his chest.

Shelley's eyes opened slowly, and she smiled when she looked into his worried blue eyes.

"My love, are you all right?"

Shelley nodded once and cuddled into his chest.

"Let me take this one off your hands, Talitha," Adrian said as he came to stand by her side.

"Gladly. You can deal with your own kind." Talitha released her hold on Gardon and focused on Braxson. She moved Braxson down the wall with her left hand and beheaded him with her sword and watched his body turn to ash. "Good riddance to bad rubbish."

"You will pay for all your indiscretions, Gardon," Adrian said as he turned Gardon around with a wave of his hand and placed invisible handcuffs on him.

Gardon tried to wriggle free as he watched Adrian open a portal to the warlock council chambers. "No!"

Adrian smirked as he pushed Gardon through and closed the doorway.

Brock, have you set the charges yet? William mind-said, knowing his coven had already dealt with all the other Debauched.

Yes, Sire. One minute and we will be ready to go.

"How is our boy?" William asked, coming to stand beside Renee now holding Samuel.

"He's okay, my love. Can we go home?"

William searched for Adrian and watched him open the portal to the Crestwell mansion. "Whenever you're ready, Renee." He gestured toward the portal. "Let's get back to our Christmas holiday celebrations, everyone."

They followed William and Renee, who held a sleeping Samuel, through the shimmering portal.

Being the last one to step through the portal, Brock watched the warehouse explode into a fireball, destroying every bit of evidence in its path. *One less drug supplier we have to worry about.*

CHAPTER NINE

With the decorated Christmas tree at one end of the sitting room on the left and all the wrapped presents under it and a warm fire roaring, Shelley watched each of her newfound Lepidoptera family chatting on the cream-colored European couches. Clinking her wine glass and standing tall, Shelley scanned the room. "I'd like to make a toast."

The room went quiet as all watched and listened to the newest member of their family.

"This year certainly has been a surprise for me, first, finding the man of my dreams"—she looked at Alex and smiled—"discovering I was a Lepidoptera, but what I think has been the most wonderful thing was to learn I have not only some awesome new friends but also a new adoring family. I want to say, thank you, from the bottom of my heart for making me feel accepted and welcomed into your family." She raised her glass. "To family."

Everyone smiled and said, "To family," and acknowledged each other before taking a sip.

"Thank you, Shelley," William said as he came to stand beside her. "I too would like to make a toast. One, to my

Lepidoptera family and coven, thank you all for saving our son Samuel. Renee and I are grateful and feel blessed to have this little boy in our lives. If it wasn't for you all, Samuel wouldn't be here today, and neither would Shelley. And two, I'd like to thank Alex and Shelley for allowing us to stay at their beautiful home and for this wonderful Christmas holiday. None of my coven have been out of Bagnolet to celebrate Christmas for so long, and I must admit I've enjoyed seeing every one of you have a good time and letting your hair down, so to speak. Here's to more years like this and our Lepidoptera families growing in numbers." William raised his glass.

"Hear, hear!" Grayson said, raising his glass.

"Thank you, William. We're glad to have you all here at our home," Alex said, shaking William's hand.

Dinner is being served in the dining room, Luda mind-said to everyone.

They filed from the sitting room into the dining room.

Luda stood near the buffet-style food tables and watched the astonishment on their faces as they entered the dining room to sit. A long glass table had been arranged with golden- and green-leaved Christmas decorations and candles placed here and there on a white and golden table runner down the middle. In front of each cream-colored with golden framed chair, each person had their own elegant place setting that included gold cutlery, fine bone china plates with gold rims, with a golden bonbon placed on top of each plate, and crystal glasses for their drinks. At the end of the table, set up in front of the windows, were buffet tables with all different types of hot and cold food. A fridge had been placed on the side of the room with blood for each Lepidoptera.

As Talitha sat at the head of the table with Violette and Michael on her left and William and Renee with baby Samuel on her right, she watched how her family interacted with each other. She felt pleased, knowing she had created this family and how

328

large it had become over the years, and was glad to still be able to not only see but enjoy watching each and every one of them.

Alex pushed back his chair and stood tall as he clinked on his glass with a gold piece of cutlery.

Everyone quietened and focused on Alex.

"I would like to propose a toast to the ones who have gone before us."

Everyone raised their glass. "To the ones who have gone before us."

"Also, to our queen, may you live a long, happy life and watch us all grow." Alex held his glass higher.

"Hear, hear!" they said together.

"And perhaps one day, we can rid this world of the Debauched and their treachery and help the humans live a peaceful life."

"Hear, hear!"

"Lastly, I'd like to thank Shelley, Luda, and Lamiae for this lovely Christmas lunch and how wonderful it all looks. You have outdone yourselves, ladies."

They smiled at Alex, acknowledging his praise.

"Hear, hear!" Everyone raised their glasses higher and sipped their drinks.

*****

With Christmas Day being a total success, Shelley proudly stood with Alex on the front porch and waved some of her newfound family goodbye.

"Have a safe trip back to Bagnolet," Alex said as he shook each of their hands. "And thank you for all you have done."

Shelley gave each of them a warm hug. "Thank you for saving me."

"Anything for family," Kelan said, returning the hug.

"We'll see you all tomorrow around lunchtime," William said as he watched Adrian open a portal for them. "Keep an eye on the surveillance cameras, Taiven, and let me know if anything's going on with the Debauched. It sure will be interesting to see who their new leader is."

"Yes, Sire."

Violette stood next to Michael and watched them walk through the portal, waving goodbye to her family. *Not looking forward to going home tomorrow because that means I'm trapped in that house again. Being a princess sure does have its drawbacks.*

Michael listened to Violette's thoughts and wondered what he could do for his life partner. He wrapped his arm around her shoulder and kissed the side of her head. *Maybe I can speak with William about letting you go on some more missions with us. After all, you are only eighteen years old and still probably want some fun in your life.*

Violette briefly smiled up at Michael and cuddled into his side.

Talitha stood behind everyone on the front porch landing, listening to Violette and Michael's thoughts. She knew from her own experiences in life exactly how Violette felt. *I don't think you'll be the only one speaking with William when we return to Bagnolet, Michael.*

CHAPTER TEN

Shelley was startled awake when she felt the thud of the airplane wheels touch down at the San Francisco International Airport.

"Good morning, sleepyhead." Alex leaned over to give her a kiss on the side of her head.

"Morning." Shelley stretched and yawned. "Where are we?"

"San Fran."

"I'm looking forward to a shower." *And some blood.*

The driver will have some for you once we're in the car.

"Great. Where are we staying?" Shelley unfastened her seatbelt when she felt the plane come to a stop.

"I've booked us a luxury suite at the five-star Grand Hyatt," Alex said, unclipping his seat belt.

"I can't wait to see our room," Shelley said, grinning from ear to ear.

*****

Once they had collected their luggage from the carousel and were through customs and heading into the terminal, Alex spotted his chauffeur, and they proceeded to the car.

"Thanks, Oliver," Alex said as he handed him their luggage to place in the trunk. With the car door already open, Alex gestured to Shelley to enter the car.

"You're welcome, Sire," Oliver said in an British accent.

"Where is the blood, Alex?" Shelley asked, impatiently searching the inside of the car.

"It's here, my love." Alex moved the middle seat armrest to reveal a secret compartment, which had a mini fridge full of blood bags. He took a glass from the side cupboard, filled it with the blood and handed it to Shelley.

"Thank you." She gulped it and watched Alex pour another glass. "Can I have some more?"

Before he could answer, she took the other glass from his hands and drank that too.

"Thirsty?"

"Mmm, yes. Think I'm a bit low." She wiped her mouth with the back of her hand.

Alex poured her a few more until she felt sated then poured some for himself as the car traveled toward downtown.

*****

Shelley placed the door keycard into the slot so the lights would turn on in the room and held the door open for Alex to bring in the luggage. As he placed the luggage on the stands provided, she waited for him to turn around. As he did so, she leaned in and kissed his lips with appreciation. "Thank you. The suite is lovely."

"You are welcome, my love. Would you like to shower first?"

"Yes, please."

"You go ahead. I have a few phone calls to make, so I'll shower after you."

*****

"Hello, my friend. What can I do for you?" William asked.

"I have a bit of a dilemma. The Debauched have killed the soldiers I had picked to guard Shelley here in San Francisco. Do you know anyone I can call to help us?"

"I don't know of anyone there, but I can send some of my coven if you like."

"That would be great. I am indebted to you."

William recalled how he had first met Alex, who had been twenty-eight and only been a Lepidoptera for about four months, three hundred years ago in the streets of San Francisco. Alex had stumbled upon a fight between William and six Debauched vampires, and they had backed William into a corner and were about to behead him. Without concern for his own self being, Alex had jumped them from behind and helped William slaughter them. "This is one of many debts I owe you, my friend. You've saved my butt more than once over the years. I'll send Violette, Michael, Grayson, Kelan, and Taiven. I'll ask Adrian to portal my coven members there. Where are you staying?"

'The Grand Hyatt in the city. We are on the twenty-sixth floor, room twenty-six ten."

"Give it about an hour, and they'll be there. Can you also organize accommodation on the same floor for them all?"

"I'm sure that won't be a problem. I'll ensure they have enough blood too. I know a manager at the hotel who can help with that, on the quiet."

"Terrific. Let me know how everything goes. Goodbye, my friend."

"Thanks, William. Bye for now," Alex said as he watched Shelley exit the bathroom.

"Were you talking with William?"

"Yes, my love. Nothing to worry yourself about though." Alex placed his phone on the bedside table.

"So, who's coming?" Shelley asked, reading his thoughts.

Shit, I forgot to block her. "Violette, Michael, Grayson, Kelan, and Taiven." He gingerly passed her toward the bathroom.

"Why?"

Alex harrumphed and leaned on the bathroom doorframe. "I had other soldiers to guard you while we are here, but the Debauched killed them last night. I got a text about it a few minutes ago."

Shelley sat on the bed. "God, that's awful. I didn't realize I'd need a guard now I've fully transformed. And I'm surprised William is letting the princess come to guard me."

"Yeah, me too. I thought she wasn't allowed to go out on missions," Alex said, scratching his head. "I'm going to shower. I won't be long."

*****

"Knock, knock," William said as he walked through the doorway into Michael and Violette's bedroom.

"Sire," Michael said.

"How would you both feel about going on a mission with Grayson, Kelan, and Taiven to help Alex guard Shelley whilst they are in San Francisco?"

"I'd love to," Violette said, glad to be going on any mission, let alone out of the house.

Michael put his hands on his hips. "Sire, do you think this is wise? I know Violette has asked if this is possible, but I'm not sure this is a good idea."

"I too have reservations about this. But, as you know, the princess is quite capable of looking after herself, and I feel she is ready to be out in the world. We can't keep her cooped up here, Michael. It's not healthy for her. Besides, she'll have Grayson, Kelan, Taiven, and yourself to protect her."

"Right. How are we getting there?"

"I've asked Adrian to portal you all there. Alex is organizing a room for everyone at the same hotel he is staying at."

"Knock, knock," Grayson said, entering the room. "So, we're all good here?"

"Yes. Have you packed the weapons?" William asked.

"Yes, Sire. The four of us are ready to go. Also, Adrian has turned up downstairs. Lamiae is making him feel at ease with some food until we're ready for the portal. We're now waiting on Michael and the princess."

"Give me five, and I'll be ready." Violette went to the wardrobe and got down the two suitcases for her and Michael to pack plenty of combat clothes and toiletries.

"Yeah, I'll be ready in a few minutes." Michael pulled up the carpet to retrieve his weapons bag from the secret floor compartment.

"We'll leave you both to it. Meet you in the sitting room in ten," William said, walking with Grayson toward the doorway.

*****

Violette felt a surge of energy as she walked from the shimmering portal onto the carpet inside Alex and Shelley's room with her bags.

"Thank you for coming," Alex said to them. "I've organized two rooms on this floor for you all. Also, in the hotel basement are three cars; two are SUVs, and the other is a limousine. Once you're sorted in your rooms, I'll give you details on where I need you each day or night to guard Shelley." Alex regarded Violette. "Princess, I know you're here to help, but I'll ensure you're protected at all times while you're here too."

"Thank you, Alex, but that isn't necessary. I can take care of myself."

"I think Alex knows that, my love. What you fail to understand is everyone in this room would give their life to save you. You forget how valuable you are to our kind and what you mean to each of us, whether that be friendship or family."

Michael watched everyone avert their gazes to the ground and bow their heads toward their princess.

"Hmm ... yes, I suppose I do. Thank you, everyone. But please remember, I'm here to help."

"Thank you," Shelley said as she hugged Violette.

"Right. Now that is sorted, let's get you all settled in your rooms." Alex handed Michael one keycard for his and Violette's room and Grayson the other one for his, Kelan, and Taiven's room. "There will be blood in your rooms in the minibar fridge, and don't worry, housekeeping are Lepidoptera's."

*****

"Do you think we might see some of San Francisco while we're here, Michael?" Violette asked as she placed her toiletries in the bathroom.

"Maybe. Although, our only priority at the moment is to guard Shelley."

"Okay. I was wondering ... are Shelley's parents human?"

"I'm not sure. I suppose we'll find out today."

"How will that work? Are we going inside with them or guarding from outside today?"

"From outside."

"How long until we leave?"

"We have about twenty minutes before we'll meet Alex and Shelley at their room."

CHAPTER ELEVEN

Oliver slowly steered the long black limousine into the dark chocolate-colored paved driveway of Shelley's parent's weatherboard house, which was painted a deep cream color and had white-painted window frames.

As Shelley exited the car, she felt a sense of belonging and remembered all the good times she'd had over the years with her parents and how supportive they had been throughout her life. "It's this way," Shelley said to Alex, pointing to the dark brown concrete stairs which went up the left-hand side of the house.

Alex nodded and followed Shelley up the stairs to the front door.

"Hello!" Shelley called out through the front screen door. A huge grin crossed her face when she saw her mom running toward her.

"Come in, come in," Shelley's mom opened the screen door and hugged her daughter tight. "I've missed you, sweetheart."

"I've missed you too, Mom. It's nice to be home again."

Alex cleared his throat.

"Sorry. Mom, this is my fiancé, Alex. Alex, this is my mom, Mary."

"It's lovely to meet you," Alex said, trying to read Mary's thoughts.

"It's nice to meet you too, Alex." Mary leaned in to give him a quick hug. "Shelley has told us so much about you that I feel I know you fairly well already. Come on, let's go in and find Shelley's father." She closed the front wooden door and escorted them through the house to the back yard where they found Shelley's dad sitting at a table, reading the newspaper.

"Don! Shelley and Alex have arrived," Mary said, her long grayish-brown hair flowing in the subtle breeze.

Shelley leaned toward her father to hug him. "Hello, Dad. How are you?"

"Hello, sweetheart. I'm good. Thanks. It's good to see you."

"I've missed you. Dad, this is my fiancé, Alex. Alex, this is my dad, Don."

Alex proffered his hand. "Nice to meet you, sir."

"Good to meet you too, Alex." Don shook his hand, considering his broad physique.

"Shall we go inside, or would you prefer to sit out here?" Mary asked.

"Inside," Alex said, noticing Grayson and Kelan standing on the road at the back of the sloping property.

"Come on, Dad. I'll wheel you inside." Shelley pulled his wheelchair from under the table.

Alex's eyes widened when he realized Shelley's father was in a wheelchair. *Why didn't you mention this to me?*

I didn't think it mattered, Shelley answered, eyeing Alex as she pushed her Dad past.

It doesn't matter, but it would have been nice to know your father was in a wheelchair.

*****

"Would you like something to drink?" Don asked Alex as he

wheeled himself to a wooden sideboard in the lounge room and opened the door.

"Yes, that sounds good. What do you have?" Alex said as he approached Don.

"Whisky, red wine, white wine, and I have some beers too."

"I'll have a beer if that's okay."

"Two beers, it is!" Don retrieved two bottles from the minibar fridge and handed them to Alex. "What about you, Mary and Shelley? What would you both like to drink?"

Shelley sat on the velour couch near the fireplace. "Umm … I'll have a white wine, Dad."

"I'll have the same, Don," Mary sat across from Shelley. "Take a seat, Alex."

"Thank you." Alex sat next to Shelley on the fawn-colored couch.

"How was your flight?" Don pulled his wheelchair next to Mary and handed her a glass of wine.

"Long. Alex brought tickets in first class, so it wasn't too bad though." Shelley watched her father place her drink on the table in front of her. "Thank you."

"It's the only way to fly," Alex said, looking from Mary to Don.

"Where are you staying?" Don asked.

"At the Grand Hyatt in the city," Alex said.

"Nice hotel. I noticed you have security guards when you pulled up," Mary said to Alex.

"Yes. They go wherever we do," Alex said.

"Why is that?" Don asked.

"Being wealthy is not all it's cracked up to be, and there are a few undesirables out there who are jealous of my empire, so I choose to have security." Alex's brow creased.

"Shelley tells us you're from Westwood Highlands. Do you still have family there?" Don asked.

"No, sir, I don't. Business is the only thing that keeps me returning to San Francisco."

What's with the twenty questions? Alex mind-said.

Don't worry, it's not you. My dad is extremely protective of me.

"What types of businesses do you have or run, Alex?" Mary asked.

"Mainly hotels and restaurants, ma'am." Alex placed his hand in Shelley's.

"How is your jobhunting prospects going, Shelley?" Mary asked.

Shelley looked from Mary to Alex and back again. "At the moment, I'm considering opening my own practice in Zurich. Alex said he'd help me." Shelley picked up her wine glass from the table in front of her.

"That will be wonderful, dear. So that means you're going to live in Zurich for the foreseeable future?" Mary asked, sadness in her voice.

"I'm not sure, Mom. I know I promised to open a practice here so I could look after you guys in your old age …"

"Have you two set a date for the wedding yet?" Mary asked.

"No, not yet, ma'am. But we were thinking we'd possibly get married in Zurich." Alex looked from Mary to Don.

Mary flashed a forced smirk. *Not sure we could afford to go to Zurich.*

"Don't worry, ma'am, sir. Shelley and I will pay for your flights and all your expenses, and you can stay at my hotel, The Crestwell."

"That is kind of you, Alex," Don said, raking his gray hair.

"Mary, Don, I wanted to ask you a question. Did you know the lady who gave Shelley to you at the church?"

Shelley and Alex tried to read their minds.

Are they blocking us? Shelley mind-asked Alex.

I'm not sure. Hey, Violette, can you hear Mary and Don's thoughts?

Yes. They sure are blocking you both. You do realize Shelley's mother is a Griffin, right? And her dad is human?

What-what is a Griffin? Shelley eyed Alex and frowned.

I'll tell you later, babe. Right now, we need to know if they know we are Lepidoptera.

"In answer to your question, Alex, I sort of knew of her. But I didn't know her personally." Mary's blue eyes shined bright as her nostrils flared, remembering that night. *Calm yourself, Mary.*

Alex stood quickly when he noticed her blue eyes illuminate and clenched his fists by his side. "What are you?"

Mary rose. "I think you know the answer."

"Mom?" Shelley stood beside Alex.

"Sit down, both of you. You too, Mary." Don regarded his wife disapprovingly.

The three of them glared at each other as they sat slowly in their designated seats.

Are you all good in there, Alex? Violette mind-asked, ready for what might happen.

Yes. For the moment, Princess.

"To clear the air, you are both Lepidoptera vampires, and my wife ... she is a Griffin. But I'm sure you know that." Don harrumphed. "How did you become Lepidoptera, my sweet daughter?"

"It happened when I met Alex—who, by the way, is my life partner according to the Lepidoptera ways. Once I met him, my transformation started to take place. But I think you already knew I was a vampire, didn't you?"

"Yes, we knew. But we never thought it would eventuate. Christ, if I had known you'd turn into a Lepidoptera in Zurich, I would have stopped you from going. This is not a life we wanted for you, sweetheart," Mary said with sorrowful eyes. "Your mother was a Lepidoptera. I think they called her a First One. She asked me to keep you safe for her. And we have all these years, until now. I hope she doesn't return and kill us for what has happened."

"That won't happen. She is dead," Shelley said, confused and saddened by the fact that Alizon had been telling the truth. Heated tears welled in her eyes for the loss of her birth mother.

"What ...? How?" Mary's brow creased.

"Once I turned, she could feel my presence. With the help of her partner, Gardon, they kidnapped me. And when I was with her, she told me that she only wanted to get to know me. But I didn't believe her. She seemed to have some other ulterior motive. God, this is so unbelievable." Shelley's brow furrowed.

She was not someone you could trust, Shelley. Believe me. I read her thoughts, and she had become evil, Violette mind-said to Shelley.

I will never know.

"You certainly have had to deal with a lot over the last couple months, haven't you? I don't know what to say besides your mother and I will always love you as ours." Don wheeled himself toward Shelley, studied her tearful eyes and leaned in for a warm hug.

"Thank you, Daddy. I love you too," Shelley said, hugging him back tightly.

As Don pulled away from their embrace, he said to Alex, "Thank you for taking good care of our daughter."

"The pleasure is all mine. As I told you on the phone, I love Shelley a lot. Don, I'm interested to find out what your ties are here."

"What do you mean?"

"Do you and Mary work? Or have family here? I'm wondering what keeps you in San Francisco."

"We are retired, so the answer is no, we don't work. We do a bit of charity work though. Family? Shelley is our only family. I suppose Mary and I stay in San Fran because we like it here. You can keep under the radar, if you know what I mean."

"Would you like to see Shelley more than you do now?"

"For sure. She means everything to us. I'm sure you know that."

"If only that could happen ..." Mary said.

"How would you feel about moving to Zurich?"

"I don't know. We have a life here," Don said proudly.

"I— We can look after you both. I can provide security for you both, and you would never have to look over your shoulder again. I have a house in Zurich which I think would be perfect for you. Would you consider this?"

Don looked to Mary for answers. "What do you think, Mother?"

"I'm not sure. You need to realize, Alex, that here"—she gestured around the room—"we feel safe, and this house is ours. Can we discuss it while you're here and give you an answer later?"

"Yes, that is acceptable. Please give it some consideration though. It would mean a lot to Shelley and me to have you with us in Zurich. As I said, I have a house where you and Don can live, and I can provide security for you both."

Thank you for being so generous to my parents, Alex.

"Let's have some lunch, and we can discuss it some more," Don said, wheeling himself to the liquor cabinet. "What would everyone like to drink with their lunch?"

"I'll have some more white wine, Dad."

"I'll have the same, Don," Mary said, standing. "Could you give me a hand in the kitchen, Shelley?"

"Sure," Shelley said and followed her mother into the kitchen.

"Umm, may I have a whisky and dry?" Alex asked.

"Sure. We'll bring the drinks into the dining room for you ladies," Don said.

"Thanks, Dad!" Shelley called out.

*****

343

"Don, I know it's none of my business, but I wanted to ask what put you in the wheelchair?" Alex asked as he sat at the dining table already made up with cutlery and placemats with Don to chat.

"I was in a workplace accident in the late eighties. Racking fell on me and damaged my spine. I haven't walked since. Actually, this was how I met Mary. She was a nurse at the hospital."

"And with modern technology now, they still can't repair your spinal damage?" Alex queried.

"To be honest, we've never looked into it. Unfortunately, these types of operations cost money, and it's not something we have a lot of, plus, we don't have medical insurance."

Alex nodded and frowned. "How would you feel if I looked into this for you?"

Don grinned from ear to ear. "Alex, I would be indebted to you."

"Leave it to me, and I'll see what we can do to get you out of that chair. Fuck, that must be …" Alex's brow furrowed. "I can't even think of a word to describe what you must be going through."

"Shitty, fucked up, etcetera, etcetera? Yeah, I know. I've been asking why me for years." Don frowned. "I absolutely hate this thing." He tapped his wheelchair wheel. "Let's change the subject, shall we? Your security, are they all Lepidoptera vampires?"

"Yes, and they are all extremely good at their jobs, and loyal too. I currently have five guarding us outside, back and front, at the moment."

"Here we go." Mary entered the room, carrying a large pot of casserole with some oven mittens, and Shelley followed with the warmed plates.

Alex sniffed the air. "Mmm, smells good."

"She's a good cook, that's for sure," Don said proudly.

Shelley placed the plates in the middle of the table.

Mary set the pot on the table and removed the lid. "Serve yourselves, dears."

*****

As day turned into night, Mary asked, "Would your security like something to drink or possibly eat?"

Yes, please, Violette mind-said to Alex.

"That would be nice, Mary. I'll organize the drink, if you can do the food. And yes, they eat anything. Will it be all right with you and Don if they eat inside? I'm sure they'd appreciate a break." *Grayson, can you bring in some blood for Shelley and me?*

Yes, Sire. Grayson walked toward the car to retrieve the cooler.

"Yes, that's fine. I have plenty of leftover casserole, so they can dig into that." Mary went to the front door when she heard a knock, expecting it to be the Lepidoptera's.

With vampiric speed, Alex stood next to Mary and placed his hand against the door. "Don't open it."

"Why?" Mary asked, frowning.

"It's not my security." His nostrils flared. *Stay where you are, Lepidoptera. We may have an issue here.*

Yes, Sire, they said together.

Mary looked through the peephole. "It's only Pastor Andrus, and he is one of my kind. It's okay to let him in."

Alex nodded and took his hand off the door.

Mary opened the door with Alex standing by her side. "Good evening, Pastor Andrus. What can I do for you this evening?"

"Good evening, Mary." Pastor Andrus looked from Mary to Alex. *Lepidoptera, hmm.* Taking a deep breath, he tried to calm himself so his blue eyes wouldn't shine brightly and reveal that he was a Griffin.

"Pastor Andrus, this is Alex, our Shelley's fiancée."

"Nice to meet you, Alex." Pastor Andrus proffered his hand.

"Good evening," Alex replied in deep voice as she shook his hand.

"Hello, Pastor Andrus," Shelley said as she came to stand next to Alex and her mother. "How are you?"

"I'm fine, my child. Your mom and dad tell me you're getting married. How wonderful."

"Yes, that is true. Umm, we were about to sit down to eat. Would you like to join us?"

"No thank you, dear. I came by to ask your mother if she could volunteer at the church tomorrow."

"I'm sorry, Pastor Andrus. I can't tomorrow. Shelley and Alex are only here for a few days, and I want to spend as much time as I can with them. Maybe next time?"

"That's okay. I totally understand. I'll call you in a couple days." Pastor Andrus stepped back from the door. "Goodnight." He doffed his hat and walked down the concrete stairs.

"Goodnight, Pastor," Alex, Shelley, and Mary said together.

"What did he want?" Alex asked, watching Mary close the front door.

"He knew you were coming to town, so he wanted to see if Don and I were all right, that's all. We Griffin are protective of our own kind." Mary walked into the lounge room.

You can come inside now, Lepidoptera's.

Within seconds of the Pastor driving away, Grayson, Violette, Michael, Taiven, and Kelan stood at the front door, and Shelley invited them inside.

"Mary, Don, I'd like you to meet my friends Grayson, Violette, Michael, Taiven, and Kelan," Alex said as they entered the lounge room.

Not even taken aback by the way they looked in their combat gear, Don rolled his wheelchair to them and shook each of their hands. "Good evening." *Wow, I didn't realize they use female Lepidoptera's as security.*

"Yes, we have a few female Lepidoptera's who go out on missions and operations now," Violette answered his thoughts.

"I'm impressed" Don said, surprised by how she had heard his blocked thoughts. "Do you all live in Zurich?"

"No, we all live in Bagnolet, in France," Violette said proudly.

"You're a long way from home. Let's get you all settled into the dining room," Mary said, leading the way. "Do you need a hand with that cooler, Grayson?"

"No, ma'am. But thank you for asking."

*****

When they had finished their meals and the Lepidoptera's had cleaned their dishes, everyone sat around the dining room table, chatting about their day, amongst other things. Much to their surprise, Mary and Don couldn't believe how easy the Gramaze coven vampires were to talk with and how much they enjoyed their company.

"Your friends are lovely," Mary said, leaning into Alex sitting next to her. "I can't say I've met too many Lepidoptera's in my life, and my life has been long."

"You couldn't meet a nicer bunch, that's for sure." Alex watched each of them relax at the table. *Lepidoptera's, don't become too complacent. I think it's time to leave. Excuse yourselves and keep guard on the house and the princess, please.*

"We must be off. Thank you for your hospitality, Don and Mary." Grayson stood and pushed his chair under the dining table.

The others followed suit.

"You're welcome. We hope to see you all again before you go back," Don said, shaking each of their hands.

"We'll see them out," Shelley said to her parents.

We might head off too, Shelley, Alex mind-said as he approached the front door with Shelley.

CHAPTER TWELVE

The next morning, Shelley woke to voices coming from the lounge room of their hotel suite. She checked the digital clock on the bedside table—6:03 a.m. She hopped from bed and quickly shrugged on a pair of light blue jeans and a white windbreaker and headed toward the lounge room.

"Good morning," Alex said as she walked toward him and his security.

"Morning, everyone." Shelley spotted the packed suitcases and sat next to Alex on the couch. "What's going on?"

Alex took a deep breath. "I have a bit of bad news." He placed his hand over hers and felt her anxiety build. "Gardon has escaped, and they are not sure where he has gone."

"What do you mean, they are not sure where he has gone? Can't they detect him some way?"

"Apparently not. And that isn't the worst of it. Apparently, the council told Adrian that Gardon has vowed that if he can't have his daughter love, he will kill her and anyone else who gets in his way."

Shelley gulped hard. "Shit. Is there any chance he can find me or my parents?"

"I'd say so. I've sent Grayson, Adrian, Kelan, and Taiven to get your parents and bring them here. They should be back any minute now. We're all going home to Zurich." Alex felt Shelley release his hand, watched her stand and pace the room.

A blue shimmering portal appeared in the suite, and Grayson, Adrian, Kelan, Taiven, and Shelley's parents stepped through.

Shelley ran to her parents and hugged them simultaneously. "I'm so sorry, mom and dad."

"Shh, my sweet child. Everything will be all right. Alex will look after us all," Mary said, hugging her tight.

"Are we ready to go?" Adrian asked impatiently.

"Yes," Alex said, standing. "The sooner, the better, Adrian."

Each one of them grabbed their luggage and weapons and waited for Adrian to create another shimmering portal.

*****

"Sire, same plan as Christmas Day?" Grayson asked Alex as they walked through the portal into the Crestwell mansion in Zurich.

"No," Alex said, setting down the weapons bag. "I'll brief everyone in the combat room, in say"—he looked at his watch—"one hour. Can you make sure everyone attends? And I mean everyone."

"Yes, Sire." Grayson nodded once.

"Shelley, could you make your parents comfortable in one of the made-up rooms? I'll be there in a minute to discuss what we'll do."

"Yes. Will everything be all right?"

"Don't worry. I won't let anything happen to you or your parents. We have plenty of security here." He hugged her tight.

"Thank you." Shelley wrapped her arms around his waist. After a moment, she pulled away from their embrace and turned to her parents. "Mom, Dad, come with me. I'll show you where your room is."

"Sire?" James asked, waiting instruction.

"James, can you take everyone's luggage to their rooms?"

"Yes, Sire."

Luda, we have extra guests, so please ensure we have enough food and blood.

Yes, Sire, Luda mind-said from the kitchen. She had already started making a list of what items she would need.

Alex took his cell from his jeans pocket and dialed Frederick. "Contact Harris and Allan and let them know I need them at my house in Zurich for an operation. I need the three of you here in about thirty minutes, no later."

"Yes, Sire," Frederick said.

Pressing the end button on his cell, Alex remembered he needed to call William.

"I already know," William said as he answered the phone. "Violette has kept me up to date with what is happening."

"Right. Speaking of Violette, do you think it would be safer if I sent her home?"

"Gardon is no match for Violette. You'll have a better chance if Violette is there for backup. Keep me abreast with what is happening."

As Alex placed his phone in his pocket, he felt the house shake. *What the fuck was that?*

Sire, Gardon is here, Annabelle mind-said, who was guarding the front grounds with Bryant.

Violette, Grayson, Adrian, I need you at the front of the house, now. Taiven, Kelan, keep an eye on the back of the house.

Within seconds, Adrian, Violette, Grayson, Annabelle, and Bryant stood next to Alex on the snow-filled front porch, watching a shimmer every few seconds as a persistent Gardon tried to push through the invisible wards Adrian had placed around the house on Boxing Day.

"The wards seem to be holding," Adrian said. "Would you like me to see if I can reason with Gardon?"

"I don't think you'll get far. By the look on his face, he seems pretty determined."

"I'll give it a go," Adrian said and approached the shimmering wall. "Gardon ..."

Gardon ignored Adrian and kept hammering the invisible ward.

"Gardon, why don't you hand yourself back into the council?"

"What? You think I'm that stupid? I know what they'll do to me. I'll be stripped of my powers." Gardon stepped closer to the shimmering wall. "Why don't you join me, Adrian? Once upon a time, we used to be friends, and now ... you think ..." Gardon placed his hand through the shimmering wall, grabbed Adrian's throat and lifted him off the ground. "Now you'll pay for helping those fuckers keep my daughter from me and Alizon."

Adrian struggled to try and pry Gardon's hand off his throat.

"Adrian!" Violette screamed as she ran with vampiric speed toward the shimmering wall. "Let him go, warlock, or you'll pay."

"If you come any closer, Princess, or try anything, I will kill him." Gardon smirked as he held Adrian in the air.

Violette held her hands in front to summon every bit of strength she had to try to help Adrian until she heard Michael scream, "Violette! Stop!"

Violette turned to see Michael approaching.

"That's what he wants you to do; take down the wards," Michael said, now standing beside her.

"Too late, Princess. I don't need you. I can do it myself." He pulled Adrian through the shimmering wall, electrocuting and killing Violette's foster dad. Gardon discarded Adrian's limp body and ran past a stunned Violette and Michael.

"No, you will pay, warlock!" Violette turned, rushed toward him at vampiric speed with sword in hand and pierced him through. "Take that, you fucker." Violette decapitated him before he even hit the ground. Dropping her sword, she ran to Adrian laying lifeless on the ground. Sobbing as she knelt next to him, Violette flipped Adrian onto his back and placed her hands over his body to try to heal him. With her eyes closed, a pure ray of bright ultraviolet light came from her hands as she chanted an ancient Buddhist healing ritual. *"Ong, Ma Lee, Bae Mae, Hong ..."*

Michael watched in awe of Violette as she eventually resurrected Adrian.

Watching his chest rise and fall and his eyes open, Violette smiled and hugged him. "Thank the Lord."

"I'm okay, Violette. Thank you," Adrian said, whose apparition had been standing a meter away, watching Violette chant.

"Grayson, Bryant, take Adrian inside," she commanded.

"Yes, Princess," Grayson said as he and Bryant stood on either side of Adrian and helped him inside.

"Come on. Let's get you inside, Violette," Michael said, picking her up off the ground with his muscular arms.

Violette cuddled into his chest as Michael carried her exhausted body inside.

"Is everyone all right?" Shelley asked, waiting for them at the front door with her parents watching them all walk through.

"Yes, everyone is fine, my love. Adrian and Violette will need some rest, that's all. But your birth father, Gardon, is dead," Alex said, closing the front door.

Shelley sighed. "Good riddance to bad rubbish. At least I, we don't have to deal with him or Alizon again. They have caused me nothing but trouble since I learned about them."

Shelley glanced at her adoptive parents and felt appreciative to have had such a good life as a child with them.

"I'm sorry to say, Shelley, that it is not the most favorable of situations, but I feel life will only get better from now on for you and Alex," Mary said.

"Yes, I know you're right, but I can't help feel a little sad though."

"That is only natural, my love." Alex wrapped his arm around her shoulder and pulled her close. "How about we all get ready for some lunch? I believe Luda is preparing a banquet for us all."

"Sounds wonderful," Mary said, holding onto the back of Don's wheelchair.

*****

As the Gramaze, Lachance, Landers, and Crestwell families sat at the long dining table, eating their lunch, Don, at the head of the table, clinked his glass with his knife. "Fill your glasses. I want to propose a toast."

They all filled their glasses, and the room quietened.

"Mary and I wanted to thank you all for keeping not only our daughter safe but the both of us as well. That was pretty scary out there today, and I don't know what we would have done if you weren't around. So, here's to family." He raised his glass.

"Family," they said together.

"Also, as you all know, Alex and Shelley have asked us if we would like to move here to Zurich with them. Mary and I chatted about this further today, and I'm happy to announce we'd like to accept your offer, Alex."

The room erupted in cheers.

Alex and Shelley pushed back their chairs and rushed to Don and Mary.

"That is the best news we've had today. I'm excited to have you here." Alex hugged Mary and shook Don's hand.

"Mom and Dad, it sure will be awesome to have you here with us. I can't wait," Shelley said as she hugged them both.

CHAPTER THIRTEEN

With Adrian now reinstalling the wards around the Crestwell manor and grounds, and with Shelley's parents living comfortably at the back of the Crestwell property, and with the Gramaze Lepidoptera's returning home, leaving Annabelle to live out the rest of her Lepidoptera life with Bryant, her new life partner, Alex reclined in his office chair with his hands behind his head and grinned. *My home and life sure have changed since I have transformed. Even though it has been a little over three hundred years, it only seems like yesterday when Mason, the California Lepidoptera leader, turned me. I'll forever be in his debt for what he did for me, saving me from my life of crime on the streets of San Francisco. With no family and having to deal with a disease like smallpox, I was so alone, until he changed me, and I transformed into a Lepidoptera. Sometimes I must pinch myself when I realize how lucky I was that Mason gave me the Crestwell Hotel for my service and dedication to him. And Shelley, who would have thought I'd feel this content at this time in my life? I still can't believe how Shelley found me and our instant attraction for one another.*

Alex's cellphone buzzing in his pocket brought him back into reality, and he sat straight in his chair. "Hello, William."

"Hello, my friend. I'd like to say thank you for sending not only my family but the princess home safely to us."

"You're welcome, William. But it is I who should be saying thank you. I appreciate everything you've done to help me. You sure have a fine family there."

"That's what family and friends are for, to help one another. Anyway, what I rang you for, is to ask you if you could portal Gardon's body to us? We have to present his remains to the warlock's council tonight."

"I was wondering if the council would request his body, so I had his remains placed in a body bag and have had him on ice. If you'd like, I can have him ready in about, say, ten minutes. Can you ask Adrian to create the portal to open in my back yard?"

"I can do that," Alex heard Adrian say from the background.

"Great. Was that all, my friend?"

"For now. I'll speak with you again in a few days when things quieten down."

"Right, if that's all, I'll get Gardon's body organized for departure," Alex said, pushing back his seat.

"Good evening, my friend," William said as he pressed End on his mobile.

*****

"Did everything go as planned with Gardon's remains?" Shelley asked as she felt Alex slip behind her in bed.

"Yes. He has now been returned to the council. Though, I have to wonder, I'm not sure what they do with warlock's bodies once they have passed over," Alex said, making a mental note to ask Adrian. Alex felt a sadness reverberate from Shelley's body.

"Are you okay?" He semi sat upright in bed and placed his hand under his head, looking down at Shelley.

Turning over, Shelley cuddled into his bare chest. "I know I don't have the right to feel sad about this whole ordeal, but I wonder what it would have been like to get to know Alizon and Gardon. After all, they were my birth parents. I have so many questions, but now, well, now they won't get answered. In a way, I feel ripped off, but in another way, I don't think …"

Alex laid flat on his pillow and pulled Shelley into the crook of his shoulder, stroking her hair. "I don't know what Gardon and Alizon were like years ago, but from what we saw and what transpired in the last couple days, I'd say we saw the worst of them. What about if I ask Talitha and Adrian to speak with you? They would know them better than any of us."

"Thank you, Alex. I'd appreciate it, and maybe then, I can make peace with all of this. I … I feel like someone has ripped a hole in my heart, that's all." Shelley cuddled him tight as a tear escaped from her eye.

"I'm sure it's confusing, but I don't want you to feel like it was your fault that any of this has happened either. Gardon and Alizon had an agenda, and I don't think anything you could have done or said would have changed what transpired, unfortunately."

"I think you're right. I'm grateful my adoptive parents took me in, because I'd hate to see what I'd become if Alizon and Gardon had raised me. It sure is funny where life's roadmap can take you."

"I agree. Just look at us, for example. Who would have thought? Speaking of us, would you like to set a date for our wedding?" Alex asked, smiling.

"I'd love to." Shelley rolled over to get her phone off the bedside table. "Let's check the calendar."

Alex placed his hand under his head. "What about August thirty-first? That would give us about nineteen months to plan. Is that enough time for you? The weather will be good then too."

"Is there any reason you want that day?" Shelley asked, who hadn't even launched the app on her phone yet.

"It would have been my birth mother and father's wedding day if they were still alive."

"Oh, right. Let's check." Shelley skipped to the date on her phone calendar. "It's a Wednesday."

"I'm game if you are."

Shelley nodded with glee. "Sounds perfect, and at least we have plenty of time to plan the ceremony and reception," Shelley said, already thinking she would ask Analyse and Bronwyn to be her bridesmaids. She gave Alex a kiss on his lips.

EPILOGUE

NINETEEN MONTHS LATER

The reflection of her visions echoed through Violette's mind as she contemplated what had transpired in her life since the night her and Danielle's parents had been killed and when Emily and Adrian LaChance had eventually fostered and moved them to Bagnolet. Leaning into Michael, Violette placed her hand in his and remembered the tall, handsome stranger she first saw from a distance in the LaChance mansion's gardens from her bedroom window, wondering who he was and feeling an instant attraction for him, not realizing he was her life partner. Her smile soon turned to a frown as she recalled learning about the Lepidoptera vampires then going through the steps of her own transformation a few year ago.

Everything alright, Violette? Michael mind-asked, feeling the waves of sadness resonating from her body. He leaned into her body and placed his arm around her shoulders.

Violette leaned into his body. *I'm fine.* She had been blocking everyone, including Michael, from her thoughts today. *With all these Lepidoptera's here today at Shelley and Alex's wedding, I am feeling a little bit overwhelmed, that's all. My memories sometimes haunt me, and then there is all their mind-chatter; it does my head in sometimes.*

I'm here for you if you need me, Violette.

Thank you. I'll be all right. Violette watched Shelley and Alex face each other and hold hands as the celebrant asked them to say their vows. *Doesn't Shelley look beautiful in her lace and satin wedding dress?*

Definitely. And Alex looks debonair in that black suit. Michael watched Alex place Shelley's gold and diamond ring on her finger. *They sure are a great couple.*

For sure. And now Shelley has her physiatrist practice next to the Crestwell Hotel up and running. Things are certainly looking good for them.

It's a pity I don't have the same choice when it comes to a job. Now that I'm a fully qualified teacher, I can't even practice my skills. Sometimes being a princess sure has its drawbacks, Violette thought to herself. She was sick and tired of all the restrictions placed upon her because she was next in line to the throne.

Michael felt another surge of sadness resonate from Violette, and even though he couldn't read her thoughts, he knew that with the passing of each day, she had become more despondent watching every other female Lepidoptera with a degree start their careers and contribute to the daily Lepidoptera missions. Even Danielle had fulfilled her dreams of becoming a sports teacher at a primary school, and Samantha had finished her studies and had recently opened a pediatricians private practice in Bagnolet.

William, who was sitting adjacent to Violette and Michael, eavesdropped on Michael's thoughts. *Do you think Violette would be interested in teaching our boy Samuel?*

I don't know, Sire. I can ask her if you like.

Renee and I will ask her at the reception tonight. See what she says.

Great. And could I ask, Sire, if it's possible for Violette to go out on a few more missions. You've seen for yourself how she handles herself, so I can't see why not.

I've spoken with the queen about this, and she agrees that we do need to let Violette participate in more missions. I can see what this is doing to Violette's mental health, but I need to be clear, Michael, the princess is valuable to our kind, and this cannot be jeopardized in any way. Am I making myself clear?

Yes, Sire, Michael mind-said as he watched Shelley place Alex's gold band on his finger.

When the celebrant announced that Alex and Shelley were husband and wife and Alex could kiss his bride, all the Lepidoptera's stood tall and clapped. They cheered as the happy couple walked hand in hand down the aisle.

*****

"It's lovely to see our friends happy and so in love," Annabelle said, standing in a long line with Bryant to congratulate Alex and Shelley.

"Yes, I'm happy to see Sire has married his life partner. Shelley sure has brought to Alex's life a change he needed," Bryant said, holding Annabelle's hand. "I know that feeling all too well."

Annabelle smiled and kissed his lips. "Who would have thought we would find love again? I must admit, I never thought I would find another life partner, someone I could share my life with, someone who makes me feel complete again."

"I feel the same way, babe." Bryant lovingly kissed the back of her hand. "And now that we have our own home, it seems even better."

"Yeah, and as much as I appreciated living at the Crestwell manor, it's nice to have a house of our own. And I'm sure Shelley's parents appreciated us vacating the cottage down the back of Alex's place so they could have a home of their own too."

"Especially now that Don can walk again. I don't think the grin has left his face since the day of his spinal operation."

"I believe, from speaking with Mary, that Alex had all their furniture from San Fran moved here too. How nice for them."

Bryant nodded and moved down the line with Annabelle.

*****

"Can I cut in?" Stephen asked Michael, who was dancing with Violette.

Michael smiled. "Sure."

"You look lovely. How are you, sis?"

"I'm fine," Violette said as she watched Michael sit with Stephen's partner, Sharina, at their table.

"Don't give me that. What's going on?"

"Not a lot, Stephen. You know, same old, same old."

"Come on. Let's go for a walk." Stephen pulled her toward the doorway.

Violette hesitated at first but followed him outside.

"I have an idea I wanted to run past you," Stephen said as he walked slowly with Violette.

"Okay, you have my attention."

"How would you feel about opening a school for Lepidoptera children?"

"What? You mean, teach them? I wouldn't have thought there were too many Lepidoptera children around. In fact, I only know of Samuel."

"Sharina and I have been looking into it, and we have it on good authority that, apparently, around the world, there are a few more." Stephen watched her face light up.

"Really? And where would this school be located?"

"At the back of the Gramaze property in Bagnolet, of course, silly."

"Right!" Violette visualized the school, trying to comprehend how this would work. "I could talk with William about it and ask if he and the queen would be in agreeance. After all, William and Renee did ask me tonight if I'd like to start teaching Samuel soon." Excitement ran through her body as she contemplated what this could mean for her future.

"No time like the present." Stephen indicated to Violette that William and Talitha were sitting on a wooden bench only across the courtyard.

My Queen, William, do you have a minute? Violette mind-asked as she looked in their direction.

Of course, the queen replied.

*****

Violette stood in front of William and Talitha and explained the idea of starting a school for Lepidoptera children and where it would be located.

"Not a bad idea. I'd have to give it some thought, Violette," Talitha said and looked at William.

"Possibly, it could work," William said, pondering the logistical side of things.

"Yeah, and maybe we could ask other supernatural creatures too. But only the ones we trust," Violette said, searching for ideas.

"You may have something there, Violette. Leave it with us, and we'll get back to you," William said.

"Thank you, My Queen, William." Violette smiled eagerly as she walked away from them with Stephen.

"Well, they didn't shut down the idea. Maybe they'll say yes," Stephen said as he approached the tables with Violette.

"I hope so. Thank you, Stephen. I appreciate what you've done for me." Violette stopped to hug her brother.

"I haven't done anything yet. It was only a thought. And I'd love to see you happy again, sis."

Michael felt the excitement and enthusiasm resonate from Violette then read her mind. Smiling, he hoped his life partner's dreams of teaching and finally doing something with her life would eventually come to fruition.

CATCH UP ON ALL THE LATEST NEWS AND UPDATES FROM SUSAN HODDY

Facebook: Susan Hoddy - Author

Twitter: @susan_hoddy

Instagram: susanhoddy

LinkedIn: Susan Hoddy

Goodreads: Susan Hoddy

Website: www.susanhoddy.com

If you would like a group or book club reading done of some chapters and/or a book signing in your store, please contact Susan via her website www.susanhoddy.com to organize an appointment.

ACKNOWLEDGEMENTS

It never gets any easier, and in some ways this book was the hardest book for me to write, knowing it is the last book in The Lepidoptera Vampire Series, and trying to let my readers know what has happened with each character. But even though it's been hard, I have thoroughly enjoyed writing it and have found that I have grown as a writer.

This book would not be here, resting in your hands or on your e-reader if it weren't for the following people. I owe all of them my deepest gratitude.

My wonderful husband, Michael and my beautiful daughter, Samantha. You have always given me time and space to write my books and have been interested in what I am writing. I could not have written this book or finalized the book cover without your continued advice, support and love. I feel truly blessed to have you both in my life. Thank you Michael and Sam. Love you both so much.

Several friends, family members, and associates, all of whom have read my manuscript and given me feedback on what they wanted to see in the storyline and book cover. Many thanks to you all.

My new editor, Brian Paone from Scout Media, whose continued knowledge, advice and support has provided me with a much-needed calming strength to keep going. I am eternally grateful to you. Thank you, Brian.

My book cover designer, Beti Bup from The Book Cover Designer, who has worked tirelessly to provide me with a truly breathtaking cover design. Thank you, Beti Bup®

Susan Hoddy is a young-adult and romance fictional writer, best known for her Lepidoptera Vampire Series. Susan was born in Perth, Western Australia in 1966, and enjoys a good chinwag with family and friends, road trips with her husband, cups of tea, day-dreaming and writing.

Susan has always worked in many facets of an office during her life, but in 2012 she decided life was too short and wanted to make a start on her passion, which was writing. After acquiring her novel writing diploma from the Australian College of Journalism, she continues to create worlds where fantasy and romance exist, with her books.

In 2019 Susan won two book awards for Attraction and Awakened in the Lepidoptera Vampire Series from New Apple Literary Fifth Annual Indie Book Awards.

'Attraction: The Lepidoptera Vampire Series – Book One' was chosen as the "Official Selection" in the **YOUNG ADULT GENERAL FICTION** category.

'Awakened: The Lepidoptera Vampire Series – Book Two' was chosen as the solo "Medalist Winner" in the **YOUNG ADULT GENERAL FICTION** category.

Susan Hoddy

ATTRACTION

THE LEPIDOPTERA VAMPIRE SERIES

Susan Hoddy

AWAKENED

THE LEPIDOPTERA VAMPIRE SERIES
BOOK TWO

Susan Hoddy

AFFIRMATION

THE LEPIDOPTERA VAMPIRE SERIES
BOOK THREE

Security

SUSAN HODDY

www.ingramcontent.com/pod-product-compliance
Lightning Source LLC
Chambersburg PA
CBHW071206250626
47159CB00001B/222